BACK UP

A Novel

By,

Marshall Welch

An Altered Ego Production

Copyright 2021 by Marshall Welch

All original songs written and copyrighted 1979 & 2021 by

Marshall Welch

Lyrics to *Just For Me* written by Marshall Welch and Donna J.

Wade

Songs performed by the author and Aimee Altamirano

For Gordon

Dear Reader –

You are invited to use the camera on your smartphone and
'take a picture'
of the QR codes embedded on these pages to hear the songs.

Back Up

1a: (noun) - one that serves as a substitute or support -- *I brought an extra pencil for backup. -- a backup plan*

b: musical accompaniment -- *The tunes include banjo and guitar backup.*

c: additional personnel who provide assistance --*The police officer called for backup.*

2: an accumulation caused by a stoppage in the flow -- *traffic backup*

3: (verb) – (to) retreat < or > (to) rise from a fall

You do what you can for as long as you can, and when you finally can't, you do the next best thing. You back up but you don't give up.

~ Chuck Yeager

Chapter 1

Tap…tap…tap.

"Is this on?" the 10-year old asked as her tiny fist gently coaxed her hairbrush to life. "OK, good. Good evening ladies and gentlemen. I'm Bessie James. Let's start things off tonight with a little number by Peter, Paul, and Mary and it goes something like this…" Leaning to her right where her record player sat on top of her desk, Bessie carefully placed the stylus on the spinning vinyl. As the crackling song came to life, she held her hairbrush just below her slightly tilted and raised chin. She closed her eyes and began singing along with the record…

Puff, the magic dragon lived by the sea…

An audience of dolls and stuffed animals sat on the floor with an enraptured gaze in front of her closet door and its full-length mirror. The ten-year old girl opened her eyes to watch her reflection gently sway back and forth to the melody. She was pleased with what she saw in the mirror but did not smile. Instead, she wistfully raised her eyebrows and continued to stoically perform for her adoring audience until the song built to a dramatic concluding crescendo with one arm reaching toward heaven…

"…in a land…called…Hon…a…lee!"

And then her blond hair suddenly draped down off of her shoulders as she took a deep bow. Just as quickly, she stood erect, smiling and shaking her long locks back behind her neck as she gazed into the mirror. Her audience sat in spellbound silence.

"Thank you! Thank you so much. You're too kind. For my next number…"

"Bess? It's time for dinner!"

A deep exasperated sigh escaped from her as she threw her head back and closed her eyes.

"Bessie? Did you hear me?"

"I heard you, Mom. Just a minute, I'll be right there."

The reflection in the mirror heaved its shoulders with another dramatic sigh and cocked its head in deflated resignation. Bessie stood there for a moment before flipping an internal switch that reactivated a smile and bubbling persona. She raised her hairbrush to her chin and spoke to her audience, "Thank you so much. I'll be right back after a short intermission – don't go anywhere."

The repetitive pulse of the record player stylus trapped in the final grove of the vinyl was finally silenced and returned to its stand. With a click, the spinning turntable on the small Silvertone portable record player was stilled. The hairbrush was tossed on her bed as Bessie dragged herself toward her bedroom door. Once in the hallway, she slid her hand along the paneled wall as her slippers silently plodded down the orange shag carpet. Her mother was placing two Swanson turkey breast TV dinners in their aluminum trays on the table just as Bessie flopped down in her seat. With a blue paper napkin unfolded in her lap, she sighed.

"How was school today?"

"Fine. How was work?"

"The same. Oh, well…there is going to be a funeral this Friday for Mildred Petersen – you remember her, don't you? Anyway, I need to make the bulletin and work with the florist."

"Uh huh."

It was yet another manufactured conversation over a manufactured dinner in a manufactured doublewide tornado magnet where both of them carried on with a manufactured existence. It had been that way since Bessie was five years old. A tractor rollover killed her father when he worked at a sugar beet factory about 20 miles away and across the Red River in North Dakota from where she lived in Dilworth, Minnesota. She barely remembered him. What she did recall or imagine came largely from photos she saw and stories she heard. Her mother never really recovered from the accident.

Her mother was the secretary at their town's Trinity Lutheran Church. Their well-meaning, yet self-destructive, pastor offered some communion wine to her mother to help settle her nerves during a counseling session intended to help her work through her grief. Instead, it was a veiled excuse for a "quick therapeutic and theological nip" on the part of the closet alcoholic minister who was eventually found out and defrocked before becoming a real estate salesman in Detroit Lakes, Minnesota. This, unknowingly, set the course for her mother's own gradual downward spiral into what psychologists characterize as functional alcoholism. Her mother's chemical dependency began and was enabled through her role as church secretary through which she could obtain and monitor sacramental wine for communion services. At first, her mother "accidently" purchased too much with the rationale it could be stored at her home for eventual transfer to the church for its intended Eucharistic purpose. That, of course, never happened. The ploy didn't last long as the ruse eventually evolved into full-blown purchase and consumption of her own bottles of wine she never intended to serve any theological purpose. Early on, she never imbibed with anything stronger than wine, fueling her own rationalization that if she really had a problem, she'd be consuming other, and more potent spirits. Bessie's mother "only indulged" as she made, ate, and finished dinner resulting in one, often, two empty bottles and an early bedtime, usually in the Lazy Boy chair in front of the flickering TV screen. And somehow she managed to roust herself up and out the door each morning making sure she was never late getting to her work.

Bessie's Mom was pretty and smart even though she had never gone to college. Both of these attributes conveniently and effectively masked the other less complimentary aspects of her mother's otherwise mundane existence. Neither was she abusive or particularly negligent to Bessie. She was mostly indifferent or otherwise preoccupied. Her outward appearance reinforced her rationalization that she didn't have "a problem" -- as the colloquial expression goes. She was, in fact, kind and supportive of Bessie's activities – at least of what she knew, remembered, or understood. The relationship between mother and daughter was essentially a peaceful co-existence consisting of little to no interactions in the mornings as each prepared to enter their day and during civil but strained conversation at the dinner table when they ultimately dined together.

This was the functional aspect of her mother's chemical dependence. Its benign symptoms were easily disguised and withheld from others both at work and at church. No one at the church had the slightest inkling of her indulgence. In that sense, the diagnosis of her mother's abuse was accurate. She functioned – barely. The only variation to this routine was on the weekends.

Friday night was special. Friday night was "girls night" when Bessie's mother would bring home a sack of burgers and fries from Burger Bash – a greasy drive-in burger joint that was kitty-corner from the church. They would play and sing along with torch songs by female singers swirling out of the cabinet speakers of the Zenith hi-fi in the corner of their living room -- Brenda Lee singing *All Alone Am I*, Billie Holiday's accusatory *You've Changed*, Peggy Lee's sultry *Fever*, Shirley Horn asking *How Am I To Know*, Helen Merrill dreaming *You'd Be So Good To Come Home To*, June Christy crooning *How High The Moon*, Blossom Dearie dreaming about *My Gentleman Friend*, Dinah Washington proclaiming *There Is No Greater Love*, and Julie London lamenting with *Cry Me A River* – to name just a few of their favorites. Bessie sat cross-legged on the floor gazing at Julie London's cleavage on the album cover she held in her hands and pondered what it must be like to be a woman in love.

"Bombshell, eh?" her mother intoned as she exhaled mentholated smoke.

"I guess," Bessie replied with a defeated sigh.

Her mom took a sip from her wine glass and tapped her cigarette on the ashtray before taking another long drag. "You're going to look just like her one of these days," her mom offered as she squinted her eyes to combat the smoke.

"Yeah, right," Bessie retorted as she tossed the compliment and album cover aside.

Her mother cocked her head. "Yeah, well…we can dream, can't we? I know I did," she said as she took another drink.

Bessie dismissed her mother's inebriated confession and unrealistic fantasy. She envied Julie London's voice more than her sultry looks. She yearned to sound like all of the female vocalists they listened to each week. Still, an occasional ballad by Nat King Cole was thrown in as the only somewhat ironic alternative to the white bread and mayonnaise repertoire. But even his voice sounded pretty creamy. Bessie walked her fingers along the album spines vertically lined up on the floor leaning against the hi-fi cabinet, finally landing on one of his albums with the sole purpose of changing the subject.

"Hey…how about *Unforgettable*? We haven't played that in a while, have we?" Bessie suggested.

"Ummm…I don't remember…get it? Remember?…Unforgettable?…Get it?" her mother cackled, amused at her flimsy alcohol-fueled joke. She threw her head back and flung her hand with her cigarette toward the ashtray on the table at the end of the sofa, only to knock over her wine glass. "Oops…silly me," she slurred.

Bessie jumped and ran to the kitchen and returned with a dishtowel to mop up the red puddle before it dripped over the edge of the table and left another stain on the carpet.

"It's OK…no big deal. I'll clean it up. So…what do you say? Are you up for some Nat King Cole?"

Her mother leaned her heavy head back, closed her eyes, and dramatically outstretched her arm as she began to sing the schmaltzy love song. Bessie took this performance as a "yes" and after returning from the kitchen she pulled the album from its sleeve and placed it on the turntable. She carefully lowered the needle on to the spinning vinyl. Soon, the two of them were singing along with Nat.

"Well…that's that. We can always count on good ol' Nat, can't we sweetie?" her mother waxed. Bessie's only response to her mother's rhetorical question was to take the album off the turntable and return the album to its place in the vertical stack next to the hi-fi cabinet. As she did, a handful of albums stashed between the back of the hi-fi and wall caught her eye. Wrangling her arm in the cramped space, Bessie managed to retrieve a handful of albums.

"What are these?" she asked as she inspected the covers.

"What are what?" her mother responded without opening her eyes as she laid her head back.

"These…these records."

Her mother peeled an eye open. When she realized what Bessie was holding, she lurched out of her chair and stupor. "What are you doing?!?!"

Bessie flinched slightly at her mother's abrupt response. Even in her fuzzy condition, her mother noticed her daughter's fright as Bessie pulled the stack of albums to her chest as if to keep her heart from leaping out of it.

Bessie's mom sighed to calm herself. "Oh sweetie…those are…*were* your Daddy's."

A rare warm look came over her mother's, otherwise, dulled eyes. Bessie averted her own back to inspect the cardboard sleeves she cradled in her arms as she began reciting a roll call of the artists.

"Johnny Cash…Hank Williams, Jr…. Bill Monroe…Chet Atkins…Buck Owens…Patsy Cline…Roy Rogers and Dale Evans…"

Her mother suddenly interrupted Bessie's rattling off the list.

"My goodness…that was really about the only one of his records I could tolerate."

"Which one?"

"That one…in your hands…by Roy Rogers and Dale Evans. All of those others were nothing but sorrowful drawling' heartaches. But that one…he and I would listen to it together…when you were just a baby. There was one song in particular we actually sang together just for fun before heading off to bed. Let me see, now…what was it? Oh yes…" And with a faint flicker of recollection, Bessie's mother began to softly sing…

Happy trails to you...until we meet again...
She stopped singing for a moment and simply stared off, retrieving an image she had buried for years. Her mother suddenly perked up with, "Wait...put it on."

Bessie removed the album from the sleeve and read the label to determine which band of grooves to place the needle on The scratchy old album came to life, as did her mother who began to sign along...

Happy trails to you...until we meet again!

"Come on...sing with me!" her mother coaxed her. Bessie stumbled along, learning the lyrics as she went. But over time, the song became etched hard and fast in her heart. No matter what their selection of records each and every Girls' Night, Bessie's mother always doused the torch songs with Roy Rogers and Dale Evans' recording, *Happy Trails to You* as the grand finale and musical nudge toward bedtime. The two of them would sit on the sofa with heads tipped together, arms wrapped around each other's shoulders and croon in unison. It was a corny fun and a tender way to wrap up their evening together.

Bessie grew up hearing, singing, and loving these songs along with the artists who sang them. It was the one thing they did together. She loved splaying herself on the sofa singing at the top of her lungs together with her mom who was sacked out in the Lazy Boy until the wine began to dull her. It was the only real moment they shared in their otherwise manufactured existence. She also loved the songs that were instrumental in shaping her idea of what it meant to be in love.

Meanwhile, her Mom spent Saturday night polishing her shoes always with a Salem cigarette dangling from her mouth. Once the shoes were polished, she would don her head in curlers in a Toni hair set for church while watching Lawrence Welk. Bessie always excused herself to her bedroom where she would perform for her audience of dolls and stuffed animals. Sunday night was devoted to watching either Bonanza or Ed Sullivan, depending on what performers were showcased on Ed's weekly variety show. Like so many her age, four shaggy haired singers from England captivated Bessie's attention on one particular Sunday night in February of 1964. In reality, she was mostly fascinated by the reaction their performance had on the audience largely comprised of screaming girls. She really couldn't make sense of it due to her pre-teen understanding of the world. She found it rather silly at the time. Looking back, she came to realize how this moment would change the world and her life.

A few years later, when Bessie was in junior high school, her mother made her way to the hi-fi as she did every Friday night. Bessie sat at the kitchen table finishing a crossword puzzle anticipating their weekly sing-along. The fuzzy static from the stereo needle was the overture to the crackle of the vinyl. Suddenly a voice far different from the silky pop singers Bessie had heard for all these years came from the speakers. Instead of the lush production of big bands and stringed orchestras accompanying a velvety torch song came a simple, solo voice of an angel accompanied by a single guitar.

Bessie raised and turned her head toward her mother who gazed at the album cover while leaning against the hi-fi cabinet.

"Who *is* this?" she gasped.

Her mom took a drag from her cigarette and exhaled before replying simply with, "Joan Baez."

Bess walked over and pried the album cover from her mother's hands and stared at it. "Where did you get this?" Bessie implored, her hands almost shaking.

"At the T.G.&Y. store – today at lunch."

Bessie continued staring at the album cover, shaking her head in wonder. "Where did you hear about this?"

"Oh, in the office. The women folding Sunday's bulletins were talking about civil rights music. They mentioned this singer. So, I thought I'd check her out. What do you think of it?

"I've never heard anything like this. What do you call this?"

Her mother shrugged indifferently taking another drag from her cigarette. "Folk music. Hootenanny music, I guess. Beats me. Frankly, I don't get it. You can have it if you want."

"Seriously?"

There was another shrug as her mother made her way to the kitchen to pour herself another glass of wine. Bessie took the stylus off the record and removed it from the hi-fi. After slipping the record back into its cover, she raced to her bedroom and closed the door. She placed the LP on her little record player and laid down on her bed, letting Joan Baez's vibrato wash over her. Thus began Bessie's own musical journey.

Chapter 2

Now a teen, Bessie began listening to Top 40 radio stations, always leaning an ear toward the speaker on her transistor radio whenever she heard a female folk singer. She saved her meager allowance and birthday money to buy her own albums – mostly Joan Baez, Judy Collins, and Joni Mitchell. Bessie convinced her mother to drive her to Sears at the West Acres Mall over in Fargo one Saturday where she bought a cheap Silvertone acoustic guitar and Mel Bay's Book of Guitar Chords. Her fingers became sore as she taught herself how to play very basic chords. Overtime, thankfully, they became hard and callused.

Soon, the Friday night Sing-Alongs with her mother faded away just as her mother did from any significant role in Bessie's life. Friday nights, as well as Saturday nights, were now spent ensconced in her room listening to and playing along with her growing library of beautiful long straight-haired, hippie female singers. She no longer lip-synced to children's songs like *Puff The Magic Dragon* in front of the mirror. Instead, she pulled out her guitar and mimed to the vinyl in front of her mirror – nodding slightly with appreciation to the applause only she could hear in her head between tracks before going on to the next song. Over time, she began to plunk out the chords while singing along with them on her own little island at the end of the hallway in their manufactured home.

The Christian Brothers and their wine had been good companions to her mother over the years but were gradually replaced by a new buddy named Jim Beam. Bessie came to appreciate the old adage that "three is a crowd" all too well. As a result, she took it upon herself to be "out" as much as possible leaving her mother alone with her "Genie in a bottle." This meant becoming involved with school clubs and church youth group activities that would keep her away from home -- Yearbook, Pep Club, Chess Club, and so on. She did, however, refrain from joining the Future Homemakers of America, otherwise known as FHA, simply because her paradigm of homemakers was based on her own experience. Consequently, she avoided anything remotely associated with becoming like her mother's role model.

She also eschewed any athletic activities, not because of a lack of athleticism, but because she lacked the necessary competitive spirit it required. She was "too nice" to "beat" anyone in any form of competition. She did, however, have a sense of discipline that served her well with her studies. Bessie would complete her homework in the library if there were no after school club activities on her docket. Her academic prowess was due to nothing more than simply completing and turning in assignments that her peers ignored or lost. Bessie devoted that same degree of focus to listening to lyrics of songs, interpreting poetry in English class, and watching classic movies for nuanced symbolism and foreshadowing. As a result, her GPA vaulted her to be Valedictorian of the Dilworth High School Class of 72.

These socially acceptable diversions kept her out of trouble – something that could have easily transpired in her situation. She was, therefore, considered to not only be a "good girl," but a "*nice* girl" by her peers and teachers. This reputation, however, had a downside. Bessie was not merely "respectable" – she was perceived to be almost saintly, which in turn, meant un-touchable.

"That Bessie James -- she's just an outstanding young lady," she had heard more times than she wanted to remember.

Yes, she did all the right things and did them well – especially singing in the choir at school and at church. This, given the combination of these admirable attributes and accolades, made her seem unapproachable by just about everyone in her class. This included rough and tumble farm boys on the high school athletic teams as well as the brainy captains of the debate or United Nations teams. She was, as the saying goes, "out of their league" even though she really wasn't. Instead, Bessie was simply out of their sphere of existence. She was rarely asked out on a date despite being pretty – not exceptionally beautiful – just…pretty.

In addition to her estrangement from boys, she had no real girlfriends. It wasn't that she was shunned. It was because she intimidated the other girls her age. They simply couldn't compete with her personality, achievements, or her budding Marcia Brady looks. Bessie did not bother with wearing make-up – she didn't need to, as there was a pure innocence about her, inside and out, that was visible to all.

She was not aloof. Never the less, she seemed unapproachable by her peers. Her classmates felt she was in a tier slightly above everyone. Still, no one resented her. She was not viewed or treated with spite or envy or even disdain and that was the problem. She was essentially invisible because she was simply "too good" and therefore seemed "too un-real" – like a specter. She had effectively projected a charade of confidence and groundedness to camouflage her reality at home. Sadly, outside her home she had no friends. She had acquaintances. As a result Bessie was an island – surrounded by empty smiles and deep neglect.

Her transition into adolescence was not particularly difficult, although her mother had offered little in the way of preparing her. The extent of her mother's efforts and involvement was helping her get her first bra and leaving on her bed a stapled pamphlet about getting her period, along with a box of pads. The rest of her education about her changing body came by stealthily observing classmates' appearance and eavesdropping on their conversations in the girls' locker room and bathrooms. She liked boys but the thought of dating or going steady sounded like too much drama and effort.

Bessie continued learning how to play her guitar as she sang along with her albums. Eventually, she stopped singing along with her idols and sang their songs on her own. She built up enough confidence to play folk songs at school talent shows that were met with rousing applause. Everyone was in awe of her talent. There was a special quality not only about her voice, but in the way she seemed to convey the songs as they shared a rich warmth that emanated from her heart. No one could articulate the special quality she exuded. The new minister, Pastor Glenn, was soon asking Bessie to play during the 9:00 morning folk worship service at her church.

Unlike her mother, Bessie was not particularly religious – she didn't even have what one might consider any kind of faith. Privately, she considered the aroma of bacon cooking to be a spiritual experience, which in turn, provided ample evidence of God's existence. Still, she had her doubts and that didn't seem to trouble her despite successfully completing Formation Class and taking first communion. She didn't pray. She went through the motions. Sunday School was a social opportunity that provided a modicum of interaction with peers. Bessie liked the Bible stories. Secretly, she appreciated them and took them as mythology and metaphors for deep values as opposed to being factual history. Her attendance at church was out of obligation and expectation – it's simply what one did in Dilworth, Minnesota. To her it didn't particularly matter what "flavor" it was although the only choice was vanilla - Lutheran.

Both her church and high school choir directors encouraged her to apply to the Lutheran college in nearby Moorhead to study music with the school's renowned choir director. She applied and was accepted declaring a major in music. She couldn't afford to live on campus, despite the rule that all first-year students must live in the residence halls. The school recognized her academic potential as well as the fact she was a "commuter student" since she lived a mere 10 miles away, along with special financial circumstances and waived the on-campus residency requirement.

Bessie had inherited her Grandmother's huge copper colored 1968 Ford LTD with a black vinyl top when Granny moved into an assisted living facility.

"Here you go!" her Grandmother announced as she handed over the car keys. "It may be an ugly beast, but the price is right, wouldn't you say?" Bessie nodded enthusiastically as she took the keys and gave the old woman, who would die four months later, a loving hug. The car seemed to be the size of a small aircraft carrier, but it handled well on icy roads. Despite being a gas hog, it was a set of wheels that not only helped get her to school, but out of the house and away from her mother.

Bessie auditioned for "*the* choir" at the college and did well competing with other equally accomplished singers who had come from around the country to also pursue her goal. She found it a strange experience to suddenly become average. There were only two openings due to returning students and despite her strong audition, she was relegated to the "B-Team" Chapel Choir. The reason they gave her was that this would enable her "to build her chops." She was definitely a shoo-in her sophomore year. Meanwhile she enrolled in a Film As Literature class along with classes in Music Theory and Music History.

Bessie was a sponge. She absorbed the information and gained insight into chord structure and harmonics. She now understood the basic chord patterns of the tonic, subdominant and dominant triads that virtually all popular songs incorporated based on the foundation of the blues. With this knowledge she was able to transpose songs into different keys as well as "pick up" melodies by ear. Likewise, Bessie grasped and appreciated the physics of sound and how certain keys sounded sadder than others as well as how space within chords created a feeling that could be altered by simply adding a "third" in between an open fifth on the keyboard. As a result she was able, without the benefit of any prior lessons, to doodle on the piano.

Like in high school, in college she made acquaintances but few friends. Because she couldn't live in the dorms, she was denied the communal lifestyle of late night pizza parties and bull sessions in the hallways. She was, however, aware of those rituals as she overheard conversations in the lunchroom and the classrooms before the professors entered. Bessie envied her co-eds. Not because she was lonely, but because she longed for a sense of community – for dialogue on both weighty and sophomoric topics. Besides, she didn't have time for a social life as she was forced to get a job as a waitress to help pay for the exorbitant tuition of the private liberal arts college she was attending.

She had perused the college newspaper and found an ad for a part-time night shift waitressing job at the Country Kitchen next to the Interstate. College students gleefully referred to the restaurant as "Quit Yer' Bitchin." Waitressing at night would prove to be a unique experience that typically involved truckers, loners, and college students – always college students who were either there to nurse cups of coffee while studying, or gorging themselves on breakfast after a night at the bars, for those who were of drinking age. Deep down inside she didn't really mind.

The salary and tips came in handy. More importantly, it was another excuse to get out of the house. After her shift, she would change out of her uniform and into her street clothes and hunker down in an empty booth to do her homework.

Bessie had also run across an ad in the school paper recruiting student talent for the campus coffee house, dubbed *The Box* for its architectural and structural confinement in the student union's limited space. Students who passed an audition were scheduled for Friday and Saturday night performances that included a modest $10 per night honorarium. The thought of auditioning, let alone performing in a college venue, made her nervous. Assuming she got the spot, she would not be performing in front of the familiar and supportive faces she had grown accustom to.

With her guitar case in tow, she clambered up the rickety wooden steps of the old house on the campus border that was the headquarters of all student entertainment. Two boys, hinting at its mission, sat on the front porch playing guitars. There was no sign to identify it – everyone simply knew its existence, location, and purpose by word of mouth and simply referred to it as "The House." Its mythical presence was magical to her. It was as if this setting was a living and breathing entity all unto itself, inviting the curious to become a part of this place. Bessie opened the door and stepped inside. The walls of the front room were covered from floor to ceiling with concert posters. Tie-dyed sheets were draped like billowing parachutes to conceal the utilitarian light fixtures hanging from the chipped paint ceiling.

Swirls of blue clouds floated from incense burners along the windowsill.

"Hi. Can I help you?" a young woman asked from behind a worn and salvaged desk.

"Yeah. I was uh...wondering if I might audition for the coffee house?"

The student receptionist stood up and walked toward Bessie with an outstretched hand. "Cool. My name is Liz."

"Bessie."

"Nice meeting you Bessie. Tony and Gary are upstairs. They're in charge of talent and concerts. Oh, did you hear? They're working on bringing John Denver here for a concert," Liz enthusiastically told her.

"Wow. That'd be so cool."

Liz looked Bessie over. "So, you're a Frosh." Bessie thought she heard an air of contempt in her voice.

Bessie nodded, "Yeah, does it show?"

Liz laughed. "Well...not really. But you *are* wearing a beanie."

Embarrassed, Bessie reached up to touch her head with her free hand to verify the presence of the humiliating yellow cap that was a tradition. All incoming first year students were "required" to wear the beanies until the first touchdown of the season was scored. It was fair game for any freshmen caught not wearing one. Students from the upper classes were known to toss unsuspecting freshmen into Prexy's Pond in front of Old Main. Bessie loathed wearing it, but given her accommodating personality, she tolerated the tradition that was supposedly intended to help bond the incoming class and create memories.

"Oh, right. Forgot about that," she said with a blush, raising her eyes to see the bill of the beanie just above her brow.

Liz smiled, "Have you thought about trying out for Frosh Frolics? It's a fun talent show."

"Hmmm – I haven't heard anything about that."

Liz began shepherding Bessie up the stairs to the attic where her student partners were lounging on a dilapidated sofa in a room where the ceiling was also draped in paisley and tie-dyed sheets and yet more concert posters that filled the walls. A cheap stereo was set on bricks and boards on one wall.

"Oh it's a kick. Besides, if you perform for the show, it will help draw an audience to the coffee house…assuming you pass the audition, of course," Liz stated matter of factually.

"Right. Of course," Bessie replied.

Two guys with scruffy beards stood up as Liz escorted Bessie into their lair.

"Guys – this is Bessie. She's here to audition for Frosh Frolics and for a gig in The Box. Bessie, this is Tony and Gary."

Bessie was somewhat taken aback by Liz's assumption that she also intended to try out for the talent show. But, it was too late now. She reached out to shake Gary's hand who merely responded with a terse, "Tip it, Frosh!"

Bessie stood bewildered. Tony, standing next to Gary, then mimed tipping a hat when Bessie suddenly recalled another dreadful component of the beanie tradition in which first year students were "expected" to tip their beanies to students in the upper classes.

Bessie offered an embarrassed, "Oh, right…sorry," as she reached up in chagrinned compliance. Gary suddenly reached over and grabbed her arm and pulled it down.

"No…I'm just kidding. It's a stupid rule. I'm just messin' with you. Come on in…have a seat."

She looked around, finding no chair or room on the sofa, and simply sat down on the rug which appeared to be expected protocol. She had mentally and emotionally prepared for an interview – to tell her life story – as it were - and to explain what songs she sang and why – all for naught.

"So…" Tony said as he lay back against the sagging sofa clasping his hands behind his head, "play us something."

Bessie retrieved her guitar from its case and settled with her guitar cradled in her lap. She licked her lips and tilted her head as she looked up toward the ceiling and leafed through her mental list of songs. She took a deep breath and eased her way into Judy Collins' song, *Since You Asked*. Bessie closed her eyes and disappeared into the song. Her head and chin were tilted up and to the side slightly as she envisioned the lyrics – entering into them and living the song. As she did, the room that she and the others were in simply vanished. The story within the haunting yet lilting melody was not a regurgitation of love songs splattered on their Top 40 radio station. It was yearning that revealed a willingness to be with another as well as laying bare a delicate vulnerability. When she finished, she took a quick cleansing breath to bring her brief performance to a close before opening her eyes. Three gazes were transfixed on the faces before her.

"What?" she meekly inquired.

Each of the trio blinked their way back to life and looked at each other.

"Jesus…what was that?" Tony posed with disbelief in his voice.

Bessie quickly turned to Liz hoping to discern some explanation to his question. Liz just sat quietly with large doe eyes and lips slightly parted in awe. Receiving no insight from the receptionist's blank stare, Bessie asked, "What was what? You mean…what was the name of the song?"

Gary sat up straight on the sofa as if to bring himself back to life. "No…it's…I mean…WOW…what did you just do?"

A shy smile of embarrassment combined with some confusion came to Bessie as she slightly shook her head in bewilderment. "I…I'm afraid I don't understand."

"That was amazing," Liz finally offered.

A tiny chuckle escaped from Bessie as she covered her mouth with her hand. "Really?"

"Really!" Tony confirmed.

Gary chimed in, "God, I've never heard…I've never *felt* anything like that."

Bessie's shoulders scrunched up with anticipation, "So…am I in the show?"

"Shit yeah…are you kidding? We'll get you in *The Box*, too! What was your name again?"

"Bessie…Bessie James."

Gary turned to his partners seeking their confirmation of smiles and head-nods and offered, "Bessie James…I love it! A real folky outlaw. Jesus, Bessie…you made our day!"

And with that, Bessie found her way on stage for both the talent show and in the tiny coffeehouse located in the Student Union her very first year on campus. It was her first, albeit modest, professional performance. She was getting paid to sing even if it was only $10 for a single 45-minute set on a school night. She didn't care. What could possibly be better than having someone actually pay you for doing what you both loved and needed to do?

Chapter 3

The handful of students in the audience for Bessie's debut at *The Box* was oblivious to her nervousness as well as to her presence perched on the stool a few feet away from them. They were there to smoke cigarettes, consume massive quantities of coffee, and share gossip. Undeterred, Bessie began singing and playing – for her own satisfaction if for no one else. Due to her jitters, she failed to notice that Tony was standing in the back intently listening and watching. It was, essentially, a live audition to see if she would break under the pressure and to see how the audience, as meager as it was, would respond. The outcome of her debut performance would determine whether or not she would have any future appearances. While generally distracted, the small crowd was polite. No one left. That was a good sign. The applause was sparse but sincere. Tony liked what he heard and especially liked what he saw.

At 9:45 the house lights went up and the single waitress began wiping down tables and bussing empty cups and full ashtrays as the small crowd wandered toward the exit. Bessie slid off her stool with a smile and heavy sigh as Tony approached the stage clapping his hands.

"Bravo!"

Bessie pulled a strand of hair from her face back behind her ear, "Oh please," and turned her back to him as she walked over to her guitar case.

"Seriously! You were great. The audience sucked...but you? You were great!" he offered as he rested one foot on the lip of the stage.

Bessie closed her guitar case, picked it up and turned to him. "Thanks. You're just being nice."

"No...I'm being honest."

She smiled, embarrassed. "Well, I don't know about that."

"Really...it was a perfectly good debut. And trust me, you'll get better."

Bessie bit her lip. "Do you really think so?"

He closed his eyes and nodded. Tony then opened his eyes and once again clapped his hands together, startling Bessie into a slight flinch that she hoped he hadn't noticed.

"Tell you what...I need to tear down the P.A. soundboard and take it back to The House...you wanna wait and walk over with me?" he asked her as he stepped up on to the stage and moved toward the wings to the soundboard to unplug it and remove the mic chords.

Bessie blinked, not sure how she should answer him. "Um...yeah, I guess...sure."

Watching him wind up mic cords and pack the equipment Bessie finally took notice of his looks. She had been too nervous during her audition to really get a good look at him. His tight faded jeans and cowboy boots made him look tall. He wore a denim shirt with the sleeves rolled up to his elbows. Wavy hair parted down the middle draped to his shoulders. A stubble of beard made him look rugged – even sexy. Bessie focused on his deep blue eyes when he glanced back at her as he closed the lid over the black box that housed the public address system and heaved it to his side.

"Great! Let's go!"

The short walk back to The House began in awkward silence. Tony noticed that Bessie turned her head away every time he tried to look at her. Amused and embarrassed for her, he broke through the tension with small talk.

"So…what are you majoring in?"

"Music."

He nodded and pursed his lips. "Makes sense."

Compelled to maintain the meager conversation, Bessie offered a succinct, "And you?"

"Business."

This surprised her. His appearance and apparent passion for music didn't seem to fit with her notion of what a business major would look like.

"Really?" she replied with disbelief.

"Uh huh." Tony enjoyed watching how the dangling conversation made her squirm. He allowed the sound of the loose gravel beneath their feet to fill in the gaps. When he sensed she could no longer tolerate his silent taunting, he finally offered additional detail.

"Yeah, I'm actually hoping to go into management…music management. That's why I get off by working over at The House. I'm a Senior and it's the closest thing to an internship that I'm going to get…at least in the field I hope to go into."

Bessie's exaggerated head nods affirmed her understanding but she still said nothing. Now it was Tony's turn to squirm in the uncomfortable impasse of conversation. Thankfully, they soon arrived at The House with what Bessie assumed to be the termination of their exchange with relief and an exit. They stopped on the steps of the front porch.

"Wanna come in for a sec?" Tony asked as he pointed to the front door over his shoulder. Tony couldn't read Bessie's widened eyes as she stood there quietly. After she sighed heavily, Tony took a step toward the door and removed some keys from his pocket. "Come on," he said with a jerk of his head toward the inside of The House. The shy singer watched him lean down to pick up and tote the bulky soundboard through the entrance as the door slammed against the case, adding yet another ding and scrape to its well-worn exterior. With guitar case in hand, Bessie slowly climbed the two steps and followed Tony who was stashing the heavy case into a storage closet.

"Whew! That was a work out," Tony gasped and wiped away the effort rubbing his two hands together as he abruptly switched gears. "Hey, have you heard the latest Pink Floyd album?"

Bessie had not heard it let alone *any* of their previous albums and replied with a coy but honest and simple, "No," that did not reveal her ignorance of the group.

"Neither have I," Tony exuded as he started jogging up the stairs. Half way up, he turned to see Bessie still standing at the foot of the stairs and called out, "Come on…we can listen to it up in the attic!" and continued his upward jaunt.

Bessie looked around for a moment and rested her guitar case upright against the wall before softly treading up the creaky wooden stairs that announced her arrival. When she walked into the open attic area where she had auditioned, she found Tony pulling the album from a black jacket with a triangular prism casting the spectrum of light on the cover. He glanced over taking note of her arrival and nodded with his head toward the beat up sofa against the wall. "Have a seat," and returned to the task of placing the stylus on the spinning vinyl.

Bessie sat at one end of the sofa and propped her head with her arm perched on the rolled arm of the dilapidated couch. A splash of light spilled in through the window from the streetlamp outside in the parking lot behind the house providing the only illumination in the room. Tony stood over the beat up stereo as a hushed cacophony of mechanical sounds and mumbled voices built up to a crescendo through the speakers. Tony gasped a hushed, "Wow!" when it all slid seamlessly into dreamy guitar chords and a lilting guitar riff. Bessie had never heard anything quite like this. It was a far cry from the angelic voices of the female vocalists that currently comprised her repertoire. She was intrigued.

Tony had to lean down to avoid bumping his head on the slanted attic roof before flopping down on the other end of the sofa with one of three lumpy seat cushions between them. He sat upright and reached to the back pocket of his Levi's and awkwardly retrieved a tin of Sucrets Throat Lozenges. Bessie's initial thought was that he was suffering from a sore throat. But that hunch quickly disintegrated when he deftly flipped the lid open with his thumb and one hand to reveal the first joint she had ever seen. He proceeded to dig a cigarette lighter out of his front hip pocket and lit the tight roll of papers. Bessie immediately liked the pungent sweet aroma that swirled from the blue smoke as she watched Tony deeply inhale. He closed his eyes to hold his breath before exhaling and silently offering the joint to Bessie with his outstretched hand. Without hesitation she accepted his offer and mimicked his behavior. Somehow, she managed not to cough as she watched him watch her. Enduring it as long as she could, she blew the smoke out and tried to catch her breath. She had never smoked a cigarette, let alone a joint, so she was surprised at how it burned her lungs. For years she had watched her mother go through a pack of Salems a day and yet it never crossed her mind that the smoke would be so harsh.

    Tony smiled. "Good shit, huh?"

    Bessie affirmed his critique with an agnostic nod and handed the joint back watching him as he quickly took another long hit. She carefully observed how he seemed to sip the smoke into his lungs as if he was sucking long and hard on a straw. Before he exhaled, he once again offered it back to her. Again, she imitated him. As she exhaled, she found herself feeling slightly light-headed and leaned back against the sofa. Retrieving their shared item, Tony let the cherry on the joint go out and placed it in an ashtray on the makeshift coffee table in front of them before leaning his head back to join Bessie staring at the ceiling. Together, they sat there letting the ethereal music wash over them. Bessie closed her eyes. She was completely blissed out. Her nervousness seemed to have lifted from her. Before she knew it, she became vaguely aware of the repetitive clicking of the stylus chirping at the end of the album. Prying her eyes open, she watched Tony pull himself off the deep cushions of the ratty sofa and return to the stereo to flip the album over. She closed her eyes again and thought she imagined hearing the ring of a cash register in her altered state. She furrowed her brow as she attempted to make sense of what she was hearing. Unsuccessful, due to her foggy state of mind, she opened her eyes to either verify or dismiss what she was hearing. When her eyes came into focus, she found Tony standing over her – smiling.

She smiled back with a slight giggle. "Hello, you," she coyly greeted him. Bessie immediately wondered if she had uttered these words or if it was someone else.

"Hello you, yourself," he replied.

He simply stood there, looking and smiling down upon her as she flopped across the sofa cushions. Bessie giggled once more as she pensively raised one hand to her mouth and shyly bit down on the tip of her finger. Tony correctly interpreted her silent invitation. He unbuttoned his shirt, tossed it on the floor, and curled up beside her on the lumpy cushions as they slowly began exploring each other's faces with their hands. Tony ran his finger over Bessie's lips and looked into her eyes before giving her a gentle kiss – her first kiss. She felt herself melt as the opening organ chords of *Us and Them* melted over their tangled bodies. Despite all she was feeling right then, Bessie seemed to take note of the sultry saxophone that offered a perfect soundtrack to the moment. She was amazed how the music seemed to envelop both of them. Their gentle, almost fragile kisses gradually became bolder as did their breathing. She felt him reach down and unbutton her jeans and she arched her back in blissful surrender. He tugged her jeans off and tossed them on to the floor. Tony slowly released himself from their cocooned embrace and stood up.

Bessie looked up at him as he began to unbuckle his belt. She pulled her hand and arm behind her head, lifting her head slightly, watching him.

"Um, have you taken care of things or do you want me to?" he asked as he pulled his jeans off his ankles.

The effect of the cannabis, combined with inexperience, confused her. She stared blankly at him for a moment without responding. Tony stood before her in his underwear as his excitement continued to grow and reached back down to gather up his wad of denim from the floor. He wrestled his wallet out of the other back pocket and opened it up to retrieve a cellophane package the size of a teabag. Tony held it up for her to inspect.

"Do you want the honor or do you want me to do it?"

Out of the haze of the pot and music, was the gradual clarity that Tony was holding a condom. Still thoroughly dazed,

Bessie flopped her head back on the sofa cushion and waved the back of her hand toward Tony implying he could have the so-called honor. Besides, she had no idea of how to perform the task. He shrugged as he ripped the package open with his teeth and unwrapped the rubber ring. With fascination Bessie watched as he removed his underwear and expertly rolled it on. Like everything else thus far that evening, this was a first. The first time she had ever seen a condom, let alone one worn where it was intended to be. He then reached over and gently removed her panties, tossing them to the floor on top of her jeans. She sat up to unbutton and remove her blouse. He reached over and expertly unclasped her bra that snapped in the front before removing his own shirt

    Bessie was unsure what she was thinking or feeling. It was a rushing wave of excitement, fear, anticipation, and vulnerability. After giving her a soft gentle kiss, Tony climbed on top of her. She released a petite gasp when he softly moaned as he entered her. Bessie began to massage his back as he slowly thrust his hips. Her senses heightened by the THC swirling around the synapses in her brain suddenly made her aware of the different length of the fingernails on each of her hands – her right longer for picking her guitar strings – her left shorter to play the chords. The sudden awareness of such a minute tactile detail fascinated her and momentarily distracted her from what Tony was doing. Then Bessie thought she heard herself purr. Purr? She had never purred before! Can pot make you purr? Or was it the sex that made you purr? Her inner conversation was interrupted as she was beginning to feel a surge within her that she had never experienced before when Tony suddenly and violently exhaled into her ear. Bessie turned her head away to escape his panting as he collapsed on top of her while the upwelling wave inside her began to subside.

She waited…and waited…and waited some more as he lay there catching his breath. She didn't dare move. She didn't know what to do. After another minute, Tony raised himself up and off of Bessie and stood beside the sofa. Still unsure of what to do or say, Bessie stayed there and looked up at him, awaiting some kind of cue. The whole thing ended before the second side of the Pink Floyd album.

Tony arched his back and sighed heavily. He then reached down to the floor and casually tossed Bessie's panties and tangled jeans to her. Startled, she flinched and stared at him.

He walked over to the stereo and removed the stylus from the album and returned the record to its sleeve. After placing the album back into the vertical file of other records, Tony turned to look at Bessie and rubbed his hand through his hair.

"Well…" Tony at last spoke only to pause dramatically, "now I can say I laid the folk singer outlaw, Bessie James before she was rich and famous."

Aghast, Bessie remained on the sofa, not moving or saying a word. Tony suddenly seemed to remember the latex accouterment he was wearing and carefully peeled off the condom and tossed it in the garbage can. Repulsed, Bessie clinched her eyes shut. He walked back over to the sofa and bent down to recover his own underwear and jeans. She opened her eyes to see him smile and stare at her as he put one leg at a time into his underwear and then his jeans. She could not read his expression.

"So…does that make you some kind of groupie?" she finally inquired.

Even in his foggy state, Tony sensed edginess to Bessie's depiction. He stood there, trying to decipher her comment. Was it an insult or some kind of clumsy compliment? He was too stoned to tell.

"I guess so," was all he could muster. He turned away, to buckle his belt and did not detect the scorn on Bessie's face. Once he had buckled his belt, Tony reached over to touch Bessie's arm. "Hey…I've got an early class in the morning. Come on…I'll walk you back to your dorm."

Bessie silently got dressed. They walked down the stairs where she retrieved her guitar case. She followed him out the front door and on to the porch.

"So, what dorm do you live in?" he casually asked as he locked the door. Bessie had not revealed that she lived at home so it was natural for him to assume she lived on campus. She cleared her throat.

"Hogan Hall," she lied.

"Cool. I'll walk you over." He grabbed the guitar case from her hand as a chivalrous gesture that merely stoked Bessie's growing consternation. Neither said anything on the walk through the campus. Lights on in dorm windows hinted at students working on homework late into the night. They finally arrived to the entrance of her alleged residence hall and stood uncomfortably toe-to-toe, waiting for the other to say something first.

Tony gave in. "You were great tonight. Really…I mean it. In more ways than one." He offered with a sly smile.

In the receding blur and haze of the evening Bessie couldn't be sure if she had been used or if it was the other way around. Either way, she didn't like the way it felt and she made a promise to herself that she'd never allow that uncertainty to occur again. She took the guitar case from his hand, cocked her head, and looked into his eyes.

"Thanks," she said flatly.

She could see the surprise gradually fade into disappointment on Tony's face when she offered no gushing appreciation or thrill in return. His smile evaporated. He glanced down as he kicked at the sidewalk with his toe.

"Well then…I've got to get going," Tony stammered.

Bessie reveled in his nervousness. "Okay…see ya," she said matter-of-factually and leaned into the double glass door leading into the lounge area of the dorm with her shoulder. She paused, conveying an impatience for him to leave. Taking the cue, Tony turned and walked away.

"Right. See ya. Good night," he called out over his shoulder.

She stood there and watched him disappear into the night. Once he was out of sight, she sighed and pulled away from the glass door. She turned toward the parking lot on the other side of campus where she had parked her car before heading over to the coffeehouse.

She mulled over the night's firsts. First solo gig. First joint. First kiss. First sex. And more importantly, she had her first real brush with regret. She was disappointed at how she had been swept away by the moment and had given into her impulses. That troubled her. Bessie had thus far managed to get through her young life with very few regrets – not that she wouldn't or shouldn't have any. The point was she didn't allow herself to entertain them. She believed that the best way to bury any hint of regret was with resolve.

Her discernment was interrupted when she approached her car to find a slip of paper tucked under her windshield wiper on the driver's side. Bessie set her guitar case down, unlocked the driver door, and pulled the flapping paper from the wiper. It was a parking ticket. She had inadvertently parked in a faculty slot. Bessie tossed her head back with a laugh. Perfect, she thought. Another first!

Chapter 4

In addition to these series of firsts, Bessie was forced to drop out of school at the end of her first semester due to growing financial challenges after her mother was charged with a DUI. This, however, meant that she could bump up her hours at the Country Kitchen and make a little more money. No one really noticed her absence from classes the following semester as she maintained a charade of continued enrollment by spending her free time in the library and café. Bessie eventually realized she could roam the endless maze-like hallway of rehearsal cubicles in the Music Hall. Not only could she hunker down to play her guitar, she could continue to figure out how to play chords on the piano as she learned songs. And no one would even notice her presence. She even made her way to The House on some afternoons where she enjoyed hanging out in the attic where she had lost her initial shyness, not to mention her virginity. She always sat on the floor, keeping her distance and dubious eye on the sofa. Despite the drama of that night after her first performance at The Box and later nights in that same room, the space always felt familiar and comfortable. The buzz in the room was from either a passed joint or what was in the latest *Rolling Stone* magazine. Sometimes the energy was enhanced with speculation of what big name act the rag-tag team of student producers might successfully snag for an on campus concert. Debates over this new guy named Springsteen vs. Dylan ensued. Arguments for and against the war in Viet Nam raged. The flames for ardent support for Women's Rights were fanned. It was so hip and bohemian. She took it upon herself to make coffee when the pot had been emptied. Ah yes, she had made herself right at home.

That was just it. Home. She belonged there. It was the first time and first place she had ever felt like being part of something. The funky old house conveyed a sense of place as opposed to merely taking up space. Bessie's own horizon of repertoire and co- musicians expanded as she jammed with other wannabe performers at The House. She learned and played songs by Dylan and the Grateful Dead, as well as other lesser-known acts of the day from the region like David Buskin and Steve Goodman. Meanwhile, during this time, Tony avoided Bessie as much as she avoided him. Their paths rarely crossed. When they did, their interaction was limited to a muted exchange of "Hey! How's it goin?" with a nod of the head as each continued navigating themselves in opposite directions and lives.

Bessie did not merely want to perform on stage – she *needed* to. She had finally learned, after a frustrating lifetime of maneuvering through her life, that this was her way to connect with others. To Bessie, it was not a matter of singing *for* people. Instead, she sought an invisible bridge that allowed her to *be with* people who would otherwise distance themselves from her. Performing confirmed her existence.

She had kept and used her lapsed student I.D. to maintain a connection with the student government's entertainment committee at The House so she could continue playing in the coffeehouse at least once a month, sharing the stage and spotlight with a handful of actual students. She managed to keep up the charade for the remainder of the academic year, juggling work and dropping in at The House. Summer was spent at nearby Buffalo River State Park just east on U.S. 10 where she could read uninterrupted for hours and later in the day jump into the river to cool off when her fingers got too sore from playing and learning new songs on her guitar.

    A year later, during what should have been her sophomore year, Bessie contacted the coffeehouse crew at The House and offered to be the entertainment during the first week of classes, knowing they would not have ramped programming up. With Tony having graduated, the group wasn't terribly organized and she figured most of the performers they had used last year would either not be coming back or were too caught up in starting school. Both Gary and Liz were still there and they, saw Bessie's gesture as a favor so they gladly offered the stage to her to welcome incoming students, even though, still unbeknownst to them, she was not a returning student herself. Bessie rationalized this was a minor detail not worthy of mentioning. And even though she was scheduled to play the first Friday night of the fall semester, she knew that Gary and Liz would have other performers take the stage, which meant she might get a single weekend once a month – if she was lucky.

    The first Friday of school of her faux enrollment, however, seemed to unravel from the outset. Her mother was too hung over and called in sick. This meant her mother would be draped across her Lazy-Boy chair nursing her pounding head with a purely medicinal dose of Bloody Marys while listening to her worn out albums of torch songs, smoking cigarettes. Bessie grabbed her backpack and packed a few things – some fruit, and the copy of *The Exorcist*, a new novel she was just starting, knowing that these items would supply and sustain her out and away from the depressing domestic reality of her life. She would head to the library to pass the time. She slung the backpack on to her shoulder and grabbed her guitar case. She was headed out the door when the phone rang.

"Hello?"

"Bessie?"

"Yeah."

"This is Rodney from work…how are you doing?"

"Fine. What's up?"

"I'm calling because I need you to fill in just for tonight. Rachel is out of town for some wedding."

Bessie sighed. "Really? Tonight? Geez, I have some plans."

"I know. I'm sorry to spring this on you. But it's actually the graveyard shift. Can you come in around midnight?"

Why did it have to be tonight of all nights? She wanted to focus on her performance at *The Box*. The silence of her deliberation annoyed her boss. "Well? Can you?"

She shook herself back into the conversation. "Yeah, I guess."

"Cool. I owe you, Bess. Thanks."

"Yeah, OK."

Resting the receiver on the wall phone was like dropping an anchor. She was now weighted down with dread. Time to move on into the day. Bessie glanced over at her mother splayed in her chair and didn't bother to announce her departure. She simply walked out the door, only to find a flat tire on the behemoth Ford LTD. Bessie dug out her keys from her backpack and let it drop from her shoulder as she unlocked the trunk and removed the jack and spare. Changing a flat tire was not on her schedule for the day.

She parked on the street off campus as her student parking sticker had expired. Bessie made her way to the library where she hunkered down in her favorite study cubicle hidden on the top floor behind dusty volumes neatly stacked on shelves. The novel – a real page-turner -- captivated her for most of the morning. From time to time she stretched and roamed around the nearly empty third floor. As she was finishing her banana outside by the fountain, she found herself watching students walking toward their classes and their dreams.

After her lunch, Bessie grabbed her backpack and guitar case and walked over to the music hall where she meandered up and down the hallway listening to a cacophony of fingers running scales up and down piano keyboards, voices warming up, and the tuning of stringed instruments – a virtual aural barrage of aspiring artists honing their talent and skills – until she found an empty rehearsal room to commandeer. She tuned her guitar and began rehearsing the tentative two sets she would perform later that night.

Chapter 5

Bessie perched herself on a stool in the spotlight on *The Box's* stage. There was a handful of students there – all excitedly talking and anticipating their impending academic adventure. She envied them. She found it difficult to shake off the day and her frustration followed her onto the stage. She caught herself nervously lamenting about her trials and tribulations on stage to the indifferent audience as she re-tuned her guitar – partially to take up time as well as to offer an excuse for her lack luster performance – but no one was really listening – except for one guy sitting in the back. He was the only person who applauded when she finished singing Joni Mitchell's *Chelsea Morning*. His modest response after each of her next songs buoyed her through the rest of her set.

While the house lights came up at 9:50 as the coffeehouse began to close up, her spirits quickly dimmed as she remembered she now had to make her way to the Country Kitchen for her graveyard shift. She had some time to kill. With her guitar packed away, she carried the case and herself off the stage. She gingerly navigated her way through the tangled thicket of chairs and tables and poky patrons to the back of the room the same way she deliberately traversed through all the bodies and events she encountered everyday in her life. There, that solitary young man sat, doodling on a table coaster. Bessie stopped at his table.

"Thanks. You were probably the only person who knew I was here tonight."

Initiating a conversation, with a stranger no less, was uncharacteristic of her – almost brazen in her way of thinking. Her statement was equally surprising to the appreciative patron who looked up and tossed aside the coaster.

"Oh, hey, I really enjoyed it."

"Really?" She sounded surprised. "Oh, I'm so glad."

"Seriously. I really did. Pull up a chair."

She put her guitar case on the floor and sat down as she offered her hand, "I'm Bessie."

"So you said."

"Oh, right," and nervously she nestled back into her chair wondering what to do with her hands.

"I'm Joey. I really liked your set."

"Thanks."

Bessie sat there uncomfortably scanning the room avoiding his stare while desperately trying to dredge up some conversation. "So…as they say…do you come here often?"

"Me?" Joey scoffed. "No, this is my first time."

"Oh, right. Yeah, me, too." She lied.

"Really?"

She bashfully shrugged her shoulders. "Uh huh. You sound surprised."

Joey *was* surprised. "You mean your first time…here…in this place."

"Yeah…but my…well…my first time *any* place really." She rolled her eyes and hunched her shoulders before dropping them with a sigh. "God, does it show that much?"

"Really? Your first ever gig? Wow!"

She offered a neutral response by simply shrugging her shoulders. While it was true she had never performed anywhere else besides at church, she didn't admit she had performed here during the last academic year. It was the first time she had ever said something that was so marginally and strategically untrue. This surprised her momentarily. Still, she rationalized that claiming this was her first-ever performance would cut her some slack from any pursuant critique this guy – this very charming guy -- might have to offer.

Joey leaned across the table. "That's so cool. Good for you! I figured you'd been doing this for a while. You have quite a repertoire."

"Well, it's easy to rack up a bunch of songs when you're sitting around with nothing else to do." Bessie continued to nervously scan the room to find a quick exit. She was now officially out of her comfort zone.

Joey seemed to notice her nervousness and continued to share his enthusiasm and conversation. "Seriously…I'm impressed. I guess I thought you were a student here."

She sighed heavily. "I was. Things didn't work out. Always wanted to be a singer and hit it big. But, you know…"

"Yeah, I know," Joey replied in solidarity. "So if you're not in school, what are you doing…when you're not learning songs, I mean?"

"Oh God, it's such a cliché. I'm a waitress at the Country Kitchen by the Interstate. In fact, I'll have to head over there for my shift pretty soon. It's just temporary, you know. Just for now."

"Well, that's what temporary means." Joey smiled.

Bessie, embarrassed yet again, "Right, well…anyway. I just wanted to come over and thank you for being so nice and all," and started to get up.

"Whoa, whoa, hold on." Joey reached over to grab her arm. Bessie looked surprised as she sat back down. "No, I'm curious. You mean to tell me you've never played in front of anybody before?"

Bessie nodded and then stammered, "Well maybe a solo in a talent show but not what you might call a real set at a real club…not some college coffee house, if that's what you mean."

"Wow. That's ballsy. Good for you. I mean…you're good."

"Oh please, you're just being nice," attempting to escape, Bessie got up again only to have Joey reach over once again to grasp her arm.

"No, I'm not…well, yeah, I am, but I'm being honest, too."

"Well, once again, thanks. I appreciate it. Well, I really need to…" She tried to make it clear that she desperately wanted to escape as she gently pulled her arm out of his grasp but Joey didn't seem to notice her intentions and interrupted her.

"Have you written anything?"

Bessie just stood there perplexed, aghast at his question. "Me? Naw. Are you kidding?"

"No, I mean it."

"I can't write." She now raised her hand to cover her blushing face.

"I bet you can!"

"No… I can't," she retorted almost defiantly.

Joey tilted his head, pondering. She could tell he was trying to decide whether to say something and finally offered, "What?" to coax him into continuing their conversation.

Earnestly leaning across the table, Joey whispered, "Can I offer a couple of suggestions?"

Skeptically Bessie asked, "Like what?" and slowly sat back down when she realized how invested he had become.

"Like, don't apologize to the audience. Don't let them know you're nervous…that just makes *them* nervous…or worse, contemptuous and ready to pounce on you."

"Uh, huh. OK," she added.

He looked over his shoulder as if someone was watching and listening. "Another thing…worth two cents so you can take it or leave it…don't tell them you've had a bad day. They don't give a shit. In fact, the reason they're here is because *they've* probably had a bad day and want to forget about it."

She eyed him cautiously. "Interesting. Good point. How do you know all of this?"

Joey sat back in his chair and shrugged, "Just common sense if you think about it."

The waitress strolled over, "Closing up!"

"Right, OK," Joey responded as he reached into his jacket pocket. "Can I offer you something else?"

"Depends." Bessie uncomfortably adjusted herself in the chair in preparation for whatever it was this guy was about to offer.

"Well, you might be interested in this," as he placed the cassette tape on the table and pushed it toward her."

She picked it up. "What is it?"

"Some songs."

She eyed the cassette suspiciously. "Some songs? Whose songs?"

"Mine."

"Yours?" she exclaimed with surprise and slight doubt.

"Yeah. I'm wondering if you'd give them a listen…tell me what you think."

"Are you serious?" She truly could not tell if Joey was joking.

"Yeah. You know…just check em' out and give me your opinion. I'd appreciate the feedback."

Bessie fingered the cassette in her hand. "I guess so."

"Cool. Tell you what, I'll come back tomorrow night. Oh, wait…you'll be here again tomorrow…right?"

She nodded.

"Great. You can tell me what you think and give it back to me. Oh, and uh, that's my only copy right now."

Bessie just sat there, taking it all in. "Wow. OK. You trust me with it?"

"Yeah, sure. Why wouldn't I? It's not like you're gonna run off and record them before tomorrow night."

"OK. Sure. Well…." looking around at the empty room, "I guess we need to go. Thanks again for listening…and for your comments."

"It was *my* pleasure. Nice meeting you. I'll see you tomorrow night."

Both stood up and walked to the door.

"Um, I'm sorry but…what did you say your name was?" Bessie asked sheepishly.

"Joey…Joey Michaels."

"Right. Sorry. I just couldn't remember after everything else you were saying." Bessie paused and patted her free hand against her leg in futile frustration to punctuate the end of the clumsy apology. "Thanks, Joey."

He just smiled before each of them headed off in an opposite direction once they left the student union. Bessie tossed her guitar case and backpack onto the back seat of her car and then pushed the cassette into the player in the dashboard. The tape player came to life as she turned the ignition key. Without ever taking the car out of park, Joey's voice and guitar transported her to a whole other place. He had a great voice. His guitar banged out some rough and ready chords on the first tune that was a sort of country rock song that Linda Ronstadt would sing. But it wasn't just a "boy meets girl" song. Quite the contrary, it was a story of a girl finding her own way after being mistreated and left by a no-good man. What immediately struck her was the fact that this man she just met was telling a story from a woman's perspective. She found herself bobbing her head and tapping the steering wheel along with the beat. After a brief pause and series of clicks, a kind of cool, jazzy guitar began as the lyrics pondered what love could be. Bessie found herself swimming in the wonder of it. There was a long silence after the second song, leaving her wanting more but that was it. Just two songs. Two amazing songs.

She rewound the tape, punched the play button and drove off listening a second time. After a few bars, Bessie could hum along with the melody – a good sign. Again, she rewound the tape and began mumbling along with the lyrics, as she seemed to sense where the story of each song was leading. She repeated this a half a dozen times as she drove to the restaurant. Upon arrival at parking lot, Bessie had memorized both melodies and had a good start on committing the first verse of the first song to memory. Bessie found herself humming both tunes as she waited on tables until dawn.

Once home, she dashed to her bedroom and closed the door. Rather than collapse on her bed after a full night on her feet serving drunken college students and tired truckers, Bessie sat on the edge of her unmade bed next to her portable tape player. She popped the tape inside the trap door and unsnapped the latches on her guitar case. With her cheap but ever-faithful guitar in her lap, Bessie began figuring out the chords to both songs. The pause button was punched off and on in between lines to jot down the lyrics. By the time the sun was shining through her bedroom window, Bessie had learned both songs and had nearly committed the lyrics to memory along with the glimmer of possibilities. By midmorning she allowed herself to get some sleep.

Chapter 6

Bessie returned to *The Box* that night and set up. Being the first Saturday night just before classes began the next week, the room was full of students who were too young to hit the bars. She eagerly scanned the crowd but didn't see Joey. Five minutes past her start time, she finally made her way to the stool sitting in the splash of a spotlight and began her regular set. The crowd was polite but preoccupied with conversation. Bessie continued to scan the room for Joey but with no luck. Before she knew it, her forty-five minute set had come to a close. She stepped off the stage and moved to the back of the room where she leaned against the wall. She felt her spirits sag, wondering if he was coming back. Then again, she had his tape – his one and only tape. Surely he'd return if only to retrieve it.

Finally, out of the shadows and din of the busy room, Bessie spotted Joey as he walked in. Before he could find a place to sit, she ran up to him with the cassette in her hand.

"You wrote these!?!?" she exclaimed.

"I told you I did," Joey replied, slightly overwhelmed by her enthusiasm.

"Seriously?"

The tables had now been turned as Joey was now as flustered as Bessie had been the night before. He finally mustered, "Don't you believe me?"

Bessie whacked her free arm against her leg. "Yeah, I believe you but...they're just so...I don't know." She continued to wag the cassette in her other hand in front of Joey.

"They're just so what?"

"Good!"

Joey sighed. "Whew, that's a relief."

She looked at her watch. "I have to get going. You're staying, aren't you?"

"Of course."

"Good!" as she handed the cassette back to him.

Bessie returned to the stage for her second set with few in the coffeehouse noticing her reappearance or realizing the fact that she had ever disappeared. She tuned her guitar and then put her hand on her brow to shield her eyes from the spotlights to see if Joey was still sitting at his table. His vague shadow was silhouetted against the wall. She took a deep breath and launched into one of his songs with no introduction.

The chatter in the coffeehouse dimmed. Heads turned toward the stage. Bessie's voice didn't sing the song – her heart did and everyone there knew and felt it. She *was* the song…the story. The audience was not merely listening. Something else was taking place. The grit in her voice, like the song itself, was both disparate and defiant. Yet, somehow both seemed warm and rugged.

Lord, won't you help me – the blues paid a call.
They're knockin' outside my door.
I'm busted and broke and fresh outta hope
And I really can't take much more
Since that no good man up a left me
I've had to make it on my own.
This big ol' world wasn't meant for this girl,
But there's no other place to go.

I'm done being a plaything to men and their games.
A woman has wants and needs.
I was a toy to a two-timin' boy
That he'd wind up whenever he pleased.
Til' the day he drove off in his Chevy. I guess playing house got old.
This big ol' world wasn't meant for this girl,
But there's no other place to go.

I need a lover and I need a friend
Who'll stick with me through All the thick and the thin.
I need to be touched and held oh so tight
In somebody's arms who's gonna stay through the night.

I'd pack up my things and start over again
But it's tough when you ain't got a dime.
So I'll just lock the door and change my name

And drink away all the old times.
But a bottle can't give you lovin' It'll suck the life out of your soul.
Yeah, this big ol 'world wasn't mean for this girl,
But there's no other place to go.

Some kind of transformation had occurred within the past twenty-four hours. Bessie was beaming with confidence in her voice and presence on stage. The room had become enveloped in the vulnerability and strength conveyed in Joey's song. The audience was not just paying attention -- they were participating in the moment and the story Bessie shared. Rather than polite applause, the crowd burst into a thundering response of whoops and hollering and table pounding. The song had touched them – they felt it. Joey felt it.

"Thank you. Wow! Thank you." Bessie was startled by the raucous reaction. She readjusted the mic stand, "That was a song written by a friend of mine." She suddenly realized she didn't know the name of either song. Bessie quickly regrouped and continued. "Here's one more of his, I hope you like it." She cleared her voice and began the song without mentioning his name or acknowledging his presence in the room. The room once again fell into raptured attention. This time Bessie's voice was shy, not out of fear or nervousness, but through the feeling the lyrics conveyed in doubting the experience of falling in love. Joey's melody was a breezy, carefree bassa-nova while the words painted a picture of longing and doubt. He had deftly and successfully juxtaposed two contradicting emotional states.

One lonely day in summer I called mine
You came my way and just in the nick of time.
Ooh, you looked so fancy -- Ooh, you dressed so fine.
Your eyes looked right at me -- I was filled with desire.

Now I never imagined that I could feel this way.
You've some kind of magic
That makes me crazy.
I just can't shake it…I just can't make it
Heads or tails or up and down
My head is spinning round and round
And it's more than just a silly crush
I've never wanted someone so much
Now could it be…Could it be…I'm in love.

Now some don't believe in love at first sight.
But they didn't see that look in your eyes.
Now I don't know what happened -- Or how I lost control.

My lips started tremblin' -- But I knew I wanted more.

Now I never imagined that I could feel this way.
You've some kind of magic
That makes me crazy.
I just can't shake it...I just can't make it
Heads or tails or up and down
My head is spinning round and round
And it's more than just a silly crush
I've never wanted someone so much
Now could it be...Could it be...I'm in love.

Both songs revealed an original voice that did not attempt to mimic familiar artists. And the tunes clearly resonated with the small but enthusiastic crowd. She was, quite literally in the spotlight and Joey was OK with that. He was, in fact, thrilled.

Unlike the night before when Bessie finished, many in the audience came up to the stage to talk to her. She shook hands and offered thanks to their compliments. One girl even asked for her autograph. Joey sat back as he took it all in. The house lights finally came up as the wait staff cleared tables and straightened chairs. Bessie packed up her guitar and bounded to the back of the room where Joey sat stunned. She put her guitar down on the floor and sat down.

"So...waddya think?" Bessie glowed with anticipation.

"I can't believe you learned and played them!"

She held both of her hands up to her chest, appearing to keep her heart from exploding. "I hope you didn't mind that I played them. Did you like them? Did I play them OK?"

"Mind?!?" Joey was blown away. "It was incredible. I loved your interpretation."

Bessie hunched up her shoulders and crinkled her face with delight. Joey just kept shaking his head and chuckling in disbelief. He leaned over the table as if to share a secret.

"Remember last night when I asked you if you had any original tunes?"

"Yeah," she whispered.

"Well, that's the thing. You sing all these covers really well and they sound exactly like the person who did them originally. Look, if I want to hear Joni Mitchell or Linda Ronstadt, I'll listen to *them*…not you sounding like them. You have a sound…a feel that's all your own. I heard that sound tonight…I *felt* that sound…everyone did!"

She nodded her head. "I know, I know. I did, too."

Joey continued. "You weren't just singing to or for an audience. You had created a relationship with them. I know that sounds crazy." He leaned back in his chair and smiled with sublime amazement.

They sat looking at each other in silence for a few minutes. Bessie took a deep breath and sighed. "Those songs…what you wrote…I can't really explain it and I don't expect you to understand this but…I felt something. They seemed…so real to me…they were like my songs. Does that make sense?"

Joey nodded, "You made them yours. They weren't covers of somebody's else songs so you were able to own them – to *be* them."

"What are you saying?" She looked deep into his eyes but listened with her heart.

"Well, now it's my turn and I'm not sure how to explain this. I heard this voice in my head as I wrote them – your voice."

"But you hadn't even met me or heard me."

"I know."

They exchanged more long, silent looks at each other. The noise of scooting chairs on the concrete floor filled the space between them like fingernails on a chalkboard.

"Now what?" she asked.

"You can have them."

"Are you serious?"

He nodded. "I'll write some more…if you want me to."

"Of course, I do."

Joey reached over and grabbed one of Bessie's hands but couldn't wrestle away the alarm in her eyes. "I know this is going to sound crazy, but…you have something. People want it. I think we could be good together…as a team."

Breathlessly Bessie uttered, "Go on."

"I know a guy here in town who runs a recording studio. He basically does radio and TV commercials. He actually owes me for doing some studio work with him. I'll ask him for some studio time…he'll go for that cause he won't have to actually pay me any cash. We'll cut a demo."

"A demo?"

"Yeah, a demonstration tape. We'll record those two songs you did tonight plus maybe one more of something familiar. If we're lucky, I might be able to round up some musician friends of mine to sit in. We could take that first song you did and punch it up – maybe add some driving cowbell. Bonnie Raitt would love it!"

"Who?"

"You don't know Bonnie?"

She shook her head.

"Well, we'll take care of that. Meanwhile, we'll knock out that demo and send it off and shop it around to some A&R guys in L.A. I'm convinced we can get you a record contract. We'll also ship it off to some venues…we'll line up some gigs and go on the road…that is…if that's something you'd like to do."

Bessie dropped her hands on the tabletop. "Joey…this is just a podunk little college coffeehouse teetering on the edge of the world. Nobody out there in the real world is going to notice me," she gestured toward the door with a nod of her head.

Joey pursed his lips. "I think they will…with a little help."

Bessie's gaze revealed her disbelief, "I don't know what to say?"

Joey could see the doubt in her eyes. "Say yes."

"Well, I mean…we don't even know each other."

Joey seemed to ponder this fact and Bessie feared he was preparing to offer some pithy clichés. To her surprise, he simply opted for the truth.

"You're right – we don't."

Chapter 7

Thirty minutes later Bessie found herself once again sitting across a table from Joey – but this time it was in a booth at the Country Kitchen where they agreed to meet. The conversation began with the exchange of obligatory "I was born in log cabin" life stories over a #2 breakfast of two eggs over medium with sausage patties and hash browns for Joey and a #7 order of French Toast for Bessie. Each of them were born and raised within 15 miles of each other. Bessie mentioned her father's death in a sentence and alluded to a peaceful co-existence she maintained with a marginally functional mother. Joey nodded sympathetically and then offered a brushstroke of growing up in Moorhead. He rattled off his musical pedigree of being one half of a singing duo in high school before playing in a handful of bands during his college days. He confessed that he majored in rock and roll more than his studies in sociology but persisted enough to graduate – barely. The history lesson changed into Joey's vision as abruptly as their impulsive decision to order home fries to cap off their breakfasts. The platter of carbohydrates merely sat un-touched, growing cold as Bessie listened raptly to Joey's plan. He was too busy talking to eat. Bessie suddenly became aware of her reluctance to reach out and grab the fries and couldn't help but wonder if this was indicative of her overall grasp of Joey's pitch.

"More coffee, Bess?" Rachel, the waitress inquired.

Having met and exceeded her quota of caffeine for one night, coupled with the adrenalin rushing through her, Bessie doubted if she would ever fall asleep later.

"No thanks, Rach."

The waitress turned to Joey, "And you, sir?"

"No – no thanks. I'm good."

"Well then…" Rachel deftly left the check on the table and reached across the table strewn with napkins scribbled in ink, "…let me get those plates out of your way." The waitress stood with their plates stained with hardening remnants of egg yoke and solidified syrup and turned to exit before flashing a knowing wink to Bessie.

Joey was oblivious to the wink, but noticed Bessie's smile.

"Friend of yours?" he inquired running his index finger around the rim of his half-full/half empty coffee cup.

"Yeah. We often share shifts here."

Joey leaned his head back against the booth's cushioned seat, "That's right…you told me last night you worked here." He thumped his forehead with the palm of his hand and muttered, "Duh!"

Bessie grinned and reached for the check. "Let me get that…"

Joey's reach intercepted her hand, "No let me."

Bessie quickly snatched the check away and held it up as she tilted her head and raised an eyebrow, "Employee discount…" she reminded him with a singsong response.

Joey raised both hands in surrender before resting his forearms on top of the table. He leaned over with a faux menacing frown, "OK. Have it your way." His expression broke into a smile but he remained leaning across the table in a slightly imposing way.

Bessie cocked her head and smiled. "Besides, it's the least I can do…especially after hearing your proposal."

Joey continued his somewhat intensive pose and said nothing immediately. After a few seconds he merely responded with, "So…does that mean you're up for what we discussed?"

Bessie took a final gulp from her coffee cup to fuel her courage. The cup clinked on the saucer as she sat it down. She waited. She liked being in control, even if it was just for a few seconds. Up to now, her head had been reeling while desperately hanging on to every word and idea of Joey's audacious plan. It was almost a jumble. Bessie decided to sort through it all by repeating it with the hope she hadn't misunderstood, let alone imagine it all.

"OK. Let's see if I follow." She paused and looked into his eyes that invited her to continue. She took a deep breath and exhaled.

"We get together every day over at your place for the next week or so to learn and rehearse some tunes…some of yours and some of mine. Right?"

"So far so good."

"Meanwhile, you're going to call your friend to get some studio time to record a demo."

"Right again."

"On top of that, you're going to line up some engagements at some…"

Joey interrupted her, "They're called 'gigs'"

"Right…gigs. As I was saying, you're going line up some gigs – at some college coffee houses to start so I can work up an act." Bessie stopped and stared at him, waiting for a response that didn't come. She continued. "You're going to do ALL that for a 25% cut of…let's see, what did you call it, again?"

"The gate…25% of the gate. A lot of these places will only pay you what they make as a cover charge or passing the hat."

Bessie cleared her voice and nodded. "Right…the gate…25% of it goes to you and I get the rest." Bessie paused and looked deeply into his eyes. "That doesn't sound like very much money…for either of us."

Joey shook his head. "It isn't."

Bessie flopped back in her seat and sighed. She gathered her thoughts and her hands, resting them almost prayerfully, on top of the table.

"Well then…I don't get it. Why are you doing all this for next to nothing?"

Joey reached across the table with one hand and placed it on top of hers. Bessie's heart leaped.

"Because…like I said before…it's all going to pay off in the long run."

Bessie looked at his hand on hers. She bit her bottom lip and shook her head in slight disbelief. "I don't know," she said almost whining.

Joey took his other hand and placed it on top of Bessie's folded hands.

"Look…I'll be honest. It's not going to be easy at first. In fact, it's probably going to suck. It's called paying your dues. But trust me…you have something…something people want. And a few weeks out on the road, you'll be able to hone and harness that…that gift of yours. In a matter of time, you…we…both of us will be comfortable. Once you get a record contract…there's nothing to stop you. Believe me."

They stared at each other with Joey's hands still on top of hers. She was, essentially, in his hands. Bessie looked around the restaurant in search of some kind of guidance but found none.

Chapter 8

Bessie pulled her gigantic Ford LTD up in front of the tiny white house next to the Power Plant along the Red River and parked. She double-checked the address scribbled on a napkin with the numbers on the side of the house. This must be the place. She got out of her car and opened the back door to retrieve her guitar and made her way to the front door that was ajar and knocked. No answer. She knocked again – harder – and called out a tentative "Hello?" through the opening. She was right on time – a curse of hers. Could Joey still be asleep at noon? Bessie turned and contemplated returning to her car to check the address one more time when a young woman wearing panties and a man's undershirt came to the door with a puzzled look on her face. Startled, Bessie raised her free hand to her throat.

"Oh my…you startled me. Uh…is Joey here?"

Bessie's surprise quickly turned to alarm as she speculated who this pretty girl might be and why she might be answering the door, clad the way she was.

Equally perplexed, the girl tilted her head and furrowed her brow.

"Joey? Is Joey here?" Bessie repeated.

The girl's frown disappeared as she lifted her head, grasping Bessie's inquiry and opened the door wider. With one hand on the doorknob, the girl pulled her hair back behind her ear and then pointed to a hearing aid.

"Jo-wee dow-ders in baysh-men. Go bah uh-wown dew duh bah-doe," she replied as she mimed Bessie to walk around to the rear back door.

Relieved, Bessie smiled and then nodded, "Oh…" as she gestured OK with her hand, "…thanks." The girl returned the nod and smiled as she closed the door. Following the deaf girl's instructions, Bessie wandered around to the back of the house and knocked on the basement door before slightly opening it.

"Hello? Anybody home?"

She could hear music coming from a stereo inside that probably drowned out her greeting. She opened the door further.

"Hello?" she repeated louder.

The volume of the stereo immediately decreased and Joey suddenly appeared at the door, looking at his watch.

"Wow…right on time. Did you have any trouble finding it?" he asked as he welcomed her into his tiny basement apartment.

"No…no problem at all. I did meet your neighbor, though."

"Vicky? Oh…right. She's cool."

After just a few steps down, Bessie was in Joey's tiny living room and sat her guitar case down. She quickly inspected the room to find her own preconceived assumptions of what his apartment would look like were completely off target. It was tidy with albums lining the floor by the stereo housed on bricks and boards and a coffee table. There was a huge reddish poster filling an entire wall above the stereo. Joey noticed how she slightly furrowed her brow as she examined it.

"Chicago. From their third album, *Live at Carnegie Hall*," he matter-of-factually explained. Bessie nodded. Joey continued to elaborate. "Yeah, I love Chicago…love the way they use horns with rock music. I was playing in a local band that covered their stuff."

This piqued Bessie's interest. "Oh, wow. What was your band called?"

"Transit. We totally ripped off their original name of Chicago Transit Authority."

Bessie nodded again as she was vaguely aware of the band and music he was talking about. She was, never the less, impressed that he had played in such a group. This partially explained some of his insight. She continued to look around, noticing a tiny kitchenette around the corner and a closed door leading to what she assumed was his bedroom. In the corner an electric guitar and an acoustic guitar stood at attention in their guitar stands next to an amplifier. Bessie had no idea of the make or quality of any of his equipment. Joey gestured her to sit down on the sofa.

"Yeah, your neighbor told me to come round back," Bessie returned to his welcoming question as she sat down as an afterthought.

Joey flopped down in a beat up but comfy looking chair across from Bessie. "Geez, didn't I tell you how to find me?"

Bessie shook her head. "No, you just gave me the address."

Joey rubbed his chin. "Sorry about that."

Bessie shrugged indifference. "No big deal. I found you. Anyway, she seems nice." She tried to camouflage her curiosity regarding the dynamics of their shared living arrangements.

"Yeah, nice girl. She works days…I work nights…or at least I used to. We pretty much keep out of each other's way. Besides…she doesn't mind me playing my stereo too loud," Joey snickered.

Bessie smiled and cocked her head with amused consternation, "That's convenient."

Joey rested his elbows on the arms of the chair and folded his hands in front of him. "Yeah well, unfortunately she isn't so good at returning the favor. She can really make a lot of noise when her boyfriend's over…if you know what I mean."

Chagrinned and relieved, Bessie just shook her head in exaggerated disgust with a smile. Without missing a beat, Joey continued. "Well…glad you made it…glad you're here. Want something to drink?"

"No, I'm good, thanks."

"You sure? Can I get you a beer?"

"No, thanks. I don't drink."

Bessie nervously shrugged her shoulders up to her ears and let them drop. Joey noticed but simply clapped his hands together, "Cool. Well, then…let's get started…shall we?"

Thus began their first week of coaching and rehearsing. Bessie was initially overwhelmed by Joey's drive and energy. This was nothing like casually sitting on the floor at The House over on campus jamming with a bunch of college kids. This was work. But Bessie thrived on it. She soaked in Joey's insights about patter on stage coupled with poise and command of the spotlight. He elaborated on the brief advice he had offered during their first conversation after he heard her perform at *The Box*.

"So…I heard the rest of your repertoire the other night. Do you have any other songs that you didn't play?'

"Yeah, a few."

"Are they all hippy dippy chick songs?"

Joey watched her face for a reaction that didn't materialize. Instead, she flatly responded with a curt, "Yeah." Now it was her turn to watch his reaction, but he just smiled.

"Do you happen to know any other songs but just…you know…don't play them?" He leaned his elbows on his knees and hunched over waiting for her reply.

"I do, actually."

"Really?"

Bessie heard the surprise, if not doubt, in his voice. "Really."

He continued to gaze at her with a boyish grin. "Like what?"

"Some Dylan…The Dead…James Taylor…even some old Stones."

Joey's eyebrows arched with approval. "Cool. We'll give those a listen." He leaned back against the chair and rested his arm along the top behind his head. Bessie decided to elaborate.

"Yeah, well, I learned them jamming over at The House."

Impressed, Joey nodded his approval. "*Very* cool. Well, like I said, let's give everything a listen and then see if we can add your own little signature to them. Maybe even come up with some oldies that everyone's forgotten about – that'll trip em'out. We'll throw in some deep cuts, too."

"Deep cuts?"

He nodded. "Uh-huh…songs on albums that were never released as singles and only aficionados would know. In any case, we'll make them your own."

That was the beauty and wonder of what happened when she sang his original songs that second night at the coffeehouse. She wasn't emulating someone else. She was just being herself and it clearly resonated with the audience. Once a tentative song list was generated, Joey tutored her on writing a set list.

"You've gotta know and understand the dynamics of the audience. Like when our band would play, the first set of songs was mostly for listening. People were just starting to drink and get comfortable. Gradually, as the night and drinking moved on, they were ready to dance. In your case, however, we can assume – or hope - there's not going to be any dancing. So…" he paused and began walking around the room holding his hands as if in prayer to his lips, "…we…no… *you…*" he emphasized as he pointed to her, "need to think about how you're going to keep their attention."

"I'm not sure what you mean," Bessie replied sheepishly.

"Think about it. People are coming into this cozy little coffeehouse after a lousy, long day at work or writing their thesis or looking for a job. They want to relax and forget about the shitty day they had. Or…it's going to be a couple…maybe on their first date, or a trio of friends getting together after a while apart. People will want to talk. Why should they listen to you?"

Bessie had never considered any of this apparent psychology before. "I don't know…introduce myself I guess…" she meekly replied.

Joey stopped his pacing. His eyes told her, "Nope."

She stared blankly at him.

Joey held up both of his hands to reveal a stage he saw in his mind. "You come out…sit down…don't say anything and start with a song that says, 'Hey, I'm here.'"

The doubt and confusion on Bessie's face slowly melted away.

And so, their daily get-togethers fell into a routine for the next two weeks. Each day began promptly at noon with quick obligatory 'How are you?' pleasantries, followed by an update from Joey on his efforts to get studio time for a demo as well as his detective work on lining up gigs. She sat in what had become her usual spot in the sofa listening to Joey detail how he'd run up to the office of his former band's agent. There, he'd pour through their directory of nightclubs and college campus entertainment offices similar to The House where Bessie no longer had time to hang out. He was putting out feelers for possible venues where she could cut her teeth once her demo was ready. With very little capitol on hand, the team of producer and performer had no money to pay for expensive studio time. Luckily, Joey had racked up some free studio time in exchange for doing local radio and TV commercials. The problem wasn't financial – it was logistical. It was next to impossible to secure actual time in the studio due to its busy schedule. Therefore, their time together was focused strictly on honing Bessie's act.

Bessie came bounding into his apartment one afternoon and began to settle in as Joey walked over with his guitar in hand.

"Here…let me introduce you to Prudence…your new axe."

Bessie reluctantly accepted the guitar and rested it in her lap. He could sense her confusion and explained.

"This is an Ovation – it's an amplified acoustic guitar so we can plug you into an amp. You're going to have to get used to the feel of the neck."

His rationale made sense, but the nickname he had given the guitar baffled her.

"Prudence?" she replied quizzically.

He stood in front of her with hands on his hips utterly aghast. "Yeah, you know…" and he began to sing, "Dear Prudence…won't you come out to play…"

Joey let his cryptic explanation hang in the air with the errant assumption she would grasp its clever significance. Her blank expression proved otherwise, prompting him to continue his lesson.

"The Beatles' White album? Second song on Side #1???" he hoped his hints would ring a bell. Instead, Bessie just bit her lip and shook her head.

"Sorry…"

Joey rubbed his hand through his hair and gasped. "You don't know the White Album?" He was as incredulous as she was oblivious. Her embarrassed shoulder shrug spoke volumes. Joey immediately marched toward his stereo.

"Well then, we're going to rectify that right here and now," he announced. He pulled a blank white album cover from his vertical stack of records and placed the vinyl on the turntable. The stereo came to life with a dull thump over the speakers as Joey punched the power button on his Marantz amplifier. "OK, we'll skip the first cut and jump right into your first lesson with the classics." He carefully placed the stylus needle on the second groove. A simple and gently picked D-chord with a descending baseline gradually emerged from the speakers. After a few introductory bars, John Lennon shyly implored Prudence Farrow, sister of Mia Farrow, to emerge from her bungalow at the ashram where they Beatles were studying mediation. They listened together. When it was over, Joey lifted the stylus from the record. He turned off the stereo and began to replace the album into its cover.

"There. You've now been properly introduced to Prudence."

Bessie beamed. "I like it. I'd never heard that before."

Joey nodded, "It's a deep cut."

Bessie returned the nod. "Cool. Is that a song I could learn?"

Joey broke into a broad grin. "It's *exactly* what you should learn and do!"

It was all so overwhelming to Bessie – not just the technical how-to's Joey was presenting, but the nuanced insight and the art of performing. The sheer level of energy and attention Joey demonstrated was unlike anything she had ever experienced or received from her mother. The accolades her choir directors at school and church heaped upon her in high school were just that – merely praise. Despite their admiration of her talent, they didn't come close to Joey's devotion. The downside to the glow she was feeling was that she did not know how to navigate such attention. Her gratitude was slowly being overshadowed by a growing sense of adoration – something she had never felt before. She suddenly found herself in the lyrics of one of Joey's songs she performed that night at *The Box* and wondered could it be that she was falling in love?

Their sessions always concluded the way they began – on time. No matter where they were in the process, they ended their sessions promptly at 5:30 pm so Bessie could make her eight-hour shift at the Country Kitchen by 6:00. Like any other night, she took and delivered orders from the ragtag patrons, some of which had become regulars so she knew what they probably would order by heart, thus earning bigger tips. However tonight, quite unlike any other night, the head cook called out from behind the serving window separating the kitchen from the dining area.

"Bess!" he barked.

"Yeah?' she called out as she refilled coffee cups along the counter.

"Ya gotta phone call."

"A phone call?"

"Yeah…make it quick…we've gotta rush of orders."

She wiped her hands on her apron and pushed through the swing-to doorway making her way to the blinking light on the wall phone. She punched the button, extinguishing the strobe.

"Hello?"

"You still at work?"

"Joey?" She paused for a moment. "Of course I'm at work…you called me here didn't you? What's up?"

"You gotta go…right now."

"What are you talking about? Are you OK? What's wrong?"

"Nothing's wrong. Mac just called me from the studio. They had a cancellation in an hour from now. He's going to be there and is willing to engineer."

"What? What are you talking about?" Bessie plugged her open ear with her finger to block out the clattering of the kitchen.

"The studio! Your demo! Come on, girl…this is it!"

Bessie was flummoxed as she had another hour to her shift.

"Now? Uh, I don't know if I can?"

"Waddya mean? Can't you get someone to cover?"

"I suppose so." Bessie bit her lip.

"Good. Here's the address. Got something to write with?"

"Hang on," she tucked the phone receiver under her chin, pulled a blank ticket from her waitress book and a pen from behind her ear.

"OK – what is it?" She copied the address Joey rattled over the phone. The studio was in an office building over in Fargo. "Got it!" she panted into the receiver as she replaced the pen behind her ear.

"OK. I'll see you there. I'll bring the ovation. Come in the main entrance of the building and you'll see some buttons on the wall in the entryway. Buzz and we'll let you in," Joey instructed.

Joey hung up.

Bessie's shock showed on her face as Rachel walked by.

"You OK?" the waitress gingerly probed.

The question brought Bessie back to the noisy din of the kitchen. "Yeah. I'm OK." She stood there for a moment letting Joey's call sink in. Once it had, she grabbed Rachel by the arm.

"Can you cover my last hour for me?"

"Why? What's wrong?"

"Nothing's wrong. Everything's good, in fact. Look I can't really explain right now. Can you or can't you?"

"Yeah, I guess" Rachel replied reluctantly.

Bessie leaned over and pecked Rachel's cheek with a kiss. "Thanks!" and pulled off her apron as she headed toward the back exit.

"Don't forget to clock out!" Rachel shouted after her. "And hey…"

Bessie stopped in mid step with the exit door ajar.

"What?"

"You owe me!"

Bessie smiled and gave her friend a thumbs-up as she clocked out and ran out the door.

Chapter 9

She bounced up and down on her toes after pressing the button in the glassed entry way bathed in blinding florescent light as she waited for a response. During the eternity that ensued, Bessie glanced at the directory noting the suite number of the studio located on the basement floor and then looked down to realize she was still wearing her waitress uniform. Embarrassed, she was in the process of running her hands down the front of her ugly brown and orange checked uniform in a vain attempt to make it disappear when there was a sudden buzz and click on the glass door. She made her way down the steps and carpeted hallway, inspected the names on each of the small door plaques until she reached the end of the hallway in front of the door to the recording studio. Bessie tentatively opened it and peeked inside.

"Hello?" she shyly announced her arrival into a standard looking waiting room. The receptionist's desk was empty.

"In here!" came a staticky response over an intercom speaker above a picture window. She turned to one side of the room to see Joey and another man on the other side of a large window. They motioned through the glass for her to step through another closed doorway and come into the control room. Bessie followed their directions and made her way into the small sound-proof room filled with all sorts of technical looking equipment, blinking lights, and cigarette smoke.

Joey rushed over to her, taking her by the arm and escorted her to the other man sitting in front of a bank of illuminated controls.

"You made it! Great! Bess…this is Mac. Mac…this is Bessie James."

The man squinted to shield his eyes as he exhaled cigarette smoke. His left leg bounced manically on the tip of his Converse tennis shoe under the console desk as he reached over to shake her hand.

"I've heard a lot about you -- glad we could make this happen." Mac reached for a can of Vernor's ginger ale and mixed it with milk in a glass before taking a swig as he kept an eye on Bess. Upon returning the aluminum can to the top of the table next to the console he quipped, "Nice outfit," with a wink.

Bessie glanced down at her uniform. "Oh yeah…sorry. I came straight from work. It's nice meeting you. Thanks so much."

"No sweat!" Mac snapped back before draining the rest of the green can of ginger ale into the glass and stirring in milk. "Well then…let's get this show on the road, shall we? We've got an hour," he announced.

Joey once again took Bessie by the arm and turned to escort her into the studio on the other side of another huge slab of glass. She was immediately taken aback at how muffled the room sounded. The sound baffles effectively deadened any and all echo. It was almost like having cotton in her ears. In the middle of the room was a stool beneath a shiny mic boom looming overhead. She spotted the Ovation guitar in its open guitar case sitting on the floor nearby. Bessie carefully climbed on the stool, continuing to take in her surroundings. Joey retrieved the guitar and handed it to her as she made a feeble attempt at getting comfortable. She kicked off her utilitarian work shoes. Once she settled in as best she could, Joey placed his hands on her shoulders and looked into her eyes.

"OK. We've only got an hour. But that's more than enough time to record the four songs we chose for the demo. Do you need to warm up?"

Bessie looked back with deer-in-the-headlight eyes and shook her head. Joey smiled.

"Tell you what, Mac's going to need to set some levels. You just start singing to warm up. OK?"

Bessie nodded.

Joey reached over to the mic boom to remove a pair of headphone off of the chrome arm extending overhead and handed them to her. She placed them over her ears before pulling the mic down just in front of her face.

"There. How's that?"

Somewhat cross-eyed, Bessie tried to focus on the microphone inches away from her lips. She then reached up with one hand and adjusted the cups over her ears.

"Fine," she suddenly heard herself over the headphones as if she were speaking in a cave and slightly flinched. Joey immediately recognized the reaction.

"That's the monitor with some reverb. You're going to hear yourself singing. You'll get used to it as you go along."

Bessie nodded, unconvincingly. Joey smiled. He then inserted a cable into the jack on the backside of the Ovation guitar. Bessie could now hear her hands rubbing the guitar strings through her headphones. The guitar seemed to come to life inside her head as she formed a chord on the neck and plucked the strings with her right hand. She smiled at the result and looked up at Joey.

"Cool, huh?" he enthused.

She nodded again when she suddenly heard Mac's voice inside her head. Bessie looked up and toward the glass window to see Mac talking to her. "OK, Bess. I want you to just start singing and playing so I can set some levels. Got it?"

Bessie gave him a thumbs-up forgetting she was miked. He returned the thumbs up through the window. Joey patted her on the shoulder and slipped out of the studio. She saw him join Mac at the soundboard. Joey put his two hands together and pointed them at her.

Bessie began playing one of his Joey's songs – one she had now played dozens of time. One she could play in her sleep. Despite this, she alternated between little mistakes in the finger picking or the lyrics. Her frustration came through the sheet of glass separating her from was obvious the two men.

"It's OK. Don't worry. You're just warming up while I get the levels," Mac assured her through the headphones.

Joey knew that Bessie singing in a studio would be a very different experience from singing to him in his living room. He didn't blame her for being nervous. Bessie continued to make uncharacteristic flubs, slowly eating away at their hour of free studio time. She knew this, which only added to her frustration until finally and quite unexpectedly, Bessie felt tears running down her cheek. She could not remember the last time she had cried. She stopped in mid-verse and covered her eyes with one hand. Joey and Mac could hear her muffled sobs through the speakers in the control room. Mac took a drag from his cigarette and a gulp from another his ginger ale and milk concoction and gave Joey a knowing look.

Joey returned the same look and said, "Give me a sec…" as he dashed back into the studio. Once again he placed both hands on her shoulders and leaned down to peer into her face she was shielding with one hand.

"Hey, hey, hey…come on…you can do this. I've seen you do this in front of people."

Bessie looked up and wiped her tears away. She sniffed and wiped her nose, giving an embarrassed glance toward Mac on the other side of the glass.

"I know. That's the problem, I guess."

Joey stood up and dropped his hands from her shoulders, looking perplexed. "What is?"

Bessie took a deep breath to gather enough strength to clarify. "That's just it. There's nobody here to sing to."

Joey put his hands on his hips and turned to look back over his shoulder toward Mac and then back to Bessie. "You've got Mac and me to sing to," Joey tried to persuade.

Bessie shook her head. "It's not the same. You're…way over there…behind that stupid window looking at me like I'm some…I don't know what…on display…"

Joey once again placed his hands on her shoulders. "OK, OK. Tell you what? How about if I sit right over here…" Joey walked over to the side of the room in front of the window where another stool sat. "Like this…and you can sing to me. Would that work?"

Bessie sniffed and nodded with a tentative "Maybe."

"OK, let's give it a try, shall we?" Joey turned to look at Mac through the glass. "Is that OK with you, Mac?" He gave another thumbs up. Joey turned back to Bessie. "There. How's that? I know…just one more thing…" Joey paused and turned back to Mac. "Can we dim the lights a bit, Mac?"

Magically the overhead lights came down while a single pinpoint of light emanated from the overhead track lighting that softly splashed over Bessie. Joey perched himself on the stool in the shadows – folded his hands into his lap and smiled.

"Now…sing to me, Bess."

Chapter 10

A week later, Bessie and Joey had a crate full of cassette tapes containing the two songs of his that she had performed in *The Box* plus a version of The Beatles' *Norwegian Wood*. They had arranged the verses in a kind of syncopated bassa nova 5/4 time signature. Bessie went back and forth between an A major and G major chord in this wonky new time meter that slid right into the original 3/4 meter and A minor for the bridge. The fourth sample on the demo was the Judy Collins' song, *Since You've Asked*, that she had auditioned with at The House. Both had been recorded in one take. The next step was getting a headshot. At the conclusion of one of their afternoon sessions, Joey alerted Bessie that a friend of his would be coming over the next day to take some pictures and suggested that Bessie bring a couple of different outfits. Excited, Bessie spent over an hour standing in front of her closet the night before debating what to bring.

Bessie arrived at Joey's apartment the next day promptly at noon, as always. "Knock-knock! I'm here!" Bessie announced as she propped the door open and leaned inside.

"Come on in – we're in here!" Joey called from his bedroom. She immediately took note of the pronoun in his reply. Bessie came in and carefully laid out a half a dozen blouses, skirts, slacks and one dress on the sofa before taking off her coat. She pulled her chestnut hair back behind her ears and walked toward the bedroom door. Standing at the threshold, she could see that Joey had shoved his bed out of the way to create an ample staging area against the wall. Next to him was a beautiful young woman. She had shoulder length brown hair. It looked like her jeans had been sprayed on to her. A white, lacy peasant top did little to conceal her figure. Bessie froze. Joey looked up after situating the wooden stool she had come to know so well just so.

"Jane…this is Bess. Bess…this is Jane, my old girlfriend."

Bessie wondered why on earth Joey added that last little detail. *Old girlfriend*???? What the hell was that supposed to mean? The girl immediately and accurately read the expression on Bessie's face. Jane cocked her head and explained with dramatic chagrin and one hand on her hip, "That was a long time ago."

Bessie's shoulders dropped along with her apprehension and stretched out her hand, "Nice to meet you."

Jane accepted and then released Bessie's hand adding, "I've heard a lot about you," as she nonchalantly turned her attention to fiddling with her camera lens.

"Oh…OK…well I sure appreciate you helping out," Bessie clumsily responded.

Jane then looked up and back at Bessie, inspecting her for a moment. "Yeah, Joey's pretty excited. But…" she paused dramatically and looked at Joey with a raised eyebrow… "he's yet to let me hear you."

"Look, I told you, we just got her demo tape made," Joey argued in his defense.

Jane shrugged. "OK…if you say so."

Bessie interrupted with the hope of redirecting the conversation. "Well anyway…I brought some different outfits. They're out there in the living room. Do you want me to bring them in?"

Jane once again put one hand on her hip as she looked at Bessie. "No…not just yet. What I *would* like to do is hear this demo of yours," the ex-girlfriend said. Joey detected the impatient annoyance in Jane's eyes.

"What for?" There was a hint of either suspicion or protection or, possibly both, in Joey's voice.

"It'll help me decide what kind of image we want to create. Before we can show people what you look like on the outside, I need to know what you look like on the inside…make sense?"

Bessie and Joey exchanged glances. Joey shrugged. "Yeah…makes sense…I guess," he reluctantly added. "OK, let's go into the other room and I'll put it on."

The three of them paraded into Joey's cramped living room. Bessie moved her wardrobe aside as she and Jane arranged themselves each at one end of the tiny sofa. Joey popped the cassette into the player and retreated to Bessie's end of the sofa. He perched himself on the sofa's arm and folded his hands together in his lap with closed eyes allowing the music to wash over him. Bessie listened with a mix of excitement and embarrassment as she watched Joey's ex-girlfriend listen deeply. Jane simply stared at the speakers, displaying no reaction whatsoever. Bessie squirmed and licked her lips. The player clicked off when the cassette reached the end of the tape. Jane's only response was a whispered, "Wow."

Bessie felt compelled to break the awkward silence and quickly reached over to grab the bundle of clothes by the hanger hooks. "So…Jane…" she made a concerted effort to call her by name in an attempt to display her feigned indifference to her past and present role… "which one of these do you think…"

Jane stood up and glanced at the clothes and then shifted her silent gaze back to Bessie. After a few seconds, Jane reached over and grabbed Bessie's hand. "Put those down. Come with me," and led Bessie into the bedroom with Joey following. Jane pulled Bessie to the stool and let go of her hand. "Here…have a seat. Joey? Do you have some candles around here?"

He swallowed hard "Uh, yeah. Somewhere. Why?"

"Go and get me some will you? Oh, and some matches, too."

Joey took his puzzled face into the kitchen where the two women could hear him rifle through drawers and cabinets. Jane turned to Bessie.

"OK, take off your blouse."

"What?" Bessie cringed.

Jane's whole face grimaced dramatically and impatiently. "You heard me."

Bessie slowly unbuttoned her top keeping an eye on the bedroom door. She shyly slipped it off and handed it to Jane, who simply tossed it on the bed just as Joey returned with some candles and matches.

Bessie folded arms across her stomach and rubbed her elbows watching Joey watch the two of them with wide eyes.

Jane turned to Joey. "Cool. OK, now light one of them and turn off the overhead light, will you?"

Joey followed her instructions and stood in a golden halo that cast a warm glow through the room.

Jane continued to choreograph. "Joey…move closer to Bess."

He slowly stepped toward the stool.

"Stop! Right there! Don't move. Now…lift the bedspread up with your other hand," Jane instructed. Joey deftly raised the bedcover up while still holding the candle as Jane continued with her direction. "There! Nice! That's blocking the glow of the candle on the wall creating a nice black background."

Joey glanced toward the wall to see the effect she described, wondering how it would look in the photo.

Jane walked over to her tripod and attached her camera. She looked through the eyepiece and uttered, "Nice," under her breath before lifting her head to look at Bessie. "OK, now…turn your body the other way…" she gestured by nodding her head.

Bessie shifted her body on the stool exposing her side and profile to the camera.

"Right. Now…pull your bra strap down."

She followed Jane's direction without a hint of hesitation or shyness as her bra strap disappeared out of the frame in the lens finder. Bessie peered up and looked through the lens to determine Jane's satisfaction.

"God! That's perfect."

The Nikon camera came alive in a flurry of snaps. Bessie maintained her pose. Joey stood breathlessly, watching. After a few minutes of minor adjustments, Jane stood up and away from her camera.

"OK. I think we've got it."

Bessie's whole body collapsed as she could once again relax and breathe. She stood up, forgetting she was in her bra, and reached for her blouse. As she began to button it, Bessie turned to Jane.

"So…what was that all about?" the model asked the photographer.

Jane leaned against Joey's dresser and let her hands flop against her thighs with a sigh. "I listened to that tape of yours and well…" she paused to search for words before continuing. "My God, Bess…I heard you bare your soul. I mean…you weren't just singing…you *were* the songs. And so, I realized I had to capture that…that…essence."

Bessie stood in silence and turned to Joey. He smiled before chiming in. "See, Bess? That's what I told you that first night I heard you. Jane felt it too…didn't you?" Joey asked, turning to Jane for confirmation.

"Well…anyway…" Jane stood and began gathering up her camera and equipment. "…I'll run this down to the dark room and print some proof sheets for you to look at. Hopefully you'll find something that works for you."

Bessie and Joey offered an enthusiastic "We will!" in unison. They smiled at each other, embarrassed at being in sync. Jane slung the strap of her camera bag over her shoulder and hefted the tripod resting it on top of the other shoulder. Together, the three of them walked out of the bedroom and into the living room.

"You wanna stay a while? Want a beer?" Joey offered in a feeble attempt as a feeble host.

Jane glanced at both of them knowingly. "No, I'm gonna head out. I'm eager to get into the darkroom to see how these turned out." Jane walked over to Bessie and gave her a quick peck of a kiss on her cheek. "Nice meeting you. Good luck." She turned to face Joey adding, "You take good care of her…you hear me?"

Joey nodded.

Jane winked at him and let herself out the door.

Joey and Bessie just looked at each other as the photographer closed the door

Chapter 11

The next day, Bessie tapped on Joey's door before letting herself in. He was sitting at the tiny kitchen table with a can of PBR. His head was cradled in one hand as he set his elbow on the tabletop. He was pouring over the proof sheet of Jane's work that she had left in an envelop he found leaning against the back door just a few minutes before Bessie's arrival. They had more than likely passed each other in transit.

Bessie removed her coat and tossed it on the sofa as she approached him. "Are those the pictures?"

"Uh huh," he mumbled without taking his eyes off the images.

She pulled out a chair and joined him at the table, craning her neck to see the proofs sprawled in front of them. Joey lifted his head from his hand and handed her one of the proof sheets and a magnifying glass. Bessie leaned down to inspect the postage stamp-sized portraits. She gasped. Joey chuckled.

"I know…amazing aren't they?"

Bessie was mesmerized by the images, barely comprehending she was looking at herself. Joey reached over to point at a specific shot.

"This is the one," he said confidently.

Bessie looked up and simply nodded in agreement.

It was a stunning black and white portrait of Bessie's half lit/half shadowed face against a black background as she turned her head and looked over her bared shoulder toward and *through* the camera lens. The picture was not provocative or alluring.

She didn't appear coy or sexy. But it did more than simply portray a singer. It captured and revealed a purity – an innocence – a vulnerability as well as a tentative boldness.

Joey had a hundred glossy 8 X10 black and white copies of the photo made and sent her promo package of headshot, intro letter, and demo tape out to nearly 100 different venues and agents hoping for a nibble of interest. Meanwhile, Bessie spent her days juggling a few hours of sleep before wandering around her former campus followed by rehearsals at Joey's and ending with her shift at the Country Kitchen, as fall began to slowly fade away. Her initial enthusiasm also began to fade in the dull routine. While appreciative of Joey's mentoring, their afternoon sessions were strictly business – at least to Joey. There was no chitchat let alone any deeper exchange.

One day Bessie heard herself sigh as she parked and turned off the ignition. Secretly, she was harboring a first hint of fatigue tinged with some dread as she lugged her guitar case around to the back door of the little white house. At the same time, Bessie was dazed by Joey's devotion. No one had ever lavished her with such attention. She was unsure what and how she felt – about their grand plans as well as what she currently felt about Joey.

She no longer knocked and waited for an invitation to come in. She simply opened the door and walked in.

"It's me!" she announced. Bessie was immediately halted at the doorway by an invisible wall of utter magic. She closed her eyes and inhaled deeply. "What am I smelling?" she asked with breathless wonder.

"Cookies," came a flat reply from the kitchen.

Bessie took another deep breath and set her guitar case down and pulled off her coat. "That…is…heavenly!" she exclaimed emphasizing each word as she tossed her coat on to the sofa. She leaned down to pick up her guitar case as Joey came around the corner from the kitchen carrying a plate of chocolate chip cookies that he set down on the table.

"No, no…leave the guitar there and come on over," he said pulling out a chair as an invitation to sit. Bessie did so, watching him return from the kitchenette with a carton of milk and two glasses.

"What's all of this?"

Joey heard the surprise in her voice.

"A celebration," he said as he sat next to her and began pouring the milk into the glasses.

Bessie gleefully rolled up her shirtsleeves in anticipation. "Celebration?" Of what?"

Joey set the milk carton down and looked deeply at her. "You…us!"

Bessie squirmed slightly in her chair. "I don't understand."

Joey leaned over the table resting his chin in his fingers as he placed his elbows on the table. He sat there for a moment.

"I have a couple of things to tell you."

Bessie cocked her head. "Yes?"

Joey sat back in his seat and let his hands rest on the table. "Well, first off...you're ready."

"Ready?"

"You're ready to go on the road. And..." he paused dramatically before continuing..."I've lined up a bit of a tour for you."

Bessie sat up in her chair and gasped.

Joey raised one his hands. "Now, now...we're not talking about a world tour or anything. In fact, it's going to be pretty low-end. I've got you booked at some college coffee houses and a few honest-to-goodness clubs here in the Midwest."

"Joey!" Bessie exclaimed.

"Like I said, it's pretty rough and ready stuff...no frills. We'll be roughing it but it'll be good for you. A good way to cut your teeth...pay your dues...build your chops and all the other pithy clichés that escape me right now," he tossed his loss of words backhandedly into the air.

"I can hardly believe it!" Bessie's gasped with her hand at her throat.

"Well...believe it. You've worked hard. It's time. We'll go over all the gory details later. After hearing them, you may change your mind," he said with a sly grin.

"Oh Joey...I can't wait to hear all about it. Thank you...thank you!" Bessie gushed. She caught her breath and folded her hands in front of her in an attempt to calm her self down. "So...you said you had something else."

Joey nudged the plate of cookies in front of her. "Here…have one."

Bessie reached over to pick up one of the cookies. It was still warm and it slowly began to fold in half in all its droopy, soft glory. She had to lean in under the drooping cookie to take a bite before it fell apart in her hand. Clumsily, she held one hand under her chin to catch the bits that crumbled off her lips. Joey watched her close her eyes and slightly lift her face up to the heavens as if in prayer to the gods.

With eyes still closed, she moaned blissfully, "Oh my God…this is amazing! And chocolate chip are my favorite!"

Joey looked at her, pleased with her response. "You like it?" he playfully probed.

"Like it? Are you kidding me?" she gushed with a mouthful of cookie.

She finally opened her eyes and reached for the glass of milk to chase down the medallion of wonder. Bessie cleared her throat as she set the glass back on the table.

"So…you were saying…"

For the first time in the weeks they had spent together, Bessie sensed some hesitation on Joey's part – perhaps even some nervousness. She worked at bridling some of her enthusiasm to allow some space for Joey to continue with whatever it was he was so obviously desperately trying to say.

He swallowed, "I guess this is a kind of confession in some ways." He stopped and licked his lips.

Bessie was taken aback. She was nervous for him more so than about what he might say. "Go on," she gently coaxed.

He took a cookie from the plate and took a bite. They both sat in silence as he chewed, swallowed, and took a drink of milk. He placed the glass down with resolve to continue.

"You see…I never told you something that first night we met."

Bessie's heart was pounding. "Yeah?"

An embarrassed smile came across his face as he looked down for a moment. When he looked up, he took another bite of the cookie to help delay his confession and fuel his courage. Bessie began to sense that Joey was gradually revealing a chink in the armor he had so ardently worn thus far during their interactions.

"That night…I sat there watching you and listening to you. I remember thinking to myself, 'My God, this is like milk and cookies' and I…" he let his words trail off.

Bessie furrowed her brow. "I'm afraid I don't understand."

Joey surprised both of them when he reached across the table and took one of her hands. "You know…it's like when you were a little kid…and when you got hurt or were upset about something…your Mom would bake you cookies. I just remembered how good it felt…not just how good it tasted…but how good it felt to warm yourself with those fresh-baked cookies and wash it down with a cold glass of milk. I don't know…it's as if cookies and milk somehow managed to make everything right. They're like the perfect comfort food for the soul. Know what I mean? That's how you. up on stage, made me feel. Your voice…your presence. You were like cookies and milk to me that night. I know that must sound stupid or corny. But I was coming out of some deep dark places and then…you came out of nowhere and rescued me."

"Rescued you? Me? How?" Bessie implored.

Joey nodded and then tried to shake away his embarrassment. "Jesus…look at me…"

Bessie squeezed his hand. "It's OK. Go on."

Joey took a deep breath. "I guess the back story doesn't really matter. The point is you…and your voice are like milk and cookies…to me anyway. You make me feel…I don't know…whole…complete. You know…just like when your mother used to make you cookies. And I want others to experience that."

Joey looked deep into Bessie's eyes that were beginning to fill with tears. She placed her free hand at the base of her throat and filled her lungs with air and the bittersweet truth that suddenly revealed itself to her.

"I don't know what to say," Bessie confessed through her tears and gasps.

"You don't have to say anything. I just wanted you to know…that's all."

Bessie lifted her eyes upward and took another deep breath. "No, you don't understand…" Bessie tried to explain.

"Understand what?"

"This..." she gestured with both hands across the table and continued, "and you...I mean... Oh, God...it's just so hard..." she paused to wipe her tears away.

"What? What's so hard?" Joey was now somewhat alarmed at Bessie's unexpected reaction.

She raised her shoulders as she took a deep breath and then dropped them along with her exhalation and secret. "My mother never made me cookies."

Joey stared blankly at her. "What do you mean?"

Bessie flopped her hand down on the table in exasperation. "I mean...she never made me cookies like this. I've never...you know ... had this...this wonderful experience before," she confessed.

Joey pulled his hand away from hers and sat back in his chair, second-guessing himself. "Jesus...I'm sorry Bess. I never would have..."

She cut him off. "No, no...don't be sorry. It's wonderful. It's lovely. I mean it. This was such a gift to me. You are such a gift to me. I don't...I don't..." she let her words dangle as her bittersweet revelation continued to sink in.

Joey got up and walked around to her side of the table and gently placed his hand on her shoulder. She turned and buried her face into her other shoulder as she reached up and rested her hand on top of his. After a few deep sobs, Bessie lifted her head and wiped away the tears with an embarrassed chuckle and smile.

"So...is it OK if I have another cookie?

Chapter 12

Thwack, thwack, thwack.

Bessie snapped her pencil in deep deliberation like a drumstick across the yellow pad of paper as if it were the head of snare drum.

"Is that everything?" Joey asked.

"I think so. That's everything on the list, anyway." Bessie consulted the pad in her hand. The page flapped in the cold October wind hinting at winter's impending arrival.

"Wow, I didn't think we'd get everything in there. Let's see…two suitcases, amp, guitar case, mics and mic stands, wooden stool, wardrobe bag, two sleeping bags, ice cooler…" Joey continued taking inventory in the trunk of Bessie's Ford LTD.

"Wait…sleeping bags?" Bessie questioned.

"Yeah, you never know what we might find in the way of accommodations. Some of these places can be a real dump and I don't plan on sleeping on or in their sheets…if you know what I mean," Joey explained.

Bessie held up her hand and mimed nervously chewing on her nails at the image Joey had provided. Then she gave one final look into the trunk. "Well, I know all of this would have never fit in your car," she surmised.

"You've got that right." Satisfied with their inspection, Joey slammed the lid of the trunk closed. "Are you sure you're OK with us taking your car?"

Bessie flopped her arms against her thighs. "We've been through this already. Besides, my beast has more interior room than your Mustang – we'll be more comfortable."

Joey leaned his head to the side. "True. Good point." He stuffed his hands into the front pockets of his jeans and paused. "So…what did your Mom have to say this morning?"

Bessie sighed and looked down the street. "Not much."

"So, is she excited for you or is she pissed off?"

"I can't really tell. That's the thing. I never can tell. She's just off in her own little world – it really doesn't matter much what I do. So, I simply said we're taking off today."

"And?"

"She said good luck." Bessie sighed once again.

Joey shook his head out of disbelief and sympathy.

To change the subject, Bessie gave the trunk lid a gentle pat for good luck. "So…there it is. Everything we're going to need to keep us going for six weeks." Her comment was not so much a statement of fact as much as it was her own attempt at assuaging her own doubt.

"Yup." Joey confirmed.

They both looked at each other for a moment. Bessie finally pulled her car keys from her front pocket and held them up by the ignition key.

"Who wants to drive first?" she smiled as Joey took her keys from her.

With that, the two of them embarked on a six-week tour that would zigzag its way up and down the map. Both the itinerary and their budding partnership would have their own ups and downs along the way. The venues varied from church basement coffee houses, which were a hot trend during the 70s, to college coffee houses, to actual clubs – some with notable reputation. As tradition would have it, many if not most, of the smaller coffeehouses offered Spartan overnight accommodation for the wandering minstrels who took to their tiny stages as part of their recompense for performing. The only exception to that expectation was a surprise on Bessie's very first gig on the road.

They drove the 90-minute trip north to Grand Forks to play at a coffeehouse in the basement of a Lutheran Church. Their first inkling that things were going to be different here was the fact that the walls were adorned with One-Way Jesus-Freak posters. The décor made both of them nervous – enough so that when Joey shook hands with the Manager/Pastor, he asked the man if he had listened to Bessie's demo tape.

"Indeed, I did!" Pastor Ray exuded. "I enjoyed it very much. The kids are going to love Bessie – Bessie James…I love that."

Joey and Bessie looked at each other before she continued the reconnaissance of the cliental as Joey had coached her. "Um, well…you know that I don't do…um…you know…I guess you'd call it, 'Praise Music'…don't you?"

The pastor, appearing to be only a few years older than the two of them, leaned back with a hearty laugh.

"Goodness sakes. Of course, I do. No, no, no…your repertoire is no issue here. Our mission is to provide some safe space for youngsters to hang out. No, in fact, I'm counting on you to do some peppy pop songs…they'll love it."

Both of them exhaled a sigh of relief.

The pastor continued his jovial banter. "So…how long have you two been together?"

Bessie glanced over at Joey. "Oh, about…3 or 4 weeks or so…wouldn't you say, Joey?"

Joey nodded while scanning the tiny stage in the corner in the basement.

"Newlyweds! How marvelous!" the pastor clapped his hands together in celebration.

Once again, the duo looked at each other wondering what to say and who would say it. Joey finally took the leap.

"Oh…well…you see…we're not…um…married. I'm her manager."

A frown swept the smile off the pastor's face. "Oh. I see. Well…then…we may have a problem with the uh…accommodations."

Joey and Bessie exchanged yet another look at each other.

"What do you mean? What's the problem? Your venue profile said you offered overnight housing for the talent." Joey inquired.

Pastor Ray swallowed hard and wrung his hands together. "Indeed. However, most of our performers are solo acts. We occasionally have duos and we put them up. However…I'm afraid we have a policy that you must be married to stay here."

"What?" Joey exclaimed. "Where does it say that it the contract?"

The pastor stammered. "Well, it's…shall we say…implied."

"That's bullshit!" Joey shouted.

The pastor raised both hands to calm Joey down. "Please, please…there's no need to get angry or raise your voice. I'm sure we can work something out."

Joey glared at the pastor, his chest heaving with anger. Bessie reached over and gently placed her hand on Joey's arm softly whispering…"Joey…" which immediately brought her ever-loyal manager back down to earth. She turned to the pastor.

"I'd really like to sing here tonight. Are you sure we can't just…you know…crash here on the floor or something?"

The pastor continued wringing his hands. "I'm afraid not. It's against church policy. I'm rather new here at the Parish and I'm dubious of violating policy."

Bessie glanced down at the floor for a moment. "I see…" as she turned to Joey.

"I don't know, Bess. But I gotta tell you…" he paused and glared at the pastor…"I think it's a little ironic that you and your flock are so damn worried about a couple living in sin when its you who's screwing us." Joey walked away.

Pastor Ray swallowed hard and pulled a handkerchief from his back pocket to wipe his brow. "My, my!" he gasped.

Bessie was embarrassed as well as eager to do her first gig on the road. "I'm sorry. He's just…you know…very dedicated to me and my career."

The pastor returned the handkerchief to his pocket. "Yes, well…I can see that."

Bessie scanned the room and returned her attention to the brooding pastor. "I want us to work something out. Is there someplace close by…and cheap…where we can stay tonight?"

With a sigh of relief, the pastor replied with a smile. "Yes, there's a Motel 6 just a block or so away. I hear they're very comfortable…and economical."

Bessie nodded. "OK. I'll do the gig tonight and we'll clear out."

He clapped his hands together. "I'm so glad. I truly enjoyed your voice when I listened to the tape. The kids are very excited to hear you. They're such a good group. I know you'll love them."

Bessie offered a smile but felt its insincerity. "OK, then. We'll set up…get a bite to eat and be back by 8:00."

"Super! There's a great little pizza joint down the block…you might want to check it out. Oh, and there's a green room around the corner for you and your…uh…manager to use before the performance and during your break."

"OK, cool. Well then…We'll see you in a little bit."

"Thanks, Bessie…God bless you."

"Yeah…thanks."

Bessie wandered out to the parking lot to find Joey leaning against her Ford LTD. She walked over and leaned against it with him – in a tense silence that seemed to last forever.

"So…are we playing or not?" he inquired flatly.

"We are."

Joey nodded while keeping his gaze on the parking lot of a Red Owl supermarket across the street. "I'll go set up then," and he turned to the back of the car and popped open the trunk with the keys to begin unloading their modest amount of gear.

"Hey…" Bessie called out as he walked away lugging the amp in one hand and guitar case in the other."

Joey stopped and turned to look over his shoulder without saying anything.

"I know where we can stay tonight…it's just a block away," she shouted across the parking lot. Joey just turned and continued walking toward the back door of the church annex. "Oh…and…" she called out again to stop him in mid-step – this time he didn't turn his head. "There's a pizza place nearby…how's that for supper?" He just continued walking toward the church. His silent indifference hurt more than if he had shouted at her the way he had at the pastor.

Bessie discerned it was best to give Joey some space, opting to take a short walk around the block to scope out the location of the motel and pizza joint. She returned a half an hour later to find the church back door propped open with an empty pop can. She opened the door and made her way to the tiny stage to find Prudence perched in its guitar stand, her amp, stool, and mic stand in place ready to go. What she did not find, however, was Joey. She made her way to the tiny dressing room around the corner from the stage. In it, she found a small dressing table and two metal folding chairs. There was a hook for hangers above a full-length mirror on the back of the door. Her wardrobe bag hung there. The room was nothing more than a janitor's closet, exuding about the same amount of warmth and comfort.

She took a seat on the cold folding chair, folded her arms, and waited. And waited. And waited some more. Bessie began to fret as she heard the murmur of a small group of teenagers in the other room. She looked down at her watch. It read 7:45 pm.

Still no Joey.

Bessie changed out of her jeans and denim shirt and into nicer pair of jeans and a softer embroidered shirt she pulled out of the wardrobe bag. She sat on the chair nervously rubbing her hands over her thighs. Bessie jumped slightly when she heard the thump of a P.A. system come to life.

"Good evening! How's everybody doing tonight? So glad you could make it. Wow…looks like quite a crowd tonight. That's great because we have a talented young lady to sing for us tonight. I know you're going to love her…so let's give a great big Fish and Loaves welcome to the talented Bessie James!"

There was a chorus of whoops and hollering with applause.

Show time!

Bessie was trembling. She could barely hold a guitar pick in her hand. Where was Joey?

117

She managed to pull herself up and off the folding chair to make her way to the stage. She sat down on the stool and looked out over about 50 teenagers who were clumped around some tables. She retrieved Prudence and cradled the guitar in her lap. She smiled and offered a modest bow of the head and simply began picking out the opening chords of *Dear Prudence*. In the back, at a counter that had served countless pancake suppers was Pastor Ray serving Styrofoam cups of coffee, smiling enthusiastically. Somehow or another, Bessie made it through her first set to a surprisingly attentive and appreciative audience of high schoolers getting wired on strong coffee.

"Thank you…thank you so much. You're so nice. Wow! I'm going to take a short break now. Don't go away…promise? OK, thanks. See you in a few minutes."

Bessie returned Prudence to the guitar stand and bounded off the stage to the bleak dressing room. She flung the door open and stood in the threshold scanning the room.

Still no Joey.

Bessie had to remind herself to breathe. Once she did, she looked over to the small dressing table. There, on a small plate were two chocolate chip cookies and a glass of milk. She burst into a mix of laughter and tears as she cupped her two hands over her mouth to mute the sound of her relief.

She spent the 15-minute break soothing her nerves with Joey's remedy. The gaggle of kids continued their loud conversations. Bessie stood up and in front of the full-length mirror for one last inspection before returning to the stage. She made her way on to her stool and began re-tuning her guitar. Once ready, she looked up and out across the crowd. The house lights dimmed slightly. She shielded her eyes for a moment. There, in the back, she could make out a familiar silhouette. The shadowy figure raised an arm and waved. Bessie released a huge sigh of relief and began her second set.

A smattering of teens clamored around Bessie on stage at the end of her first official tour gig. They oozed their youthful admiration with well wishes and a handful of requests for her autograph. Joey stealth-fully began rolling up mic and guitar cables in the background. As the crowd disappeared, Pastor Ray approached the stage.

"That was so amazing! The kids loved you. *I* loved you. We must have you back again in the future!"

Bessie demurred a modest and cautious, "Thanks...we'll see."

Detecting the guarded tone of her response, the pastor wrapped his arm around her shoulder and lowered his voice. "I'm so sorry about...well, you know...the mis-understanding we had earlier. I'm glad we worked that all out."

Bessie just nodded her head. "Yeah, me, too."

She glanced over to Joey who was literally wrapping up everything with the hope of him rescuing her. He caught the look she flashed to him.

Joey leaned down to pick up the stool...the last of the gear to be packed up. "OK...we're good to go!"

Pastor Ray reached into his pocket and pulled out an envelope, handing it to Bessie. "Here you go, my dear."

"Oh, thanks…that should go to Joey."

The pastor blinked. "Of course," and he walked over to Joey. "Here you go, sir. Thanks ever so much." The pastor walked back to Bessie and took both of her hands. "Best of luck to you…" and then he turned to face Joey waiting patiently on stage and continued, "…to both of you. I'm sure you'll go far!"

Joey replied with a terse, "Thanks," and began walking toward the exit.

Bessie shook the pastor's hand. "Thanks. I had a good time."

"Good, I'm so glad. God bless you…both of you!" he waved and walked toward the kitchen humming one of the songs Bessie had performed.

It was a silent five-minute drive to the Motel 6 a block or two away. Joey went in to register while Bessie waited in the car with the engine running. He returned and slid into the seat with a single room key in his hand. He backed the car up a few feet and parked in front of their first floor room. Joey handed Bessie the room key as he walked to the back of the car and opened the trunk to gather their two suitcases. Bessie unlocked the door and walked into the small but efficient room to see two beds. She stood there inspecting the room as Joey walked in, past her, setting her suitcase down beside her. He tossed his suitcase on one of the beds.

"I guess this one's mine," he announced.

He unzipped his suitcase, pulled out his shave kit and headed into the bathroom and closed the door. Bessie shut the room door behind her and heaved her own suitcase on to the other bed and sat down next to it. She sat nervously with her hands in her lap. A moment later, Joey exited the bathroom in his underwear and t-shirt with his shave kit and the wadding of the clothes he had been wearing balled up in his arms. He stuffed them into the suitcase with little finesse. Joey then moved the suitcase on to the floor before pulling back the bedspread and crawling into bed. He propped himself against the orange padded headboard bolted to the wall. Joey reached over to the table in between the two beds to snatch the TV remote. The beat up black and white Zenith television screen flickered to life with the farm reports on the late news.

Bessie looked at him. He could feel her stare but ignored it. "Well...are we going to talk?" she asked.

Without taking his eye off of the television, "If you want."

"Well then..." Bessie waited for him to turn his attention away from the TV screen. He correctly interpreted her and clicked off the TV and turned to her.

"Sure...let's talk." He sat with his arms folded across his stomach.

Bessie rearranged herself on her bed. "Thanks for the cookies and milk...that was such a nice surprise," she said sweetly.

Joey struggled to maintain his stoic façade even though Bessie detected a smile cracking in the corners of his mouth. "I'm glad you liked it."

Bessie cocked her head and sighed to acknowledge the weight in the room. "I'm sorry," she finally offered.

"About what?" Joey faked his confusion.

"About tonight."

He continued to play dumb. "Why? You had what I'd call a successful debut on your tour."

She folded her arms across her chest and furrowed her brow. "You know what I mean."

Joey decided he had let her squirm long enough. "I think we should get a few things ironed out."

Bessie looked at him. "I agree."

Joey pulled one of the pillows on top of his lap and bounced his hands down on top of it. "You're the talent and I'm the manager."

"Right."

"Well…I wasn't so sure."

Bessie sighed deeply and punched her bed. "I said I'm sorry. Look…I was just so looking forward to my first gig. I didn't want to walk out."

Joey stared at her and said nothing.

"Yes, you're right…you're the manager. But don't I have a say in matters?" Bessie shook her head in doubt.

"Sure. But you sideswiped me in front of that asshole," Joey sniped back.

"He wasn't an asshole," Bessie responded calmly.

"Yeah…he was an asshole. The point is…you're right…you do have a say. We discuss these things together and make decisions…*together,*" he emphasized the word.

Joey's point was slowly dawning on her. She had unilaterally given in to the pastor without truly consulting Joey – not that he necessarily would have gone along with her proposal. None-the-less, he was right – they hadn't discussed it…together. At the same time, Bessie had a sudden epiphany about her own agency…or perhaps the lack of it. Ever since that night in the attic at The House, Bessie promised herself that she'd never let anyone – even Joey – take control of her life. But his argument was well taken – they didn't discuss it even if she ultimately had the last word. She decided to try and make light of the moment.

"Well…you didn't ask me which bed I wanted…did you?" she quipped.

A smile gradually emerged, but not his grasp of what she had implied with her remark. "No, I suppose I didn't. Touché."

Bessie stood up and walked over to the side of his bed. "Look…I'm sorry. It won't happen again. You're right…we're partners."

"Promise?"

"I promise.

Bessie extended her hand. Joey reached for it with fake suspicion and shook it. "Deal."

"OK, then. I'm going to take a bath…I need to relax and come down off my high."

Joey reached over and grabbed the TV remote. Johnny Carson soon joined their discussion. "Yeah, I don't doubt that. Go on...chill...enjoy your bath."

He then folded his arms behind his head, getting settled in. Again, her subtle invitation eluded him.

Bessie returned to her suitcase to gather her toiletries and a nightgown. She made her way to the bathroom, closed the door and turned on the bath water. After several moments, she felt her whole body sink into bliss as she submerged herself in the hot water. Nearly a half an hour passed -- she may have even dozed off in the tub. She got out, dried off, and put on a nightgown that she hoped might catch Joey's attention. Bessie felt her pulse quicken as she opened the bathroom door and returned to the room. The blue flicker of the TV screen bathed the room. She stood in the bathroom doorway and turned to see if Joey noticed her entrance. He was quietly snoring.

Chapter 13

"So…I see you brought a book tonight."

A young woman sitting at a table near the stage looked up – blinked, and turned to survey the room to determine if Bessie was speaking to her. Once she realized that Bessie was, in fact, talking to her from the stage, she replied with a guarded, "Uh huh," as she had been reading it through Bessie's entire first set.

Bessie nodded as she leaned against Prudence resting in her lap. "What is it…what's it about?"

Bessie's inquiry from the stage in front of the sparse crowd slightly un-nerved the reader. The woman nervously glanced around the room.

"Uh…it's *Rosemary's Baby*," she replied sheepishly.

"Oh, I love that book. Kinda scary, though. You clearly have good taste. Tell you what…I'll sing something just for you…how's that sound?"

The woman's skeptical frown slipped into an embarrassed smile. "Yeah, OK, sure."

"OK, then. This one's just for you and Rosemary's Baby."

Bessie quickly checked the tuning of her guitar and then dug down deep into her catalogue of songs to pull out *Friend of the Devil* by the Grateful Dead – a tune she had learned jamming at The House. The room burst into applause when she finished the song – the bookworm clapping the loudest. The woman never picked up her book again for the rest of the night.

In truth, Bessie had never cracked the spine of the novel before. Joey stood in the back, leaning against the wall, marveling at what he had just witnessed. He enjoyed watching Bessie break through the 4th wall and dismantle it brick-by-brick to build a bridge to the audience as she was slowly developing a style and presence on stage every night. As he originally sensed the first night he saw her, she had a way of connecting with people. The interaction he had just observed was a glimpse of things to come. He had seen Bessie slyly glance down at the table to see the book cover as she returned to the stage after her first break. She knew all along what the mildly dis-interested patron was reading. Clearly, Bessie took note of it as well and decided to act upon it. Instead of calling the woman out on it, she used it to draw an otherwise dis-interested audience member into her moment.

By the middle of the tour, Bessie chose to roam the venue rather than retreat to a ratty dressing room. Joey watched as, on her own volition, she began to "work the room" by shaking people's hands and chatting. She'd ask students what they were majoring in or where they were from or what year they were in school. It was a combination of connecting and reconnaissance that sometimes resulted in more than she bargained for – like the night she approached a solitary young woman at the Grinnell College coffeehouse.

"Hi. Thanks for coming out tonight" Bessie enthused.

The girl did not look up. She merely rotated her empty coffee mug in her hand, deep in thought. Bessie stood there for a moment debating whether to move on or wait. After a moment, Bessie gently placed a hand on the back of the empty chair at the table.

"You mind if I join you…just for a minute?"

Bessie's question made the woman look up and shyly nod her head.

Bessie chuckled. "Well, does that mean yes you mind and you want me to get lost or…does that mean yes, it's OK if I sit down?"

An embarrassed smile came across the woman's face as she gestured to the empty chair with her hand. Bessie sat down and the two of them sat through an awkward silence for a moment.

"So…what's your name?" Bessie finally asked.

"Jeri."

"You go to school here?"

She nodded.

Bessie gradually began picking up on the vibe. "Rough day?" Bessie gingerly probed.

Another nod.

"I'm sorry."

Bessie waited for details but only received more silence.

"Well…like I said…I'm sorry you've had a rough day. I'll let you alone now…" and started to get up from the table. This elicited an animated response from the girl.

"No…wait. You don't have to go," as she outstretched her hand to keep Bessie from leaving.

Bessie lowered herself back into the wooden chair. She detected a tear in the corner of Jeri's eye who apparently did as well, as she quickly wiped it away with a sniff and a sigh.

"Yeah...you could say it's been a bad day. It's been a bad week, actually."

Bessie uncharacteristically reached across the table and placed her hand on top of one of her hands. "I'm sorry." Bessie didn't try to pry any other information out of the girl. She simply wanted to be present and accompany her wherever her sadness was taking her. The safe space seemed to open a door for the patron to walk through.

"My boyfriend had to go home – his Dad died. So now he has to help out on their farm. He had to drop out of school."

Bessie sighed deeply and squeezed the girl's hand.

"I miss him...know what I mean?"

Bessie nodded, but privately confessed that no, she didn't know what the girl meant as she had never ached the way she was aching. In an odd way, Bessie found herself slightly envious of the girl. Jeri inhaled deeply and dropped her shoulders.

"And this awful weather...God, these grey skies are so depressing...that doesn't help either...know what I mean?"

This time, Bessie *could* relate to the girl's sense of gloom with winter approaching. But again, Bessie said nothing. She just sat there – being *with* the girl – who was now becoming self-conscious. Jeri glanced at her watch.

"Oh, God. I'm taking up your break. You don't need to stay here and take care of me. Really. It was nice of you to…you know…" the forlorn girl let her comment drift.

Bessie gave one more squeeze with her hand. "No…thank *you*…for sharing."

By the time they had exchanged their thanks and goodbyes, it was time for Bessie to return to the stage. She took her place on the stool and looked out at the sad girl of the north sitting at her solitary table a few rows back. Bessie slowly began picking the strings on her guitar and sang Bill Wither's bluesy song, *Ain't No Sunshine When She's Gone*, exchanging the pronoun 'she' with 'he." Bessie had always liked the song and figured she'd eventually include it into her set one of these nights. Tonight was the night. She closed her eyes and climbed into the song. When she finished, she looked out toward Jeri. She was still there at her table, holding both of her hands as if in prayer up to her mouth. When the two of them made eye contact through the smoke, the girl dropped her hands and mouthed, "Thank you." Bessie just nodded and smiled.

Chapter 14

Life on stage was wonderful for Bessie. She attributed her joy and growing confidence to Joey's tutelage and the plate of two good luck cookies – always chocolate chip – he left in the dressing room before each and every performance. Life *off* stage, on the other hand, was a bit more mundane, and at times even a bit muddy, but always predictable. Joey had warned her of this inevitability. But due to her inexperience and completely unrealistic vision of what 'going on the road' entailed, she couldn't really grasp the accuracy of his prophecy. Meals were barebones, consisting mostly of grocery staples they could fit in their Coleman ice chest in the trunk. Breakfast consisted of bagels and cream cheese washed down with instant coffee. Lunchmeat sandwiches on day-old white bread and fruit were for lunch. Supper was slightly more sophisticated by serving up cans of Chef Boyardee spaghetti or La Choy Chop Suey they could heat in a saucepan in the kitchen at the venue with the occasional treat of pizza or McDonalds.

Accommodations, especially at churches, were particularly Spartan, although they could usually access the kitchen space for meals. Sometimes a church offered nothing more than a couple of cots, so they were glad they had included their sleeping bags as an after-thought. Most of the time there were beat up single beds in an attic or basement. A bathroom was down the hall, often without a shower, let alone a bathtub, forcing them to take 'spit baths' in the sink. Digs at actual coffee houses were somewhat better. Colleges typically provided a room in a guesthouse on campus or sometimes a guest room in a dorm. Neither Bessie nor Joey ever complained because it helped cut down on costs. There were, however, a handful of times they had to spring for a motel room where Bessie could luxuriate in a bathtub.

    Post-gig itineraries were the least predictable aspect of being on the road. The only real constant was the obligatory debriefing afterwards with the venue manager and that was about it. Some nights they'd return to their modest accommodations together and collapse, especially if they had spent the day driving. Otherwise, Joey would often stay longer to converse with the manager to talk shop and indulge in beverages stronger than the caffeine that was peddled all night. Sometimes he would not return until morning and usually hung over. If there was a television in their space, Bessie would watch *The Tonight Show* or old movies and fall asleep. If not, she read. There were the occasional sexual advances and overtures from men, and sometimes women, but Bessie always politely declined with the standard excuse that she had something else planned. What she wanted was a long-standing relationship. She longed to make love with a life-long partner rather than give into a short-lived, generally disappointing carnal conquest like the one she had in the attic at The House with Tony. It wasn't her ego or libido that needed to be caressed – it was her heart.

    Their tour continued to bounce back and forth between college towns in Minnesota, Iowa, and Wisconsin. This was so Bessie could continue to cut her teeth in the generally polite confines of college coffee houses. Joey knew she also needed to take it up a notch by playing some actual clubs where the crowds would be older and possibly less gentile and attentive. Their first foray into this realm of venues was a brief side trip across the border to Fort Frances, Ontario.

"Now we can legitimately call this an international tour!" Joey joked.

She had to play one night in this border town that reeked of putrid fumes from the paper mills. Joey hesitated at taking the gig at first, given it was only for one night. It was, however, at an actual club, not a church or college coffeehouse, aptly called the *Paper Moon* at the Prince Edward Hotel. This was one of the first gigs Joey had actually booked, nearly 3 months earlier. Being focused on the rest of the tour, he hadn't checked back with the management to confirm details and logistics once he received the contract. The crossing of the border at International Falls went without a hitch. Unfortunately, one was waiting for them when they pulled up in front of the hotel late at night, exhausted. Even in the dark and haze of their fatigue, they immediately sensed something was wrong.

"This is the main entrance…isn't it?" Joey asked as he peered through the dirty windshield.

"Looks like it. But…I don't see any lights on inside, do you?"

Joey heard the confusion in her voice that was gradually becoming tinged with concern.

"Hmmm – let me hop out and take a peek," he said as he opened the driver's door and walked up to the glass doors. He cupped both hands along side his face to blot out the other city lights as he peered inside. Joey turned around, with his head down, shaking it side-to-side trying to make sense of the situation.

"Well?" Bessie inquired as Joey got back into the car.

"It's closed."

She stared blankly at him. "What do you mean, it's closed? Hotels don't close…do they?"

He shrugged, "Well, evidently this one does. It looks like it's gone out of business. It's essentially empty."

Bessie's jaw dropped open. "So what does that mean?"

Joey clamped both hands on the steering wheel and stared ahead through the windshield.

"Look, there's a phone booth across the street," Bessie observed.

Joey rummaged through his bundle of paperwork and finally located the contract. He scanned the page for a moment. "Here's the phone number…I'll give them a call," he told her as he hopped out of the car once again.

Bessie sat in the car and watched. Joey hung up the phone and then entered the drug store next to the phone booth. Within a couple of minutes, Joey trotted back across the street, and he once again plopped down behind the steering wheel.

"Well?" she probed.

"No answer. I checked with the drug store. The guy behind the counter said the place got closed down."

"Closed down? What does that mean?" Bessie was near tears.

"I guess that means there's no gig. We have no place to stay tonight."

Bessie flopped back into her seat and ran her hands through her hair. "That's crazy."

"Yeah… it is," Joey nodded.

"I mean…didn't you call and check before we went on the road?"

Joey took his hands off the steering wheel and flopped them into his lap. "No. I mean…they signed and returned the contract so I assumed we were good to go. Why would I check? Since when do hotels just shut down?"

They sat in the idling car saying nothing, letting the reality of their situation sink in. Bessie asked tentatively, "So where are we going to stay? Our accommodation was part of the deal, wasn't it?"

"Yeah. But here's the thing, Bess…" Joey had to find the courage to break the truth to her.

She looked at him, waiting for him to continue.

"I hate to say this but…we don't have enough cash to pay for a hotel…not even a cheap motel. I've been counting on this accommodation being thrown in and well…this gas-hog is taking a bite out of coffers."

She gulped. "But...we've been so good at getting groceries for the ice cooler instead of eating out."

"You're right...we have. It's just..."

"It's just what?" she interrupted.

"We've been paid with checks and I haven't been able to cash any of them. So, it's not like we're broke...we're just low on liquid cash."

Bessie began digging through her purse. "I only have ten bucks."

"Well...that's more that I have right now. Besides, what we *do* have are US dollars."

"Geez, that's right. What were we thinking? Wait...what about your credit card?"

"It's maxed out. And no...I wasn't thinking. Besides...from the looks of things as we drove into town, most of the motels had No Vacancy signs lit, so there's no place to go anyway. Something must be going on here in town...a convention or something," he added as he hunched down and surveyed the street through the windshield.

"So what are we going to do?"

He turned to her. "I guess we'll have to boon dock it tonight."

"Boon dock?" she repeated.

"Yeah, you know...head out of town...park the car somewhere and sleep in it."

She stared at him blankly, trying to picture what he was suggesting. He could see that nothing came to her eyes and tried to make light of it.

"Now…aren't you glad we drove your car and not mine? Tell you what, you can take the back seat and I'll take the front. How's that sound?" Joey offered.

Bessie's headshake of disbelief was her only response. Joey put the Ford into gear.

"Okie dokie…let's go find us a place to crash."

"Bad choice of words, Joe!" Bessie sniped.

He chuckled. "Sorry…let's go find a place to spend the night."

Joey could sense Bessie's anxiety as she silently rode shotgun.

"Come on…it'll be fun. Think of it as an adventure."

She just glared at him. A dense fog crept in as they drove toward the outskirts of town. The headlights barely cut through the heavy shroud until they flashed across what appeared to be a levee. Joey pulled up beside the mound of dirt and killed the engine.

"Home sweet home," he announced.

Bessie sat quietly for a moment. Joey just looked at her.

"I gotta pee," she announced.

Joey extended his arm toward the wide-open expanses of Ontario outside their windows. "There you go!" he gestured.

She got out of the car and slammed the door, making sure he felt her consternation about the whole situation. She then made her way behind some bushes along the levee to relieve herself. When she returned, she could see both car doors were open as the interior light glowed in the fog.

"You want front or back?" Joey asked.

Without a word, she crawled into the back seat and began fashioning a pillow out of her pea coat. Joey just shook his head as he stepped outside. Now he was glad they had made room for their sleeping bags. He yanked them out of the trunk and tossed one to Bessie.

"Thanks," she grumbled as she pulled it up over her.

"Well…goodnight," he wished her as he wrangled his way into the front seat, wedging his legs in front of the steering wheel. Joey offered one last comment with the hopes it would lighten the weight of the moment.

"Well, I guess you're going to need to learn some blues."

Bessie finally broke her indignant silence. "Why do you say that?"

"Cause you're officially payin' your dues now, lady."

Joey heard a muffled chuckle rise from the back seat.

Exhaustion blanketed them and they quickly fell asleep.

About an hour later, a rumbling sound gradually filled the silence of the chilly autumn night. Suddenly, a bright light penetrated the dense fog, creating a gauzy, pulsating glow in the dark. The car began shaking, almost as if an earthquake was happening. Bessie shot up straight out of her sleep and the back seat.

"My God! What is it?" she screamed.

Joey bolted up out of the front seat.

"Jesus!" he gasped.

The two of them stared helplessly at a massive, vibrating structure crawling a mere few feet away from the car.

"Oh my God…it's a UFO!" Bessie exclaimed out of her stupor.

Joey was now bracing the passenger door shut with his two feet in a futile attempt to barricade whatever it was from entering the car. The bright light had passed them. The bellowing rumble began to fade, replaced with a clacking sound. Bessie strained her eyes, trying to see through the dense fog. Sparks were flying here and there. An awful grinding of metal shrieked. After a moment, Bessie finally found her voice.

"It's a…train!"

What they thought was a levee was the rise of a railroad track. The car was parked a mere four feet from the spinning wheels of a freight train.

Once they realized what was happening, they both broke out in laughter.

"What else can happen tonight?" Bessie blurted.

"My heart is absolutely pounding," Joey confessed.

"I'm glad I peed when I did, otherwise, we'd have another crisis to deal with!" Bessie joked.

Their laughter gradually faded, along with the freight train that had moved on into the distance. Each of them lay back down in their makeshift beds. Soon, Bessie could hear Joey's breathing get slower. She exhaled deeply. Her brush with death emboldened her.

"Joey?"

Her whispered call to him elicited a slight gasp, bringing him up and out of the twilight zone of sleep he was starting to descend into.

"Yeah?"

She lay there staring up at the darkened interior light on the ceiling of her car as she cautiously probed for some illumination. "Can I ask you something?"

"Yeah."

She paused to carefully choose her words. Her silence evoked a prod from him.

"What is it?"

Bessie licked her lips. "Have you ever…you know…been in love?"

She could hear him mull over her question.

"Why do you ask?"

"Oh…just wondering. So…have you?"

The chirping crickets outside the car muffled the sound of her beating heart as she waited for his answer.

"I think so."

His vague answer surprised her. She had expected either a yes or a no.

"What do you mean…you *think* so?"

"Well…I mean there's a difference between being in love and loving someone."

Bessie pondered the truth of this for a moment.

"Well…have you…been in love, I mean."

"Yes. Once."

"Was it…Jane?"

"No."

"So you just…loved her…Jane, I mean."

"I guess."

"But you weren't *in* love with her…right?

Joey didn't respond.

"I imagine there's been…you know…lots of girls with you playing rock and roll and all that…right?"

More crickets. Within a few more minutes, Bessie could hear the slight snoring come from the front seat.

Chapter 15

Bessie stared out into the half-filled room. She waited. The chattering that had gone on all night continued. No one was paying any attention. They hadn't all night. This was rare. The crowd at *The Natural High* in Kinosha, Wisconsin was self-absorbed with its own jibber-jabber and ignored her music playing in the background of their personal dramas. At first, she was frustrated, as she had looked forward to this gig. This was a club with a reputation. But clearly, for some unknown reason, it was an off night. Bessie looked to Joey at the side of the stage and offered a bewildered look. He answered by shrugging his shoulders. She had essentially spent the second set entertaining her self by trying out some new tunes. So, out of a combination of desperation and defeat, Bessie dug down deep to pull up a tune that would at least entertain her, if no one else.

"Well...tonight I want to close tonight with a tune my Mom taught me a long time ago and it goes something like this..."

She plunked out a poky cowboy tune on her guitar and began to serenade Joey with the old Roy Rogers and Dale Evans song, *Happy Trails to You*, she used to sing with her mother.

"Come on, everybody...join in with me now!" she shouted with mock enthusiasm as she began to repeat the first verse, expecting to continue doing a solo. All of the sudden, a small circle of patrons toward the stage actually began singing along. Surprised, Bessie let out a cowboy holler! "Ye haw! One more time!"

To her amazement, nearly the entire room that had ignored her for the past two hours began singing along. When the song came to its triumphant conclusion, the room burst into cheers and applause. Dumbstruck, Bessie smiled and took a bow.

"Thank you…thank you so much. Hey, I'm Bessie James and I'll be here tomorrow night so tell all your friends…I hope to see you again. Good night!" And with that, she went into a reprise of the old Roy Rogers and Dale Evans tune. The room once again went nuts.

She bounded off the stage and into Joey's waiting arms. When she pulled away from his embrace, he smiled and said, "I think you're on to something."

The next night, the room was full and the crowd much more attentive and engaged. Somehow…someway…she had connected and the word was out. Like the night before, she ended by inviting the crowd to join in to sing what was to become her signature closing for the remainder of the tour. Next stop – the renowned Amazing Grace Club further south along the shore of Lake Michigan in Evanston, Illinois.

Chapter 16

"This place is…" Bessie searched for words – "…amazing!"

Joey walked in from behind and stood next to her. "Tell me about it."

The immense space did not swallow them as much as it graciously received them. They slowly made their way in, scanning the array of beautiful silkscreen posters of artists who had graced the stage – John Prine, Steve Goodman, Randy Newman, Odetta, Mimi Farina, John Hartford, Jerry Jeff Walker, Bonnie Koloc – and so many other unfamiliar names that included her poster. There was an ebb and flow of people lining up at a serving counter to receive soup and bread.

"Big, isn't it?" Joey observed.

Bessie continued to gaze at the space with her mouth open. "My God…it's more than that," she feebly acknowledged.

Joey nodded and put his arm around her shoulder. This foreign gesture was the only thing that could pry her away from surveying the venue where she'd be an opening act for the next two nights.

"Yeah…this is more or less the pinnacle…the Mecca of folkies. And here you are, Bess," he pronounced with a sense of pride as he continued to let his eyes roam the room. Their tandem awe was suddenly interrupted by a chirpy female voice come from behind them.

"Welcome to Amazing Grace. I'm Margot – the assistant manager here" and she extended her hand to Bessie.

The two of them spun around. "Oh...Hi! I'm Bessie and this is Joey."

A revelation came across the young woman's face. "Wow...you must be Bessie James – we've been expecting you. And you must be her manager, right?" she said as she turned to shake Joey's hand.

"Right. Nice meeting you," Joey responded politely – almost reverently.

"You're first time here?" Margot intuited.

Bessie chuckled and raised a hand to conceal her embarrassment, "Does it show?"

Margot just shrugged and smiled. "A little."

Bessie continued to take in the room. "I've never been in a place like this. I mean...there's so much going on here. You can feel it...or am I just imagining it?"

Margot nodded her head. "Yeah, it's real. Everybody calls it magic. We hear all the musicians say they came back to get..." Margot made quotation marks in the air, 'some magic' and our regulars feel it, too." Their host let them continue soaking in the magic before continuing.

"Come with me...I'll give you a quick tour and history lesson."

The three of them slowly thread their way through the afternoon crowd.

"There's so many people here...and it's the middle of the day!" Bessie said with surprise.

"Yeah, they're here for the grub. We're a food cooperative...we actually started off as a food coop before we became a music venue."

"Seriously?" Joey was aghast.

Margot nodded as she continued to guide them. "Yup. We started off over in Scott Hall on the Northwestern Campus. We started making and serving soup, bread, granola and serving a full meal for a buck."

"Really? On campus."

"Yeah. We have sort of a love/hate relationship with Northwestern. They more or less put up with us. We did have to move out of Scott to here – Shanley Hall – not too long ago but that's cool. It's sort of a dump but at least we have a decent commercial kitchen here." Margot escorted them by the kitchen. "It's a happenin' place for sure. I started out working in the kitchen. But naturally, the music is the main draw these days."

They gradually made their way toward the stage and Margot motioned to take a seat at a table where the trio sat down.

"It's crazy to think about how many big time artists have played up here," Joey confessed with a nod toward the stage that was adorned with a big easy chair, a floor lamp, and a side table.

Margot nodded once again. "Yeah...sacred space, really."

"So, what's with the furniture on stage?" Bessie asked.

"Oh that? Yeah, that's part of Martin's thing. He does his whole gig as if he was in your grandma's living room."

The image and feel of the cozy heavy chair and lamp on stage, along with the ambiance of the whole place was etched in Bessie's mind.

"Martin?" Joey furrowed his brow in an attempt to place the performer.

Margot glanced at the stage and explained. "Martin Mull. He's a hoot – combination musician and comedian – more comedy than music. Pretty unusual act, really. Kind of quirky and cerebral. He plays guitar. In any case, that stage is sacred space…like I said."

Bessie glowed.

"It's amazing," Bess enthused before shaking her self back to the moment. "So…speaking of being amazing…how did it get to be called Amazing Grace?"

Margot leaned back in her chair, tipping the front two legs off the floor.
"Funny story. We had this duo playing – Norman Schwartz and Carla Reiter – you've probably never heard of them – nobody has, really. Anyway, one night they impulsively ended their set singing *Amazing Grace*. The whole place joined in. It was pretty cool. Did you notice the mural outside?"

Both of them shook their heads. Margot continued.

"Well, it made its mark. By word of mouth, the name just stuck. Nobody planned it. It just took root organically, like so many things about this place."

"That is so cool!" Joey added.

"It is," Margot confirmed and glanced around the room. "Yeah, it's taken on a life of its own. It's a combination food coop, music venue, and counter culture nest. It's a community really. A bunch of us Gracers live together in a house over on Colfax. In fact, that's where you'll crash tonight and tomorrow."

"Gracers?" Bessie repeated.

"Yeah, that's what folks call us lifers who can't seem to shake this place."

Bessie sighed. "God, don't you just want to bottle this and take it with you and clone this?"

"Well, a bunch of Gracers sort of did that. A handful of them took off to create Amazing Grace West in Eugene, Oregon."

"That's so cool!" Joey repeated.

Margot seemed indifferent and dubious. "We'll see. I'm not so sure you can actually clone something like this. But, who knows. Anyway…" she teetered her chair back to all four legs on the floor, letting her hands come down on the table, "I've got to get back to work. You can set up your gear on stage if you want. Sparky's our sound guy – he'll run sound for you and help you set up. Like I said, you'll crash over at Colfax." Margot rose from the table with Joey and Bessie following suit.

"Where do I change?" Bessie asked craning her neck to spot a possible green room.

Margot responded with an embarrassed chuckled. "Oh, right. Well, here's the thing. We don't really have a dressing room. You sort of hang out in the kitchen until you go on and you'll have to change in the bathroom. Sorry about that. But hey, most acts just walk up on stage and play in what they're wearing. It's pretty casual here."

"Well thanks so much. It's been great!" Bessie said.

"You're welcome. Glad to have you guys here as part of the family. You'll do the first set at 8:00 opening for Martin who'll come on at 9:00. Then you'll do a second set at 10:00 and Martin will close at 11:00. Well, gotta go. Somebody will look after you later tonight. Nice meeting you!" And off she went to the kitchen.

Bessie turned to Joey with wide eyes.

"I don't ever want to leave this place!"

Chapter 17

Happy trails to you...Until we meet.... Again!

"Thank you everybody! Thanks so much. Stick around...you don't want to miss the quirky world of Martin Mull – he'll be coming up next. Thanks, and good night!"

The crowd in the Amazing Grace exploded into whoops and hollers as Bessie bounded off the stage. Joey was seated off to the side waiting for her. She nearly bowled him over when she leapt into his awaiting embrace.

"You nailed it, Bess. Absolutely nailed it. They loved you!"

She peeled herself away from his congratulatory hug. "You really think so?"

Joey contorted his face in utter disbelief. "Are you kidding me? Did you hear that response? Seriously, you had them...you had them right here," he said as he laid out the palm of his hand. "Come on, sit down, catch your breath. Here's some hot tea for you. How's your voice?"

They pulled out the chairs of the table Joey had commandeered and sat, Bessie with a deep cleansing breath. Neither of them spoke. They just smiled at each other. Joey was just about to offer some observations about the set and the audience when a gentleman approached their table.

"Excuse me. Sorry to intrude. I just wanted to come over to introduce myself and tell you how much I enjoyed your set."

"Oh...that's so kind of you. Here..." Bessie pulled out the third chair. "Have a seat."

"Thank you. I won't stay long." He extended his hand first to Bessie. "My name is Bob Gibson."

"It's nice meeting you. I'm…"

Mr. Gibson interrupted, "Yes, I know who you are," and turned toward Joey, "and you sir are?" the question hung in the air.

"Joey…Joey Michaels. I'm Bessie's manager."

"Well then…congratulations to both of you. Well done!"

They offered a "thanks" in unison.

"As I said, I won't take up too much of your time. I just wanted to say hello. Tell me…are you recording with anyone?"

Bessie's eyes widened. His abrupt question shocked her. "No. Not yet. We put out some demos," she replied.

Joey chimed in. "Yeah, we're hoping that going out on the road will get some attention."

"Well, you certainly caught mine, I can tell you." He turned to Bessie. "You're quite good, young lady. Not just your voice, but I must say, you have a very nice rapport with the audience. I'm sure you'll go far."

The man reached for a paper napkin from the silver dispenser on the table and then retrieved a ballpoint pen from the inside pocket of his jacket. He scribbled a name, address, and phone number.

"Here…" he said as he pushed the inky scrawl across the table to Joey.

"This is a friend of mine. He's just opened a studio in L.A. and has launched a fledgling record label. He's looking for talent. *Good* talent!" he emphasized.

Joey glanced at the napkin and handed it to Bessie.

"Wow. I don't know what to say?" Bessie gushed.

"Thanks. That's awfully kind of you," Joey added.

Mr. Gibson waved off their appreciation. "It's my pleasure. Just trying to help a newbie." The man began to rise from the table. "As I said, I think you'll go far and I think you and Benny will hit it off. He's hungry for talent right now. He'll pound the pavement for you. Good to have a producer like that. Anyway…I must be going. It was nice meeting you."

"Nice meeting you," Bessie replied shaking his hand.

"Thanks again," Joey said standing up.

"My pleasure. Best of luck to you," and he turned away, disappearing into the crowd of over 250 patrons.

The two of them stared at each other with mouths agape.

"What just happened?" Bessie asked slightly dazed.

"Must be some of that magic Margot was talking about," Joey said with a grin.

Sparky, the soundman, suddenly appeared at the table. "So, I see you met Bob."

"We did!" Bessie answered gleefully.

Joey cocked his head, "So who is this guy? Is he legit?"

Sparky guffawed his disbelief. "Legit? You don't know who Bob Gibson is?"

Both of them shook their heads.

The soundman consulted his watch and glanced at the stage in anticipation of the second set for the headliner act before bending down and replied conspiratorially.

"Ever hear of Joan Baez?"

Bessie nearly came out of her seat. "Yeah…" she replied enthusiastically and with awe.

"Well he introduced her at the Newport Folk Festival – quite literally introduced her to the world. He was a folky himself – first as a solo act and then a duo. He hung out with Albert Grossman and his corral of talent – Odetta, Pete Seeger, and Dylan. He also discovered Peter, Paul, and Mary. Jesus, he's like the Godfather of the folkies. He's totally connected. Bob's based out of L.A. now. Rumor has it he's fallen on hard times. He's way into..." he hesitated, "…well, let's just say he's in a scene that's not all that healthy. A shame, really. Anyway, he pops in here whenever he's in town. In any case, he's got the golden touch…or ear, should I say. Oops – gotta go." Sparky hustled back toward the stage.

They looked at each other once more and then gazed at the ink scrawled on the napkin. **Benson Leavitt was the name. The name of the record company was Moonshine Records.**

The very next morning, Joey popped a demo tape, Bessie's headshot, and cover letter, dropping Bob Gibson's name as well as the padded envelope into the mail. The tour ended that night with Bessie's second night as an opening act at The Amazing Grace coffee house. She spent the bulk of those 48 hours soaking in the magic of the space. It was nothing like the other venues she had played. In many ways, she felt at home there. The food, albeit modest, fed her soul more than her stomach.

The trip home was a swift ten-hour drive on I-94. Some of it was ridden in silent reflection. Other times were spent chattering about specific gigs. They agreed to take a week off to recover and give each other some much-needed space. Neither of them broached the subject of the napkin they still carried with them. There was an unspoken understanding not to hope or dream or talk about it out of risk of disappointment. They didn't want to 'jinx' things. Better to simply wait and wonder. It also meant returning to her mother's mobile home and navigating that space.

One morning, with her mother at work, Bessie sat on her bed fingering out chords to some new songs she was considering. She figured the down time was a good opportunity to learn some new tunes. The phone interrupted her dabbling. She made her way down the hall and grabbed the avocado green receiver off the wall phone – expecting it to be her mother.

"Hello?"

"Are you sitting down?"

"Joey?"

"Well...are you?"

"Yes," she lied.

"Good. You'll never guess who I just got off the phone with."

She folded one arm across her chest and began twirling the phone cord with her free hand impatiently. "You're right. I have no idea."

"Benson Leavitt."

"Who?"

"Benson Leavitt…the guy in L.A. with the studio and record label."

Bessie could suddenly hear her pulse pounding in her ears, threatening to drown out what Joey was telling her.

"And?"

"*And…*" Joey paused dramatically, "…he wants us to come out to L.A."

"What!?!?"

"He listened to the demo. He wants us to come out to check out the chemistry in the studio…to see if everything clicks. If so, he'll offer a one-album contract."

"Oh my, God! This is incredible!"

"I told you this would happen…didn't I?" Joey exuded confidently.

Despite the exciting possibilities, it was a gamble on everyone's part – theirs and this guy in L.A. whom up until now had just been a name printed in ink on a napkin. The modest $200 travel stipend he offered was, however, a good sign. That wasn't a whole lot to go on, but it was a start. Neither one of them ever debated the option of not going.

Joey sold his Fender Stratocaster guitar and Twin Reverb amp to pay for the trip. Bessie and Joey packed what they could of their possessions into each of their cars – his 66 Ford Mustang and her Ford LTD and headed toward the Promised Land. Driving separately meant they could not relieve each other when highway fatigue set in. All they had to keep them alert were cassette tapes when radio stations faded in and out along the way. The three-day journey zigzagging across the country to avoid early winter storms did not offer much of an opportunity for conversation. When they finally arrived at a cheap motel along the highway, they had enough money for one room to share but not enough energy for conversation or anything else and quickly fell asleep, sharing a bed and exhaustion from concentrating on the wintery road and future ahead of them. But nothing more than that.

Chapter 18

They were both exhausted and ill prepared when they finally arrived in L.A. late the third night. Both vehicles pulled up in front of what appeared to be the office of Moonshine Records housed in an old warehouse located in a run-down industrial area in the heart of L.A. just south of US 101. They were on the outskirts of Little Tokyo only to find the building where the studio was located locked and closed. Joey had to fumble and ransack through the pile of things in his car to find the name and phone number of Benson Leavitt. With letter in hand, Joey left Bessie and both cars to find a pay phone. Naturally, no one answered the office phone as it was closed at that hour. With nowhere to go and with no more than a few remaining bucks between them, the two of them looked at each other wondering what to do. It was dark. They knew no one and had nowhere to go. They drove both of their cars around for a few blocks and found Union Station and paid what seemed an outrageous amount to park.

The convenience of restrooms balanced out the restless night they spent trying to sleep on the hard benches inside the Art Deco train station. Besides, it was safer to sleep inside under the guise of travelers waiting for their train rather than in their cars. The aroma of coffee wafting through the cavernous waiting room aroused them out of their stupor the next morning. Together, they cobbled enough change for two small Styrofoam cups of strong coffee and one Danish they split between them. Light began filtering through the tall windows. They passed the time entertaining themselves by watching people shuffle into the train station. When the clock suspended above them chimed 9 o'clock, they went in search of a pay phone.

After nearly a dozen rings and just as Joey was about to hang up, a woman's voice answered. "Moonshine Records...This is Maxine. How can I help you?"

"This is Joey Michaels and Bessie James. We just arrived in town."

There was a pause on the other end of the line.

"Who?"

Bessie could tell by the look in Joey's eyes that something was up. Joey gulped and regrouped. He realized the label was interested in Bessie as an artist rather than him. Joey quickly handed the phone over to Bessie. She shook her head no and refused to take the phone.

"Take it! Tell them it's you...go on!" Joey whispered.

Bessie reluctantly took the pay phone receiver in her hand and licked her lips. "Hi. This is Bessie James. Benson Leavitt had invited me to come out to cut...uh...some..." she drew a blank on the term. Joey whispered, "Trial tracks."

"Uh...some trial tracks after he heard my demo. Anyway, I'm here, wondering when we...I...should drop by."

"Oh Bessie! Great! So glad you made it into town. We've been expecting you. Well, Benny isn't here right now. And the studio time is booked. Gee, I wish you had called earlier to plan the logistics. Tell you what...can you give us a call tomorrow...when Benny's here...to figure out a schedule?"

Bessie was holding the phone receiver up so Joey could listen in. She turned to him and shrugged her shoulders in confusion. Joey nodded yes. "Uh...sure. OK. I can do that."

"Great! I'll let Benny know you're in town. He'll be so glad to see you. Thanks...talk to you tomorrow."

The phone call both resolved and created some mystery. The main question now was what to do and where to go until then. They had enough money to pay for another day of parking near Union Station and for some modest fast-food meals. Joey scouted discarded newspapers and magazines they thumbed through when people watching bored them. While uncomfortable, sleeping at the train station was safe and not especially unusual, as many passengers would sleep while waiting for their trains. For the moment, they were relieved and reassured their journey was not yet a bust and so they opted to wander around downtown Los Angeles. This inconvenience and uncertainty was chalked up as paying more dues – one of those things they hoped they would look back on and laugh with fond memories. Secretly, both Bessie and Joey wondered what they had gotten themselves into. To escape her nagging doubt, Bessie broke the silence.

"Where do you see yourself...you know...when we hit it big?"

Joey returned her optimistic grin. "What do you mean?"

"I mean...once we've made some money, where do you see us settling down?"

Bessie was shocked when she heard herself utter the plural pronoun in her question and wondered if Joey had noticed it as well. He turned his gaze toward the buzzing mass of travelers making their way through the train station on their own journeys to collect his thoughts.

"Not sure. Maybe someplace where the mountains meet the ocean?"

His reply surprised her. "Why is that?"

"I've never lived any place that had either."

"You mean like here in L.A.?"

Joey shrugged. "I dunno. It seems kinda big and crazy here. Maybe someplace a bit more mellow."

"Like where?"

Another shrug from Joey as he thought some more before adding, "Maybe Santa Barbara."

Bessie wrinkled her brow. "Santa Barbara? Why there? Is it nearby?"

Joey nodded his head out toward the main entrance of the train station. "It's up the coast about 100 miles. I once saw a coffee table book that had lots of photos of the place. Looked pretty amazing – like heaven as a matter of fact."

Bessie felt her heart drop listening to his solitary vision of the future. There was no "we" or "us" in his response. Worse was what he said next.

"What about you? Where do you see yourself once you've hit the big time?"

Bessie struggled to maintain her composure. She took a deep sigh and made something up. "Oh, I don't know. Living along the coast sounds kind of nice. Who knows…maybe I'll settle for the island life."

"Well, go for it." Joey returned his attention to the magazine he had picked up from one of the empty benches in the waiting area.

Bessie sighed deeply. "Guess I'll take a walk…stretch my legs a bit."

"Cool. I'll be right here," Joey assured her.

She wandered around the train station, looking at the massive electronic sign listing destinations, arrivals, and departures wondering where she was headed.

Chapter 19

The next morning, they repeated the routine from the day before. The difference this time was they were relieved to hear Maxine the receptionist tell them there had been a window opened in the studio schedule for that morning and asked if they could be there by 10:00. Without hesitation, Bessie said yes, despite the fact that singing in the morning was not necessarily the best for vocal chords that had not been warmed-up.

Their convoy of two cars crammed with all of their earthly possessions made its way through the morning traffic back to the studio. Bessie warmed up her vocal chords singing along with songs playing on the KHJ radio station as she drove, keeping Joey in her sight. They parked in the lot behind the building and pulled themselves from the drivers' seat of each vehicle. They faced each other toe-to-toe and silently hugged before heading through the studio doors.

"There they are!" Benson announced. He bounced his way to them, giving each of them a kiss on their cheek. He added, "I'm so glad you're here!"

"So are we!" Bessie glowed.

Benson Leavitt was bald and as big around as he was tall. He reminded Bessie of Humpty Dumpty. He didn't look anything like what Bessie assumed a producer or record executive would look like. Benson was, none-the-less, urbane and sophisticated in an effeminate sort of way. He was rarely seen without a cigarette dangling out of his flailing wrist covered in silver and gold bracelets. He was as flamboyant as he was enthusiastic.

"I see you made it one piece. How was the trip?"

"Well, we…"

Benson impatiently high jacked Joey's report of their cross-country journey.

"Well you're here now and that's all that matters. Let's not dilly dally," and he turned toward the receptionist who had watched the welcome. "This is Maxine. She really runs the place. Don't know what I'd do without her. 'Take it to the Max' as we say around here."

"So nice to finally meet you," she oozed with a welcoming outstretched hand.

Bessie shook her hand, "Yeah, I guess we met on the phone."

Joey took his turn shaking her hand.

"Nice meeting you."

"Welcome to L.A.…Welcome to Moonshine," Maxine smiled.

"Well, well, enough of the formalities. Let's do this thing, shall we? This way my dears!" Benson called out as he turned.

Bessie and Joey followed Benson as he waddled down the narrow hallway. He escorted them into a studio where a bored drummer and bass player sat smoking cigarettes. A session for a radio commercial had been cancelled, freeing up the studio and sidemen. The group exchanged handshakes and names before tossing around some titles of some standards they might jam on. This was, essentially Bessie's audition.

Benson was astute, as he wanted to see how malleable and creative she could be improvising on a song with strangers. These were seasoned session players who could improvise and riff on anything. Simply name the song and pick a key and then stand back to watch the magic happen. Benson invited Joey to pick up a guitar and join in. Bessie rattled off a list of songs from her repertoire she had developed over the past month. The first song they landed on was *Daniel* by, Elton John. It went well – moody yet tender. Benson stepped in with a suggestion, "Hey how about mixing things up a bit. Do you know Steely Dan's *Do It Again?*"

Bessie pursed her lips in thought. "I know it…I mean I know the tune but I don't know the words except for the hook."

"No sweat, we can get you the words." Benson bounded over to a file cabinet and instantly pulled out a lyric sheet and placed it on the music stand in front of Bessie. "Let's play with it. Let's see how you can make it your own. Let's see what happens."

Bessie settled-in on the stool and let her voice caress the microphone. Amazingly, the impromptu ensemble rendered a smooth, jazzy yet mellow rendition of the song with Bessie's voice sounding much like it did on the other song Joey had written for her. Benson's rationale was to break out of the cliché folksy chick singer genre to see if she had any breadth. When the jam ended, Benson took note of the sidemen's approving nods and nonchalant posture.

Bessie beamed. They moved through the song gently with Bessie melting into it. Benny just shook his head with disbelief and rapture. Joey leaned against the wall with his arms folded across his chest – smiling.

Benson was enthusiastic and straightforward. "OK. I think we're on to something. But I have to be honest with you. I don't have any hot talent signed – yet. You're it. That said, you have my total and complete attention and energy. I'll pound the pavement getting your record played. I'm all in. We're a small label. That can work against us or it can work for us. My bet is it will work for us. I'm going into this as a team. I need you…you need me. So, what do you say? Do we have a deal?"

Bessie glanced over to Joey who smiled and shrugged his shoulders implying the decision was hers.

"Really?" she asked.

"Really."

"And can Joey help produce?" she asked Benson.

"Absolutely. You know and trust each other. I can feel that here and now. The audience will hear and feel it on the vinyl. So…are you in?"

Bessie hopped off her stool and ran over to Benson with a hug.

"I take that as a yes! Cool. We'll get started on the contracts. Meanwhile…
where are you guys staying?" her new producer inquired.

"Uh, nowhere really," Bessie stammered.

Benson took a long drag off of his cigarette. "What do you mean?"

"Well, uh, we've parked over at Union Station and have crashed there…using the bathrooms, sleeping…" Joey was attempting to explain.

"Are you fucking kidding me? That's nuts," Benson flailed his hand in the air dismissively.

Both shrugged at the reality of their situation.

Benson raised his index finger to his dimpled chin in thought. "Tell you what…I'll give you an advance of, oh, let's say two-grand to get an apartment and buy some groceries. I know somebody over in Hollywood…not too far from here who runs an apartment building. I think they actually have an opening that came out of the blue due to some eviction or accident or police raid…some weird shit. Anyway, you'd be doing them a favor. I'll give em' a call and say you're on your way over. How's that sound?"

"That's great! Wow! We appreciate it more than you know," Bessie gushed.

Benson turned his cheek upward and closed his eyes dramatically. "What can I say? This is what partners do for each other…am I right?" Then he leaned over to give yet another quick kiss on the cheek of both of them. "This way, my dears," he chirped as he turned toward the hall. They followed Benson out to the receptionist area.

"Hey Max – will you take 2K out of petty cash for these two?" Benson asked.

"Sure thing, boss."

The two of them watched in amazement as Maxine pulled out a wad of $100 bills from a strong box in the bottom drawer of her desk and handed it to them. Joey glanced over to watch Benson light yet another cigarette while taking his pinky finger from his free hand to deftly press and clear each nostril of his nose with two quick sniffs. Joey quickly surmised that Mr. Leavitt might have had another enterprise on the side that could possibly explain the amount of cash he just saw.

Benson exhaled a cloud of smoke into the air. "That should get you started and hold you over for a couple of months while we record. Oh…and there is one other thing…" he paused.

The two of them looked at him anxiously.

"Yeah?" Joey asked.

"Call me Benny."

With that, Bessie and Joey moved into a modest two-bedroom apartment next to the Landmark Hotel in Hollywood, where Janis Joplin had overdosed. Their domestic arrangement, while providing shelter, also generated some tension. They were, essentially, still roommates and really nothing more. Bessie shyly and cautiously observed Joey's behaviors as they moved into their new digs. She wasn't sure how she would respond to any overture he might make regarding the bedrooms. Thus far, their relationship had been strictly business – artistically speaking. Joey had made little to no gesture of any other motivation on his part. And while appreciative of his prowess of music and performing, Bessie felt a tug of something else as well. How could she not? He had poured so much of himself into her music career, she couldn't help wondering if he would extend that to her as a person…as a lover. And while they had safely arrived in Los Angeles, their journey and adventure was really just beginning.

Bessie marveled at the experience of being in a studio with seasoned session players. They knocked her first album out in three weeks. The album included the two songs Joey had written and given to her. The remaining songs were cobbled together consisting of a handful of new tunes written by local aspiring songwriters and some covers. Joey bristled at the idea of covering someone else's song based on his own frustrating history playing in a cover band. But as co-producer, Joey was pleased, as well as relieved that Benny and the sidemen were open to re-arranging the songs to fit Bessie's style and personality. Both of them were thrilled to have *Big Ol' World* as the first single – Joey's song that Bessie sang in the coffee house where they first met. Admittedly, it was selected as the single to ride the coat tails of Linda Ronstadt's current slew of country-rock hits and that strategy seemed to be working. It was soon getting a lot of airplay. Hearing it on the radio as they drove around L.A. was thrilling to them. Bessie would pull over to the curb so they could listen and sing along.

Chapter 20

Ding, ding, ding.

The tiny Coke spoon chimed against a wine glass half full of Chablis from a Santa Barbara vineyard. It was a feeble attempt to call for everyone's attention with little effect.

Ding, ding, ding – again.

"Listen up! Hey! Everybody…*please!* Listen up!" The murmur of the party dropped a notch. Someone turned down the volume of the music blaring on the stereo. Attendees craned their necks to see and hear Benny make the announcement. "Thank you! I'm so glad everyone could make it. Hope everyone's having a good time. I know there's at least one person here tonight who's majorly stoked…Bessie? Where are you, babe? Stand up!"

And now…finally…they were celebrating the release of her album in a house tucked away in Laurel Canyon. Advance sales of the album to record distributors and stores provided Bessie enough money for a place of her own – *finally* – after the brief but tense two months sharing an apartment with Joey and before that co-existing with her mother. But for now, she was here – taking it all in – a long way from Dilworth, Minnesota.

Whoops of joy and adoration following Benny's announcement suddenly brought her back to the room. She shyly stood up from the sagging sofa that seemed to swallow her. Once she made it to her feet, she lifted her wine glass to acknowledge the crowd and smiled. Benny continued with the celebration once he spotted her hiding in the back of the room.

"There she is! All right! Congrats on the new album. I know I can speak for everybody here; I've practically worn out my copy already. What a score! We can all say we knew Bessie when she hit it big. To Bessie!"

"To Bessie!" the room roared back with assorted drinks held high in the air. After another brief whoop-ti-do the crowd returned to their conversations. The air hung heavy with weed, cigarette smoke, and patchouli. The stereo needle scratched across the vinyl that was currently on the turntable, bringing a brief respite from the volume. Moments later Bessie's new album wafted through the speakers and was once again greeted with cheers from the crowd.

A few of the attendees, some famous – some wannabes – wound their way through the bodies in the crowded space and smoke to Bessie to peck a kiss on her cheek or give her a hug. Embarrassed by the attention and the fact she knew no one there, Bessie graciously received their congratulatory oozing. In all honesty, she didn't really want to be here. Laurel Canyon was a million miles away from her comfort zone of the Red River Valley in western Minnesota. Soon after the trail of well-wishers waned, Bessie folded her hands between her knees and scanned the room for the one person she did know and wanted to be with. Joey was nowhere to be found. He was here – somewhere. He had been engulfed in the whole scene and was thriving on the vibe.

Suddenly, a guy with shoulder-length hair and a mustache wearing an unbuttoned denim shirt and jeans holding a joint plopped down on the couch beside Bessie.

"I'm Kevin."

"Hi…I'm…"

"Yeah I know who you are," Kevin interrupted. She watched him pull a joint from his front shirt pocket and lit it. "Want a hit?"

"Naw…thanks, though."

"It's good shit…you sure?"

After a shrug, she reluctantly took the joint and made a half-hearted toke on it. She recalled the effect cannabis had on her that night in the attic with Tony. The faux-toke she took was more of a polite gesture and an attempt to send this guy on his way. After a few seconds, she exhaled, "Thanks," and handed it back to the guy. She then turned her attention away from him and continued to scan the room for Joey while he lustily scanned Bessie. He took note that she was wearing a denim shirt and jeans, like she always did. He offered an enthusiastically stoned nod before speaking over and above the loud music.

"I see you got the memo."

Bessie turned to him. "What?" She had trouble hearing what he said over the party's blaring soundtrack which only complicated deciphering what she thought she heard him say.

"The memo…I see you got the memo and came dressed in the appropriate attire," his hand gestured toward her. She looked down and then at him.

"Oh yeah, right." Despite her flat tone, the fact that she responded at all only emboldened her new companion.

"So...waddya say we get out of here and have our own little party? I've got some Columbian blow at my place. I don't like to carry that stuff around with me, know what I mean?"

No, she didn't know what he meant, although she knew what he was proposing. Her Midwestern upbringing kicked in with the appropriate degree of civility, as she didn't want to be rude.

"Oh, thanks, but I'm waiting for someone. Thanks anyway."

The denim-clad admirer tilted his head back and threw up his hands in gracious defeat, "Have it your way," and walked away.

Bessie felt the need to pinch her self to confirm she wasn't dreaming. Here she was, rubbing shoulders with some of the hottest musical acts in a funky little cottage in Laurel Canyon. The attendees were a virtual constellation of every star that was part of the L.A. music galaxy. A few months ago, she was listening to *their* albums and now they were listening to *hers*. It was all quite unbelievable. It all happened so fast. Bessie got up from the sofa and navigated her way to the patio where she leaned against the railing that kept her from falling over into the canyon and lights of L.A. below.

She turned to scan the crowd on the patio. Finally, she spotted Joey who was engaged in an animated conversation with two superstars. He was definitely working the room. He was in his element. She knew she could not, or perhaps *should not*, get his attention. Tired and somewhat un-nerved by the scene, she went into the kitchen and called a cab to take her to her own place.

Chapter 21

To Bessie, Los Angeles was a sprawl of freeways and people and she could not get her bearings. When the time came to look for a place of her own, Bessie's first impulse was to drive to San Fernando Valley. It was the only geographical location within the tangled ribbons of asphalt, other than Hollywood where she and Joey had crashed, that she knew. Roy Rogers and Dale Evans had sung about finding a home in the San Fernando Valley on the album she used to listen to as little girl. After studying a Rand McNally map, Bessie built up her courage to steer her lumbering Ford LTD on to U.S. 101 and anxiously thread her way through the cascade of traffic headed north to explore the fabled valley. Once there, she was immediately underwhelmed by the amount of asphalt and strip malls. She pulled into a Denny's Restaurant on Sepulveda Blvd in Van Nuys for some coffee. In the lobby area was a newspaper-style vending machine that dispensed free real estate magazines. She thumbed through the pages and prices at the counter while nursing her coffee.

"Looking for a place?"

Bessie looked up from the glossy pages. The waitress stood there with a coffee pot in one hand and the other hand cocked on her hip.

"Uh, yeah. Not having much luck, though."

"You looking around here in the Valley?"

"For a start anyway."

The waitress glanced around cautiously. "Want some advice?" she whispered coyly.

"I guess," Bessie replied.

"You don't wanna live out here. This is the porn capital of the world."

"What do you mean?"

"What I mean is, all these creeps who make porn movies come here to the valley to shoot them in cheap apartments. They move around. And when the scum peddlers aren't trashing the neighborhood…the drug dealers move in."

"Wow. I had no idea," Bessie confessed.

"Yeah well…it's up to you. But if I was you…I'd check out some other places."

"Like where?"

"I dunno…someplace with a little more class…a little more life."

"Sounds expensive."

The waitress shrugged. "It doesn't have to be. It's all about connections, really."

"Yeah, well, I don't have any…connections, that is. I'm new in town."

"Really? Where from?"

"Minnesota."

"No kidding! I'm from Duluth!"

"Seriously? I'm from the Moorhead area."

The waitress nodded and finally put the coffee pot down on the hot plate. "Good God, you can see the edge of the world from Fargo-Moorhead. Yeah – I came out here to be an actress and look at me…slinging hash in nowhere land."

Bessie nervously ran her finger around the rim of her coffee cup. "That's a drag."

"What about you? Why are you out here?" the waitress probed as she stashed a pen behind her ear.

For the first time in her life, Bessie was actually self-conscious of her good fortune and at a loss. "Oh, I got a job," she hedged.

"Doing what?"

"In the recording industry." She hoped her cryptic response would adequately disguise her new, albeit, fledgling notoriety. Her mid-western sensibility wouldn't allow her to gloat at her new career.

"Good for you. Well, then for sure you don't want to crash out here in this shithole valley. Tell you what…" Once again, the waitress looked cautiously about before continuing. "You look like a nice kid…from back home. I have a friend in Venice…not too far from the beach. She's got a place she needs to sublet but she doesn't want to let it out to just anybody…know what I mean? She lives in Venice Beach. Besides, she's in a rush."

The waitress pulled a ticket from her order book and began writing down a phone number.

"Here…give her a call. Mention my name…" she pointed to the name badge on her waitress uniform, "Stacie." She shoved the paper across the counter.

Bessie reluctantly picked it up and inspected it. "Gee…I don't know what to say. I mean, you don't even know me."

"I know enough. You've got that good ol' Midwestern personality. Honestly, you'd be doing her a favor. Besides, you got nothing to lose…am I right?"

Bessie continued to stare at the phone number.

The waitress tapped the countertop with her pen. "Go on…do it. Call her right now. There's a phone booth in the lobby."

"You mean…like…right now?"

Stacie read the look on Bessie's face. "Yeah sure. Why not?"

Chapter 22

Venice was not just another suburb in the sprawl of Los Angeles. It was another planet to Bessie. True to its name, there were canals built as a Bohemian enclave in 1908. The concrete water channels were lined with cute, funky bungalows. Access to the tiny abodes was via a maze of one-way alleyways. The city streets were not much wider. They were lined with boutiques, bookstores, cafes, head shops, and art galleries – basically establishments that sold things people really didn't need to survive. The collection of residents was made for people watching. Some were swathed in California beauty as they roller-bladed or biked down the promenade lined with palm trees along the beach. Others preened lifting weights in parks that were no more than slivers of green crabgrass between the sidewalk and sand. There was also a motley posse of the homeless rummaging through garbage cans and panhandling.

The place Stacie proposed as a possible living space was in the heart of Venice. The 1000 square feet was not the only modest thing about it. It was a charming, unassuming one-bedroom studio apartment on top of a garage on Linnie Canal off of Dell Avenue. One could almost catch a glimpse of the ocean, depending on how far one's neck could be craned. Otherwise, one could not help but catch the Venice vibe. The living area had a balcony that looked out on to one of the canals lined by sidewalks and exotic flora. It also had a spinet piano and Bessie found herself tinkling the keys as much as she did on the strings on her guitar.

Jackie – Stacie's friend – was a model who spent more time on the road, traveling with her photographer lover/manager than in the flat. The bungalow had been an investment more than a residence. But, like the owner, Bessie would also be spending a lot of time on the road. The price, given the pristine location of the place, was extraordinarily reasonable – something Bessie could easily pay given advances from touring and album sales. The only apparent downside as far as Bessie was concerned was the challenge of driving her massive Ford LTD down the alleyways and into the tiny single-car garage. She could barely squeeze between the wall of the garage and car to get out. Still, Bessie marveled at the fact that her tiny abode was technically on an island defined by the maze of alleys and lanes bound by the man-made canals. She had, for the moment, forgotten about her prophetic conversation with Joey in the train station. For now, the notion of island life suited her as she had essentially lived as an islander her whole life.

Chapter 23

With the album out, Benny and Joey worked together to secure Bessie some opening slots with a handful of other artists on tour. It was a far cry from their odyssey in her Ford LTD across the Midwest. They tagged along with whatever headliner they were supporting in a tour bus and stayed in hotels. Gone were the days of eating canned spaghetti, singing to highly caffeinated hipsters, and sleeping in cheap motels or the back seat of a car. But the shimmer quickly dimmed.

Youth is a time devoted to imagination. Bessie, like most aspiring teens, had imagined adoring fans cheering as she took the stage or scampering crowds clambering to get her autograph backstage after a performance. Those images, however, rarely (if ever) included the drudgery of being on the road promoting an album or going from gig-to-gig. After-parties were always scripted the same – thanking and acknowledging adoring fans and hangers-on while Joey "worked" the room either scouting for new talent or talking shop with promoters and other managers.

While the sexual parade grew tedious, predictable, and downright disappointing for Bessie, Joey relished it. She was actually taken aback with the realization that guy groupies existed as well as chick groupies. Initially, the idea of fawning boys hoping to crawl into bed with her was exciting. Early on in the tour, Bessie eventually succumbed to the temptation of the groupie scene – with both men and women. The latter was out of convenience and curiosity. The only thing that came out of her foray into rock star sex was awkward and nothing more than a meaningless, mindless and nameless frolic. The morning after was always an embarrassed parting of the ways. She yearned for so much more. The urge and primal drive for sexual conquest was not embedded within her libido like it was for most guys playing in or working for a band. In time, she refrained from on-the-road sex the same way she abstained from alcohol and drugs. All three indulgences always spiraled into her feeling out of control of her life. The slightest hint of any motivation to indulge in these escapades was a combination of expectation, loneliness, and spite – all of which were a meager and futile attempt to get Joey's attention. It didn't. He was preoccupied with his own sexual conquests.

    She let the road crew know of her disdain for the hopeful hangers-on waiting backstage after the gigs. They dutifully played the role of bulldog, shielding her from the carnal circus that gathered backstage after a gig. Meanwhile, there were plenty of girls backstage who were happy and willing to vicariously hang on to the coat tails of famous recording stars by having sex with their manager.

    Boredom quickly surpassed glamor on a crowded tour bus and in cookie-cutter hotel rooms that served either as a cell or a sanctuary. Bessie found herself spending most of her time in her hotel room – alone. She quickly lost interest. What she truly yearned for was down the hall in another hotel room.

    Regardless of the size and location of every gig, there were always two things she could count on. First, Joey always made sure that a plate of chocolate chip cookies were waiting for

Bessie in her waiting room before going on stage. The second thing she could count on was that she could always glance to stage-left and see Joey smiling and nodding his head. As important and special as both of these were, Bessie longed for something more from Joey.

Much of their next year was spent on tour. Despite the relentless schedule, Bessie was never the headliner act. She always opened for other bigger names, but even those acts were second-tier stars rather than super-stars commanding huge crowds and money. She knew that being a backup act had its ups and downs. The ups obviously being the exposure that helped album sales. Bessie always got goose bumps when the audience would chime in and sing along on her two big, and only hits. The downside was the crowd was primarily there to see and hear the headliner. Those fans were, at best, distracted or subdued and at worst impatient and rude. The only real fiasco was when she was added at the last minute to the bill of a hard-hitting country rock band out of Montana (of all places) called *Haywire*. They were a bunch of good ol' boys that liked to party as much as their fans. Bessie's soft stories and docile voice simply did not resonate with the rowdy crowd who came to 'rip it up' with a band that was simply a Lynyrd Skynyrd knock off. Luckily, that shared bill didn't last more than a few weeks as the promoters ultimately realized the mismatch of the two acts.

The rare exception when Bessie was the solo headliner was a special homecoming concert at the college where Joey first heard her sing and play at the campus coffee house. Despite spending only a semester as a student, the campus had adopted her as one of its own once she had become a star – no matter how modest. She was looking forward to this gig primarily out of sentimental reasons. Even Joey confessed his excitement at the symmetry the event presented. Bessie had invited her mother to the concert and had even arranged a backstage pass. But, her mother had declined – saying that wasn't "her thing" but told her to "break a leg." Bessie was disappointed, but not surprised. Nothing had changed.

Backstage before the show, there was a shy knock on the door. At first, Bessie hoped her mother might have had a change of heart – but she didn't hold her breath. Bessie looked to Joey who simply shrugged before he drifted over to open it. Standing there were the three students Bessie had auditioned for nearly two years ago. Joey held the door open allowing the trio to see Bessie sitting in a lounge chair in the green room.

"Uh…Hi, Bessie. Remember us?" In unison, the three of them offered a shy little wave and smile.

Bessie stood up. "Of course I do! Come on in!" she waved them in. She gave each of them a hug while she and Tony exchanged a knowing smile. Bessie introduced each of them to Joey as they passed him, "Joey, this is Liz…and Tony…and this is Gary." They were thrilled to have her call them by name. She embarked on a history lesson for Joey. "I auditioned for these guys way back when. They're the ones who let me sing at *The Box* coffee house."

Joey smiled and folded his arms across his chest. "Well, I guess we have you to thank. Without you, Bess might still be waiting on tables at the Country Kitchen."

Bessie interrupted, "This is Joey Michaels, my manager. He actually discovered me at *The Box*."

"Really?" Liz responded with a thrill. "That's so cool!"

Gary chimed in, "Well then, I guess you could say we discovered Bessie," his beaming smile dimmed slightly when he saw Joey's flat expression and added, "…so-to-speak," as an olive branch to Joey.

Joey just smiled and unfolded his arm, "Yeah, I suppose you could. Well come on in…Bess has a few minutes before she goes on."

Tony glanced over at the small table off to the side and noticed the plate of cookies. "Looks like the Girl Scouts have been here."

The group exchanged confused glances of which Tony took note. He nodded toward the cookies. Bessie followed his nod with her eyes.

"Oh, right," Bessie was embarrassed. "No, that's just a little thing Joey and I do before each gig…sort of a good luck ritual."

Tony looked at Joey and then back at Bessie with a smile. "Cool," Tony quipped. "It appears to be working for you."

The conversation shifted to polite tales of how their life trajectories had diverged in directions other than original intentions framed in the wonder and promise of college.

"Well, we're Seniors...hoping to graduate this year," Gary said as he nodded to Liz standing by him.

Joey turned to Tony and asked, "What about you?"

The question brought Tony out of his gaze of Bessie. "Oh, me? Well, I went corporate but I didn't completely go to the dark side. I handle establishing franchises for Tower Records stores around the country. Its headquarters is in Sacramento so I get to travel a lot. But hey, I figure it's job security that's borderline hip...know what I'm saying? Besides, it's not like records are ever gonna disappear so I figure it'll be a good long ride."

"So, I assume your stores are selling Bessie's albums, right?" Joey half joked and half speculated.

"Of course. Flying off the shelves. But like I say, I don't handle sales – I help establish franchises," Tony explained.

Bess and Tony continued exchanging coy glances throughout the chatter that went un-noticed by everyone in the room except Joey. At one point during the reminiscing, Bessie glanced over to Joey to see him leaning against the wall with arms folded across his chest, arched eyebrows, and a Cheshire Cat grin on his face. She returned it with a scowl and furrowed eyebrows as she turned her attention back to the enthusiastic patter. Doing so, she found herself attempting to advert her eyes from Tony's gaze that she could feel against her flushing cheeks.

Joey took note of Bessie's subtle shift in redirecting her attention to the other two of the trio and erected himself from his inspecting posture against the door. He shifted his own attention to thinking about the gig that was about to begin in a matter of minutes. Bessie, on the other hand, was basking in the moment, not in the glow of notoriety, but in the fact this was a tiny community of shared experience. She was suddenly grateful to these three people she had lost track of. In some ways, she wrestled with slight pangs of guilt in that she had, more or less, forgotten "the little people" (as the cliché goes) who helped her become what she had become.

Bessie also admitted to herself that she had forgotten about the night with Tony in the attic of the production house just off campus. She was surprised in some respects but not in others. That impulsive tryst was important in many ways as it served as her own sexual awakening, to say the least. More telling was what she took away from that carnal exchange. Despite her sexual naivety, Bessie came to accept that night for what it was -- an experience, really, and nothing more. Perhaps it was only a notch in his belt of sexual conquests. Then again, perhaps it was she who used him. She was unsure. If nothing else, it was the threshold she had to cross to embark on her own adulthood. All in all, it was really nothing more than that. It wasn't love. It wasn't even passion. It just was. She had gradually come to realize that it had really been nothing more. At the same time, she admitted to herself that having sex with Tony was exciting and she eventually convinced herself that she enjoyed it – even for as brief as the whole encounter was. But it didn't take long for her to realize that was just part of the scene she was now a part of. To her there was a difference between having sex and making love – at least she hoped there was a difference. Sex was more or less a given in the world of rock and roll – as much as the booze and drugs were. Regardless of what she had or did with Tony that night…let alone what went on most nights on the road – it wasn't what she longed for. She yearned for something else that eluded her.

Joey checked his wristwatch. "OK, folks. It was great seeing you…really it was. But Bessie needs to get ready," as he began shepherding the trio toward the door.

"It's just so cool to see you! We're so excited to hear you again!" Liz exuded.

"Well, it was so sweet of you to come out tonight." Bessie was sincere.

"Geez – we wouldn't have missed it for the world," Gary added.

"Break a leg!" Tony intoned as the three of them exited the dressing room. He offered one final smile and glance over his shoulder as he caught a final glimpse of Bessie through the narrowing doorway.

Joey closed the door, spun around, leaned against it and raised his eyebrows.

"What?" Bessie asked defensively in a vain attempt to defuse Joey's accusatory stare.

"Nothing," he said glibly.

Bessie detected the knowing, nonchalant tone in his voice but simply glared at him. He merely grinned at her until her scowl melted away. She finally succumbed to his uncanny clairvoyance with a curt retort, "That was a long time ago," in an attempt to douse his smugness.

He just continued to smile before he responded with a matter-of-factual, "It's show time!"

Chapter 24

Bessie glowed on stage. She fed off the adoration from the crowd of college students and locals who now saw her as their own. Joey looked out at the adoring faces from the wings of the stage, recalling how he felt when he first heard her sing in the coffee shop that was located just a short walk across campus from the auditorium where she stood now. He couldn't help but admire Bessie as she stood in the spotlight all alone with no safety net. A solo act has no one to lean on. He could hardly imagine what that must be like. Still, Bessie was able to be with the audience, especially this one here tonight. As she finished her final encore, someone from the crowd tossed up a yellow beanie – the same kind that all incoming first year students wore until the first touchdown of the home game – the same one she had donned when she auditioned to play the campus coffeehouse. Bessie leaned down to pick it up. The crowd roared their approval as she adjusted the tiny bonnet on her head and walked off stage.

After the concert, a small throng of vague names and faces from high school congregated backstage. Bessie was both pleased and perplexed at the attention. These people, after all, hardly gave her the time of day when she was in high school. They hadn't necessarily been mean or cruel. They simply didn't acknowledge her existence when she clung to the sidelines of school and church events. And now, here they were, clambering to talk to her and get her autograph. Bessie, of course, was gracious, calling each of them by name when she chatted ever so briefly with them. She took delight rather than revenge. Joey watched with a knowing smile. Bessie finally lifted eyebrows as an S.O.S. to Joey who stepped in and rescued her.

"OK, OK…thanks everybody. Thanks for coming! Good to see all of you. We need to get going now." Joey's wrangling was met with a chorus of disappointment.

After closing the door behind her fans, a collective sigh of relief escaped both of them in unison just before they chuckled their delight in the sanctuary of the dressing room.

"Well, that was interesting," Bessie exclaimed as she returned to the oversized lounge chair.

"So, how'd that feel?" Joey smirked.

"It was nice," she said almost in a whisper.

"Was it?"

"Yes," Bessie shifted to a tone of exasperation and emphasis in her voice to counter Joey's apparent doubt.

He stood looking at her with a grin. "I thought you told me you didn't really have any friends from high school."

Bessie twirled a strand of her hair. "Well…I knew a lot of people."

Joey slightly shook his head. "That's not the same thing."

She turned her head away and continued twirling her hair when there was another gentle knock on the door. Joey turned toward the door and opened it slightly ajar.

"Yeah?"

It was the road manager. "There's somebody here who'd like to see Bessie."

Joey craned his neck in an attempt to see who the guest was. "Well, I think Bessie's finished seeing folks for the night," and started to close the door. The promoter blocked the door with the toe of his boot.

"Uh…I think it might be a good idea if she took a moment to meet this gentleman."

Joey's interest piqued, he stood back from the door. "Alright then…just for a minute. Go ahead…send him back." Joey closed the door.

"Who was it?" Bessie asked.

"Not sure…somebody important, though. I guess we're both about to find out."

In less than a minute, there was another knock on the door. Joey cracked it open with a somewhat curt, "Yes?"

A clean-cut, handsome middle-aged man wearing a vest stood almost nose-to-nose with Joey in the gap of the open doorway. The man was slightly taken aback by Joey's bulldog behavior but managed to offer a polite smile.

"Hi. I'm Bobby Vee. I just wanted to stop by and pay my respects to a hometown girl."

Joey's mouth dropped. He simply stood in the doorway long enough for Bessie to call out from inside, "Joey? Who is it?" When no answer came, she lifted her voice in an invitation, "Come on in…whoever you are!" Joey stood back and opened the door as the guest smiled and entered Bessie's dressing room.

He extended his hand, "Hi. I'm Bobby. I won't take long. I just wanted to swing by to congratulate you on the show tonight and your career. I really enjoy your music."

Bessie stood up to accept his hand and compliment. "Why thank you. I'm so glad you like my work."

"Oh please, I wish…I mean…I hope you never call what you do 'work' as I can tell it's much more than that."

Taken aback, she glanced at Joey who remained standing shell-shocked at the doorway hoping for some kind of indication as to whom her guest might be. Seeing nothing coming from her manager who was paid to take care of her, Bessie took on the role of host.

"Come in won't you? Have a seat," she gestured to the only other chair in the room as she walked toward the dressing table to retrieve her half-empty plate of cookies. "Cookie?" as she offered the plate to her guest.

Amused, he said waving off her gesture, "No, no thanks. I'm not going to stay that long. I just wanted to stop by. It's so good to see something hot come out of Fargo-Moorhead. I'm really happy to see how things have turned out for you."

"Well, you're too kind." Again she turned to Joey hoping for him to bail her out of her apparent but cleverly camouflaged ignorance, but he offered nothing. She quickly began to fake her way through a sincere but one-sided conversation with the mystery man. Bessie had thus far surmised he was of some importance and evidently was a performer himself – at least he had the look of one – whatever that might entail. She launched into the banter she had come to memorize and employ during the round of after-parties she had endured on the tour with some generic chitchat. "So, do you have any projects right now?" That standard line was always a safe venture into a tête-à-tête. She had learned a long time ago to flip the focus of conversation around back on to someone else.

He shrugged. "Nothing major. I did a comeback tour a few years ago. It turned out to be pretty much a nostalgia tour." He sighed before continuing. "It was nice to have a crowd at a State Fair sing along with my songs. But I began to realize all of this has a shelf life, you know what I mean? After all, the Rolling Stones aren't going to be doing shows forever, now will they? Come to think of it, though, I did that tour with a local band - a seven-piece band with horns called *Transit*. Did you ever hear them when you were still around?"

The name of the band rang a bell. She now recalled Joey mentioning the name when she saw his Chicago poster hanging on the wall of his apartment. He had explained he had been in a seven-piece band that took their name from the original moniker of the famous band – Chicago Transit Authority. She glanced over to Joey's face to detect any recollection of the band on his part. His flat affect was an attempt to hide the fact from their guest that he had actually played in that band at one time. However, he left the group to play in another local band, Yellow Press, just before Bobby Vee invited Transit to be his backup. Joey's departure from the group was not due to his performance on stage as much as it was his behavior off the stage. The culmination of his alcohol-fueled antics and sexual escapades combined with artistic differences on how to "cover" songs led the band to – as the expression goes – 'ask him to submit his resignation.'

"No. I don't think so," she answered.

Bobby continued. "Too bad. Good guys. Anyway after that, I did some producing – dabbled a bit with some local talent. Just taking it easy now days. I've got a little studio at my place out near Detroit Lakes." Bobby turned to see Joey who had now eased his way into the room and extended his hand to him with a simple, "Hi…I'm Bobby."

Joey shook his hand. "Nice meeting you."

It was Bessie's turn to rescue Joey. "Joey's my manager. He's from around here originally."

"Really?"

"Yeah," Joey confirmed.

Bessie continued, "Yeah, Joey used to play in a band here, too."

Bobby was curious now. "Really? What was the name? Maybe I heard you guys."

Joey cleared his throat. He debated whether or not to share his previous tenure with Bobby's backup band and decided to skip over that page in his history. "Uh - Yellow Press. A cover band." Bessie gave him a knowing look.

Bobby looked up at the ceiling in thought. "Hmmm – no…I guess not. Sorry."

Joey shrugged off Bobby's apology.

Bobby turned his attention back to Bessie. "Well...like I said, I just wanted to stop by...say hi and tell you how much I like your music."

"Thanks...Joey wrote much of it," Bessie nodded in the direction of Joey.

Another, "Really?" from Bobby followed by a quick, "Impressive," before turning back again to Bessie.

Joey finally mustered up a few words. "So, Bobby...I'm wondering...*we* were wondering if you have any words of advice...you know, since you've been there, done that."

Bobby turned his head back and forth, surveying each one of them with a smile. "Not really. Enjoy the ride...while it lasts." He pulled a pack of Juicy Fruit gum from his vest pocket, unwrapped a stick, and popped it in his mouth.

Deflated, Joey pressed for more sage insight. "Seriously. We'd truly like to hear it."

This time Bobby looked Joey up and down. He turned back to Bessie. "Well...like I said...enjoy it while it lasts." He paused to consider adding more. "Because it won't." He saw the stunned look on both of their faces and tried to soften the reality he predicted. "It never does." He walked over to Bessie and took her hand to offer a goodbye as well as a cushioned apology, "No offense."

"None taken," Bessie replied looking him in the eye. He returned her gaze debating how and if to continue. He felt the warmth emanating from Bessie and caved in.

"I guess one last thing…if I may be so bold…" his arched eyebrows and head cocked to one side in speculation, inviting permission to continue.

"Sure…of course…we asked you to share with us. What is that?" Bessie asked now holding both of his hands in hers.

Bobby glanced over his shoulder at Joey and then back into Bessie's eyes. He whispered, "Have a backup." He glanced down at his feet and kicked an invisible object with the toe of his cowboy boot while still holding hands with Bessie before looking back up to continue. "Trust me…" he chuckled, "I'm the poster child for backup plans." He grinned and winked. With that, he dropped both of her hands and walked passed Joey toward the door. He placed a hand on the doorknob and turned back to both of them. "It was nice meeting you. Take care now." He closed the door behind him.

After a few seconds of stunned silence, Bessie tilted her head toward Joey. "Who *was* that?" Joey heard the confusion in her voice.

Joey wandered over to plop down into the oversized lounge chair. "*That…*" he said with a dramatic pause, "…my dear, was Bobby Vee."

Indignant, she put both hands on her hips. "Well, I know that. But who's Bobby Vee?"

Joey leaned his head back in a combination of disgust and disbelief. "Bobby Vee is the local boy who filled in for Buddy Holly." He paused for a moment to look at Bessie suspiciously. "You've heard of Buddy Holly, right?"

The question required Bessie to rummage through her memory banks but the blank look on her face gave her ignorance away.

"You've heard the song, 'American Pie' haven't you?" There was an edgy-ness to Joey's response – not just in his voice, but also in the question itself.

"Who hasn't? Wait…did he write that?" She was naively aghast.

Joey chuckled. "No, but he certainly plays a role in the back story of the song." He paused again to assess Bessie's knowledge of rock and roll history. "You know what the song is about, don't you?"

Once again, she considered her response only to reply with, "It's something about the day the music died, whatever that means. I never really understood it."

"Exactly. That's the day Buddy Holly died in a plane crash. And guess where he was headed in that plane."

"I have no idea." Bessie's tone revealed her impatience with Joey's guessing game.

"Here."

Bessie blinked. "What do you mean?"

Joey took a deep breath. "Buddy Holly was supposed to play here in Fargo-Moorhead but died in a plane crash on the way. And can you make a guess at who had the unenviable role as backup to stand in for one of the hottest stars of the time might be?"

A revelation grew across Bessie's face. "Bobby Vee?"

"Yup. He was the backup. And it launched him into his own career. He had a handful of hits. He was pretty squeaky clean. He didn't last too much longer when the likes of the Rolling Stones or Dylan came along. As a matter of fact, Dylan even played bass in Bobby's band for awhile under some stage name…long before going on to become who he is today."

A muffled, "Wow" was all Bessie could say.

Joey stared at her for a moment before repeating, "Yeah…wow."

Bessie raised her fingers to her lips in thought. "So that's what he meant when he said he was the 'poster child' of backup plans."

Joey just nodded with a raised eyebrow.

Chapter 25

During the second leg of her promotion tour, Bessie was opening for yet another balladeer the likes of Jim Croce and Harry Chapin. His name was Clifford Diggs. She privately worried if his fate was destined in the same way as the other two singers. His music tapped into and fused folk, country, and rock. Cliff was a nice guy and always treated Bessie with respect. He was also a Jesus freak. As a result, prayer circles and Bible study replaced after-concert parties. These un-nerved Bessie almost as much as the stereotypical debauchery that took place on most rock and roll concert tours. She wasn't opposed to the spiritual gatherings. In fact, privately she respected Cliff and his band for being true to their values and beliefs. She simply didn't feel inclined to participate. Instead, it became her habit to do one of two things after a gig.

One routine was to quietly veg out in her hotel room alone watching classic movies on TV while eating ice cream. She tended to gravitate to movies about places and how those places shaped those who occupied that space – films like *Casablanca, Roman Holiday*, and *The Last Picture Show*. Bessie also liked quirky rom-coms – *Annie Hall* being her favorite – as she yearned for a relationship just as she had growing up on the isolated desert island of her youth. Instead, she had merely filled in the space of her lonely existence with activities.

The other habit of hers was to wander near the venue, on foot if possible, after the gig to discover clubs and hangouts. She was usually able to do this incognito. Upon arrival, she would soak in the music and ambiance from the margins feeling somewhat a part of the scene without any fanfare.

That routine took a detour one September night in Champaign, Illinois after a concert in the Auditorium on the University of Illinois campus quad. The gig was billed as a "Back-to-School" event. The audience was enthusiastically polite. The crowd of twenty-somethings listened and roared their appreciation after she performed her two big (and only) hits. As was the case with all of Bessie's backup gigs, the audience was there to hear the headliner act. Regardless of that fact, she knew Joey was in the wings. That particular night, she took a quick peek to the side of the stage in between songs as she tuned her guitar. As expected, Joey had taken his predictable position. Tonight, however, he was not alone. In her fleeting glance she saw him leaning into and talking to a beautiful woman as he pointed toward Bessie on the stage. She had never seen this woman before and her sudden presence momentarily rattled Bessie. Being the professional she was, Bessie quickly refocused and rejoined her audience that was as eager for her to end her set as she was.

After her 40 minute set, Bessie went back stage where she found Joey – alone. He gave her a big hug. "Great gig…as always!"

"Thanks." Bessie bit her lip to keep from asking where his 'friend' was and decided a better tact would be to wait and let him volunteer the information. He didn't. This bothered her. He had to have known that she saw the two of them in the wings and that she was bound to be curious. But true to Joey's manner, he stuck to business and never gave a hint as to the identity of the mystery woman. All that mattered to Bessie right now was that the woman had vanished as quickly as she had appeared.

The experience put her off enough that she decided to nix Cliff's set altogether. She had heard and seen it countless times before. Joey noticed her heading to the dressing room.

"You're not going to watch?" he asked.

"Naw – been there, done that. Think I'll go for a walk."

Joey shrugged and wandered over to Cliff's manager who was standing nearby, supervising the quick stage change. Secretly she had hoped this would tip him off that she was…well…what was she feeling? She wasn't sure. Her failed tactic simply made her feel worse. All the more reason to get some fresh air.

Bessie dropped her guitar off with a roadie and made her way to a back stage door exit. The hotel was just a few blocks away so she decided to wander in that direction with hopes of finding a campus hangout along the way. The air was thick and muggy with flashes of heat lightning illuminating the sky. The night reminded her of summer nights growing up in Minnesota – all that was missing were the lightning bugs.

She stumbled upon Kam's as she strolled down Daniels Street in the general direction of her hotel. It was not a cozy, intimate speak easy playing cool quiet jazz or folk music – the type of venue she would typically seek. It was, instead, a rowdy college bar with no live music – just deafening tunes coming from the jukebox inside. She shyly poked her head inside the door where an imposing bouncer asked to see her I.D. and didn't seem to notice or care about her name nor her notoriety – regardless of how minimal it was. She was, essentially, just another college-age girl. An appreciative and somewhat envious grin came to her face as she made her way through the throng of students and saddled up to the bar. Oh, how she missed the college experience – the intensity of friendships forming that could last a lifetime and survive the drama of entering adulthood through a kind of academic kindergarten designed to teach life skills more than disciplinary skills. Bessie watched young men and women only slightly younger than herself play pool and throw darts as they swilled pitchers of beer and smoked cigarettes.

Her appreciative survey of the room was interrupted with a tap on the elbow she had rested on the bar. "What can I get you?" the bartender shouted over the din of the room.

"Just a coke – with a straw – thanks."

The bartender nodded and quickly filled a tall glass with ice and shot the inky syrup from a bar gun over the frozen cubes. He shoved the drink toward her as she handed him a five-dollar bill, "Keep the change!" she shouted. A silent nod of thanks came from the barkeep.

Bessie turned her attention back to the melee and sipped through her straw. She soon felt the stare of three pairs of eyes on her. Three coeds were huddled together in a booth across from the bar, unsuccessfully trying to camouflage their whispers, nudges, and discrete finger pointing. It was one of those very rare moments when Bessie had been recognized. She simply smiled at them to acknowledge their attention and pretended to continue surveying the room by looking away. After some encouraging nudges from her two friends, one of the girls gathered up enough courage to crawl out of the booth. Halfway to the bar, she turned back to her friends to garner encouraging nods and waves of their hands in their attempt to steer her to Bessie. She nervously approached Bessie from the side, slightly out of her peripheral view, as she didn't appear to notice the appearance of the coed.

"Um...excuse me..."

Bessie turned toward the girl sipping on her straw. "Yes?"

"Um...right...well...I was just...I mean...my friends and I were just wondering..." the embarrassed girl stammered. Bessie smiled and tried to respond with a supportive coax.

"Yes?" she repeated.

"Uh, well we just wondering if you're Bessie James."

Bessie set her glass down on the bar and turned back to the girl. "Yeah...it's me." She reached her hand out. "What's your name?"

Amazed, the girl almost offered a curtsey before taking Bessie's hand. "Oh my God! It *is* you. This is so cool!" She turned to her companions sitting wide-eyed in their booth. "Guys...it is her!" she called out over the crack of a cue ball at a nearby pool table. Meanwhile, the girl continued to pump Bessie's hand as Bessie just chuckled.

"Do you have a name?" Bessie repeated.

Embarrassed, she replied, "Oh, right. I'm Suze…Susan."

"Nice meeting you, Susan."

"Oh please, call me Suze…everybody does. And these," she paused long enough to look over her shoulder and then back to Bessie, "are my roommates."

Bessie craned her neck as she gave a dainty wave of her hand that was met by the duo with embarrassed hands cupped over their mouths. Suze was beaming. "Would you like to come over and join us?"

Bessie pondered the invitation for a moment and then shrugged. "Sure, why not?" She turned to retrieve her Coke, but the bartender had snatched it away leaving her empty handed. Meanwhile, Suze took Bessie by the arm and escorted her to the booth where her roommates squirmed with anticipation.

"Guys, this is Bessie James. Bessie -- these are my roommates, Julie and Christie."

"Nice meeting you," Bessie shouted over the jukebox that was, for some unexplainable reason, playing *Mack The Knife*.

"Here, let us skooch over so you can sit down," Julie bubbled.

Bessie sat on one side of the bench with Christie as Suze scrunched in beside Julie. Bessie sat with her hands on the table, fiddling with a beer coaster. "So…you guys go to school here?"

All three nodded in unison as Julie provided additional information. "Yeah, we're all juniors," which was followed by some awkward silence despite the blaring music.

Bessie pursed her lips and nodded, "Is this your main hang out?"

Another silent, unison nod from the star struck trio until Suze finally contributed the first hint of an actual conversation. "We have your album. We love it. We play it all the time."

"Yeah, we've nearly worn it out," Christie chimed in.

Bessie smiled. "Great. Thanks. I'm glad you like it."

Suze sheepishly looked at her two roommates. "We wish we could've made it to your concert. We wanted to…but we couldn't get tickets in time…it sold out before we had the bucks."

Bessie lowered her chin with a smile. "No worries."

"We wanted to go," Julie added apologetically with good intentions.

Bessie leaned across the table and cupped her hand to her ear. "What? What did you say?"

"I said…we wanted to go!" Julie enunciated loudly.

Bessie nodded and waved off their apology. She looked down to see the girls' pitcher of beer and glasses were empty. "So, can I buy you guys another pitcher of beer?"

The three coeds nearly burst with appreciative surprise. "Oh, you don't need to do that," Suze graciously responded. "Besides, it's too noisy in here to talk. We should just let you go. You probably have an after-party to go to."

"It was nice of you to come over and talk to us," Julie added.

Bessie shook her head, "Well, I don't have any place to go except back to the hotel and to bed."

"Are you staying at the Century 21 Hotel?" Suze asked.

Bessie raised an eyebrow. "I guess so. They all begin to blur together."

"Well that's the only decent hotel near campus and it's just down the street, right by our place," Christie explained as she pointed in a non-descript direction.

Suze and Julie looked at each other seemingly to confirm their telepathy. Suze then suggested, "Yeah…we could walk you back. Would that be OK?"

"Oh, you don't have to do that. I can find my way back. Besides, I don't want to take you away from your fun." Bessie began to crawl out of the booth.

"No, no. We don't mind. Like I said, it's on our way. We'd love to walk with you, if you don't mind," Suze exuded.

Now standing by their table, Bessie shrugged again, "Sure, if you want."

The trio simultaneously clapped their hands with delight and then began inching their way out of the booth. "This is so cool! Wait until I tell Paul about this," Julie chirped.

Bessie smiled at her new friend's exuberance. "Your boyfriend?"

Julie nodded and looped her arm through Bessie's to escort her out of the bar and on to the sidewalk in the muggy night. Bessie inhaled and exhaled deeply to clear out the second hand smoke she had ingested and to revel in the release from the ever-booming bass coming off the jukebox. The girls began down the sidewalk, engaging in chitchat detailing where they were from and what they were majoring in. Bessie politely listened and nodded for the three blocks they strolled. The entourage stopped at the corner in front of the hotel.

"Well, here we are!" Suze announced, stating the obvious.

"Yup. You got me here safe and sound. Thanks for the escort," Bessie replied.

Suze suddenly piped up. "Hey. I know…you want to come up to our place? It's right over there, across the street."

"Jesus, Suze…she doesn't want to hang out with us," Julie chided and then turned to Bessie. "You've been so nice. It's so cool meeting you. We'll let you go now."

Bessie turned to look at her hotel and then turned back to crane her neck as she looked down the street. She took a deep breath. "Yeah, sure…that'd be kind of fun."

"Are you serious!" Christie exclaimed.

Bessie chuckled as she nodded. "Sure, why not?"

The trio of roommates released a scream in unison. "Far out!" Suze shouted. "Come on, it's right over here," as the foursome walked down the street.

It was an old house that had been converted into typical off-campus student housing with one living quarter on the first floor and another on the second. They unlocked the front door and climbed creaky stairs to the upstairs apartment.

"Ta da! Here we are!" Julie announced. "Just take a seat. Can we get you something? A beer?"

"No, I'm fine, thanks," Bessie replied as she made her way to a dilapidated sofa rescued from Goodwill. Settling in, Bessie soaked in the vibe – having never shared the experience of living together with girlfriends either in a dorm or an apartment. Her rather spontaneous artistic journey essentially emancipated her from living with her mother into her first shared apartment with Joey until she had made enough money to buy her own place.

The room reeked of patchouli incense. The walls were covered with a hodgepodge of posters adorned with inspirational, albeit cliché, quotes and rock groups. There was a braided rug on the floor and a director's chair in front of a makeshift shelf consisting of cinder blocks and wooden boards that housed a stereo with a vertical stack of albums.

Bessie noticed and gestured toward a mini electronic keyboard standing on its end at the end of the shelving with a cord running into the back of the stereo receiver.

"Who plays the keyboard?"

Julie had to think about what Bessie was referring to before she responded. "Oh that...Christie won it in some raffle. None of us actually play. We just dink around on it when we're bored or when we try to play along with an album."

Bessie just nodded. Suze walked over to open the window wider. Bessie couldn't tell if she had merely allowed muggy air from the night to enter the little apartment rather than waft the stuffy air out. Suze then plopped down on the other end of the lumpy sofa from Bessie. Julie sat in the director's chair while Christie sat crossed-legged on the carpet.

"This is so cool. I can't believe you're here with us when you could be off having some wild party," Suze confessed.

"Geez, I can't even imagine the scene you're used to," Julie purred with envy.

Bessie rolled her eyes. "Trust me, it's not nearly as glamorous as you think."

Christie let out a dubious guffaw, "Yeah, right. I don't believe that. It must be one non-stop party."

Julie chimed in, "Yeah, the whole sex, drugs, and rock n' roll life style."

Bessie took in a deep breath and sighed heavily. "Yeah, that's there. But even that gets old. Besides, I've never really been into all of that."

Suze perked up. "I knew it! I can tell just from your albums and the way you sing that you were…I don't know…different."

A chuckle and shake of the head from Bessie amused her admirer who continued. "I mean it. Your music isn't like most of that shit out there. You tell stories."

Suze's compliment and characterization of her as a storyteller was gratifying and validated Joey's mentoring and approach to her performance. "Well, I'm glad you think so."

Suze got up from the sofa and headed over to the album collection. She pulled out Bessie's album and began fishing the vinyl out of the cover intending to play it.

Bessie sat up. "No...no...you don't need to do that. Please?"

She saw the bewildered look on the impromptu DJ's face who then turned to look at her two roommates with the hope that their expressions might help her understand Bessie's request. They, however, looked just as confused, if not disappointed, compelling Bessie to explain.

"Really...it's nice you want to play it, but really...I'd rather just talk. I never get to visit with...you know...regular people...no offense," Bessie added apologetically.

Suze slid the album back into its cover and returned it to the vertical stack and sat back down. "OK. Sure. We understand...don't we?" as she turned to her roommates who concurred with head nods.

Christie cleared her throat. "Well, I have to say that I just love how you seem able to convey a feeling in your songs. Not just in the lyrics or the melody...but the chords and choice of instruments. I don't know...I can't explain it. Sometimes I literally get a sense of...um, let's see...space in your songs."

Bessie was pleased with Christie's complimentary comments and astute observation. She leaned her elbow on the end of the sofa as the palm of her hand cradled her cheek. "It's interesting that you use that word...space. That's exactly what I try to do."

"Really?" Christie was visibly pleased at Bessie's confirmation.

Bessie nodded. "Really." She paused and surveyed her adoring hosts for a moment.

"Would you explain what you mean by 'space' to us?" Christie asked.

Bessie blushed. "Oh, you don't really want me to do that, do you?"

A chorus of enthusiastic "Yeahs" sprang in response.

Pleased, Bessie shrugged and smiled. She took a deep breath. "Are any of you musicians?" Bessie's question was met with three shakes of the head.

"I'm studying architecture," Julie responded. "We study space all the time."

Bessie nodded and smiled. "Well then, you get…how to put it…the physics of space then, don't you?'

"I'm trying to, anyway." All of them chuckled at Julie's confession before Bessie continued.

"Well…there's some physics of space in music as well. It has to do with chord structure, mostly." Bessie quickly assessed the faces of her hosts who were hanging on to every word. Reassured, she decided to proceed. Bessie pointed to the keyboard. "Can I use your keyboard?"

"Sure!" Julie scrambled to pull it out and set it on the makeshift coffee table with a cord running to the stereo. The stereo thumped to life when she pressed the power button. The keyboard came to life through the stereo speakers as Bessie tapped one of the keys.

"Do any of you know how to play chopsticks on the piano?" Bessie asked.

All three of them nodded and turned to each other exchanging confused glances as to where Bessie was headed.

"OK then. Well..." she paused to take a deep breath, " that little ditty nicely illustrates our aural desire for space. The first two notes, F and G, are smack dab next to each other are played together six times." She held up two fingers and began plunking them on the plastic keys. "These two notes that have such close proximity together with little space between them create an "interesting" yet not altogether "pleasing" sound. But after the sixth repetition, we change one of the notes, lowering the F down to an E." She paused long enough to play the notes and then continued. "And 'ta-da!' – we have generated some space that resolves the tension created from the first two notes being 'too close.' Make sense so far?"

The class of three nodded, encouraging Bessie to continue.

"OK. Chopsticks continues by creating more space after a series of six repetitions until we create eight steps between the notes to achieve an octave, which to our ear sounds finished or resolved. Composers will intentionally place notes "too close" to create what is musically termed as "dissonance" to create psychological tension. You've most certainly have heard church hymns and the traditional "Amen" ending...right?" She placed her hands on the keys and played the familiar chord and paused once again waiting for the trio of roommates to affirm her question.

"Sure, who hasn't?" Julie responded.

"OK, then. The 'amen' is composed by first placing two notes 'too close' to each other that creates this tension we want resolved, followed by dropping or moving one of those notes "down" to create the space – notes evenly spaced out that we subconsciously yearn for, thus creating resolution. This, in turn, evokes an emotional response within us. We're subconsciously reacting to how space is used with musical tones."

"Ooh – just like the opening guitar on The Who's *Pinball Wizard*," Suze added.

"Exactly!" Bessie replied with a clap of her hands for emphasis.

"Wow! That's so cool. I never knew any of this stuff!" Christie exclaimed.

Julie chimed in. "You said something about architecture. Where and how does that fit in?"

Bessie nodded. "Right. Let's use architecture, then. In a sense, composers are architects of sound...creating space. Just think about the physical and architectural space of a cathedral. It echoes...right? The space creates the echo, which generates that spiritual sense of space. I'm betting you've heard Gregorian Chants...you know...monks walking around singing in a monastery. It all sounds so...religious...to our ears anyway. That's because we subconsciously 'hear' or sense the distance or space between the notes the monks sing and chant. That space is referred to as an open fifth…here, let me show you."

Bessie placed her right thumb on middle C on the keyboard.

"Let's call this note number one or "DOH" and this note number five or "SO" -- like the song from the *Sound of Music*." She placed the little finger of her right hand on the G note. Before she could continue, Julie spoke up.

"God, I love that movie."

"I think I wore out our album of the soundtrack when I was a little girl," Suze added.

"Shh – you guys," Christie hushed, "let her finish." She turned back to Bessie. "Go on…you were saying…"

Bessie suddenly felt self-conscious. "Oh, I don't know…I'm afraid I'm getting a little carried away. You don't want to hear this," Bessie said.

"Yeah we do. Please?" Suze pleaded.

Chagrinned, Bessie continued. "OK. Well anyway…this space…in between these five notes…is what we call an open fifth and *that's* what creates this auditory sense of openness. The composers were aware of this and used it to reflect and create a sense of space between heaven and earth. It is what makes the music sound "holy" to our western ears. Now…add the note right in the middle…the third and you create a triad or a chord which more or less 'fills in' that space that we're used to hearing."

Julie broke into a smile. "Totally makes sense! I never thought of composers as architects."

Bessie clicked off the keyboard and sat back. Their conversation then shifted from Bessie's pedantic discourse to exchanging stories about certain songs and what memory or feeling they conjured. Tunes wafting from the radio during summer jobs – songs they listened to with boyfriends or danced to at school dances. And while Bessie relished the conversation, she once again felt on the margins, as she could not share their experiences of romance or proms. Yes, there were certain songs that reminded her of people and places. However, many of her memories that songs generated were often framed by moments and periods of her life she'd just as soon forget. She envied the young women sitting across from her as she listened to their stories.

Bessie closed her eyes, silently debating how much more to share. Up to now, everything she had said was so...so theoretical and academic. She was building up her nerve to cross over into something much more personal. This meant she ran the risk of revealing too much of herself, making her vulnerable. When she opened her eyes, she saw three pairs of eyes focused on her and for a moment, she felt the same way she had felt in the coffee houses she once played. Bessie took a deep breath.

"Songs – I mean *good* songs that tell a story – have a soul. They're almost alive because we can crawl into them and live through them. That's what I'm trying to do with my music.

That's what I mean about space – not just in terms of chords and notes. It's about creating a shared space with a room full of strangers – like what we're doing here...right now. When I'm on stage, I'm trying to share a moment with the audience. Something they can relate to and say to themselves, 'Yeah...I know that feeling' and that's when they form a relationship with the singer...with *me*. So when I say a song that tells a story has a soul, that also means it has a heart. That's why a story – or a song in this case – has to come from the heart and not just out of a good voice."

The three girls sat silently, hanging on Bessie's every word. Bessie was on a roll. She got up and walked toward the stack of albums. She ran her hand across the spines and pulled out a blue album. "Take, for instance Joni Mitchell's album *Blue* – she absolutely obliterates the boundary between her and listener by baring her soul."

Suze immediately added, "God, I love that album. I cry every time I listen to it."

"Have you heard this new guy...Bruce somebody..." Julie asked.

"Springsteen...Bruce Springsteen. Jesus...there's another story teller who pours his heart and soul into a song," Christie added.

Bessie nodded. "Ever seen him perform?"

Christie placed her hand over her heart to keep it from pounding out of her chest. "I saw him on TV once. God, I wouldn't even call it a performance...it was an experience. It was almost like a revival meeting. I mean, my God, he had the audience in the palm of his hand."

Bessie leaned into the conversation. "*That's* what I'm talking about…breaking down walls and boundaries to create some shared space…that's what happens when a singer sings *with* an audience rather than *to* or *for* them. It can be a raucous experience like Springsteen or a mellow, almost serene thing the way Joni does it on her *Blue* album."

"Geez, how do you know all this stuff?" Suze asked.

"I have to confess that I didn't come up with most of this on my own. The technical stuff came out of music theory classes I took my freshman year in college. The rest of it came from my manager."

Bessie paused long enough to wrestle with irony of the heart. Joey had taught her so much about the heart in so many ways – many through unintentional lessons. He knew so much and yet so little about the heart.

The three Illini coeds walked Bessie back to her hotel as the sun was coming up. The gaggle of girls stopped and stood quietly in front of the entrance.

"Well, ladies…I certainly have enjoyed my time with you," Bessie announced.

"So have we!" Suze replied as she reached over to hug Bessie. The other two roommates joined the group hug.

Bessie wiped a tear away as she pulled away from the adoring scrum adding an embarrassed, "Oh my!" as she realized her emotional state and chuckled. The other girls sniffed in tandem with their equally embarrassed chuckles.

Bessie sighed heavily and dropped her arms against her sides. "Well…I guess I need to get to my room."

The girls nodded their understanding.

Bessie smiled. "Thanks again for a lovely evening."

"Thanks for joining us," Christie added. "I'm glad Suze was brave enough to approach you." Suze let out a muffled laugh.

"Me, too," Bessie said. Then she smiled, waved, and opened the door to the hotel.

Chapter 26

Bessie took the stairs rather than the elevator to her hotel room where she ordered coffee and a croissant from room service. She was just emerging from the bathroom in her bathrobe after a shower when she heard room service knocking on the door delivering her breakfast. Bessie sipped her coffee and took intermittent bites of her flaky pastry as she packed. The bus would be leaving in less than 30 minutes.

The bus was eerily quiet and empty when Bessie climbed aboard. She took her usual seat and stared out the window. Across the street she could see the old house where she had talked the night away with three charming college girls. Joey climbed aboard and took his usual seat across the aisle from her. The bus door closed behind him with a hiss and the driver put the beast into gear, slowly pulling out from the covered entrance to the hotel. Bessie glanced around the nearly empty bus.

"Where is everybody?"

"A little change in plans."

She stared at him, waiting for him to elaborate.

"We're done," Joey flatly replied.

"What do you mean?" she asked.

"The tour – well except for tonight."

"What are you talking about?"

"It seems Mr. Diggs was discovered in his hotel room with a 16-year old boy. Evidently he hasn't just been bible banging. He has a preference for young boys. And all the kneeling that goes on isn't for prayer – if you know what I mean.

We've got a three-hour drive south to Carbondale. You're going to headline a street festival – very family friendly event. Then we head home."

On the long drive back to California, the scenery outside the tour bus window was as fleeting as Bessie's thoughts. She had always been a solo act – the pretty girl with the pretty voice and her guitar. And yet, there had been a backup band on her album. She envied watching the camaraderie of musicians in the bands she opened for on the various legs of her tour. Linda Ronstadt had backup band. Why couldn't she have one of her own?

Bessie diverted her attention from the world outside and quickly surveyed her inner world within the confines of the bus. There, across the aisle, a row ahead of her was Joey – asleep – of course.

Chapter 27

Once back in her little bungalow on Venice Beach, Bessie had lots of time on her hands. She bought a vintage bike and rode along the promenade donning a lacy cover shawl, a sundress, and wide brim straw hat. There were all kinds of crazy people seemingly right outside her face. The hustle and bustle was a spooky kind of shuffle that some called the human race. Out of the madness was a little bit of sadness that made Bessie feel out of place. Surely there must someone who could offer a little love and pull her back from outer space. Bessie found it easy to be lonely when trapped inside the beach crowds. But still a tiny voice inside her wanted to shout aloud. She knew that to many out there in the world it was all a big joke. But it wasn't funny to her. And until she found someone special, she'd continued to live her life inside out. Once back inside the four walls of her tiny bungalow, Bessie tried to capture all she was feeling and experiencing in the spiral-bound notebook she used as a journal. The exercise was primarily therapeutic rather than artistic. However, as soon as she got into the shower, she discovered some of what she had written was gradually making its way into a melody she was humming to herself.

A few days later, on a whim and out of boredom, she decided to make an impromptu trip to their old apartment in Hollywood where Joey still lived. She wanted to talk about a backup band when she took to the road again. She pulled into the apartment complex parking lot, seeing Joey's car. She still had her own key to the place. The key quietly rattled as she opened the door.

"Anybody home?" she called out.

She closed the door behind her.

"Hello? Joey?"

Bessie wandered over to the breakfast bar that separated the tiny kitchen from the living area as she surveyed the room. She could hear the shower running. Coffee was on so she went to the cabinet to grab a mug. She sat down on one of the two stools with her coffee. Waiting, she organized her rationale for a backup band – something that would require more money and logistical coordination. She figured it might be a hard sell. The water stopped running so she prepared her self for a possible argument. Sipping from the hot mug, she stared at the collection of dirty dishes in the sink while collecting her thoughts waiting for Joey to emerge from the other room. Bessie was so focused on her preemptive strike, that she failed to hear the bathroom door open. What she *did* hear was a petite shriek of "Oh, my God!" come from behind her.

Bessie turned to see a beautiful girl with a towel wrapped around her and another serving as a turban standing barefoot in the doorway – one hand grasping her throat in shock. Once she caught her breath, she gasped, "Who the hell are you?"

"I was just about to ask you the same thing," Bessie snapped back.

The woman just stared at Bessie, clearly struggling to recognize her. Bessie craned her neck to see into the bedroom through the open doorway and asked, "Where's Joey?"

The mystery woman dropped her hand from her throat and clutched the towel knotted around her bosom. "He ran around the corner to the convenience store. He should be back soon." Gradually the woman's eyes widened. "You're Bessie."

Bessie's glare seemed to confirm the woman's speculation as well as coax an introduction from her.

"Oh…I'm Gypsy…well…Tammy actually…Gypsy's my new name…I'm breaking it in…still getting used to it…know what I mean?"

"Uh huh," was all Bessie could muster in response to the woman's blathering.

Emboldened, the woman approached Bessie but stopped just short of joining her on the other stool. The two of them sized each other up, groping for any snippet of conversation. Gypsy…Tammy…whoever she was -- suddenly became aware of her attire and continued clutching the towel in place in embarrassment. The sound of Joey's keys rattling in the door quickly broke the awkward silence. He stepped into the apartment, stuffed his keys into his front pocket, and looked up to see two women in front of him.

"Well…I see the two of you have met." His attempt at levity did little to reduce the tension in the room. Bessie just folded her arms across her chest. Taking this as a cue, the woman elaborated.

"Yeah, well…Joey's been helping me with my brand."

"Your brand?" Bessie repeated. Joey heard the incredulous tone in her voice but Tammy continued jabbering before he had a chance to respond.

"Yeah…you know…my image. That's why we landed on Gypsy…you know…kind of mysterious sounding. Better than my real name, that's for sure. Cool huh?" The woman's banter was equaled only by her impish grin.

Joey was compelled to interject his side of the story. "Well…that's part of it. We've also been arranging some tunes…"

Bessie's head snapped when she turned to face Joey. Shocked, she once again repeated, "Arranging some tunes?" in disbelief.

Before Joey could explain, the woman chimed in.

"Yeah. He wrote some new tunes for me and we're…"

Bessie's glare silenced his apparent protégé in mid-sentence. It was all coming back to her. The woman standing in front of her had been standing off in the wings with Joey during a performance. Bessie struggled to maintain her relatively calm façade. She cleared her throat.

"I see. Well…that all sounds very…" she searched for the right words.

"Exciting!" the woman exclaimed.

Bessie gave Joey a condemning look. "Well…I was in the neighborhood…thought I'd just stop by. Didn't mean to…interrupt anything. I'll let you two get back to work." Bessie slipped off the stool and walked past the woman.

"Good luck," Bessie quipped as she walked by Joey. He felt the sarcasm brush him as she walked toward the door.

"Thanks! It was so nice meeting you, Bessie!" the woman gushed, obliviously.

Bessie looked back over her shoulder toward Joey as she opened the door. He averted his eyes to the floor as she closed the door behind her.

Chapter 28

Bessie was mortified over the way Joey seemed to be falling all over himself to "groom" – if that's what one would call it – this wanna-be poser. His authenticity and straightforward, no-nonsense approach had always impressed her. In all her years of navigating relationships, she had never experienced, let alone encountered someone who recognized and appreciated her for what she was the way he did. That was one of the things that drew her to him. It allowed herself to essentially pack up all her belongings and follow him to L.A. – completely trusting and putting not just her career, but also her life into his hands. She couldn't believe how oblivious he was to the fact that he was being played by this…this *chick*.

Her pent-up energy launched her into relentless pacing around her tiny apartment. She knew what kind of woman this Gypsy was. Why couldn't he see? The more she thought about it – the more appropriate she deemed the stage name. She was the kind of "lady" that men seem to think they want but can never have. She knows what to say…she'll tell a man she loves them but that's just words. She'll say it to get what she wants and then move on down the line to get whatever it is she wants next. A woman like that drives men crazy and brings even the strongest men to their knees.

She finally relented to the pressure and picked up her guitar. At first she just let her fingers roam over the fingerboard. Then she pounded out some chords as if she was exorcising some demon that had possessed Joey as well as purging her own jealousy. In the process, lyrics began cascading from her lips. Bessie set her guitar down long enough to retrieve her cheap Sears cassette tape recorder. She set the microphone on the table and punched the red button. After what seemed like a few moments, she clicked off tape recorder. Bessie began transcribing the hodge podge of words on the back of a brown paper lunch sack she hastily salvaged from the garbage. The minimal amount of space quickly filled, nudging Bessie to search for the yellow legal pad. Turning the tape on and off, she began arranging the words and lines into a song. She popped open the door of the tape recorder and flipped the cassette over. She arranged the yellow pad in front of her and Prudence in her lap before reaching over once again to punch the red record button. With the faint whirring of the cassette, Bessie sang. When she reached the end, she rewound the tape and listened.

She's that kind of lady – that turns your head around.
She will drive you crazy until she brings you down.
She tilts her head so slightly and looks into your eyes.
She bites her lip so childlike then tells you a woman's lies.

She'll tell you that she loves you.
And that you've got what she needs.
She says she'll bring you happiness
But she brings you to your knees.

It comes to her so natural…she's got all the moves.
And it's so matter-of-factual that she's got something to prove.
It really doesn't matter if you know her name
Cause places and faces go through some phases
But the end result's the same.

She'll tell you that she loves you.
And that you've got what she needs.
She says she'll bring you happiness
But she brings you to your knees.

And she knows by the way that you watch her
You want her so damn bad.
She's got so much to offer
If she can find the time.
She'll make a rich man a pauper
Then move on down the line.

She'll tell you that she loves you.
And that you've got what she needs.
She says she'll bring you happiness
But she brings you to your knees.

Pleased and somewhat surprised, she set Prudence aside in search of her spiral bound notebook now that her creative juices were flowing. Once she found it, she set it down on the table in front of her and sifted through the pages. Landing on one page in particular, she found what she had captured from her walk along the Venice promenade a few days earlier. Once again she set Prudence in her lap and punched the red button.

There's all kinds of crazy people standin' right outside my face.
This hustle and bustle and spooky kind of shuffle
Is what some call the human race.
And out of this madness comes a little bit of sadness
And I'm feelin' so out of place.
I'm looking for someone to give a little a lovin'
And pull me back from outer space.
It's easy to feel lonely when you're trapped inside a crowd.
But still that voice inside me wants to shout…to shout.
Well I know that some folks think it's one big joke
The way the world is spinnin' around.
So until I find my baby things will seem a little crazy
And I'll live my life from inside out.

Maybe I'm the one to blame, it's really hard to say.
What's fair is fair and I'll take my share, but the price is too high to pay.
And maybe on a whim, I can start up again
By diggin' up a piece of the past.
But I might get in trouble and maybe burst the bubble
And you know I wouldn't really like that.
Insanity is just a state of mind…there is no doubt.
But still that voice inside me wants to shout…to shout
Well I know that some folks think its' one big joke
The way the world is spinnin' around.
So until I find my baby things will seem a little crazy
And I'll live my life from inside out.

She had just written her first two songs.

Chapter 29

"You wrote this?"

Bessie nodded sheepishly.

"Have you played it to Joey?" Her knowing stare provided Benny the answer as well as his sudden epiphany as to the inspiration for the song. "Jesus, Bess…this is hot."

"Really? You think so?"

"God, yes. I didn't know you had it in you."

Somewhat dazed by this revelation, she ran her hand through her hair. "Neither did I."

"Are there any more?" Benny asked.

Bessie shyly nodded. "One more – some others in the works."

"Well Hell's Bells – let me hear it for Christ's sake."

Benny sat riveted as Bessie played the other song to him. He was seeing a whole new side of her – a darker, edgier side. This was no demure songstress warbling a folksy melody. Never the less, this was the same Bessie – the same heart that sang more than her voice – and clearly this heart was breaking.

"Bess – these are good. Seriously." He paused. Bess looked down to disarm his gaze. Together, both were secretly pondering the same thing. Daring the unspoken to be said. He bent over and leaned into her. "Bess – we need to record these. This is what we've been looking for…waiting for Joey to deliver."

Bessie didn't know what to think or say so Benny did the thinking and talking for her.

"You don't need him any more."

She stared at the floor in search of some kind of response. "We're a team."

"You *were* a team. And what you've shared with me here today reveals a treasure that needs to be unearthed. Look…your contract with me is up. I'm willing to offer you a new two-album contract…if…" he paused dramatically.

She turned her gaze up from the floor to look at Benny. "If what?"

"It you cut Joey loose and let me produce these. We'll bring in some new eyes and energy to help manage. Joey's taken you as far as he can."

Deep down, Bessie knew Benny's words rang true. He had struggled to wedge her out of what she had been and into a new niche. Joey seemed to have lost the magic touch – perhaps due to his shift in energy toward managing, leaving composing and producing to fall by the wayside. The whole scene, especially for women, was changing. With the advent of punk, everything was getting a bit edgier. Meanwhile, "old school" performers – the ones who had dominated the charts from the late 60s and early 70s were beginning to sound docile at best and embarrassingly passé at worst. Both of them knew the milquetoast sound of Olivia Newton John, Anne Murray, Helen Reddy – all current mainstream 'phenoms' would quickly become quaint. Besides, these mainstream singers lacked the heart of Bessie. But given that the public was gradually digging out of the turmoil of the war in Viet Nam only to now wallow in the mire of Watergate, audiences were longing for something else. Some preferred to be anesthetized with mindless ear candy. Others wanted something edgier. Besides, the era of the folkies was fading. Carole King and Laura Nyro, the darling female singer/songwriters of the early 70s had gone on hiatus. Even Joni Mitchell was morphing into jazz with her *Hissing of Summer Lawns* album – an album Bessie devoured. Meanwhile, the Wilson sisters from Seattle, Pat Benatar and Blondie were rocking the charts. Kate Bush was pushing the envelop with an avant-garde style that couldn't be categorized – it was too "over-the-top" and British for Bessie's taste. The tunes that escaped from within Bessie were somewhere in between what was on the radio, which appealed to Benny as they fell into a niche that made them unique.

    Bessie noted Benny rubbing his chin in thought.
    "What?" she probed.
    "Well, I noticed they don't really have a bridge."
    "So? Dylan doesn't use a bridge."
    "Good point."
    Bessie perked up. "Look – you said yourself you didn't want to pigeon-hole me and yet you're anchoring me down to some random sonata format from the 1800s."
    Benny had never seen or heard this side of Bessie before. This was a good sign as far as he was concerned. She was

emerging from both her mousy demeanor as well as Joey's influence.

Bessie gradually realized that this Gypsy chick – or whatever she was calling herself this week – was manufacturing her own persona rather than a voice under his guidance. Perhaps that's what disappointed and hurt her most about Joey – he had diverted his energy into creating something – an image – rather than nurture authentic talent and heart. Perhaps Benny was right. Perhaps it *was* time to move on – especially if she wanted to be true to who she was and what she was feeling now – although deep down inside, she wasn't sure what that was.

Chapter 30

"Hello?" Bessie answered the phone tentatively.

"It's me. Listen my dear; I've scheduled an impromptu business lunch. I want you to join me at Ship's Coffee Shop on the corner of Olympic and La Cienega at noon...today."

"Business lunch? What are you talking about Benny?"

"I've scheduled an appointment with someone. I want you to hear what he has to say?"

"An appointment? With who?"

"Nobody you know. But trust me, this guy has his finger on the pulse of all that matters."

"I don't know, Benny. I'm still kind of…"

He cut her off. "Listen to me, Bess. I've let you wallow in your artistic angst long enough. You can mourn for just so long before you become maudlin. You and I both know there's some momentum building out of your…shall we say…grief. It's time to tap into it. Think of Joni Mitchell and her album, *Blue*, for Christ's sake. You're there. I'm just following up on our previous conversation. And this is the guy who can take you to the next level."

There was a long silence on the other end of the line prompting Benny to continue.

"Look – just meet the guy and listen to what he has to say. If you like what you hear – great. If not…you got a free lunch out of it."

"Alright. Since you put it that way."

"Great! I'll see you at noon. Be there or be square."
Click.

* * *

Ship's Coffee House was a far cry from the glitz of L.A. and the nouveau chic of Venice Beach. It was unintentionally 'retro' by sheer virtue of never renovating the aging space-age décor of the 1960s that once exuded the glamor and possibilities of Kennedy's New Frontier. Its nostalgic appearance was not hip. It was merely old fashioned and out of date, serving staples such as meatloaf sandwiches and chicken pot pies with free coffee refills.

Bessie arrived – 20 minutes late – and found Benny sitting on the tuck and roll naughahyde cushioned booth facing her with another man whose back was to her. Benny spotted her and maneuvered his girth out of the tight booth to stand and greet her with a kiss on her cheek.

"There you are, my dear! Come! Sit and join us, won't you darling?"

The other man remained seated.

"Sorry," Bessie moaned pathetically…"Traffic." Her one word excuse was quickly understood and accepted as she outstretched her hand. "Hi, I'm Bessie."

The man accepted her handshake. "I'm Ron Speilman. It's so nice to meet you, Bessie. Please…have a seat." The man shifted to make room for her on his side of the booth as Benny descended to re-swallow the space on his side of the table. This also allowed Benny and Bessie to maintain eye contact to silently consult with each other during the lunch meeting.

"Wow, this is some place," Bessie scanned the room.

Benny chimed right in. "It's one of the few real places left in L.A. wouldn't you say, Ron?"

Ron nodded. "I guess you could say that. What you see is what you get."

"Exactly. None of that pretentious bullshit this town is so adept at manufacturing. Now dear, check the menu so we can get down to business. They have a Chicken Pot Pie here to die for," Benny raved.

Bessie quickly scanned the menu with her eyes landing on the breakfast section.

The waitress arrived in a huff. Bessie turned to her.

"Are you still serving breakfast?"

"Absolutely. What can I get you?"

"I'll have a ham and cheese omelet, hash browns, and coffee with cream." She closed the menu, handed it to the waitress and turned to Benny. "I just love breakfast, don't you?"

"I'm not sure, I'm never up that time of day to indulge." Benny sniped before turning his attention to the waitress. "And I'll have the Chicken Pot Pie."

The waitress scribbled his order and turned to Ron. "And you sir?"

"Burger. Medium rare. Fries and a coke."

"Okie dokie," the waitress replied and vanished.

Bessie nervously folded her hands on top of the table. "I used to waitress."

Benny chuckled, "That was then and this is now, my dear. Ron's here to talk about the future, aren't you, Ron?"

Ron smiled and rotated his empty coffee cup in between his two hands until the waitress suddenly returned with a coffee pot to refill their cups.

"That's right." His calm demeanor did little to calm her skepticism.

Bessie adjusted herself in the seat. "Well then…" and settled back to listen.

Benny jumped in before Ron could make his pitch. "Ron, here, is one of the…if not the top agent and manager in the business…isn't that right, Ron?"

The gentleman glanced down embarrassed. "I'm not so sure about…"

"He's just being modest," Benny interrupted. "Go on…tell Bessie some of your ideas."

Bessie turned awkwardly to face the man sitting a few inches beside her.

"Well, you see, Bess…you're quite special. I've heard you. I've seen you in front of people. The problem is this…you haven't been in front of *enough* people. There are only a handful of people who've ever heard of you. That's not your fault…it's the fault, or should I say the result of management." Ron backpeddled, trying to soften his critique of Joey.

Bessie exchanged the first of several raised eyebrows across the table with Benny.

Ron sensed her discomfort and regrouped.

"I'm not saying your current support is poor. I would, however, venture to guess that he's now a bit out of his league. Clearly, he helped you get started but I'm not sure he can help you expand your audience or take you to the next level. Benny let me listen to your new songs. They're good."

Benny held up both hands to deflect her damning glare. "Now, now...I wanted him to hear what *you* wrote...*your* material."

Ron bailed Benny out. "I'm glad he did, too. Those two songs he played for me were...how can I put this...less folksy than your previous stuff. A bit more eclectic. That breadth is going to have a broader appeal. We'll focus on AOR..."

"AOR?" Bessie interrupted.

"Album oriented radio. And so, like I told Benny here, we need to expose you to a broader audience." Ron's pitch was momentarily high jacked by the delivery of their meals.

"Will there be anything else?" the waitress inquired.

"No, I don't believe so. Thank you. Now...as you were saying, Ron..." Benny nudged as the waitress left the check on the table.

"Well, as I was saying, we start the next phase of your career with a new album. We'll feature your new stuff and some other covers that go beyond the folky repertoire and..."

Bessie interrupted again. "But won't that disappoint my current fans? Won't they being buying it expecting that...folky repertoire, as you called it?"

Ron and Benny exchanged knowing glances as Ron continued his pitch.

"Not necessarily. We'll keep one or two on an album to satisfy that demographic. But as I'm sure Benny has shared with you, styles and tastes are changing. Even Joni Mitchell is shifting over to more jazz-fusion. So we launch the album with at least two sure-fire hits along with a mix of styles that fit who you are. But that's only one prong of the two prong strategy I'm proposing."

Bessie stabbed at her omelet with her fork, took a bite, and swallowed before asking, "And what would this second prong entail?"

Ron perched his elbows on the table on the outside of his plate and pressed his two hands together. "Television."

Bessie grimaced. "Television? What do you mean?"

"I mean a TV special that will showcase you to a whole new audience."

Bessie furrowed her brow at Benny and slightly shook her head. "Uh...I don't..."

Benny jumped into the conversation. "Have you looked at prime time television lately, my dear?"

"No," she replied indignantly, not attempting to disguise her disgust at the thought, let alone actually watching it.

"Well, it may be time you did. It's a whole new thing. All the up and coming have their own shows," Bennie argued.

"Yeah? Like who?" she sniped.

Ron re-entered the discussion armed with a list as convincing ammunition for his argument. "Like Cher…Helen Reddy…The Carpenters…Tom Jones…Glen Campbell…Johnny Cash…The Captain and Tennille…Mac Davis…Tony Orlando and Dawn…Mama Cass…just to name a few."

The blood drained from Bessie's face. "You're suggesting I have my own TV show? I'm just a one-hit wonder. No one would watch a series of me."

Ron calmly explained. "No…not a series…a one-time TV special. Something folks would tune in once to see and hear and get to know you."

"But all those shows you rattled off…they're so…so…" Bessie searched for the right word.

"Vanilla? Mainstream? Corny? Which one of those words were you looking for?" Ron asked flatly.

She just looked at Ron, debating how to answer. He could see where she was headed just as Benny chimed in with his own additional rationale.

"What about The Smothers Brothers? They're hardly what you'd call square or mainstream. They're counterculture. They're pals with the Beatles, for Christ's sake," Benny noted.

Bessie continued to struggle with the whole idea being pitched. "I'm just not sure that's me. Besides, what am I going to do for a whole show that's what...an hour long? You're not suggesting I sit there and do a set in front of a camera, are you?"

"No, no, no! You'd host. There'd be guests. You could tell little jokes in between acts." Ron clarified.

"But I'm not funny!"

Ron tilted his head slightly to acknowledge the truth of her statement before continuing. "TV writers would write some banter you'd read off cue cards when you introduce and interact with another act – kind of like Sonny and Cher do. You'd do two...maybe three of your songs and the rest would be guests singing their songs – perhaps you could do a duet. That's the beauty of it. You'd only have to give what you've always been best at – your voice. It's actually a pretty big return on a relatively small investment of energy on your part."

Bessie shot a look at Benny. "Did you know about this? Are you in on this?"

Benny did his best to lean across his belly and table in earnest with an uncharacteristic hushed voice. "My dear, dear girl...we don't have to get into the nuts and bolts here and now. The point is this...I believe you can see that Mr. Speilman here has a vision. Dare I ask if your current...uh...partner has looked into his crystal ball as to what your future might entail?"

The weight of his question jolted Bessie into the back of the booth's cushioned seat. Joey had indeed offered next to nothing in the way of 'what's next' with the exception of what she had stumbled on in his apartment a week earlier and that apparently did not involve her. Ron offered a gentle smile.

Bessie's eyes flitted back and forth between the two men. "Well, I must admit the album intrigues me. Will Benny produce it?"

"Of course," both men replied in unison.

She cocked her head directly addressing Ron. "Would we go on the road to promote it?"

"Yes."

"Can I have a backup band?"

Ron glowed with absolute confidence. "You can have anything you want. You can even have a say in the venues."

Bessie mulled this over before continuing. "Would I be the headliner?"

Ron cocked his head. "It depends. Probably not at first as the album is released. But as the singles gather momentum, that would probably shift…when you're bankable."

Bessie tried to conceal the smile emerging on her face as Benny gave her an "I-told-you-so" look. Ron noticed the exchange. It was now his turn to approach his pending client with earnest.

"Bessie…concerts are very different from the coffee house circuit where you built your chops. Let's be honest – you were essentially background music to that crowd. But because of you…your voice…your heart – you managed to get the audience's attention. That's rare. I watched you and saw how you connected in that setting. That's why I'm so thrilled at the idea of representing you."

"You saw me? Where?"

"At U of I in Champaign. I had been in Chicago with one of my other clients and missed you at the Amazing Grace so I dropped downstate to catch you there. Granted, that was an auditorium and larger than the intimate coffee houses, but it was a smaller venue and you did, indeed connect with the audience," Ron explained.

Bessie was aghast. That gig was etched in her memory for so many reasons. It was where she first sighted Joey's new protégé standing off in the wings. It was where she talked the night away with a gaggle of girls in a college apartment. It was where the tour had come to a crashing close. And now this. That particular gig seemed like a crossroads she felt compelled to pay attention to, as well as the continued pitch from Ron.

"Concerts are a whole different thing. People are paying money to see and hear you. They want to hear those songs they hear on the album."

"I know. But I have to tell you…" Bessie paused gathering her thoughts and memories.

"I'm listening," Ron gently responded. She was slightly un-nerved by his willingness to entertain her thoughts. This was a new experience for her.

"Those coffee houses you talked about…I could be *with* that audience. I didn't just sing *at* them. I connected with them. We actually had a conversation – literally – in those intimate spaces. I loved that. In fact, I missed all of that once I was opening for acts in concert venues. I couldn't make the leap across the void between me and the audience sitting so far away in the dark. I couldn't even see them, for goodness sake."

Ron raised an eyebrow at Benny. He knew all too well that this was Bessie's raison d'etre. He worried this could be a deal-breaker.

"Well…that may be true. But the same could be said about recordings. There's no audience sitting there on the vinyl. That doesn't seem to have stopped you from recording."

Ron had a point and it showed on her face. Albums were really no more intimate. Had she been fooling herself all this time? Being her record producer, Benny quickly took note of Bessie's deflating posture and intercepted the subject.

"Bessie, my dear…this a lot to spring on you. You don't have to decide right this minute, does she, Ron?" Bennie's expectant eyes were coaching Ron's response.

"No. Of course not. Think it over. There's no rush. We can make this up as we go. I just wanted to give you a glimpse of the future I see," Ron added.

Bessie sighed with relief and looked to her record producer.

"I'll think it over."

Chapter 31

The next morning, Bessie sat alone at a patio table at the Candle Café on Ocean Front Walk in Venice with her morning coffee and a magazine she had randomly grabbed from another table. She casually thumbed through the pages dividing her attention between the surf and articles on the glossy pages. One article did, however catch her eye. It reported a new kind of coffee shop in Seattle along the waterfront that apparently had created a whole new scene and buzz. Reading about the hotspot, she was reminded of the warmth and vibe she felt when performing in the funky coffeehouses with Joey. Bessie's melancholy envy was suddenly interrupted by the doppler effect of her voice trailing off in the distance bringing a smile to her face. It was not necessarily a smile of satisfaction as much as irony. A muscular beach bum had just hurtled past her on roller blades with a boom box perched on his shoulder. Little did he know that both he and his pastime were the inspiration and topic of the song that was blaring from the boom box perched on his bare bronzed shoulder. Neither was he aware that he had just breezed by the composer and performer of the song that was the second single off her new album. The song she wrote about crazy people right outside her face was doing modestly well on the charts. The off and on gigs scheduled at small venues appeared to stoke album sales. Concert ticket sales were adequate as opposed to disappointing given that Bessie was not a superstar. She was, none-the-less, now a star in the Galaxy Entertainment family of Ron Speilman's constellation of clients.

Ron was slick, efficient, and competent. He had, as promised, delivered everything she had asked for. He was also very busy caring for his other clients. Most, not all, of the communication with him was through his face-less secretary over the phone. When they did meet one-on-one, the brief, stilted conversation was on logistics. Gone was the intimate dialogue that she and Joey had. Still, Ron had ably crafted an itinerary of small yet venerable theaters, some on college campuses, around the country -- *The Blind Pig* in Ann Arbor, *The 40 Watt Club* in Athens, Georgia, the *Gammage Auditorium* at Arizona State University in Tempe, the *Ohio Theater* in Columbus, and the *Tennessee Theater* in Knoxville, just to name a few. These were dispersed over a year to minimize burnout.

There were no more grueling road trips in a bus. Bessie and the backup musicians Benny had lined up for the album all hopped on a jet to a city where they played and spent the night at a four-star hotel before flying back to L.A. so everyone could be in their own beds by the next night. The backup band was another one of the things Ron delivered. These four guys were seasoned sidemen who could pick up, read, and play charts as easily as chewing gum. They were solid. They were tight. They were also union session musicians who simply punched the time clock. Bessie gradually came to discern the difference between backup musicians and a band.

A band formed organically resulting in a bond between the personalities as much as musical synergy. These guys backing her up were nice enough and highly competent, but they weren't invested. They engaged in conversation, but it was either small talk while in transit to and from performances or geek-speak with each other on topics as mundane as the latest special effects pedal that bored Bessie.

Audiences were receptive, especially when she introduced another one of her songs as her next single, which thrilled her. But to Bessie their receptivity felt like a one-way transaction in which they had paid money in exchange for a product to be consumed – to be entertained. And while the venues were generally small and considered intimate by industry standards, the darkened halls were cavernous to her and seemed to swallow the *people* – rather than the audience -- sitting in the seats. There was no bridge for Bessie to cross and be *with* such a large crowd in such a large setting the way she had in the grimy coffeehouses. All in all, Bessie was getting all she could ever want or hope for in her new partnership. The one thing that was missing was a plate of chocolate chip cookies before each show.

Chapter 32

"Hello?"

"Hi, Mom."

"Hi honey. Where are you?"

"Oh, I'm in Salt Lake City…I think. The gig is in a nice old fashion theater on campus here at the University…Kingsford Hall…Kingston Hall…I don't know…something like that. "

"My, my you do get around don't you?"

"Yeah, I suppose. So…what's on the program for tonight?"

"I'm listening to *At Last* by Etta James. You remember that album don't you?"

"Of course I do. Let's see…I think *Sunday Kind of Love* was our favorite on that one."

"Good girl! Oh, how you used to let loose on that one."

"Well, Mom, I can't stay on too long…it's almost time to go on."

"Of course, I understand. I always appreciate your Friday night calls to check in. You be a good girl now…you hear?"

"I hear. OK…gotta go."

"Okie dokie. Take care, Bess. Love you!"

"Love you, too. Bye-bye."

Chapter 33

The last of the scattershot schedule of gigs across the map was scheduled close to her home base at the Ambassador Auditorium in Pasadena. Bessie was excited that Benny made his way from his Hollywood den to her performance and dressing room afterwards.

"Bravo, my dear, bravo!" he shouted as he kissed both of her cheeks.

"Thanks."

"Oh and to think I played a tiny role in your triumphant performance," Benny said with closed eyes and a dramatic flurry.

Bessie mimicked his melodramatic pose with her own placing the back of her hand to her forehead. "And how can I ever repay you?"

Benny's face flattened with an obvious glare. "By having a late-night dinner with me."

"You mean now?"

"Yes now. How does sushi sound? I know a late night place about two blocks away."

Bessie grimaced. "Sushi? At this hour?"

"Sushi is good at any hour. Come along now, gather up your…whatever needs gathering and let's go."

"But I have a limo and driver waiting…"

Benny raised both of his hands and flitted them backhandedly, "Send him on his way. His service is no longer necessary. I shall be your chauffer and safely deliver you to your abode."

"Well, I..." Bessie stammered.

"Well, I nothing. You owe me. Now, quit dilly-dallying. I'm famished." Benny bowed deeply, extending an outstretched arm toward the door, "After you, my dear."

It was a short, brisk walk across the bridge over the freeway from the auditorium to the sushi bar that was apparently a popular 'after concert' hot spot. Bessie and Benny drew stares from attendees of her concert as they walked into the crowded restaurant. On top of that, everyone in L.A. seemed to know Benny. He was greeted enthusiastically by the tiny hostess who escorted them to a small table toward the back of the bustling restaurant, handing each of them a menu.

"Uh, Benny..." Bessie cautiously probed.

Benny perused the menu and offered an inquisitive melodic "Yes?"

"I've never had sushi. You forget I'm just a Midwestern girl. The only fish I eat is a can of tuna or a walleye pulled out of a lake."

He never took his eyes off the menu. "Trust me. You're in good hands."

Bessie smiled and sighed. "Yes. I'm in good hands. And yes...I trust you."

The sincerity in her voice coaxed him to lower the menu from in front of his face. He gave her a warm, appreciative smile just as the waitress came over to take their order. Once he gave it for the both of them, she left, and the two quietly took each other in.

"So…how has it been on the road?"

"Good."

"And the backup?"

"They're good."

Benny gave her a knowing look from under his eyebrows. "There's something you're not telling me."

Bessie fiddled with the wrapped chopsticks. "I mean, they're tight and all that. I have no complaints."

"But?" Benny let the pitch of his interrogation rise.

"Well…I don't know. It just hasn't turned out the way I thought it would."

He cocked his head to one side. "And what way would that have been?"

"You know…chummy."

"Chummy?" Benny repeated dubiously.

"I just thought we'd all be…you know…closer."

Benny shook his head with impatient disdain. "My dear…they're backup. That's what you asked for."

"I know. I guess that's not what I wanted."

"And what was it you wanted?"

"A band…I guess."

Benny nodded his grasp of her longing. "I see."

There was a long awkward silence. Benny let Bessie squirm before continuing.

"And how about the itinerary and venues…are they what you…" he paused dramatically, "…wanted as well?"

Bessie took a drink from her glass of water. "Yes…for the most part."

"Ah ha. And what part seems to be missing?"

"I don't know. I guess I just expected a little more…you know…intimacy."

"Well my dear, one can hardly characterize an audience of 10,000 or more as intimate."

"I know, I know," Bessie replied indignantly.

Their eyes met. Bessie could see him look through her.

"Well, my dear, it seems to me that our friend Mr. Speilman has given you *exactly* what you…wanted."

Bessie looked down and nodded sheepishly.

"Bessie…look at me…" Benny whispered across the table.

She reluctantly raised her eyes.

"What did Joey say when you told him you were signing on with Ron?"

She ran her fingertip over the rim of her water glass.

"Well?" Benny coerced.

"I didn't tell him."

Benny folded his hands together on top of the table. "I see."

Their plates arrived, rescuing Bessie for the moment.

"What is this I'm about to put in my mouth?" she asked with slight disgust.

Amused, Benny pointed to the various dishes, naming them.

"Uh huh," Bessie responded with uncertainty.

"Here...start with this California Roll. You'll like it. Trust me."

Bessie bit into the rolled ball of avocado and rice and shrugged with surprised satisfaction.

"So, let me see if I understand...your contract with Joey was broken?"

Bessie continued chewing and shook her head.

"There was no contract to break," she replied once she swallowed. She then averted her eyes to survey the strange food arranged on the table but she could feel Benny's eyes on her.

"So...what *did* break?" he asked with arched eyebrows.

Chapter 34

"OK. Quiet please, everyone. Ready? Roll tape...speed...and...ACTION!"

"Hello! I'm Bessie James and welcome to my world!"

"CUT! Let's do that again. Remember, Bess...look *through* the camera to your audience and don't forget to smile. Got it? OK then. Take Two...ready...and action!"

The past 15 months had been a concerted effort on Bessie's part to ignore the TV special with the expressed hope it would somehow go away. It didn't. The project had been strategically delayed to allow album sales and concert appearances to generate some momentum and interest.

"Hello! I'm Bessie James and welcome to my world!" she repeated.

What followed was more reading of inane blather to hint at special guests off of cues cards. The manufactured banter did not expressly mention specific names of performers because the producer had yet to nail down the talent. For now, they could shoot around the guest spots and fill in the gaps later. They would temporarily focus on the opening, some transitions, and Bessie's performance of her songs – a total of four – two from her first album and two from the new one. This went on for two days.

"That was great, Bessie. Why don't you take a break and come into the booth to take a look?" the invitation from the director crackled through a speaker suspended over the stage.

She handed her guitar to a stagehand and made her way to the production booth. Inside, next to the director and various technicians sat Ron Speilman.

"Come on in. Have a seat. Let's take a look!" Ron beamed.

The videotape flickered on the monitors as it was quickly re-wound. Bessie sat silently, watching herself go through the motions of singing one of Joey's songs she sang on the stage of the college coffeehouse that seemed a lifetime ago. When the painful rendition thankfully ground to an end, one of the technicians punched a button on the control board illuminated by an array of colored lights. Over the speakers erupted canned rousing applause from a non-existent audience.

Ron stood and smiled at Bessie. "Nice! Well done, Bess. So, what do you think?" he asked brimming with enthusiasm.

This was her first real look at herself on the TV monitor. She realized there was a reason that the powdered mask on her face was called 'make up' as it was a futile attempt to "make up" an image. Bessie hardly recognized herself. She rarely wore make up. She didn't need to. Meanwhile, she was mortified as she was forced to watch her awkwardly recite manufactured banter about a manufactured world on a make-believe set in front of a manufactured audience that consisted of nothing more than manufactured recordings of manufactured applause. How, she wondered, had she allowed herself to lose control -- to be manipulated into becoming something she was not.

"I'm sorry," she choked on her words.

"Sorry? About what? What's wrong?" Ron implored.

"This. All of this." She motioned with both hands to the control booth and monitors. She swallowed hard. "I'm sorry. I can't do this. I just can't." She turned and walked out of the control room.

Chapter 35

Tink, tink, tink.

Bessie gently swirled her spoon against the porcelain mug as she watched the cream cloud the black coffee. She impulsively grabbed a magazine from the stack on the countertop as she took her usual table on the patio at the Candle Café. A whole week had passed since she had run out of the TV studio. The phone in her bungalow rang and rang. She simply let it ring, assuming it was either Ron or Benny. She had unplugged her answering machine. That was one of the reasons she was at the café – to escape the incessant ringing and the inevitable apology and making excuses. Bessie gazed out at the comings and goings of the parade of characters on the Venice Beach promenade.

She sighed.

She didn't fit in here any more than she did anywhere else. That was her problem. She was unsure of where she did. The episode at the TV studio was merely the finale of the crescendo that had been building over the past two years.

She was stuck.

Bessie suddenly found herself recalling Bobby Vee's advice – have a backup. While at the time she wasn't sure what that might be – she definitely knew what it would *not* be. There was no way she would return to Minnesota or to waitressing. College was out. Bessie began to take inventory of what she had. Luckily she had plenty of money stashed away even after buying the Venice bungalow. Bessie had refrained from impulsive buying splurges that plague so many new and upcoming stars. Likewise, her financial windfall had not gone up her nose or down her throat or into therapy like so many others in the business. She took slight comfort in knowing that she wouldn't go hungry. She also had a roof over her head. Then again, she thought prison cells have meals and a roof. Bessie gradually realized she spent most of her time out of her abode, walking around Venice Beach. This revelation meant she had a lot of time on her hands. Time could be either a curse or an asset. Perhaps she should spend a little bit of it to get away for a change of scenery where a backup plan might present itself.

    She took another sip of coffee.

    Frustrated and bored, she began thumbing through the magazine that was now sitting on her table. She quickly realized she had perused this issue once before when she landed on an article describing a hot new trend of coffee shops in Seattle that had caught her eye once before. The piece mentioned one shop in particular down on Pike's Place. In all her gigs, she had never made it up to the Pacific Northwest for some unknown reason. It was probably just a fluke of the calendar. Bessie wondered what it was like up there in that corner of the country. The story in the magazine rekindled the warm memory of some of the coffee houses she had played in before performing concert venues. Of all the cozy little dives she played in, the *Amazing Grace* still amazed her. Perhaps that's what she needed – a funky coffee house fix.

Part II

Chapter 36

Pat, pat, pat.

Bessie gently patted the top of the dashboard of her Ford LTD for good luck and turned on the ignition. Her suitcase and guitar case sat in the backseat. Bessie guided her huge car on to U.S. 101 heading north. Alone. A first for her in some ways. While she had navigated life on her own, she had never literally ventured out on to life's highway by herself. Even during their journey to L.A. she had always safely been in Joey's rearview mirror – never truly solo. Today she had Linda Ronstadt, Bonnie Raitt, Karla Bonoff, Laura Nyro, James Taylor, Dan Fogelberg – to name a few – in a shoebox full of cassette tapes riding shotgun to keep her company. More than listening to and enjoying their music, their voices drowned out the one inside Bessie's head – the voice that kept bringing up and rehashing the past – the voice that kept wondering and worrying about the future.

Within an hour or so, she was passing through Santa Barbara. The white Spanish mission-style buildings with their red tiled roofs glimmered in the sun against the backdrop of the mountains. This was the town Joey had mentioned long ago during their conversation in Union Station as a possible landing spot for him. For a moment she wondered if he might possibly be here. She didn't know. She hadn't seen or heard from him since that day nearly two years ago in his apartment with that…that Gypsy woman – or whatever the hell she ended up calling herself. Joey had once said that the photos he had seen of the city made it look like heaven. From what Bessie could see flashing by her window, trapped in her purgatory on four wheels, she had to agree.

This was Bessie's first real excursion through California. It was a respite from the noise, smog, asphalt, and star-maker machinery of the L.A. basin. She also could actually sense what the Golden State actually smelled like. She recalled once hearing Benny say that California had its own "smell" – a tangy, organic aroma. When she heard other people make similar claims, Bessie did not understand what they meant. But here, driving with her windows down, she did. It was a mix of salty air and the combined fragrance of oak, bay, and eucalyptus leaves. Santa Barbara did, indeed, seem perfect. *Too* perfect in her way of thinking. Bessie speculated that the perpetual perfection would become boring over time. After all, how much sunshine and beauty could one take? Didn't one need to have cloudy days to make one appreciate the sunny ones? All in all, Bessie appreciated the city for its beauty the same way she admired works of art that she could neither afford nor have in her home. So, she drove on.

A little past noon, Bessie passed the threshold of the San Francisco Bay Area softly singing to herself, *Do You Know The Way To San Jose* channeling Dionne Warwick. Staying on course, U.S. 101 threaded through the heart of the city as she marveled at the hodgepodge of culture, buildings, and the whole vibe as she drove. Even from the confines of her car, she could feel that it was nothing like L.A., despite being in the same state. The freeway surprised her by suddenly spitting her out on to a large, bustling street. She carefully followed the white shield signs demarking U.S. 101 along Van Ness Avenue that led her over the Golden Gate Bridge. The route didn't afford any specific opportunity to pull off. Besides, the amount and frenzied flow of traffic un-nerved her so it was best to just keep going with the flow. It was exciting to cross the landmark but she couldn't really enjoy it. She reflected on how similar her journey on tour had been – going with the flow but not really enjoying it and never really arriving to the artistic nirvana she had envisioned. She continued to nervously focus on driving. She was unable to take her eyes off the road to peer out across the Bay as she drove. It was yet another bridge in her life to cross without really knowing where the road was leading. Once across the bridge, she stopped in San Raphael where traffic had eased enough for a quick lunch of the sandwich she had made before leaving.

    After lunch she continued to wind her way up the coast. She preferred the older highway over the newer, faster, and straighter Interstate that served as the spine of the state. The older route still passed through towns where she could get a fleeting feel of the place whereas the Interstate bypassed most of the smaller towns altogether. Besides, U.S. 101 hugged the coast. She felt that she was teetering on the edge of the continent. That seemed to run parallel to the bearings of her internal compass as she was navigating the edges of her life.

    After nearly ten hours of driving, she pulled into a motel in Eureka, California. Bessie hoped the namesake of the town might provide some kind of a discovery and insight to her journey. It didn't. What it did give her was a surprising sense of comfort – as if the fog had wrapped itself around her and embraced her. Following a quick supper of chili and cornbread at a café near her motel, Bessie fell into one the deepest night's sleep she had ever experienced. As she drifted off, she told herself that she would continue her pilgrimage along the Oregon coast to Seattle the next day fully rested.

Chapter 37

"Hi! What can I get for you?"

Bessie stood frozen at the counter staring at a chalkboard covered with strange words and prices printed in an array of brilliant colors. The chalk was not the only source of sensory overload. The rich aroma of roasted coffee beans overwhelmed her.

"Oh, gee. I'm afraid I don't know where to start," she replied shyly with a nod of her head upward to the chalkboard.

The woman at the counter smiled patiently. "No worries. You're right…there's a lot to choose from."

Bessie gulped. "That may be true but I don't even know what it is I'd be choosing," she confessed not taking her eyes off of the chalkboard.

"Yeah, it's more like a chalkboard in your high school geography class, isn't it?" the woman in the green apron commented.

Bessie nodded and began reading the names of the countries aloud, "Sumatra, Kenya, Uganda, Colombia, Mexican Java, New Guinea…"

"These are where our blends come from. Each of them has a different taste," the friendly but slightly manic server explained.

Exasperated, Bessie added, "Geez…who knew ordering a cup of Joe could be so complicated?"

"Well, do you like your coffee strong or mild?"

"I don't really know." Bessie began digging her wallet out of her purse.

"OK, how about I give you our house blend?" Her suggestion was more of a tactic to move on to the next customer than to actually assist Bessie with her coffee conundrum.

"Sure, I guess. Oh, and with cream."

"OK. Cream's over there on the service table," she nodded in the direction behind Bessie and then added, "What size?"

"Oh, just small, I guess. Thanks."

"Name?"

Bessie's confusion showed, prompting the woman to clarify with a slight edge of irritation in her voice. "Your name?"

"Oh, right...Bessie"

The woman scribbled her name on a paper cup and tossed it down the counter to another person, also clad in a green apron, and shouted, "One short, house!" as her coworker snagged the empty cup with one hand.

"That'll be $1.50."

Slightly shocked at the price, Bessie handed over two dollars and glanced around the room. She then attempted to engage the server with some reconnaissance, much like she did on the road in the early days with Joey. "Interesting place. I love the aroma. I've never seen a coffeehouse quite like this. Been here long?"

The woman stashed Bessie's cash into the cash register and handed her two quarters along with an answer to her question.

"Yeah, we've been at this location a few months now. We moved from our original shop over on Western Avenue, not too far from here. It was basically a shop where we sold fresh roasted beans but too many customers asked for drinks to go so we expanded our market a bit." The woman then lifted her eyes up and over Bessie, taking note of the line of customers forming behind her. "Well, thanks for coming in. You can pick up your drink over there at the other end of the counter. Can I help the next person?" she called out, looking past Bessie.

Feeling verbally shoved aside, Bessie migrated to the end of the counter and joined a small claque of caffeine addicts awaiting their fix. The rich wooden décor had an antique charm but the room itself lacked warmth. And as crowded as the shop was, it consisted mostly of individual customers who appeared very much alone. People rushed in empty handed and rushed out with their disposable paper cups in hand filled with an elixir of short-lived intoxication. There was no place to sit or to talk. She saw no staging area for performers other than the waiting area for individual customers playing out their own little private dramas.

Bessie felt disappointment wash over her. She had driven all this way with the hope of finding a haven – a place where people came together for a shared experience. Instead, it was essentially a conveyer belt dispensing expensive and exotic doses of caffeine.

"ONE SHORT HOUSE FOR BESSIE!" came a shout, snapping Bessie out of her daze. She retrieved her cup, added cream, and slowly made her way toward the exit. She nursed her coffee as she strolled along Pike Place Market en route to where she had parked. The grey clouds hung low, matching her spirits.

The coffee house had been her destination. Now that she had arrived and departed, she had no place in particular to go. She figured she'd just point the Ford south and head back to California. Unfortunately, a maze of one-way streets confused her, re-directing her on to State Highway 99 and heading in the wrong direction. She continued driving north watching for some kind of sign on where to go next – not just for the night – but for a lifetime. In her confused daze, she managed to miss a turn and found herself on yet another state highway that literally ran out of road in a small town called Mukilteo. She had come to a ferry crossing. On an impulse, Bessie paid the toll, pulled into the queue, and waited. She had never been on a ferry. She had never been on island, despite being one herself. She told herself it would be an adventure. There was a satisfying sense of order and comfort to the whole experience, reminding her of kindergarten's socialization of taking turns and being patient. A woman in a yellow vest waved her onto the ferry and upon arrival on the other side the same woman calmly directed Bessie off the vessel. If only life could be as calmly structured in getting from Point A to Point B as taking the ferry, she pondered.

The crossing was easy – even fun. She sat in her car and watched out the window as lovely homes lining the waterfront passed by. The water looked like shiny grey glass, reflecting the grey sky above. Sea gulls dashed and called out above her. Twenty minutes later, the traffic disgorged from the ferry with a noisy clatter. The narrow channel she had just crossed seemed like a mote, safely separating her from what she had left behind. The paved exit from the ferry dock magically rejoined the state highway that now continued into and through the town of Clinton. It wasn't much of a town and she soon found herself driving through the dark. A green traffic sign to the right pointed toward Langley, another six miles. Bessie decided it was time to find a place to spend the night.

Langley was a sleepy hamlet on the water. It consisted of two main streets hugging the waterfront. What it lacked in size was replaced by charm. She meandered her car through the handful of side streets with the goal of finding a place to eat. Instead, she happened upon a hand-painted sign announcing the Country Road Cottage outside a lovely craftsman house. She took it to mean more than just a sign for an accommodation. It appeared to be a cute little bed and breakfast. She had no reservation as well as no other options. She pulled up into the driveway and parked.

Knock, knock, knock.

A porch light came to life. The door squeaked open.

A woman in her late 40s wearing an apron and a pleasant smile stood in the doorway. "Yes? Can I help you?"

"Uh, yes…well I hope so, anyway. I was wondering if you had an opening."

"For how many nights?"

The question caught Bessie off guard. She had not thought that far.

"Gee, I'm not sure…for tonight at least."

"Well, we do have one tiny cottage open, we call it the Hen House that's really quite charming…cozy and comfortable."

"It sounds lovely."

"So does that mean you'll be staying with us?"

Her response surprised herself. "Yes, I believe so."

"Wonderful. Come on into the foyer to sign in and then I'll walk you over to your cottage. My name is Dottie. And yours?" Dottie let her question hang in the air.

"Bessie."

"My, what a lovely old fashioned name. Is it short for something else?"

"Nope. Just plain ol' Bessie." Bessie smiled as she began filling in the registration form. "I'm wondering if you could tell me of place nearby where I could get a bite to eat."

"Oh let's see…what's open this time of night?" Dottie cradled her chin with one hand. "Well there's a small café just down the road about three blocks and there's a pizza place across the street. That's about it. We're such a little patch in the road we don't have too much to offer. Then, there's Doc's Diner, but it only serves breakfast and lunch. You might want to check it out if you're here for lunch tomorrow. Meanwhile, breakfast will be served here in the parlor tomorrow morning between 7:00 and 9:00. I hope you like quiche -- that's what I was preparing when you knocked on the door," she wiped her hands down her apron as part explanation/part apology.

"Oh, I'm sorry to trouble you," Bessie said as she stood up from filling out the form on the tiny desk in the entryway.

"It's no trouble at all. Well now, I'll walk you over to your cottage. I hope you enjoy your stay."

"Thank you. I'm sure I will."

Chapter 38

Bessie took her usual spot at the counter in Doc's Diner. She had laid claim to this particular stool every day for the past two weeks just as she had laid claim to her little cottage with Dottie for a long-term stay. A few others sat at the counter. Only a handful of customers were scattered about in the booths along the wall, as it was so late in the afternoon – nearly closing time for this breakfast and lunch venue. Breakfast was her favorite meal, so she didn't mind indulging in a second after the one that was included with her room. She didn't bother to look at the menu – she knew what she wanted – the same thing she always ordered. Doc's Special Omelet -- snow crab meat, vermicelli pasta, avocado, tomato, green onion and cream cheese, topped with hollandaise sauce. This was Bessie's way with many things – why take chances and try something new when you already know what you wanted? She didn't consider this being in a rut as much as settling into a comfortable routine. Apparently, the approaching waitress, who according to the badge on her blouse was named Denise, had noted this tendency of hers.

"The usual?" Denise appeared to be already writing the order down on her pad before Bessie even spoke. Her telepathy slightly startled Bessie at the realization she had, in such a short period of time, become so utterly predictable to a perfect stranger.

"Uh…yeah. Doc's Special Omelet. Thanks."

"Coffee?"

"Yes please."

"With cream – right?"

Denise pointed to a tiny stainless steel creamer next to the salt, pepper, ketchup, and napkins perched on the counter directly in front of Bessie and walked off without another word. Funny – all the times she sat at this very spot and ordered the very same thing – she had either forgotten about or failed to notice the creamer. After the initial surprise of being so predictable, Bessie settled into the comfort this place offered. This revelation, along with her usual seat at the counter with her back to the rest of the diner, also revealed that she had not really soaked in the ambience of the place. Up until now, it was simply a matter of coming in, sitting down, ordering, eating, paying, and leaving. Given that Denise knew more about her than Bessie knew about Doc – assuming there was someone by that name – and his diner, Bessie decided it was time to rectify things.

She spun around on her stool once again to survey the place. The walls were covered in pine paneling. Crafty knick-knacks were perched on little shelves protruding from the walls. Booths with squeaky Naugahyde seat cushions lined two of the walls while small tables covered with plastic red and while checkered tablecloths cluttered the remaining floor space. Ceiling fans spun lazily overhead. The patrons – all seemingly regulars – appeared to be just folks – a distinct departure from the beautiful people who frequented the fru-fru, chi-chi cafes along Venice Beach.

After craning her neck to take in her surroundings, she spun back around on her stool and gazed ahead of her. She simply stared at the stainless-steel wheel suspended from the kitchen window, watching the order slips dangling as the waitress spun the wheel. She was caught up in one of those blank stares that simply burned a hole through one of the dangling order slips until she suddenly noticed a pair of eyes peering out from underneath the wheel. Bessie blinked herself back into reality while she adjusted herself on the counter stool and sighed. Her eyebrows arched in an attempt to rediscover the world she had momentarily blocked out. A deep sigh and drop of her shoulders successfully anchored her back to the moment.

"Order up!"

Bessie shuddered slightly to the sudden bark from the cook on the other side of the tiny serving window. She placed her hand to her chest to calm her startled heart. After another deep breath to gain some composure, she noticed the cook smiling at her. Embarrassed, she dropped her hand to the countertop and offered a meek smile. He winked at her. He had seen her come in before – always alone, always sitting at the same spot, and always ordering the same meal.

Denise raced to the serving window and expertly balanced four plates across her arm before turning to serve a table near the entrance. She was the only waitress working. This offered a potential explanation for Denise's manic behavior. Having been a waitress herself, Bessie knew how demanding hauling plates of food on two tired feet could be.

"Order up!" the cook barked again.

"Yeah, yeah!" The frantic waitress shouted as she clomped back behind the counter to the tiny serving window. She glanced at the ticket next to the plate under the hot lamp before performing a near perfect pirouette, deftly placing it on the counter in front of Bessie and asked, "Anything else?"

"No, I'm good. Thanks."

"Enjoy," Denise offered with a flat unconvincing invitation.

Bessie watched the waitress strut over to the archway leading into the kitchen where she tapped on and peeked into a half-open door just off to the side.

"Ruthie? Remember to order some ketchup – we're just about out."

Bessie heard a strong voice respond, "Got cha. Thanks."

Denise continued her ballet with an arabesque by standing on one foot with her other leg stretched out behind her as she peered into what must of have been a tiny office. "You look cute today. Who did your hair?"

"Oh, some new gal over in Clinton. I'd never tried her before. Does it look OK?" the disembodied voice from behind the door asked.

A fork full of gooey omelet dripped from Bessie's smile as she was eavesdropping on the conversation that could be heard over the clatter of dishes and silverware throughout the diner. She reveled in the shorthand conversation of two co-workers – more like friends – that develops over time. It wasn't small talk in her way of thinking. Bessie thought it was more than chitchat.

It was two souls touching base – connecting – even in the mundane way that made it special. The friendly banter was suddenly interrupted when the diner door behind Bessie opened and slammed shut.

"Denise! Where the hell are you?"

Bessie and the remaining customers turned to see a tall man standing at the doorway with his legs spread and arms splayed along his long legs as if readied for a shoot out in a western. A few days of beard splotched his face and his greasy hair was slicked back. His dull eyes scanned the room.

The waitress turned around. "Darrell! What the hell do you want?"

"What do you think I want?" He relaxed his hands and placed them in the front pockets of his dirty Levis.

Denise defiantly placed her hands on her hips. "I told you last night I wasn't coming back. We're done! It's over!"

The patrons were frozen, looking at the drama as if it was a side order of fries they hadn't ordered.

Denise walked out to the end of the counter and leaned against it with one hand merely inches away from where Bessie sat. Denise and Darrell burned holes into each other with their fiery glares. The cook peeked out from underneath the order wheel. But before their standoff could go any further, the office door from the back slammed against the wall. Denise actually flinched as the disembodied voice from behind the closed door emerged with a shotgun. A middle-aged woman with grey hair stepped up beside Denise and pointed the gun at the ceiling to gasps in the room as patrons scurried to take cover.

"Darrell – you son-of-a-bitch! I thought I told you not to ever step foot in here again!"

Clearly taken aback, Darrell shuffled his feet and ran his hand across his stubbled chin. He nervously cleared his throat, "This here is between Denise and me – you stay out of this, Ruthie!"

The woman pumped the shotgun with it still pointed toward the ceiling. "I'm telling you for the last time to leave this poor girl alone. You get your sorry junkie ass out of here before I fill you with buckshot. You hear me?"

Darrell and everyone in the diner stared with bewilderment at the woman with the shotgun. He surveyed the room and pursed his lips in thought before outstretching his arm and pointing at Denise.

"Alright. You win. That's why I'm here…to say I'm out of here. I'm gone. For good! And I mean it. You can just go fuck yourself." He paused, glancing around the room before continuing. "You too, Ruthie – you can go fuck yourself, too!" Bessie looked over her shoulder to see the cook on the phone. Darrell evidently noticed this as well, assuming the Sheriff was now on his way. He dropped his arm, spun around on his boot heel and walked out the door, slamming it behind him. Almost immediately, from the parking lot came squealing tires and spewing gravel as a beat up Chevy pickup truck roared off into the distance.

There was a collective sigh of relief in the diner. Denise dropped to her knees and began sobbing. Ruthie carefully laid the shotgun down on top of the counter in front of Bessie who gingerly nudged it away from her. The woman kneeled down next to the sobbing waitress and put her arm around her.

"It's OK, honey. He's gone. You're gonna be alright."

By this time, the cook came out from the kitchen and carefully stepped by the two women on the floor in front of him. No one in the diner had moved. They were emotionally trapped in their seats.

"Is everybody alright?" The cook raised both arms in front of him, gently patting the air in an attempt to comfort his regulars. Then he ran his hands down his apron and sighed heavily. "Jesus, folks – I'm sorry about this."

"Hell's bells, Doc – it ain't your fault," offered a man wearing a dirty sweatshirt, jeans, and Wellies on his feet.

"Is she OK?" asked a middle-aged woman sitting in the only occupied booth with three other men.

Doc turned to look behind him. Ruthie looked up and gave him a nod.

"Looks like it. Well – the sheriff's on his way. I'm betting they're going to want to ask you some questions so can you folks just sit tight? Everything's on the house today. Here…let me get everybody some fresh coffee." Doc turned toward the coffee station behind the counter but was blocked by the two women still kneeling on the floor.

"Here – let me," Bessie called out from her stool. She was as dumbfounded to hear those words come out of her mouth, as was everyone else in the diner. Bessie got up and went around the other side of the counter to retrieve the coffee pot from the burner. By this time, Denise and Ruthie were up off the floor and shuffling into one of the empty booths. Bessie began floating about the room filling coffee cups.

The cook shook his head in amazement and stammered, "Uh…thanks."

The man wearing the Wellies cleared his throat. "Uh, Doc? Do you think you might want to clean up the counter a bit…you know…before the Sheriff gets here?"

Doc walked over and deftly retrieved the shotgun. "Good idea, Carl. Thanks." The cook began walking toward the back room with the weapon. He stopped and turned back toward the handful of diners, holding up the shotgun. "Uh, I don't suppose any of you saw this now…did you?"

A spontaneous but unconvincingly naïve unison response of "Saw what?" came from the motley crew of regulars.

"I didn't think so. Thanks," Doc said as he left the room with the evidence.

After Bessie had completed her rounds of coffee refills to the shocked customers, she returned to her solitary stool at the counter and poked at the massive omelet with her fork before finally dropping it on the plate. She was drained, now that her adrenalin had stopped flowing.

The cook returned to the counter in front of Bessie with an outstretched hand.

"Doc."

"Bessie," she replied just as nonchalantly grasping his hand.

"Thanks for your help."

"Hey, I used to be a waitress – guess it's in my DNA."

Doc shook his head and smiled just as everyone in the diner could hear a siren approaching. "I'm wondering if you can stick around…after all this is over."

Bessie rocked her head back and forth in thought. "Sure…I guess."

"Good. I want to introduce you to Ruthie."

"OK."

Chapter 39

The sheriff deputy came and went after gathering statements from the witnesses – all of whom reported that Ruthie had merely chased the intruder away with her verbal threats to call the authorities. Denise tagged along with the sheriff deputy to file a complaint against her ex. The patrons filed out, shaking Doc's hand and hugging Ruthie. Doc locked the door and put up the closed sign. He turned to Bessie who remained perched on the stool.

"Come on. Follow me." Doc motioned with his hand and began walking back through the kitchen as he shed his dirty apron. Ruthie walked up to Bessie and extended her hand.

"I'm Ruthie. I don't believe we've met."

A grin exploded from Bessie's face as she took Ruthie's hand into hers. "No, I don't believe we have. I'm Bessie." They both stood there grinning at each other until Ruthie chuckled and locked her arm through Bessie's and escorted her through the kitchen and out the back door.

Behind the diner was a lovely covered patio protected by a hedge of native plants and trees. Doc flopped down into one of four Adirondack chairs and motioned to an empty one next to him. "Come. Sit. Join us."

Bessie sat down on his right and Ruthie sat down on his left. A collective, audible sigh escaped from the trio. Doc looked at Ruthie. She reached over and took his hand before turning to Bessie.

"It wasn't loaded." Ruthie could see the confusion on Bessie's face. "The gun..." she paused and then continued, "...it wasn't loaded."

"Oh, right. Well...OK." Bessie's nervous laugh was an attempt to accept Ruthie's statement as a simple explanation of a seemingly common, everyday occurrence. It was almost as if this minor detail somehow negated the fact this woman had threatened someone with a firearm – in front of witnesses. She presumed there was a law against that kind of behavior, no matter how seemingly justified to this Mama Bear of a woman.

Doc could hear the uncertainty in Bessie's response. "Ruthie isn't really dangerous. A little crazy and over the top, perhaps...but not dangerous," he calmly offered his perspective to ease Bessie's uncertainty.

"Well...good to know," Bessie meekly responded.

"Now tell us...where are you from? How long have you been here on the island?" Ruthie's interrogation was calm and as natural as it could be, despite the fact she had threatened a clearly distraught man with a shotgun as if it was no big deal and water under the bridge.

"Uh well...I've been here about two weeks now."

"That sounds about right...I've seen you in here about that long," Doc added.

"And where are you staying?" Ruthie asked.

"At the Country Road Cottage."

Ruthie chirped, "Oh, that's such a lovely little inn. Dottie's done such a nice job making that place so cozy. So, where did you say you're from?"

Bessie was attempting to climb out of her disbelief at how casual the afternoon had become. Doc was simply sitting there, quietly listening to Ruthie as she chattered away. Meanwhile, Bessie's hands had only now stopped trembling. She readjusted herself in the comfortable chair.

"L.A."

"Well now…how about that? And what did you do there?"

Ruthie's question caught Bessie flat-footed. She didn't want to reveal too much, too soon. She had to quickly manufacture a story.

"Waitressing. Thought I wanted to be a star…you know…the whole thing of going off to Hollywood to become rich and famous. But, it seems a lot of other people have the same dream. It got old after a while. I decided I need a change so I headed up here."

Doc finally piped up. "Ah ha. That explains it. It sure looked like you knew your way around the diner."

"Yeah, I suppose so. I don't know what came over me," Bessie confessed.

"Well, whatever it was, we sure do appreciate you jumping in like that. Sharing a cup of coffee is what brings people together. You really defused the situation…calmed things down," Ruthie said as she inspected a broken nail on her left hand.

"Well I'm not sure I did all that much – Ruthie, here, seems to be the hero…or should I say 'she-ro' of the day," embarrassed, Bessie redirected Doc's compliment to acknowledge the heroics of the small-framed lady sitting next to her, as well as deflect any further curiosity into her own past.

"Goodness sakes – everybody around here knows me. They know I wouldn't actually shoot anyone. It was all show. Besides, that Darrell is so jittery. He's tangled with me before and knows better than to mess with me." Ruthie reached over and opened a small wooden box sitting on the tiny table to her side. She retrieved two cigars. Ruthie then removed a small tool from the box and punched a hole in the end of each cigar before handing one to Doc. He held the cigar to his nose and deeply inhaled its earthy aroma. Ruthie pulled a lighter from the front pocket of her jeans and began to torch the end of her cigar before suddenly stopping.

"Oh how rude of me…would you like one?" she asked as offered her smoldering cigar to Bessie.

"No…no thank you."

Ruthie offered an apologetic explanation. "I'm afraid this is a bit of a daily ritual for us and I was simply operating on automatic pilot. I didn't even think to offer you one."

Doc reached over to grab the lighter from Ruthie's hand and began to slowly twirl the cigar over the blue flame coming from the lighter. "Ever indulged?"

"I don't smoke."

"Ah well, that's the thing. It's not about smoking. It's about indulging…indulging the senses. It's about partaking in a good hour-long conversation with a good companion," Doc explained.

"And you can't rush a cigar," Ruthie interjected.

Bessie blinked her confusion – not merely at the track of the conversation and turn of events – but confusion over the fact the three of them had just emerged from what seemed to be a somewhat traumatic event while the two of them were casually smoking a cigar as if nothing had happened – just another day on the island.

Doc sat back and held his cigar in the air as he admired it. "It's very Zen."

"Zen?" Bessie repeated seeking clarification as well as to confirm she had correctly heard Doc. She had always imagined tea as akin to Zen – not *cigars*.

Doc took a puff and exhaled a blue cloud of bliss. "Indeed. I can taste the soil, water, and sun within this little bundle of leaves that were hand-picked and hand-rolled." He paused long enough to admire the stick in his hand before continuing. "It's a lot like wine in a way. The elements all influence the taste, the body, and aroma – be it grapes or leaves. " Doc gestured with his cigar toward his companion. "And, like Ruthie says, you can't rush a cigar. It's the perfect excuse to indulge in conversation. It's an investment of time…a commitment to listen and be heard. Ain't a whole lot of that going on much these days."

"I never thought about it that way," Bessie confessed.

"Most people don't," Ruthie added.

Bessie looked at both of them, trying to make sense of the duo. "So, are you two married?"

Ruthie scoffed with a wave of her hand, "Goodness, no."

"But we do live together," Doc clarified. "Going on, what…ten years now?"

His partner nodded as she let some smoke drift from her O-shaped mouth.

"Where and how did you meet?" Bessie could feel her body easing back into the comfort of the wooden chair, relieved that she was finally able to relax.

Ruthie tilted her head back, took a puff and exhaled, "At the bocce club."

"The what?"

"Bocce – you know – sort of like lawn bowling," Doc clarified.

Bessie nodded. "Oh yeah, right. I know what you're talking about."

"Yup, very relaxing entertainment with a smidge of competition thrown in. But it's really more of an excuse to gather with some kindred spirits and drink wine together."

Bessie quickly scanned the backside of the building. "How long have you had this place?"

"About as long. We went in together. Decided from the get-go to just run breakfast and lunch. That gives us the afternoon and evening to do our thing – closed on Mondays."

Bessie settled in for the story by crossing her leg. "So what were you doing before running a diner?"

Doc chuckled, "Well, I used to get into people's heads."

Bessie blinked. "I'm afraid I don't understand."

Ruthie waved off a cloud of smoke and came to Bessie's rescue. "Oh, come on, Doc. Don't be so oblique and tell the girl."

He leaned both elbows on his knees as he ashed his cigar into the ashtray sitting on the table. "I was a neurolinguist. Ever hear of one those?"

Bessie shook her head.

"Yup, I didn't think so. I used to glue electrodes to folks' skulls and measure their brainwave activity."

Bessie pulled her chin to her chest in an attempt to grasp what he was describing and asked, "What were you looking for?"

Doc took a long, leisurely puff from his cigar, "Average evoked potential in phoneme acquisition and discrimination."

"In English, please," Ruthie chided him.

Doc rolled his eyes. "Sorry. Well, I assume you know about brainwaves, right?"

Bessie nodded.

Doc then used his index finger to draw a brain wave in the air. "Every wave has a peak…and a valley…just like the waves on the ocean," as his finger bounced in mid air and he continued his explanation. "Well now, there's a distance between that peak and valley...albeit just a nanosecond...in which the brain is processing the stimulus it just received. I was looking at the tiny space of processing time in between the waves to see how efficiently the brain 'learns' sounds that lead to language acquisition."

"Wow. That's incredible!" Bessie exuded.

Doc looked at her flatly. "No. It's boring. Well...that's not entirely true. What *did* fascinate me was what was happening in that space...that tiny little space. You might say it was sort of my own little version of space exploration in some respects. Anyway, I was well on my way to tenure, doing all the right things...getting publications and making conference presentations about something that was so...so modestly significant – statistically speaking – until one day, I just sort of stopped."

"You stopped?" Doc could hear the incredulity in Bessie's voice.

"Yup. Walked away from academia."

"To run a diner?"

Doc set his cigar down in the ashtray to let it rest and put both hands behind his head as he explained. "Well, there was some down time...time for some soul searching. I was sitting along the water not to far from here – watching the waves. I started thinking back to when I was happy...*really* happy. I tried to remember what I really enjoyed doing...and it had to be fulfilling for me as well as provide some kind of sustenance to others. All the sudden, I found myself back in college…my senior year."

Doc raised his eyes to see back into the past. He leaned down to retrieve his cigar and took another puff, letting it rest in his hand.

"I lived in an old house just off campus with two other guys. We all had girlfriends. We had this weekly thing we called the 'Friday Morning Breakfast Club' where we invited friends over for breakfast. The whole idea was to greet the weekend. The extra feature was champagne. We made amazing omelets, waffles, and crepes…whatever struck our fancy while we played music and talked. Of course, the champagne gradually kicked in as our first morning class loomed large and we'd merely raise our glass and toast, 'Better never than late!' and proceed with the festivities. We even invited a couple of professors we liked to join us." Doc stared off.

Ruthie reached over and gently patted his hand bringing him back to the moment.

"So, as crazy as it sounds, I realized *that* was what I wanted…*that* was what I needed to do. Not so much the cooking, although that was part of it. It was the whole idea of creating space where friends could come together and break bread, so-to-speak. It was a moment…a pause in between the peaks and valleys where we could ride out the waves of life. That's where the diner comes in. Make sense?" Doc paused to puff his cigar and waved off the smoke as he continued. "And…like the Zen of cigars…I discovered the Zen of cooking.

When I'm in the kitchen, I'm focused on the here and now of combining these elements that will literally sustain someone else. That's all there is in that moment. I don't fret about the chaos and the noise out there," he nodded toward the world behind him.

Bessie was mesmerized by Doc's heartfelt journey. More than that, it resonated with her and ignited a dying ember within her. She wasn't sure what that flicker was at that moment. Never the less, she knew Doc had touched something within her. She turned to Ruthie, "And what about you?"

"Doc and I are like salt and pepper. We go together and compliment each other but we're really quite different. Opposites attract – as the saying goes. So, that being the case, my story isn't nearly as dramatic and engaging as Doc's."

"And so?" Bessie encouraged Ruthie.

Ruthie waved Bessie's curiosity off. "Oh my dear, I was a book keeper. It was the proverbial daily grind with the commute and the whole thing. I worked 9 to 5 at a book publisher that specialized in erotica, if you can believe that. I'm still a bookkeeper for that matter. I sit in our office and run the numbers, order the supplies, take care of running the place. I have an eye for details. Doc is so much more, esoteric. I'm mundane. But we make it work…don't we sweetie?" She squeezed his hand.

"So…what about the shot gun?" Bessie asked tentatively.

"Oh that? I like to go skeet shooting." She chuckled and continued. "I know…that sounds crazy. I don't actually go hunting to shoot any birds. No, I couldn't ever bring myself to do that. I do, however, like the challenge of shooting those darn ol' clay pigeons out of the sky. Therapeutic, too. Don't know why. Just do. I went down to the skeet club one day and tried it. Been hooked ever since. My shotgun just happened to be back in the office."

Skeet shooting. Bocce. Cigars. Brain waves. Erotica. It had been an interesting conversation, not to mention an interesting afternoon. A sweet silence cradled the patio. The cigars were nearly spent. Bessie *certainly* was spent emotionally. It had been a roller coaster of an afternoon. Bessie knew she'd be back for another ride.

Chapter 40

The very next afternoon Bessie carefully calculated her arrival at Doc's Diner to coincide with them beginning to shut down for the afternoon in the hope she would once again be invited to join the quirky crew behind the diner. She took her usual stool at the counter around 2:45 leaving fifteen minutes to order and be served. Bessie was somewhat surprised to see how quickly Denise had rebounded from yesterday's drama as she swept by Bessie at the counter with order pad in hand.

"The usual?"

Bessie nodded.

Denise put her hand down on the counter to lean in long enough to whisper, "Hey – thanks for…you know…the backup yesterday," and spun off to place Bessie's order on the wheel. Bessie leaned her head down slightly to peer through the order window, catching Doc's eye as he spun the wheel to take a peek at the order Denise had just put up. He winked at her. She returned a meek little wave. Bessie twirled around on her stool noticing the same old regulars who were slowly finishing up their cups of coffee and heading out the door. Bessie marveled at the little community of regulars who frequented the diner.

DING! "Order up!" Doc shouted as he slapped the tiny silver desk bell. Denise flew by and delivered Bessie's omelet in one fell swoop. "Hey…"

Bessie looked up from the task of unwrapping the paper napkin around her silverware with raised eyebrows. "Yeah?"

Denise stood there with both hands on her hips. "I've seen you come in and out of here the past few weeks but I've never properly introduced myself." She offered her hand and her name, "Denise."

Bessie smiled and shook Denise's outstretched hand, "I know. I'm Bessie."

"Like I said, I appreciate you helping out yesterday."

Bessie took a bite of her omelet and waved off the waitress' gratitude as she swallowed. "I didn't do anything…really."

"Well, that's not how I remember it. Anyway…I just wanted to introduce myself and invite you to join us for our afternoon stick."

Bessie furrowed her brow. "Afternoon what?"

"Stick…you know…cigar. Doc and Ruthie told me you joined them yesterday after all the drama." Denise shifted her weight on to one leg. "Didn't they explain the three of us smoke a cigar together everyday right after closing?"

"I guess I didn't realize it was a daily ritual."

"Yup…you bet your ass it is. That hour lets us decompress and then we finish closing up shop. Anyway…I just thought I'd invite you…as my guest."

Bessie nodded and smiled, "Sure, that'd be nice."

Denise patted the countertop with her hand. "Cool. Just sit tight as we toss the stragglers out of here," and off she went.

Bessie once again savored her omelet as well as the new invitation while Denise locked the door behind the last customers and switched off the 'Open' neon light in the window. On cue, Ruthie came out to close up the cash register. Noticing Bessie at the counter, Ruthie folded her arms across her waist in mock inspection. "Well, look who's here."

Bessie scrunched up her shoulders and smiled with innocent glee as she chewed the last of her sourdough toast. Ruthie called out to Denise, "Hey you'd better watch out for this one, Denise...she seems to know her way around a diner. She might be out for your job." Ruthie shook her head and smiled before pulling the cash drawer out of the register.

"I know...that's why I invited her to join us," Denise explained as she whizzed by with a bussing tote full of dirty dishes.

"Well that's just fine with me," Ruthie replied. She turned and looked over her shoulder as she shouted into the kitchen, "Hey Doc...gotta a guest joining us today!"

Doc sauntered from the kitchen pulling his apron over his head with a big grin. "You again?" Bessie nodded with a smile, acknowledging his friendly ribbing. "Geez, we may have to put you to work around here," he added sarcastically as he turned to go back through the same door passing Denise in the process.

"I know," quipped Ruthie, "that's what I was just telling Denise."

Denise squeezed by Doc and locked her arm through Bessie's. "Come on," and tugged her off the stool and towed her through the kitchen to the patio. Each of them settled comfortably into the four Adirondack chairs and let out a collective sigh. Bessie leaned back and closed her eyes, soaking in the serenity of the moment. Doc got up and went back inside, leaving the three women alone.

Bessie turned to Denise, offering a cautious, "So…everything alright?"

"Me?" Denise asked with surprise as she put a hand to her chest as if to calm a palpitating heart and then waved Bessie's inquiry off, "Hell yeah. He took off…again. He does that."

"I hope to God he's gone for good this time," Ruthie snarled.

"Well…I wouldn't doubt it, seeing how you threatened to shoot him," Denise said, unpinning her hair that had piled up for work.

Ruthie rendered a scoff, "I did no such thing."

"Jesus, Ruthie, you came out and pointed a gun at him, for Christ's sake. You scared the shit out of him…and everybody else for that matter," Denise exclaimed, sitting up in her chair with indignation.

"I did not point that gun at him. I just happened to have it in my hands at the time and it was pointed at the ceiling. You can ask anybody who was there…isn't that right, Bessie?" Ruthie turned to Bessie for support.

"Uh, yeah…that's true," Bessie shyly confirmed.

Denise closed her eyes in disgust and disbelief as she waved both of them off. "You're crazy, Ruthie…that's what you are," in an attempt to close the subject Bessie now regretted bringing up.

"Well…" Ruthie stretched in her chair, "there's a lot of that going around these days," and turned to wink at Bessie just as Doc returned with the small wooden box in his hand. He set it down on the wobbly table in front of the foursome and opened up the cigar humidor. The rich aroma of the cigars immediately wafted up from the cedar-lined box. Doc reached in, retrieved one and offered it to Bessie.

She stared at it. "Uh, I don't know how to smoke a cigar," Bessie explained.

"Wanna learn?" Doc smiled.

Bessie turned to watch Ruthie and Denise roll their cigars under their nose, inhaling deeply to savor the earthy scent.

"Won't it make me sick?" Bessie wondered.

"Not if you smoke it right," Doc assured her.

The sight…no…the feeling that Bessie suddenly felt suggested there was something more to this experience. She was getting a sense of what Denise meant when she suggested this was a daily ritual. Bessie nodded shyly.

"OK, then," Doc replied as he handed her the cigar. "This is a nice, mild cigar for beginners – a Romeo Y Julietta Corona from the Dominican Republic." She took it and examined it before holding it under her nose.

"Smells good," Bessie confessed her surprise.

Doc nodded and proceeded with his tutelage as Ruthie and Denise cut and lit their own. "Now…you cut the end off…this is called the cap…." he explained as he snipped the cap off his own cigar before passing the cutting tool over to Bessie to successfully mimic his action. "Good. Now to light it...you hold it in one hand and then essentially torch it with this lighter..." he clicked a small butane lighter that gave off a faint hiss of blue flame..."and hold it just below...not *on* the end and twirl the cigar like this...." he demonstrated. Then he clicked the lighter off and examined the even red glow on the end of his cigar before passing the lighter to Bessie who effectively replicated the process.

"Good job. Now...just lightly pull the smoke into your mouth...don't inhale...you're not sucking air in or toking on a joint. Just let the smoke more or less enter your mouth and rest there before blowing it out...like this..." Doc took a puff and leaned his head back, letting a cloud of blue smoke drift out of his slightly opened lips. "There...now you try it."

Bessie aptly repeated what Doc had demonstrated and what the other two women were already doing after lighting their own sticks with another lighter. She let the smoke drift out of her mouth and turned to scan their faces for an assessment of her performance.

All three smiled. "So...what do you think?" Ruthie asked as she took another puff from her own cigar.

Bessie nodded. "I think I kind of like it."

Denise chimed in. "It grows on you. It's really not about smoking...not like you would a cigarette. It's all about this...sharing the moment and space."

"It's like I always say...a cigar is an opportunity for a good hour of conversation with good friends. That's what this…" Doc gestured to the three of them with his cigar in hand, "is all about."

Bessie sat back, relaxed, and enjoyed the company and conversation that ensued – mostly chitchat about the day and gossip about neighbors and long-time customers. At one point, during a slight lull in the conversation, Ruthie turned to Bessie who now looked like an experienced cigar aficionado.

"So…how long do you plan on staying here on the island?"

Bessie was slightly taken aback by the question. She looked at each of them as she considered her response. "I'm not sure." Her pensive gaze to the outdoor deck prompted Ruthie to flash raised eyebrows at Doc sitting across from her. The three of them sat there, holding the silence, as well as her deliberation. "I'm not sure of anything right now, to be honest," Bessie finally confessed. Her confession surprised herself – not just by the revelation itself, but also by the fact that she had verbalized it aloud to three people who were essentially strangers.

"Are you looking for a job?" Doc inquired.

"No. I'm doing OK financially."

Ruthie gently rolled an ash off her cigar into the ashtray on the table in front of them. "Are you one of those trust fund babies?"

Bessie smiled and chuckled. "No. But I have had a sudden windfall and I've been careful with it…considering what to do with it."

Denise took a puff from her cigar and let the smoke spiral from her mouth. "Planning on sticking around?"

It has been nearly two weeks since Bessie had arrived to Whidbey Island. She found it to be comfortable. It was a world away from L.A. and the industry Bessie had left behind. After a few moments, Bessie slowly began nodding her head – almost as if to give her entire body a chance to rev up to the response she was about to make.

"Yeah. I think I might just do that."

Ruthie gave a knowing smile to Doc. "We sort of thought so. Go on…tell her about the house, Doc."

Bessie raised an eyebrow and turned to hear what Doc had to share.

"Well…I don't know what you're interested in. But we thought we might mention there's a nice old craftsman style house going on the market some time soon."

Ruthie chimed in. "It's absolutely adorable. And it's so you!"

"So me? You hardly know me. Why would you think that?" Bessie scoffed.

"Oh, I think I know you better than you think. In fact, I might even know you better than yourself," Ruthie smiled coyly.

Bessie sat there and smiled at Ruthie's bold statement with amusement and a degree of suspicion mixed in with some skepticism. Then, within a few moments, her smile began to fade. She placed her cigar on the lip of the ashtray. Her eyes began to fill with tears and her lips began to tremble just as Bessie buried her face in her hands.

Both Ruthie and Denise reached over to pat and comfort Bessie. The brusque bookkeeper offered a motherly coddle, "It's OK, sweetie…it's OK." Bessie sobbed as the three of them looked at each other and waited for their new companion to compose herself.

Bessie finally came up for air and gasped, "Oh, I don't know…I don't know anything anymore." She sniffed and wiped her nose. "I don't know what to do," and she fell back limp into the Adirondack chair.

Doc set his cigar down in the ashtray and cleared his throat. "Look, we don't want to pry. It's none of our business and we don't need to know what you've been…shall we say…dealing with." He stopped and looked up to receive a supportive nod from Ruthie to proceed. "I guess…" he stammered, "I guess all I can do is offer you this little suggestion…something I had to do a long time ago." He paused.

Bessie sniffed again and wiped her eyes. "Yeah? What was that?"

"I…we…can't solve your problems for you. We don't even know what they are…we don't want or need to know. So, here's the thing…I invite you to stop…" Doc somewhat dramatically paused creating an almost uncomfortable silence before continuing. "Now…" another pause. "Back up. Back up and recall a time…a place…a moment…a thing that brought you deep satisfaction. Can you do that?"

Bessie nodded and took a deep breath. He watched her as she closed her eyes and searched inwardly for that moment Doc intoned. "OK. Are you there?" the old man asked,

Bessie kept her eyes closed and nodded.

"Now…let me ask you…what feeds your soul? What makes you feel…warm and complete?"

A smile slowly came across Bessie's face. She kept her eyes closed as Doc continued.

"Now don't think about this or analyze this too much. Just let the image sit there for a moment. Trust me…the image will lead you to something…somewhere…if you let it. It's down there…it's deep…you just have to let it bubble up. It will hint at the direction you need to go…then you can recalibrate."

Bessie opened her eyes and turned to Doc.

"Cookies."

Doc smiled and tilted his head, "What?"

"Cookies…warm cookies coming out of the oven," she elaborated.

The trio of new friends exchanged glances. Ruthie reached over and touched Bessie's hand. "What do you mean? Eating them or baking them?"

"I'm not really sure. Both maybe. All I know is that's where I landed." Bessie admitted as she wiped a tear from her cheek.

Doc looked at Ruthie. "Well, that's a start anyway."

Ruthie gave Doc another knowing look before continuing. "Tell you what…why don't you let me close out the till and the books for the day and then you and I can go in the kitchen and mix up a batch. How does that sound?"

"It sounds...kind of fun, actually," Bessie chuckled. "But won't we be in the way? "

Doc shook his head and picked up his dwindling cigar, "Nah, Bruce is finishing up the dishes right now. By the time Ruthie's finished in the office, he'll almost be clocking out."

"It *does* sound fun. I wish I could stay and join the party but I've gotta run and pick up my daughter, Sheila, from day care," Denise shared as she laid her dying cigar to rest in the ashtray and stood up.

"I don't want to be a bother," Bessie quickly added. "I'll be OK...really. You don't need to..."

Ruthie cut her off, "Nonsense. It's no bother. I can't remember the last time I made a batch of cookies. It'll be good for all of us. I'm sure we can drum up some oatmeal to make some oatmeal cookies."

Doc stood and joined Denise who was headed for the door. "Well, help yourself. Knock yourself out ladies. Just make sure I get one."

Newly recalibrated, Bessie and Ruthie puttered in the kitchen after the financial chores had been completed. They chattered and giggled like mother and daughter. They made up a batch and dolloped the dough onto cookie sheets. Ruthie carefully slid the commercial-sized tray into the massive Hobart oven and peered through the glass door.

Bessie cleared her throat.

"Ruthie?"

"Yes?" she replied still peering into the oven window.

"What did you mean earlier when you said the house for sale was…how did you put it…oh, right…you said it was so me" Bessie tilted her head waiting for clarification.

Ruthie turned and smiled. "It's a cute little bungalow…built back in the 1920s when houses had character. It's so warm and cozy. It even has a lovely patio area, a tiny garden area and – if you can believe it – a shed with a kiln. We knew the lady who used to live there – she was a potter. She died not too long ago and the family wants to put it on the market. I don't know…it just looks like a space you'd thrive in."

Ruthie's chose of words made Bessie jump slightly. "What makes you think that?"

The older woman reached over and took Bessie's hand. "Sweetie…I recognized you the very first time you came into the diner. I can't imagine what would drive a successful singer like you to run off to a place like this. But I've heard you sing. I 've heard your heart tell lovely stories. I just knew those songs were a window into your soul."

Bessie shook her head in disbelief. "Does Doc or Denise know?"

"I don't think so. They haven't said anything and I haven't mentioned it because I wasn't absolutely sure."

Bessie's eyes widened as she looked toward the floor with embarrassment as Ruthie continued. "I don't want to pry, dear.

But clearly something has happened. And I can't tell if you're running away from something or running toward something."

"I think it's a little of both," Bessie muttered.

Both of them leaned against the stainless steel countertop and Ruthie put her arm around Bessie. "Tell me, dear…if you could write the script…here and now…what would it be? What is it you think you want? What do you need?"

With little thought, an image immediately came flowing out of Bessie, surprising her as much as Ruthie. "I guess…I want a space. A comfortable, cozy, warm space that wraps its arms around you." She paused for a moment. "I think I know what the cookies are all about now."

Ruthie tilted her head, waiting and listening.

"Cookies and milk," Bessie calmly stated.

Ruthie smiled. "Cookies and milk?" she repeated.

Bessie nodded and wiped a tear away. "Yeah, you know how good it is to dip a cookie in milk…not just the taste of it…but the way that makes you feel?"

Ruthie nodded. "I *do* know that feeling. It's comfort food."

"Exactly! Comfort food! Well, I don't know…I got to thinking…what if…"

"Yes?" Ruthie nudged.

"What if there was a place where people could go and not just indulge in fresh cookies and warm milk…but experience it? Does that make sense?"

"I suppose it does," Ruthie tried to confirm Bessie's epiphany. In doing so, Bessie continued to describe what she imagined.

"It's sort of like your diner with Doc…a space where people go…not just to eat…but to gather. Know what I mean?"

Ruthie nodded with eyes wide and eyebrows arched. "Uh huh…it's food for the soul…not just the stomach."

"Right! And the conversations! I love how people talk…I mean really talk and listen to each other. Like today…on the patio with the cigars. Nobody does that anymore."

"I'm beginning to see a little cottage for cookies…conversation…a comfort zone, so-to-speak," Ruthie offered coyly.

The image rested comfortably in the momentary silence as Ruthie stood up and opened the oven door. She grabbed a kitchen glove and retrieved a tray full of warm, golden cookies. "Ooooh…" Bessie cooed. Ruthie handed Bessie a spatula, "Here…put two of these on a plate so we can deliver them while they're nice and hot with a cold glass of milk to Doc…he's out back."

Bessie obliged gleefully. Together, they carried the plate of cookies and glass of milk out to Doc, who was sitting and staring off into space. He sat up as he noticed them making their way with their treasure.

"Well…look at this would you?" he happily exclaimed.

Nearly bursting, Bessie sat the plate down on the little table in front of Doc. She turned and smiled at Ruthie who returned her joy with a smile of her own. Bessie folded her hands in front of her and slightly bounced on her toes.

"Doc?"

"Yeah?" he muffled with a mouthful of cookies.

"Do you think you could take me over to look at that house you were talking about?"

Chapter 41

"Good Morning...Galaxy Productions. How may I help you?"

"Hi. Is Ron in?"

"I'm afraid he's not available at the moment. May I ask who's calling?"

"Bessie James."

There was a deafening silence on the other end of the phone.

"I see. Could you hold for just a moment?"

Bessie continued to rehearse what she was going to say listening to MUZAK recordings of Ron's artists while on hold. Just as one of her own songs came on the loop of recordings, there was a click that abruptly shut down Bessie in the opening lines of her song. She swallowed hard, worried that this was some kind of foreboding sign for the ensuing conversation she was about to have.

"Bess! It's so good to hear from you. How are you? *Where* are you?"

"Hi Ron. Thanks. I'm OK. I'm actually relieved you're glad to hear from me."

"Why wouldn't I be?"

"For Christ sake, Ron...I ran out on you. I'm so embarrassed. I'm so..."

"Don't be. I completely understand. I tried to take you someplace you didn't want to go. It's all on me."

"Seriously?"

"Seriously. I'm just glad you're OK. So…can I ask what you've been up to?"

"I had to get away. A change of scenery."

"I hear you."

Ron allowed Bessie to settle into her thoughts. He did not want to rush or crowd her into a corner.

"Ron?"

"Yes, Bessie?"

"I need a break."

"I understand."

"But what about my contract? What about…"

"All I care about right now is you and how you're doing…that you're OK."

"Really?"

"Really. Where are you? Everyone…including Benny…has been worried about you."

"I'm up in the Pacific Northwest right now."

"Doing what?"

"Oh, I don't know…sorting through things…coming up with a backup plan."

"Listen my dear…you're golden. You're evolving and maturing. The next iteration of Bessie James will be the new, improved version of the original everyone knows and loves."

"Do you really mean that, Ron?"

"Listen, Bess. I'm not the heartless machine you and everyone else in this business thinks I am. And you're not just a cog in that machinery. I care about you as a person. And…to be quite honest…when you're happy and healthy as a person…you're a happier and healthier artist. I know that sounds selfish on my part, but my first priority is you…as a person. You'll be back. I know you will. It's in your DNA. I'll be here for you…when it's time…when you're ready."

"I don't know what to say."

"You don't have to say anything. You just take care of yourself. You're still part of the Ron Spielman Galaxy of stars as far as I'm concerned. The dark clouds have just obscured you from view right now."

"Thanks, Ron."

"Promise me you'll take care and keep in touch. Will you?"

"I promise."

"OK, Bess. Take care."

"I will. Thanks. Bye."

Chapter 42

Doc was right. His invitation to simply stop…back up…and recalibrate allowed the alchemy of the cigars, conversation, and cookies to magically conjure a golden new trajectory for Bessie. It was, indeed, an enchanting craftsman style house shaded with trees. It was painted a rusty burgundy color and the trim around the windows and doors stood out in creamy beige. A huge front porch with a picket railing ran along the front of the house on both sides of the steps. The property had withstood the modest spurt of commercial development that grew up around it yet it was also within commercial zoning. Somehow it had maintained its domestic charm. On a whim, she applied for and obtained a business license but had no inkling how it might be used. Behind was a lovely patio area under a canopy of cedar tree branches. There was a small patch of ground in the sun to provide a space for tomatoes but not much else. The kiln was a surprise find. She loved the earthy, organic quality of pottery. Still, Bessie doubted she would take up throwing clay, but the art and potential was intriguing. Her initial thought was to rent out the space and perhaps provide a venue for potters to sell their wares. The cottage was in good shape overall, even the electrical wiring and plumbing, despite being built in the 1920s. The few updates and modifications that had been made did not detract from the style or personality that exuded from it. It was essentially a turnkey find.

Bessie moved in a month after first inspecting the house with Doc. She was able to quickly and easily get a loan to cover the purchase until she could sell off her beach house in California – which she knew would be easy. There would be, no doubt, a bidding war for her prime property so close to the beach. She essentially settled in upstairs of the cottage as she had little in the way of furniture or other items to fill the downstairs. The one thing she did have was a large, well-loved leather chair she had found at an estate sale on the island for $100. The lower floor was mostly a large open parlor space with cute nooks and crannies that made the room interesting and cozy. She placed the leather lounge chair in the corner next to the fireplace where she could settle in and enjoy the ambiance of the room. It became her special spot. The lower parlor had built-in shelves with glass doors. The walls had rich, wooden wainscot paneling that warmed the room as much as the fireplace and a hearth that took up an entire wall. There was a lovely arched window that divided the kitchen space from what served as a dining area off the main parlor. The previous owner had been serious about cooking and baking as evident by the commercial-grade appliances in the kitchen. Meanwhile, Bessie occupied the east-facing bedroom upstairs with dormer windows, leaving the other bedroom to serve as office space. The two rooms were separated by a bathroom fit for a queen, complete with a beautiful claw-foot bathtub.

  The cookie baking moved from Doc's kitchen to hers. Bessie began baking cookies almost as an obsession. She found the process to be therapeutic as well as an outlet for her imagination and creativity. She had never really been "into" baking growing up – there had never really been an opportunity to do so. Growing up, she didn't mind making her own meals, as modest and unimaginative as they were. But cookie baking was a new and entirely different experience for Bessie. She didn't fully understand where this sudden fascination and obsession had came from, other than recalling how Joey had said her voice reminded him of warm, freshly baked cookies. That image resonated with her and she cherished the memory of him leaving a plate of chocolate chip cookies in her dressing room before each gig. This obviously explained their sentimental significance. And while chocolate chips cookies may be considered quite ordinary and common by most, they were special to her, with an almost sacred aura. Thus, they were never on her 'to-do' list, with an unspoken "off limits" status. Meanwhile, her imagination created an array of unique and amusing cookies that almost seemed to take on a life of themselves.

She created a selection of 'kookie' cookies that exuded their own personalities. Her first creation was decorated with a peace sign – not terribly original but it sparked more oddities over time. Soon she decorated one as a beach ball – another as a stop sign that inspired her to create a trio of cookies on a plate called the 'traffic light' special. It consisted of one red gooey cookie made from red velvet cake + a yellow lemon cookie + a green zucchini-based cookie. Tapping into her musical interest and past, she created a cookie that resembled the 45s she used to play on her record player growing up. She cleverly stacked smaller versions of them on a "spindle" and dubbed it "Stack of

45s." As her confidence and imagination grew, she even created mandala-decorated cookies. One day, when she couldn't make up her mind about what kind of cookie to make, she opted to bake several kinds and decorate them as 8-balls for patrons who couldn't decide what kind of cookie to get. They simply pointed at one and received what they got. All in all, Bessie was not only baking cookies, she was also creating baked pieces of art.

 Ruthie and Denise often came over after hours to either watch or help her as she baked. Both of them had the presence of mind to offer selling them at the diner. Due to their artistic quality coupled with their gourmet taste, they were pricing them at a premium that didn't seem to dissuade customers from indulging their sweet tooth as an after-thought when they paid their bill at the cash register. These "Kookie Cookies" had become a hot item and were flying off the display case at Doc's diner each day. What began as a therapeutic exercise literally evolved into a cottage industry.

 Their gatherings also always allowed time for chitchat between the friends. One afternoon, the gaggle of gals had gathered at Bessie's to experiment with some new variations. One was a "twinkie-shaped" cookie and the other was a smaller round cookie – about the size of a Vanilla Wafer. Bessie removed the first beta-batch off the cookie sheet and on to the cooling rack. A row of the longer cookies was lined up next to the smaller round cookies.

 Denise suddenly began howling with laughter, pointing at the cooling rack.

Perplexed, Bessie and Ruthie looked at each other. Denise finally asked with an embarrassed hand covering her guffaws, "Does that remind you of anything?" Denise watched their faces as the two of them inspected the cooling cookies when Ruthie finally broke out in a broad smile.

"Looks like the family jewels if you ask me," Ruthie chuckled.

"God, I must be horny if I'm starting to hallucinate men's genitalia in a batch of cookies!" Denise confessed.

The phallic image gradually took root in Bessie's imagination and she began to laugh.

"Well…I'm betting this could be your best-seller!" Denise speculated.

"We'd have to set them off behind a curtain and check for I.D. before we sold them," Bessie suggested with a giggle.

Ruthie chimed in. "Seriously, you ought to consider adding this to your menagerie of kookies. Hey, I know…you can make some to look like boobies. Call them 'ta-tas'" as the three women bent over in laughter.

Curiously, Bessie did just that. And true to Denise's hunch, her pornographic 'kookies' were her biggest sellers that eventually inspired other knock-offs from other bakeries in the Pacific Northwest in the years to come.

Chapter 43

There was a knock on her front door one afternoon. Bessie came to open the door from the kitchen wearing her apron to find a woman standing there. She was wearing a Washington State Ferry uniform. Bessie thought she recognized her. "Yes? Can I help you?"

The woman was of average height and appeared to be in her late 30s or early 40s. Bessie noticed her wringing her hands and shifting her weight back and forth to each of her feet. "Uh, yeah. Sorry to bother you. Uh, are you Kookie?" she asked.

Bessie was taken aback by the question and initially wondered if this woman was looking for someone else before it dawned on her that the lady from the ferry was referring to her. The revelation and apt moniker brought a smile to her face. It didn't however bring a coherent response to mind so she chose to deflect it.

"Is there something I can help you with?"

The woman inhaled deeply as if an invisible set of bellows were filling her with courage. "Well, yeah…maybe. I just stopped at Doc's as they were closing up. Anyway, I was hoping to get a cookie but they told me they were out. They said you lived just up the road. So…anyway, I was wondering if…if it wasn't too much trouble…to see if you happened to have any cookies I could buy."

Bessie blinked and rubbed her hands down her apron. "Well yes, I was just pulling a batch out of the oven." She opened the door wider. "Would you like to come in…sit and wait while I get some for you?'

"That'd be nice. I hope I'm not bothering you," she said as she wiped her feet and stepped over the doorway threshold. She surveyed the room, not merely to find a place to sit, but to soak up it's cozy warmth. Bessie noticed and offered the woman her special leather chair that was large enough to swallow her. This was more than a gesture. It was gift to share her beloved chair. "Have a seat…it'll just be a minute."

"Thanks," she said as she eased into the comfortable chair.

Bessie walked toward the kitchen and called back over her shoulder, "So, you work on the ferry?"

The woman nodded.

Bessie continued, "What's your name?"

"Charon.…spelled with a 'Ch'."

That was that. She offered no further information and so Bessie left it at that, turning her attention to sliding the cookies off the cookie sheet and on to the cooling rack.

"I'm afraid I only have snicker doodles right now…is that OK? How many?"

"That's fine. They're my favorite anyway. Can I get a dozen?"

"Sure. Can I get you anything else? How about a nice glass of milk…cookies always taste better when you can dip them in warm milk."

"That sounds lovely," Charon responded and as she did, Bessie detected a slight quiver in the woman's voice.

Bessie returned with a sack of ten cookies and two on a plate with a large cup of milk. She placed them down on the side table next to the leather lounge chair and sat down on the sofa sitting in tandem with a chirpy announcement, "There you go." Bessie placed both of her hands in her lap, anticipating at least a thank you. Instead, the woman stared blankly at the floor. Bessie tilted her head, attempting to catch the woman's eyes. The woman suddenly noticed Bessie's concerned gaze and slightly flinched back into the moment, sitting upright. Bessie continued to wait for some kind of verbal acknowledgement of her delivery or even an inquiry on how much she owed for the cookies. But nothing came except for a single tear, slowly running down Charon's cheek.

Bessie reached over and gently put her hand on the woman's knee. "Are you alright?"

The woman sniffed and inhaled deeply, nodding her head without saying a word. Then, she turned to the plate of cookies and milk. She slowly lifted a cookie to her mouth and took what seemed like a cautious bite before chewing with equal caution. After a deep sigh, she reached over to pick up and cradle the mug of warm milk in her hands without bringing it to her lips. Instead, she turned her gaze to her host.

"Thanks. This is exactly what I needed right now," and then slowly sipped at the milk in her mug. After a swallow, Charon ventured further explanation. "I just needed some of this, you know what I mean? I needed those cookies to make me feel better." She dabbed her nose with the paper napkin that accompanied the cookies. "I know that must sound crazy."

Bessie gently patted the woman's knee and said nothing. She merely accompanied her in that moment with a calming smile. After another sip, the woman set the mug on the side table. She placed both of her hands in her lap as she deeply inhaled, raising her shoulders up to her ears before letting them fall down. Then, she once again scanned the room with great seriousness for what seemed like a minute or more, making Bessie slightly uncomfortable before speaking.

"You know…" Charon paused as she clearly struggled to formulate what she wanted to say, "you ought to consider how to offer this…" she gestured to the room with both hands, "along with the cookies."

Bessie removed her hand from the woman's knee and placed them in her lap. "I'm afraid I don't understand."

"This…this space," Charon offered as she took another survey of the comfortable room. "You're not just peddling Kookie Cookies…you've got something else going on here, you know?" The woman could tell by the look on Bessie's face that she didn't know, so she continued. "Right here and now…you let me into a…I don't how to put it…a comfort zone. After the day I've had…that's exactly what I needed." She paused and pondered for a moment. "I think there's a lot of people who need this. It's…" again the woman struggled to articulate what she was experiencing. "It's almost like a sanctuary…sacred space."

She stopped and then dropped her chin to her chest with an embarrassed chuckle. "God, listen to me. You really must think I'm nuts."

"No, no I don't. I'm sorry something happened to you today. But I'm glad you found your way here. I'm glad my cookies made you feel better," Bessie offered.

The woman chuckled again. "Well, I gotta tell you…it's not just the cookies, although that's what I came looking for…comfort food…know what I mean? But sitting here…just now…I found…oh, I don't know. Whatever it was…it wasn't what I was expecting. This space itself is as healing and as comforting as your wonderful quirky cookies." She paused and raised an eyebrow as she looked at Bessie out of the corner of her eye. "You're definitely on to something here, Kookie."

Charon's words launched a series of changes into motion, including the acceptance of her new nickname and the identity that came with it. Over the next few weeks, she watched the house begin to transform into a – well she wasn't quite clear what it exactly evolved into -- there didn't seem to be a name that adequately captured the essence and purpose of the shop. Eventually, she invited Charon to help decorate and arrange the space. It was, after all, her inspiration to create a comfort zone. For the first few weeks, her new friend came on her days off to putter in the house. She would often arrive with an armful of knick-knacks she had stumbled on at estate sales and always found the perfect place and way to display them throughout the house.

There was no grand opening. There wasn't even a sign out front to announce the existence of her quirky little space. That really didn't matter at the time, as she had yet to come up with a name for this place. She was confident it would present itself. For now, she simply placed a hand-painted sign that read, "Come on in!" on the front porch. People trickled in. The unique space and kookie cookies accompanied by the mugs of milk were gaining an almost cult-like reputation, purely by word-of-mouth. This budding entrepreneur was violating every textbook tenet of basic marketing and it didn't seem to matter. Patrons – guests as she referred to call them – were coming in droves. And as they did, they quizzically scanned the cozy cottage to assure themselves that they were, in fact, at the right place. The shy visitors who would invariably either ask, "Is this the Kookie Cookie place?" or "Are you Kookie?" As she expected, the name of her cottage enterprise – literally – became known as Kookie's. It also confirmed this would also become her new moniker, allowing her to take on a new identity, giving her permission to leave Bessie behind as she moved forward into her new life.

Over time, the personality of the space emerged much like a figure emerging from the sculptor's slab of marble. Kookie would back up, consider what she saw and then allowed it – whatever 'it' was – to happen. She rarely intentionally or strategically planned anything. She let her intuition do the work for her. For instance, one Sunday afternoon a small silver haired lady, no more than five feet tall, came in and lugged an antique accent chair from the other side of the room that Charon had acquired at a yard sale to the fireplace hearth. She placed it on the other side of Kookie's beloved leather chair and faced the room. Once settled into the wing-backed chair, she reached down into her satchel to remove a book and simply started reading *The Secret Garden* aloud to anyone – or no one – who happened to be in the room. When she finished reading the passage, she set the book down with a bookmark on the candlestick table where it stayed until someone else came along to continue. That evolved into a weekly story time when patrons took turns reading aloud, picking up from where the previous week's reader had left off.

Another time, Kookie noticed a young woman who came in, ordered some cookies with tea and sat surveying the walls of the room. As the woman began to get up, Kookie came over to take her empty plate, cup, and saucer.

"Thanks for coming in. I hope you enjoyed it.

"Oh, I did. I love your cookies…and this place."

Kookie tilted her head and paused. "I couldn't help but notice the way you were looking around the room. I'm wondering what it was you saw…or didn't see, for that matter."

The patron was taken aback by Kookie's astute observation. "Uh, yes. I guess I was, wasn't I?"

"And?"

"Well…it's such a lovely room…such warmth. It also has quite a lot of wall space. I was wondering if you ever considered hosting an exhibition of local artists' work – you know like a gallery."

The woman clearly noticed Kookie's quick shake of her head as the suggestion washed over her like an artistic tsunami. "What an incredible idea!" Then Kookie offered a sly smile, "Do you happen to know any local artist who might be interested?"

The woman returned an embarrassed smile, "I do, as a matter of fact. I have all these pieces with no place to show them."

"Would you be willing to bring a few of the pieces for me to take a peek?"

The woman beamed. "I'd love to. How about tomorrow?"

"That would be fine. I'm excited and looking forward to it. Now, I don't believe I know your name," Kookie said as she extended her hand.

"Dori…Dori Crockett," she replied as she shook Kookie's hand. "And you are Kookie – right?"

"Yes, I am," Kookie smiled, amused at hearing herself publicly claim that name for the first time before continuing. "Well, then, I'll see you tomorrow. Thanks for coming in, Dori."

And that was the genesis of the weekly art gallery for local artists.

Likewise, the kiln in the back yard came back to life. Kookie offered it to local potters for free with the caveat that they donate plates and mugs. Their artistic contributions provided earthy, organic, and thoroughly unique serving ware to compliment the equally earthy, organic, and thoroughly unique space.

As warmer and drying summer weather arrived, Kookie opened the back patio as "cigar-friendly" space with a very small platform that served as a modest stage. Each Thursday night, she hosted free Celtic music. Guests came to listen, chat, play backgammon, and munch on Kookies' cookies. Little girls in cotton summer dresses climbed the tree and dangled their legs as the musicians sang and played. Little boys wearing no shirts or shoes played tag. The pastoral scene throbbed with charm and delight.

Over time, Kookie's hands were full as she juggled baking cookies and managing the logistics of the place. She relied more and more on Charon to help with odds and ends. Eventually, she offered Charon a job, who leaped at the offer and joyfully threw herself into the adventure.

Charon's initial epiphany regarding the little cottage proved to be prophetic as well as right on the mark. Kookie's Place was not merely a little shop selling cookies, as clever and delicious as they were. As Charon had said, there was an ambiance about the setting that no one could truly put a finger on or label.

In some ways, the product was an experience. But how does one package an experience, let alone market one? Indeed, Kookie had created an enigmatic space. It exuded a sense of place as people gathered to share the space and experience. Her little cookie house was a lower-brow version of *The Eagle and the Child* – the gathering place of the Inklings – a collection of erudite writers such as C.S Lewis and J.R.R. Tolkien at Oxford, or the *Shakespeare and Company* salon where the bohemian artists of the 1920s gathered in Paris.

This was what Kookie had always longed for growing up. Despite signing up and participating in every conceivable club at school or church, the organized settings of her youth lacked an authentic sense of community. She was "there" but always on the margin. She always participated, but much like a cog in a machine. The ever-growing clientele of the shop seemed to confirm that others sought a similar comfort zone as well. Kookie was astounded at the number of guests who ventured into her place.

Chapter 44

One evening Doc and Ruthie stopped by the patio. They came with a man Kookie had never seen before. Bessie rushed over to their table before they sat to give her friends a quick hug.

"Hi guys! Good to see you," Kookie announced.

"Good to see you, too, Kookie. It's been a while. Too long, in fact," Ruthie replied squeezing Kookie's arm.

Kookie then turned her attention to the gentleman who stood off to the side.

"And who's your friend here?" she inquired.

Doc gently placed the palm of his hand against the shoulder of the stranger.

"This is Rocky. He's been a friend of ours for years. He has a little farm not far from here," Doc explained.

Bessie extended her hand.

"Nice meeting you, Rocky. I'm Kookie. Well, actually my name is Bessie, but everyone around here calls me Kookie." Rocky extended his left hand to shake hers. Taken aback slightly, Bessie shook it, noticing he kept his right hand in his front pocket. "Have a seat you guys," she gestured to the empty chairs around the wooden table.

Rocky was six feet tall, clean-shaven, with hair just over his ears. His eyes were chocolate brown. Boots peeked out from his straight-legged jeans and the shirttails of a well-worn blue and grey plaid shirt out. Kookie immediately tried to determine if his name matched his appearance. While he had a strong, chiseled jaw, his face and gaze were soft – almost gentle in appearance.

As they took their seats, Doc pulled a small leather case from his coat pocket and set it on the table. Without permission or invitation, Ruthie reached over and slid the cover off to reveal four cigars inside.

"We came bearing gifts," Ruthie announced as she began dolling out the cigars around the table. "Nice mellow maduros from Nicaragua," she added.

Kookie reached for one and raised it to her nose. "Nice. Mind if I save this for another time?"

Doc waved his hand, "It's yours. Enjoy it when the time's right."

Meanwhile, Rocky reached across the table to retrieve one of the sticks. He held the cigar up in his left hand, turning to Doc. "Do you mind doing the honors?" Rocky asked.

"Not at all," Doc replied as he took the cigar from Rocky to cut and light it, handing it back to him.

"Doc and Ruthie told me you indulged," he shared as he exhaled his first puff.

"Yup. Mostly celebratory indulgence, though, for certain occasions," Kookie explained as she twirled the dark brown roll of leaves in her hand.

Rocky gave an approving nod and smile before he gazed about the patio. Then Kookie noticed the stump just below his right wrist where his hand used to be as he gently tapped it on the table in time with the music being performed a few feet away on the tiny stage.

"Nice place," he stated in a matter-of-fact way.

"Thanks," Kookie responded.

Ruthie chimed in. "We take full credit for her finding this gem, isn't that right, Doc?"

Doc took another puff from his cigar and tilted his head back to let the smoke drift upward.

"Yup."

Now it was Rocky's turn to take a puff. "Cool," was all he offered in the way of a response. He then turned his eyes directly at Kookie. She felt herself blush and attempted to defuse her embarrassment with polite conversation.

"So…you have a farm?"

His eyes remained fixed on her. "Oh I wouldn't call it a farm. I'm more of a hobby farmer, really." It was as if he was watching how she would react to his response – like it was test of some kind.

Doc jumped in. "Rocky, here is what you call a gentleman farmer. Nice little spread."

Kookie smiled. This man intrigued her. "Nice. What do you grow?"

Rocky set his cigar in the ashtray to let it rest. He folded his hands behind his head and leaned back. "It's pretty low key, really. Apples, blueberries and tomatoes mostly."

"He has goats, too!" Ruthie added.

"How fun!" Kookie responded with a chuckle.

Rocky picked up his cigar and took a puff. "Yeah, they're pretty mellow. I make cheese and soap with their milk."

"Wow. That's pretty cool."

Doc interrupted. "We wanted you two to meet." He turned to Kookie and continued. "You once mentioned you considered expanding your menu of comfort food. I recall something about pancakes – blueberry pancakes would be amazing."

Ruthie joined the conversation. "I thought it was tomato soup with grilled cheese sandwiches," she corrected her partner.

Doc waved Ruthie off with his hand, letting smoke from his cigar trail behind.
"Either way, we just thought you might be interested in his produce."

Kookie considered the suggestion to expand her menu. She had, indeed, mentioned this in passing, but only as a possibility. Rocky continued his survey of the patio area. Kookie took advantage of the moment and gave Ruthie a knowing glare. The old woman just returned the suspicious look with a grin. Kookie back-peddled and regrouped.

"Well, yeah, sure. I could always use some fresh local produce. Can I come over for a visit sometime?"

Rocky returned his attention to Kookie. "Absolutely. Any time." He smiled.

Kookie cleared her throat. "Well, then, let's set up a time. In the meantime, how bout I go get us some cookies and some drinks. We made a new batch of Chai tea today. Or can I get you a cup of the house blend coffee."

"Chai sounds good," Doc replied.

"Make it two," Rocky added.

"I'll give you a hand," Ruthie offered as she rose from her seat. Kookie felt herself flinch at Ruthie's choice of words, hoping Rocky didn't notice. As the two women entered the back door of the house, Kookie turned and grabbed Ruthie's arm.

"What do you think you're doing?"

Ruthie faked her surprise by lifting her hand to her throat. "You said you needed some tomatoes."

"Don't give me that. You know what I'm talking about," Kookie chided.

Ruthie gave a sly grin. "So what do you think of him?"

Kookie put her hands to her hips and tilted her head derisively. Silently, she found him beautiful – if that adjective could be used to describe a man. He was rugged, exuding a gentle confidence, but she chose to keep this to herself. Instead, Kookie just wagged an accusatory finger at her friend.

The two women returned to the table with the drinks. As Ruthie took her seat, Kookie stood next to the table and leaned on the back of Ruthie's chair with one hand.

"Well, I need to get back to work. It was nice meeting you, Rocky."

He nodded. "Nice meeting you as well. I hope you'll come over for a visit." He gave her an impish grin.

"I will. I promise. Well, enjoy your drinks and the music."

Chapter 45

Late one afternoon, a grungy looking young man on the top edge of his twenties came into the shop. He had a surfer look with his dirty blond hair and a scraggly whiskers that framed a boyish smile. A t-shirt hung on him as well as the odor of cigarettes. But what Kookie truly noticed was his blue, penetrating eyes. He didn't merely look at her as he came to the counter – he looked through her. She smiled through her modest intimidation and greeted him.

"Hi. What can I get you?"

He tilted his head and stared at her for a moment – long enough to make Kookie slightly uncomfortable and uncertain. She offered a nervous smile. In return, he squinted his eyes slightly, seemingly in an attempt to add some clarity. He placed both hands on the countertop and leaned forward." I know you," he said as if he was still trying to convince himself of his tentative revelation.

Kookie merely raised her eyebrows that elicited further comment.

"Yeah, give me a sec…didn't you used to be…Bessie James?" He seemed to doubt himself, rubbing his chin as he speculated her past identity.

Kookie chuckled and lifted her amused gaze upward, "Yeah, I suppose I was."

"Yeah. That's it. Man, I grew up looking at your face on the cover of my parents' old albums. Wow, you haven't changed much."

Kookie felt her face turn warm as she rolled her eyes. "Oh...trust me...I've changed," she said, trying to deflect his compliment.

"No, I mean, you pretty much look the same," he grinned.

"Hardly."

"What a trip!" He swatted the side of his leg as an exclamation mark.

Kookie became self-conscious and tried to divert his attention to maintain her anonymous new identity. She lowered her voice hoping it would bring the volume of his, as well as his enthusiasm, down a notch. "Well...thanks for noticing. What can I get you?"

The young man just stood there, still shaking his head in disbelief. "Bessie Fucking James...I don't believe it. I grew up listening to my parents play your tunes. *Bring You To Your Knees* was one of the first songs I learned to play on guitar. This is crazy!"

Kookie nervously glanced around hoping no one was taking in their exchange. She decided to be more proactive and redirect the conversation.

"Well...now that we've established who I used to be...can you tell me who you are...for now at least," she said with an impish grin.

"Kurt."

"Nice meeting you, Kurt. What brings a young fella like you out to the island and to my shop?"

"Oh, I was just crusin' – I hopped on the ferry as a whim – just to get a change of scenery. Thought this was a coffee shop."

"Well, we roast and serve coffee and some tea – we make our chai tea from scratch."

"Cool. I'll have one of those."

In an attempt to limit the public nature of their conversation, Kookie added, "Great. I'll bring it over to you. Have a seat. Make yourself comfortable. There's room out in back on the patio, if you'd like." Her re-direction to the outside was an effort to curtail any further discussion of her past in the public setting of her shop.

"Cool. Thanks. And keep the change," he told her as he handed her a five-dollar bill and headed to the patio. Before he could reach the door he glanced down at the variety of kookie cookies on display, taking special note of the 45s and the family jewels. "Insane!" he exclaimed, shaking his head as he walked out the door.

With a sigh of relief, Kookie made his chai tea and delivered it to him a few moments later along with a freebie 8-ball kookie. He had the outdoor space to himself. As she approached, she noticed he was rummaging around in his backpack.

She set the cup and plate down. "There you go."

He pulled himself up from his backpack sitting on the bricked flooring next to his feet. "Cool. Thanks." He then placed a portable CD player with a headphone cord dangling from the side on the tabletop. "Hey, I'd like you to listen to something…if you have a few minutes."

Kookie's curiosity was aroused. "OK. I guess. What is it?"

"It's a demo me and my band made. Here, have a seat," he gestured to the empty chair next to him.

She looked around before easing herself into the patio chair.

Kurt then offered the headphones to her. "Here…take a listen."

She deftly placed the headset on top of her head, smiled, and sat back. He punched a button that immediately emitted a blast of thrashing that could be heard without headphones.

Kookie yanked the headphone from her ears. Her eyes bulged.

"Sorry. I know…it's a bit intense."

"You could say that."

He adjusted the volume that did little to lower the intensity of the pounding of drums and grinding of power chords on the guitar. "I want you to listen to the lyrics…Okay?"

Kookie gave him a hopeful look, "I'll try," she said as she replaced the earpieces over her ears. She stared down at the table, concentrating as she attempted to decipher the lyrics over the grunge. She even bobbed her head slightly to the beat, generating a smile from Kurt. She removed the headphones at the conclusion of the song and rolled her eyes a bit to recover.

"So? Waddyathink?"

"Are you playing on this?"

"Guitar. And singing."

"Well, it certainly is intense, that's for sure."

"It's supposed to be."

"Uh huh."

"So what did you think of the lyrics?"

"Well, I have to say you certainly poured out your heart and soul. I could feel that."

"Cool. What else?"

"There's lots of…how to put this? Angst in it."

"Excellent."

She smiled at him. "Look, I can't really give you a critique because I don't know enough about this…this type of music."

He didn't need to say anything. His face said it all. Kookie wished she could take it back, but it was too late. She pursed her lips and rattled her memory trying to come up with some sage advice…any kind of tidbit that might be useful.

"I just find it hard to believe you would have any interest in me or what I have to say. My music is like the dark ages to you."

"That may be true, but I'm still blown away meeting you. After all, I did grow up hearing your voice on my parents' stereo. It's sort of cool meeting someone who, you know, made it big."

"I wouldn't call what I did 'making it big' – I made a few records and was on the road for a few years. That's it."

"Still…I'd really appreciate hearing anything you might think."

Kookie's smile betrayed the shaking of her head in disbelief. She finally caved in.

"Alright. It's clear you have something to say. I guess the only thing I can offer is to keep your authenticity. Be real. Be who you are and you'll make a connection with your audience. Oh, and there is one thing I learned and I think it applies here, even with your music and audience."

"Yeah? What's that?"

She took a deep breath and exhaled. "Don't play *for* or *at* your audience…be *with* them." She paused long enough to tilt her head at him. "Does that make sense?"

He sat quietly for a moment, looking unflinchingly into her eyes. She was awestruck with his uncanny ability to see her. This was an additional revelation to her.

She leaned into the conversation, "There! Right now. I can see that you're here…with me. You have my total attention. That's what I mean when I say you need to be *with* the audience. If they feel that – if they sense that you're connecting with them rather than putting on a show for them – well, that's what matters most."

Kurt took a sip of his chai tea, licked his lips, and leaned back in his chair. He slowly nodded as he twirled his thumbs.

"I think I get it."

He reached across the table to retrieve his CD player and headphones and stuffed them back into his backpack. He readjusted himself in his seat and turned back to Kookie. "Where did you learn this?" he asked.

"From my agent and manager."

Kurt sighed and took a quick look at his empty cup. Then he raised his eyes, but instead of revealing gratitude, Kookie sensed something else coming from his gaze that was as intense as his music.

"So...I have to ask..."

"Ask what?"

"Why this?" he gestured with both arms to the pastoral space and tossed his head in the direction of the shop. "Why did you leave your fame and fortune playing music?"

Kookie gently shook her head once again with a wry grin. "I wouldn't call what I had 'fame and fortune'."

"You know what I mean. If being with an audience is as important and special as you say it is...why did you stop?"

Kookie widened her eyes in an attempt to shake off the impact of his interrogation. "Jesus, Kurt," was all she could muster in the way of a response. He continued to burn a hole through her with his eyes until she finally relented with a response.

"You don't pull any punches, do you?"

He grinned at her.

She shook her head and decided to search for an answer. "That's a good question. One I've been answering...trying to answer for several years now." Kookie paused and lifted her thoughts and gaze to the sky, in search of a reason to share. "I guess it goes back to what I said earlier…about being *with* an audience rather than be 'on' and playing 'for' them. Playing little venues when I was first starting out did that for me. It felt good…it felt real. Then came the albums. That was exciting and all that. It's cool to think people…like your parents…were actually listening to me. But that was really the beginning of the break down. Hearing someone on vinyl…putting yourself on vinyl… isn't the same as being in a room with people who want to share that moment with you." She paused and turned to Kurt. "Make sense?"

He nodded and she could tell he was trying to understand.

Kookie ran her hands through her hair and sighed heavily before continuing. "But the real deal breaker was when someone…a well-meaning manager…talked me into doing things I simply didn't want to do…all to help with record sales. It wasn't me. But I caved in. It was awful. I was miserable. That's when I realized I had become something else. I was a product….a cog in a machine…the business side of it.

Kurt leaned back, allowing Kookie's sage words to wash over him. "What about the touring? Wasn't that being with your audience?"

"Yes and no. The coffee house gigs were the best. I could actually see the audience. But, the venues got bigger as did the crowds. It was harder to connect. I realized I was getting sucked into an image of who they wanted me to be. I was starting to buy into that and pretty soon you lose who you are. I saw that happen a lot during that period. It poisoned a lot of talented folks…that and the drugs. People idolize you. Just keep in mind what an idol is…"

"Which is?" Kurt let his question dangle.

"A false god. And don't confuse adoration with true admiration. A 90-minute exchange on stage with several thousand people isn't a relationship…it's a business transaction. I wanted…needed something more than that."

Kurt sat nodding with insight. "And so you found that here," he gestured with an outstretched arm.

Kookie nodded. "Yup. As hard as that may be to believe." She paused and it was now her turn to gaze into his eyes. "It's all fleeting, Kurt. Don't forget that."

He squinted as he considered what she had said. Then he smiled. "I won't." He stood up gathering his things and the cookie. He swung his backpack over his shoulder and took a bite. "Thanks. I appreciate you making some time for me." He outstretched his hand.

Bessie glanced down at it with a half-smile and shook her head rather than his hand. She reached out both arms and gave him a hug. "You're welcome. You take care."

"I will."

She watched the scruffy young man depart with his dreams. She recalled her own. Then she suddenly recalled the night she spent with the college girls in Champaign, Illinois. That conversation, coupled with the one she just had, generated warmth in her bosom. It slowly began to dawn on her that she did, indeed, miss the music. Later, after the shop had closed up,

Bessie went upstairs to her bedroom closet and liberated Prudence from the dark. With the guitar in hand, Bessie returned to the parlor and placed Prudence in a guitar stand by her big old leather chair in the sharing area by the fireplace with the hope it might call out to someone – perhaps even her.

Chapter 46

One particularly busy day, Charon was working the counter while Kookie was baking in the kitchen. A mother and her 10-year old son approached the counter.

"Good Morning! Welcome to Kookie's. What can I get for you?" Charon asked.

"What do you want, honey?" the mother asked her son as she surveyed the menu.

"I want a chocolate chip cookie!" he whined "…and some chocolate milk," he demanded. His mother squinted her eyes at the list of cookies on the chalkboard.

"Hmm – I don't see them listed. Excuse me…" she turned her attention back to Charon.

"Yes?"

"Tell me…do you have any chocolate chip cookies?"

Charon shook her head. "No, I'm afraid not. But we do have white chocolate chip with macadamia nuts."

The woman frowned. "You don't? Why on earth don't you have chocolate chip cookies?" she asked with great disdain.

Charon cocked her head. "That's a good question. I really don't know. I'll have to ask Kookie."

The woman raised her eyebrows. "Well…that seems rather strange."

Charon raised both hands in confused wonder. "Yeah, well…we try to bake cookies that are a bit…unique. I'm betting that's why. So…have you decided?"

"Hey Mom! Let's get those traffic light cookies!" the boy shouted.

"Those look good, don't they? OK, we'll take those and a glass of chocolate milk and a coffee."

"Coming right up!"

After serving the mother and son, Charon was poised to ask Kookie about why they didn't bake chocolate chip cookies, but the phone rang.

"Can you grab that?" Kookie called out to Charon as she was up to her elbows in cookie dough.

Charon walked over to the phone on the wall and shouted, "Got it! – Kookie's…how can I help you?"

There was a pause until a man's voice tentatively asked, "Uh, is Bessie there?"

"Who?" Charon asked as she cupped one hand over her ear to block the noise of the mixer.

"Bessie…is Bessie James there?" the man asked.

Charon pulled the receiver away from her ear and stared at it for a second as if looking at it might provide clarity. When it didn't, she replaced it to her ear and spoke into the mouthpiece, "There's nobody by the name of Bessie here."

Kookie's neck whiplashed as she turned toward Charon standing off to the side of the kitchen. She grabbed a towel and began wiping her hands. "Who is it?" she asked.

"May I ask who's calling?" Charon politely inquired to a now totally confused caller on the other end of the line.

"Um…this is the Reverend Henry Glenn calling from Minnesota."

Charon cupped her hand over the mouthpiece and whispered to Kookie, "It's some Reverend Glenn in Minnesota."

With an outstretched hand, Kookie walked toward Charon. "Here, let me take that."

Befuddled, Charon handed the phone to her boss and watched her as she spoke into the phone.

"Hello…Pastor Glenn…this is Bessie. What a surprise!"

"Yes, well…I suppose it is. My, my, I have to say that it took quite a bit of detective work to track you down."

"I don't doubt that. How *did* you find me? What's up?"

There was a long silence on the other end of the phone line.

"Well, that's the thing. I found your number at your mother's house. And…well…that's why I'm calling," he informed her followed by a long pause that told Kookie all she needed to know.

"Is she…" Kookie paused to search for the words.

"I'm afraid I have some bad news, Bess."

Another long pause occurred before she replied, "I see."

"I regret to tell you that your mother has crossed the bridge to be with our Heavenly Father."

Charon saw the look on Kookie's face and walked over to her. She gently put her hand on Kookie's shoulder.

"Oh. I see. When? How?" Kookie stoically inquired.

"Peacefully, I'm thankful to say. It appears she just died in her chair while watching television last night. Evidently it was due to hepatitis. She was late coming into the office and she didn't answer the phone. It was so unusual for her not to be at work or at least call in, so I drove over to check on her. As a result, I found her."

Kookie raised her eyes from the floor and glanced at Charon.

"Well...I'll head back there just as soon as I can. I appreciate you calling me."

"I'm sorry, Bess. I wish I had a better reason to reach out to you. All of us miss you. We're all very proud of you and your career. We wish we heard and saw more of you and the wonderful gift God gave you. And I just wish we had reconnected under better circumstances."

"Thanks."

There was another awkward silence.

"Bess? Are you alright?" the pastor checked in cautiously.

"Yes, yes. I'm OK. Just letting it sink in, I guess."

"I understand. Well, I assume you'll want to have her service here at the church."

"Of course."

"Well then, we can discuss details later when you get here. Your mother is at the Korsmo Mortuary in Moorhead. Is there anything else I can do for you right now?"

"No, no. You've been very kind. As I said, I'll hop on a plane and get there as soon as I can. I'll call you when I know the details of my arrival."

"Very well, then. Safe travels, Bess. God bless you and again, I'm so sorry."

"Thanks, Pastor Glenn. See you soon."

Kookie placed the received on the wall phone and looked at Charon, saying nothing.

Chapter 47

Bessie sat on the floor surrounded by boxes filled with her mother's things wearing what she wore to the funeral service. A truck from Goodwill would be picking them up and all the furniture tomorrow. There was nothing she wanted to keep for herself. This included the remnants and artifacts of her childhood and adolescence she had also boxed and stacked in her bedroom. Walking into her bedroom she found everything as she had left it. Dolls and stuffed animals she used to serenade still lined the floor behind the bedroom door. The only thing in the entire doublewide trailer that held any redeeming value was the box of albums she set apart from the canyon of boxes that would disappear in less than 24 hours. These were the albums she and her mother used to play and sing to each other on lonely Friday nights.

Since it happened to be Friday, Bessie had driven her rental car over to Burger Bash to pick up a bacon cheeseburger, fries, and a chocolate shake earlier that evening. This would serve as a makeshift picnic dinner on the living room floor. Sitting on the orange shag carpet, she randomly selected an album from the box and put it on the ancient Zenith hi-fi. In between bites of her dinner, Bessie sang along with the songs, but for the first time in her life, by herself. When an album reached its scratchy conclusion, she selected another and played it. This went on into the night. As the sky began to brighten with the dawn, Bessie closed and taped the box of vinyl shut. With a marking pen, she addressed it to be mailed to her home on Whidbey Island.

Chapter 48

"Hello?"

"Benny?"

"And who is this?"

"It's me…Bessie."

"Bessie my dear! My God, it's been 20 years. How are you?"

"Not so good actually."

"Oh dear. Whatever could be the problem?"

"My mom died."

"Oh, I'm so sorry to hear this, my dear."

"Yeah, I'm in Minnesota taking care of things. I'm actually at the airport in the Twin Cities right now. I have a flight to LAX in about an hour."

"How wonderful! So you're returning to the City of Angels at last!"

"Yes and no. I'll be in L.A. but I'm just passing through. I was wondering if you could meet at the airport."

"What time does your flight get in?"

"Peak rush hour I'm afraid…around 5:00 pm"

"Don't you fret about that? I'll be there. Give me the flight info."

* * *

Bessie looked out at the patchwork quilt of farmland below her. She tried piecing together her own patchwork quilt of events that had transpired – not just over the past few days – but also over the past few years. While she pondered who she had become, she also realized she would need to make a kind of schizophrenic shift and return to being Bessie when she would meeting Benny. In what seemed like no time at all, the plane was descending over the sprawl of Los Angeles.

"There she is!" Benny announced to the entire airport as she exited the jet way. The two friends embraced.

"Thanks for coming, Benny. My God, I hardly recognized you. You look so…so…"

"Trim is the word you're looking for my dear. I've managed to shed nearly a hundred pounds as well as those nasty cigarettes. And you! You look absolutely ravishing. So earthy!"

"I don't know about that."

"Well I do. Now then, let's get out of this zoo and have a nice dinner to catch up. Any of your favorite haunts or shall I surprise you with some place new?"

"Um, well, how about just getting something here?"

"Here? At the airport? Whatever do you mean?"

"I mean I have a flight to Seattle in a few hours. Can we just grab a bite to eat or a drink here? I have an idea I want to bounce off of you."

"Aren't you just full of surprises? Well, if we must, we must. Thank God for my frequent flyer miles – we can pop into the Executive Club for a drink and hors d'oveurs."

Benny took her carry-on bag from her and together they slipped through the whooshing of the glazed sliding doors into the airport lounge. Benny ordered his standby Manhattan while she ordered a club soda with a lime.

Benny settled into the deep cushioned booth. "Well now…this is all very mysterious. What is it you want to bounce off of me?"

She twiddled her thumbs on top of the table. "I still owe you an album, don't I?"

"Technically, yes."

She searched his eyes. "But you've never pressured me to make it in all these years…despite my contract."

"No, I haven't."

"And why is that?"

Benny raised his eyes for a moment and returned his gaze to his protégé. "We both know this town…the people…this business can be pretty cut-throat. Dog eat dog, as it were. And I must confess I can be as self-serving as the next. But you my dear…you took a chance with me as much as I took a chance with you. I would not be where I am today had it not been for you."

"So…I'm not sure I understand. If I was so…so instrumental to your career, why wouldn't you have put the screws on me to deliver more?"

Benny tilted his head back and stared at the ceiling. "I suppose I could have. But…deep down inside I couldn't. You, my dear, are…how can I put this…different."

"Different?"

"Okay – unique. I always knew you would deliver and make good on your commitment. You just needed time. And…I knew that when the time was right, you'd present me…your audience…a special gift. And I do believe now might be that time."

The folksinger turned cookie queen averted her eyes for a moment and then turned to look at him. "I have an idea for an album."

Benny raised an eyebrow. "Which is?"

"How about some old torch songs from the 50s with a small jazz trio?"

"Interesting."

She was surprised and disappointed by his flat response. "You don't sound enthused."

"I'm mulling it over," he replied swirling the ice in his empty glass.

"Do you think people…my listeners would like it?"

"I think your fan base will always love you and what you do. You could read out of the phone book and folks would fall all over themselves to hear it. And, to be honest, there seems to be somewhat of a trend for nostalgia. It seems aging Baby Boomers, like ourselves, yearn for the good ol' days – although I can't say for sure these so-called 'good ol' days' ever truly existed…it all seems like a blur to me. Never the less, you may be on to something. So, my dear, what led you to…a) deciding it was time to record after all these years and b) deciding to go nostalgic?"

"I'm not quite sure. I guess it's for my mother."

"Your mother?"

"Yes."

"I sense this may be part of your grieving," he speculating as he ran his finger around the rim of his glass.

She sat back against her chair. "I'm not sure grieving is the right word. But yes, I suppose she does...*did*," she corrected her choice of tense with emphasis, "have something to do with this idea."

"I'm afraid I don't fully understand. But that's irrelevant for the moment. What does matter is you want to get back into the studio – *my* studio."

"Here's the thing...I'd like to do this under the radar."

"Whatever do you mean?"

"I was thinking you could come up to Seattle and we could record there."

"My dear, as much as I love you and the idea of working with you again, I equally love my sound board and the acoustics of my humble little studio. As you well know, it has it's own...personality and feel. Recording elsewhere would be like being unfaithful. I hope you understand what that space means to me."

The singer bit her lip and nodded. "Yes, Benny...I do understand. It totally makes sense to me." She turned her head away in thought and returned her gaze with a Plan B. "I guess I could take some time off and come down to L.A. and knock it out in a week or so. But I don't want anyone to know."

"Why the stealth?"

"Lots of reasons."

"Such as?"

"It's hard to explain."

"Try me."

"This isn't really who I am anymore."

"Nonsense." Benny swatted her statement away with a dismissive flip of his hand. "It's who you've always been and always will be. You have a God-given gift."

She folded her hands on top of the table and stared at them. "Seriously. The people who know me now...those I live with and work with...they all know someone else – not Bessie James the singer."

"Pray tell who this 'someone else' might be?"

"Just a regular ol' person. And I want to keep it that way."

Benny shook his head. "I'm afraid I don't understand. You wish to remain incognito and yet you wish to return to your true vocation."

"I know...it's hard to explain. I don't want to do this project for me."

"For whom might I ask?"

"Like I said, for my Mom, I guess."

"I see. At least I think I do. Have you run this by Ron?"

"No. I haven't spoken to him in years."

"Well then, have you run this by Joey?

She just stared at Benny.

After a moment, he continued. "You know, my dear...Joey's now up in Santa Barbara."

"Really?"

Benny nodded. This news did not surprise her. She knew he'd eventually make his way there.

"Yes, really. He's managing talent there."

"So?" she feigned her indifference.

Benny reached across the table and gently slapped her wrist. "Oh, don't play cat and mouse with me, my dear. Don't you think it's time the two of you patched things up?"

"Are you suggesting Joey have a role in this project?"

"Not at all. I'm suggesting you go and see him. He may also have some insight."

Benny continued to rattle the ice cubes in his empty glass as she nervously twiddled her thumbs building up the nerve to press her long-time friend. "So? What do you think of my idea?"

"I think I like it...the concept, that is. We'll need to think about the actual material as well as who we get for back up."

"So you're saying you'll produce it for me?"

"I didn't say that. I said we need think about it."

She broke out into a broad grin.

Benny leaned his head back and closed his eyes. "No, no, no...please don't do that to me, my dear. You know I can't resist that smile of yours."

The Mona Lisa sitting across from him cocked her head and bit her lip.

Benny could see a question forming. "Yes?" he inquired dramatically.

"What about touring?" Bessie asked sheepishly.

"What about it?"

"Would I need to go on the road to promote it?"

"It depends."

"On what?"

"On if that's what you want to do."

"It's not."

"Fine. Don't. Not all artists tour to promote their albums. Steely Dan never did. You do know, however, that will definitely impact sales."

"Yes. But I don't really care about sales."

Benny grimaced, "Please don't say that aloud – especially around Ron."

The two of them stared at each other, pondering where this plot was leading.

She suddenly glanced at her watch. "Geez…I need to make my way over to my flight. Will you walk me over to my gate?"

"My goodness, I just barely finished my drink and I know there is another one with my name on it. I must say, you were very clever in plotting this little rendezvous…you managed to craft just enough time for your proposal and then…poof…off you go again into the ether!"

Standing up, she began gathering her purse and carry-on bag. "Honestly, I didn't plan this, Benny. It all just sort of happened."

"Oh don't give me that. I know perfectly well you could have taken a flight from Minneapolis straight to Seattle or wherever it is you've cloistered yourself these days. You choreographed this little reunion with precision and subterfuge.

Thank God that Mother Nature cooperated on giving you enough time between your flights to seduce me into making an album."

"So you'll do it?"

Benny's defeated expression provided the answer. She gave him a hug and a kiss before grabbing his arm as they walked toward the gate for her next flight. He carried her carry-on bag for her.

"Tell you what…you make a list of the tunes you're thinking about. We'll have to check for copyrights and permissions. That's the first step," Benny instructed.

"I will. And once you get the back up musicians, you'll let me know…right?"

"Yes my dear. We'll keep it very minimalist...very tight but sweet. A trio will do quite nicely."

Upon arrival at her gate, Benny set her carry-on bag on the floor beside her as the two old friends stood toe-to-toe taking each other in.

"I'm so pleased you reached out to me, Bess. I've missed you."

She could see tears coming to his eyes. She reached over and pecked him on the cheek. "You had faith in me."

Benny grabbed her hand. "We do make a good team, don't we my dear?"

"We do."

With a dramatic flair, Benny lifted his head and eyes. "Well then, I must dash. Traffic will be appalling at this hour. If I leave now I may actually get home before dawn."

"Thanks again for coming out and meeting me like this."

"I'd do anything for you, my dear – you know that." He threw his arms around her and kissed her on the cheek. "Take care. We'll be in touch."

Now alone, she watched Benny turn and wind his way through the current of harried travelers. Once he was out of sight, she approached airline personnel at the check in desk.

"Hi. I'm sorry…I know this is last minute…but something's come up and I need to cancel my reservation on this flight. Perhaps you can rebook me on another flight."

"Certainly. I hope everything's alright."

"Oh, right…nothing's wrong…just a sudden change of plans."

"I see. Do you have your luggage with you?" the woman asked as she peered around the desk.

"I do."

"Well then, we can cancel your flight and apply it to your new destination…which is?" the counter person professionally inquired.

"Santa Barbara."

Chapter 49

Knock-knock.

The door opened. Bessie popped her head in, "Anybody home?"

"Bessie!" Joey came to the door to exchange hugs and kisses. "Come in, come in…have a seat." It was strange to hear her abandoned name.

She wore a flowing grey sweater draped over her shoulders with a long equally flowing skirt. Bessie sat down and quickly surveyed the room before turning to Joey. "It's been a while."

"Too long."

They sat quietly, smiling, taking each other in. At first, the silence was far from awkward and they nestled comfortably into it. It was an opportunity to take stock of each other. In his eyes, Bessie had taken on an air of sophistication over the years, overcoming her initial insecure mousy-ness Joey had first detected years ago. She now seemed confident rather than self-assured or haughty. She was no deva, but she had garnered respect, if not devotion, from fans and the industry alike, despite her hiatus. In fact, her sudden disappearance seemed to have fueled the flames of her passionate fan base. Her sustained popularity was due to the sheer authenticity that she had managed to maintain in a business that was typically built on a foundation of carefully constructed facades. She had, in other words, advanced to an upper echelon of performers, which essentially meant she was now out of Joey's league – a reality they both had privately come to accept.

Knowing this, Joey was convinced that her rise to fame and adoration was not due to his ability as a manager. Instead, it was due to the sincerity that came through on stage that forged a profound and unique relationship with her audience – something he saw and sensed all those years ago in that tiny college coffeehouse where they met. Bessie was a storyteller. She sang stories everyone could climb into and live for them selves. That part of her, he hoped, had never changed.

Eventually, despite their history and the nostalgia that enveloped them in Joey's office, the ease began to fade as Bessie started to feel exposed as she watched him watch her. She had always felt somewhat intimidated by Joey, though she never really knew why. Perhaps it was his uncanny professional insight that awed her, as she never fully understood what he saw in her. And all the while she longed for and hoped he would see something besides talent. The edgy, although familiar, discomfort prompted her to break the silence with small talk.

"Well, you seem to have done well for yourself," she said averting her eyes from him and to survey his office.

"I manage."

She turned her gaze back to him chagrinned, "Doesn't that joke ever get old?"

Joey shrugged his shoulders and began to alter the direction of the small talk. "You look good."

"So do you." She seemed to mean this and was apparently somewhat surprised at how he had maintained his looks and overall health. Clearly going on the wagon had taken him on a healthy ride after she had moved on. Then again, he had not lost his hair like so many men his age, preserving his appearance and her memory of him from long ago.

They continued their knowing gazes, peeling away the years and their history until Joey decided it was time to talk some shop. "I guess Ron Speilman has treated you well."

Bessie sighed, resigned in anticipation of where the conversation seemed to be headed. "I can't complain."

"You happy there...with him at Galaxy?"

"Why do you ask?"

She wondered if he knew how she had drifted away from his replacement.

Joey noted the suspicion in her voice. "Just wondering." He casually played with a pen at his desk to disguise his own nervousness.

Bessie nodded her head. "Where's this going, Joey?"

He let the pen drop out of his fingers and folded his hands together, as if in prayer. "You're way too suspicious, Bess. Can't two old friends get together to catch up?"

"Yes, they can. But somehow I get the feeling you want something more than that." She let her fingers walk up and down the arm of the chair.

Joey leaned back in his chair and folded his hands behind his head. His open posture was a subconscious attempt to assuage her suspicion. "I'm not poaching, if that's what you're thinking. No, I respect your history with Ron. He's been good for – umm to you." Bessie continued to stare at him with a knowing smile. She finally folded her arms as if she was defending herself, waiting for Joey to be honest. Joey caved in. "I guess I'm just wondering if you have anything in the works…any plans…you know…a new album? A tour?"

With a degree of disdain, Bessie asked, "You mean a comeback?"

"No, I didn't say that."

"But that's what you meant," she snarked.

"No, no. Honestly. I was just curious, that's all."

A brief hesitation allowed her to once again scan Joey's face in search of a motive. "And what if I did…have a project in mind, I mean."

"Oh, I don't know…I guess I wondered if you had some material," he finally removed his hands from behind his head and folded them across the desk.

Bessie unfolded the shield her arms had provided and sat up. "Why do you ask?"

Joey let out a big, content sigh. "Well, I've been dabbling a bit."

"Really?"

"Really."

Bessie seemed to be doing some mental calculation. "Geez, how long has it been since you've written anything?"

"Too long. I've been too busy managing and producing."

"Anybody I know?"

"Not really. I did stumble across something a while back. Very interesting trio...very outside the box." Joey smiled looking very pleased with himself.

"Sounds intriguing. Are you composing for them?"

"Nope. They don't need me."

Bessie once again tilted her head and looked at Joey. "Uh, huh. So are you suggesting I might need you?"

Joey began swinging his office chair to and fro. "No, no...you don't need me...you've proven that...you've done just fine without me. But..."

"But what?"

"But it's been a while since you've done anything."

Joey had ruffled Bessie. "I've been busy... raising a family."

This was partially true. She had, indeed, created a family of kindred spirits.

He stopped swinging his chair as he grimaced and raised both of his hands pleadingly. "Oh, you know what I mean. I'm talking about an album. When was your last album out?"

Bessie squirmed a bit in her chair and somewhat defensively replied, "It's been over ten years."

"There. That's what I mean. Ron's asleep at the wheel. I love your voice, Bess. Everyone loves your voice. And everyone wonders where you've been."

She turned her embarrassed gaze to her lap where she fiddled with her hands. "I don't know about that."

"I do. It's time."

Exasperated, Bessie began, "Oh, Joey..." Bessie looked up and smiled just as two knocks were heard on the door before a young woman opened it and barged in.

"You wanted to see me?" The woman, more like a girl really, halted in mid-step when she saw Joey was not alone. "Oh, I'm sorry...I didn't know you were with someone," Laurel said as she quickly stepped back away from the door.

Joey quickly stood up and invited her in. "No, it's OK, Laurel. Come on in. I want you to meet someone. Laurel, this is Bessie James. Bess, this is Laurel. She's doing an internship with us here until the end of December."

The two women exchanged hellos and handshakes. Laurel stood nervously and struggled to respond, "Wow, this is so...I'm so excited to meet you. I love your work."

Bessie waved a gracious but dismissive hand, "Oh my dear girl, you're way too young to know my work, let alone love it."

Joey interjected, "No, it's true, Bess. She *does* know your catalogue. Laurel has quite unusual taste for her demographic. She has a unique eye and ear...a very different way about her." He smiled at her. Bessie noticed.

The girl, suddenly embarrassed, stood there nervously wringing her hands in front of her. Bessie noted how nervous the young woman appeared and made an attempt to rescue her. "Well, how sweet. Thank you," and extended her arm to the chair next to hers, "Here, sit down."

"Oh no, I don't want to interrupt. I imagine you two have a lot to…"

Joey cut Laurel off in mid-sentence. "It's OK. I wanted you two to meet. Besides…" he said with a dramatic pause as he pulled a cassette and two sheets of paper out of his desk drawer and walked over to the cassette player on the credenza behind them, "I have something I want both of you to hear." Joey had yet to obtain a CD player. He popped open the player door, inserted the cassette and hit the play button. As he returned to his desk, he handed each of them a lyric sheet. A solo acoustic guitar began a tender introduction as Joey sat down in his chair. All three of them listened to the rough demo he had made at his house, following along with the printed lyrics.

I carved my initials on the sky one day
Erased by the night in a tug-of-war game
With a sun that seemed too tired to fight…

It surrendered to the strengths and the shove of the night
So I drove away.

Swallowed up by a cold autumn night
Stabbing the darkness with these two headlights
As they tow this poor lost soul around
That's been filed away in the lost and found
In someone's dreams.

CHORUS: And the night seems to call me...it calls me by name.
Darkness is my blanket, my lullaby the stars...
It rocks this weary soul to sleep in its loving arms.

An orange full moon seems to wash my face
As the highway drags me to another place in
Time
And space just seem to jell
In a one-night stand that's a prison cell.
I'm midnight's child.

Passing signs along the way,
They fill my eyes but what did they say?
And you'd think I'd learn from past mistakes.
I've gambled at hope and at very high stakes,
I guess I'll never learn.

CHORUS: And the night seems to call me...it calls me by name.

Darkness is my blanket, my lullaby the stars…
It rocks this weary soul to sleep in its loving arms.

Some xeroxed smiles hung up on a wall
In my mind like a long dark hall
Framed by a moment in a memory
It's something to cling to when you can't find sleep…
Guess I'll drive some more.

I've thrown my popcorn box away
The credits have rolled in the daybreak's haze
'Cause the curtain call comes with the dawn,
I've taken my bows and now it's time to move on.
It's another day.

CHORUS: And the night seems to call me…it calls me by name.
Darkness is my blanket, my lullaby the stars…
It rocks this weary soul to sleep in its loving arms.

Both of them recognized Joey's voice. Despite his middle age, here he sounded so young and timid – almost tentative or reticent. Bessie just closed her eyes, letting the song wash over her. She opened them when the 3-minute demo clicked off.

"Well, what do you think? It might have a little too much reverb on it but it's only a rough demo. It's not really in my key," Joey apologetically inquired.

"Wow. I don't know what to make of it. It's not a love song. It's not about falling out of love. It's stark and yet...I don't know how to describe it...it's somehow comforting...resolved," Bessie mused.

Joey smiled and turned to Laurel. "What did *you* think?"

"Oh, my God! It's...it's the poem."

Bessie turned to Laurel, "The poem?"

"Yes! It's the poem you wrote...that day in the library!"

Joey beamed with her response while Bessie remained confused.

"In the library?" Bessie repeated.

Joey nodded toward Bessie and said to Laurel, "Tell her the backstory."

With that, Laurel began recounting their first excursion to the library in great detail. She described how Joey had magically pulled a narrative out of the photographs to create a poem. And now he had transformed it into a simple, yet haunting melody.

Despite her detailed explanation, Bessie remained perplexed. "So let me get this straight...the two of you wrote this on a date?"

Laurel waved her hands dismissively. "No, no, it's nothing like that. It's...well, it's part of Joey's therapy."

"Therapy?" Bessie furrowed her eyebrows, thinking hard and trying to follow.

"Well, not really...it's more like an internship." Laurel attempted to clarify.

Bessie was now even more befuddled. "An internship? I thought that's what *you* were doing?"

"I am, I mean, yeah. But so is Joey. Kind of..." Laurel was clearly unsuccessful at clearing things up for Bessie.

Joey intervened, "We go on field trips...adventures...creative safaris, if you will...anything to spark our imagination and creativity. Purely an artistic and recreational endeavor. Isn't that right, Laurel?" She nodded in agreement as Joey continued, "And this song is a perfect case-in-point...an outcome of such an excursion."

Bessie sighed and sat back in her chair seemingly flummoxed. "Well, I'm not sure I get the picture. I like the song. But I'm still trying to figure it out."

Laurel jumped in, "It's about that shadowy space people find themselves – the dark night of the soul. It's all about searching."

Bessie just looked at Joey with astonishment while he simply smiled. "See? I told you Laurel had a way about her."

Bessie turned to look at Laurel once again who was sitting in her chair ready to pop with enthusiasm. Laurel continued to clamor, "I can't believe it! I just can't believe you did this, Joey! It's so...so...wonderful! And to think, I was a part of it."

"So...what do you think, Bess? Do you like it?" Joey asked.

"Well yes, it's lovely. It's so...different. Quite a departure from your other stuff."

Joey couldn't tell if this was a compliment and offered a neutral explanation, "I guess you could say I've matured over the years."

Bessie remained cautious. "I guess so. It's sort of cryptic, but I like it. Still...I'm not sure it's me."

"Perhaps it can launch a new version of you," Joey suggested.

Bessie just looked at him blankly. Joey finally broke the silence by smacking his hands on his lap. "Well, it's yours, if you want it."

Laurel gasped and clasped her hand over her mouth. Bessie was taken aback at the offer and by the young woman to her right reaction. "Goodness. I don't know what to say." How was it that Joey could possibly know or sense that she was mulling over the idea of making an album after all these years?

"Say yes." Joey clipped.

The three of them sat in strained silence for a few moments. Laurel suddenly looked at her watch. "Shit, um...I mean, shoot...I've gotta go. I'm going to be late," and rose from her seat. "This is the most amazing day ever. Meeting you...hearing the song...Joey offering it to you. Oh my, God. I just can't believe it." She began walking backwards toward the door. "I'm sorry. I have to go. But it was such an honor...it was nice meeting you."

Bessie stood up, "It was nice meeting you too, Laurel. I hope this guy is treating you right." she said as they shook hands.

"Joey? Oh absolutely. Anyway, I need to go…traffic, you know. Bye…again. It was nice meeting you," she once again said as she closed the door behind her.

Amused, Joey looked at Bessie who looked at him with a raised eyebrow as she sat back down asking in trepidation, "What just happened?"

Joey lifted his shoulders in innocence. "What do you mean? I wrote a song…I played it for you…I offered it to you."

"That's not what I'm talking about."

"What then?"

Bessie glared at Joey. "You God-damn well know what I'm talking about."

Joey was truly stunned by Bessie's chiding. "No, I don't"

Bessie shook her head in disgust and disbelief, continuing her interrogation. "What the hell do you think you're doing?"

Joey, not reading her, was still focused on pitching the song to his former client. "Jesus, Bess…do you want the song or not?"

Bessie got up from her chair and began pacing around the room. "I can't tell if you're just an idiot or an asshole…or maybe both."

"What?" Joey groaned.

"Are you blind? That girl is smitten."

Joey feigned his shock. "Oh come on."

"I know what a love-struck girl looks like."

"And how would you know that?"

Bessie stopped and glared at him before continuing to scold him. "Joey! You don't get it do you? You never have. After all these years you still haven't figured it out."

His stare and blinks in total oblivion did not stop her.

"Don't you know why I left you and went to Ron Speilman and Galaxy Talent? Huh? Don't you?"

Joey continued to sit, eyes wide in absolute confusion. Bessie tossed the lyric sheet onto Joey's desk. "Jesus, you *are* an idiot. I won't let you do to her what you did to me."

"What did I ever do to you?" Joey's indignation didn't come as a surprise to Bessie.

"Exactly! It was all business to you. I was just talent to you…a product to sell."

"So, what exactly is she to me?" Joey inquired.

"Good question!"

"She's a just college student for God's sake. I'm just an old man in her eyes."

Bessie shook her head. "That's not what I see in her eyes."

"What do you see then?"

"Adoration. Infatuation."

"Oh, please," Joey said as he waved off her assessment.

"Any young girl who has a handsome, talented man…or in your case, half-way handsome and talented…shower her with attention the way you do…on these so-called 'excursions' or 'field trips' or whatever the hell you call them…" she stammered and failed to complete her argument, giving Joey an opportunity to respond.

"All of that is just…whimsy."

Bessie was aghast. "Whimsy? My God, you wrote her a song!"

"The song is not about her."

"It may not be about her, but it's her song, that's for damn sure."

"She was there when I wrote the lyrics…that's all. I thought she'd get a kick out of hearing it set to music." Joey said as he struggled to catch and calm his breath.

Bessie continued to shake her head, "You don't get it, do you?"

Joey had become irritated and impatient with their conversation. "It's just a song…you can have it…or not…it's up to you." He walked over to the window, turning his back to Bessie.

Bessie stood erect, breathing like a bull ready to charge. "Before I make any decision, you have to decide what that girl means to you. I'm not about to record a song she thinks is hers if you're going to hurt her."

Chapter 50

She began scratching out ideas for the songs that were boxed and en route via the U.S. postal service on the back of a cocktail napkin that came with her hot tea during the flight out of Santa Barbara back to Seattle. And while the cassette Joey had given her was in her purse, his new song was not on the list. After all, it wasn't an oldie that she and her mother sang. Besides, she didn't feel right about singing a song that she could only think of as belonging to that sweet girl, Laurel. Still, she found it curious that Joey had even brought up the idea of making a new album. How could he have possibly known she was considering just such a move? Was it coincidence or did Joey truly have a sixth sense concerning her – knowing she was pondering a comeback? Either way, she didn't bother to mention to him what she and Benny were plotting.

Looking out the plane window, she regretted how her reunion with Joey had ended. She had truly hoped it might rekindle things. Benny's not-so-obvious nudge may have very well resurrected their creative partnership, if not a flicker of hope from the embers of affection she had felt for him so long ago. Instead, her indignation seeing him obliviously toy with that young girl the way he had abruptly terminated what might have been. They stared at each other for a few moments without saying a word after she rejected his olive branch of a song after nearly two decades of being apart. She simply turned and walked away without saying another word, just like she had in his Hollywood apartment the last time she had seen him.

Meanwhile, as she jotted down potential songs at 25,000 feet above the ground, Benny was equally productive, mentally creating a short list of competent studio musicians to make up the trio that would be the backup band as he wove his way down Wilshire Blvd back to his Hollywood apartment. In the process, he pondered what his protégé had shared with him – that she had somehow evolved into someone else over the years. He was captivated by this and tried to imagine how that could be depicted visually on the album cover. Recalling her headshot photo that Joey had sent him years ago, Benny had always been enthralled by her mysterious half-shadow profile. He would arrange for a photographer and direct the shoot. The dark shadow on the cover, reminiscent of Elton John's self-titled album, would not completely reveal her but rather, merely offer a hint of who she had become. This approach would ultimately prove to be effective, both artistically and strategically, as the inhabitants of her island would never put two and two together to recognize their own little cookie queen. This brought a smile to his face as he imagined what was to come.

Clearly, the project was meant to be by the sheer inertia and momentum it had taken. It was recorded within three months of the conversation with Benny at LAX. She had been able to slip away for two days at a time on her days off, with Benny footing the bill for her airfare. During the recording sessions, Benny put her up in the spare bedroom of his own apartment that he shared with his boyfriend, Lance.

However, just as she and Benny thought the recording process was complete, her journey took her on a slight detour when her phone rang one afternoon.

Chapter 51

Kookie grabbed the phone after the first ring. "Hello?"

"So…are you ever going to come over to see my farm?"

She had to think about the question for a moment.

"Rocky?"

"You didn't answer me."

"Oh, I'm sorry. I've been…" she paused long enough to think of what to say until Rocky completed her sentence.

"Away."

"Yeah…away."

"Everything OK?"

"Yeah. It is. Thanks for asking."

There was a long silence over the phone line. Rocky finally continued his clumsy invitation. "Well, anyway…would you like to come over?"

"Uh, gee, yeah…sure. What's a good day for you?"

"How about now?"

The pause on the other end of the conversation revealed her surprise, prompting Rocky to amend his question. "I mean…if that works for you."

Kookie swallowed. "Uh, well yeah, I guess."

"Great. Do you need directions?"

"No…I think I can find it."

"Well then…"

Another awkward silence spurred Kookie to fill the gap. "Well then, I'll see you soon."

"Great. I'll watch for you."

It was a rare, celebratory sunny late winter day in the Pacific Northwest where the natives are normally resigned to celebrate the rain this time of year. Kookie hopped on her bike and peddled over to Rocky's spread. Upon turning onto Shady Lane, she momentarily gasped. Before her was a bucolic scene of a little white farmhouse with a white picket fence and red barn taken straight from a Norman Rockwell painting. A gated arbor covered in Wisteria welcomed her on to the sidewalk leading up to the covered front porch where Rocky sat in a rocking chair, waiting for her.

"You found it!"

"Oh my, God, Rocky. This is beautiful."

He surveyed the front yard proudly. "It is, isn't it?"

"How long have you had this?" Kookie asked as she climbed off her bike and leaned it against the porch steps.

Rocky got up from his chair and walked over to the top of the steps to greet his guest. "Oh, about five years. Well…actually all my life. I grew up here. My parents left it to me. I'd left home and was kickin' about doing this and that here and there. My mother died first and my old man seemed to die right along with her – from loneliness. He didn't last more than another 15 months. My sibs have their own lives, families, and careers…one in Chicago…the other in Atlanta. They weren't interested in coming back to island life. So…here I am."

Rocky looked at her. The top two buttons of his denim shirt were unbuttoned. Kookie felt her face flush and her heart skip a beat. His rugged looks did not match his gentle spirit. The combination of the two had rekindled something long extinguished deep inside her. She turned away as if to continue scanning the property, but in reality, it was to deflect his gaze and hide her embarrassed glow.

"Would you like a tour?"

"I'd love one."

Rocky outstretched his left hand. "Come on, then."

Kookie accepted his invitation. His strong fingers curled around hers with a slight squeeze. She had a sudden revelation in that chivalrous moment that while naturally she had taken a man's hand into her own during an introduction, she had never *held* the hand of a man – not even a boy in her youth – making her heart flutter.

Along the front of the raised porch was a perfectly manicured flowerbed. The inside of the house was not outdated as she had expected, but it still exuded country charm. It could pass for a quaint bed and breakfast inn. To her surprise, along one wall was a spinet piano. The kitchen did not have the latest appliances, but neither did it consist of an antiquated wood stove or icebox. After a cursory tour of the interior, Rocky took her out the back door to inspect the five acres of apple orchards, blueberry bushes, and a decent-sized garden, which would, in summer showcase tomatoes the size of tennis balls. There was a small red barn that stored a small tractor and housed three French Alpine goats – Larry, Curly, and Moe, who produced quality milk – that meandered in and out of a fenced area.

"But those are guy names," Kookie argued when he introduced the trio to her.

"They don't know that," he reasoned. "I gave them those names after watching them frolic with each other – sort of reminded me of the Three Stooges," he added. Kookie couldn't argue with his reasoning.

After a half an hour or so of strolling his property, Kookie and Rocky returned to the front porch when the tour was completed. Rocky offered her the rocking chair and he sat on the top step. She melted into the moment as well as the comfy chair and began to gently rock.

"Well, you certainly have a lovely place. I'm so glad you invited me over."

"Thanks. I'm glad you came." He paused for a moment. "I noticed you've been in and out…couldn't help but wonder if everything is OK," he nervously mentioned his concern once again.

Kookie was surprised that he had noticed her absence despite her efforts for her jaunts to L.A. to go undetected.

"No, everything's fine. I had some business to tend to. That's all," she explained truthfully, omitting details. To avoid further elaboration as to what the business entailed, Kookie pivoted the conversation with her own curiosity.

"So…what were you doing before you moved back here?"

Rocky seemed to expect this and appeared to have rehearsed his cryptic reply.

"Oh, like I said, a little of this and that. Nothing exciting or glamorous. Traveled here and there but the road was rocky…no pun intended…and it was full of holes taking me nowhere fast." He chuckled at his own joke before continuing. "So, when the folks died, this seemed like a good idea."

"I see," she lied. Kookie's curiosity was not quenched. His life remained a mystery – as did hers – not to mention the story about his hand.

He sensed her confusion and debated for a moment as to whether or not to elaborate. "I suppose you're wondering about this," he said as he raised what he knew she was curious about.

Kookie silently raised her head with a cautious invitation. "Only if you want to tell me. I don't mean to pry."

Rocky smiled. "Oh, I don't mind. I know it creeps most people out so I just keep it to myself, unless of course, they ask…and then I tell them. But even then, I never quite know what to say – my tongue gets tied and the words get in the way."

"Well…what happened?"

"It was crushed. I was working on a fishing boat up in the Bering Sea. I was in more danger up there than I was in Nam. I put my hand in the wrong place at the wrong time and that was that. It happened right about when my folks died and left me this place. So, this was as good as place as any to rehab."

"Geez," was all Kookie could muster in the way of a response.

"Like I said, I bounced around a lot. You name it, I've done it all once or twice."

"Like what?" Kookie was genuinely interested.

Rocky sighed deeply. "Well, I as I said, I was in Nam right after high school."

"Did you see any action?"

Her host smirked. "Yeah, but not the kind you're thinking. I was loading payloads on jets at a nice safe airbase near Cam Ranh. I may not have pulled any triggers, but I've had to wrestle with the role I was ordered to play. Anyway, I came back in one piece and not nearly as fucked up as so many guys. I was definitely lucky in that respect. When I got back, there was this girl – for a while. But…that didn't work out."

Rocky paused, anticipating a follow up question that didn't come. He watched for some kind reaction on her face but saw none. Relieved, he regrouped and continued.

"So, I took off not sure of where I was going or what I was going to do. There were a lot of green lights but I couldn't seem to get going…know what I mean? I was getting nowhere fast. Over time, I lost the meaning of what I was feeling. I just kept waiting and watching for something…anything to happen. So I finally got off my ass. I've been a truck driver, gravedigger, rough neck on an oilrig in Wyoming, construction worker doing trim work, and then I got the gig in Alaska. I did that for nearly a year. And then…" Rocky raised his arm to continue, "…this happened." After a silent moment, he stuffed his stumped wrist back into his front hip pocket and watched Kookie.

Kookie was enthralled by Rocky's Dylan-esque cryptic stream of consciousness, sprinkled with euphemisms. The mishmash of mixed metaphors somehow managed to fit together, like pieces of a jigsaw puzzle, to create a complete picture. She smiled sympathetically and appreciatively. "I'm so sorry."

Rocky shook off her sympathy. "I manage. It took some time, though. I was bitter at first. I had played by the rules and I paid up my dues. But I still got the blues. Then I guess I decided I liked the color of blue and moved on. Eventually, there was some financial payoff from the fishing company after the accident. That helped. And then, the farm dropped into my life. That's what grounded me. I can't complain."

Kookie arched her eyebrows in disbelief. "Wow! I wouldn't be nearly as…accepting…as you are."

"Would it help if I didn't accept it?"

Kookie was taken aback by his calm disposition and question. "I suppose not."

To change the subject, Rocky nodded backward toward the open front door. "I noticed you admiring my Mom's piano. Do you play?"

"I dabble."

The word made him smile. "Well you're welcome to come over anytime and…*dabble*," he emphasized the word.

"Seriously?" she confirmed.

"Absolutely. I never lock the place. You can gather some produce for your menu. Hell, you can milk the goats if you want. I can always use an extra hand around here…pun intended," he said with a wry grin.

Kookie nervously waved off his awkward joke and offered a meek smile. "Well, I'll definitely take you up on your offer."

"Cool. Just drop by."

Kookie tilted her head and finally built up enough of her own courage to look into his eyes. "OK. I will."

The two of them looked at each other for a few silent moments. The pause implied that it was now her turn to share her story – her past – but she chose to ignore the invitation. She wasn't ready.

"Well, I need to get going. Thanks for the tour," was all she offered. She sensed his deflated expectation when she did not reciprocate.

Still, he offered a brave and polite, "Well…thanks for coming over" in response.

She was smitten by his quiet strength and grace.

She walked over to her bike and gave him a timid wave as she peddled out of his driveway. On her way home, she pondered the mystery of their combined lives. She, too, felt as if she had played by the rules and paid her dues but she still wrestled with the blues – wondering how and why life had taken her on the journey it had. In some ways she felt like both of their lives had been framed by fits and starts, taking them nowhere in particular. And yet, their arrival on this island in the Pacific Northwest seemed meant to be.

Over the coming days, these thoughts rattled a hodge-podge of lyrics loose in her head. This surprised her. She hadn't written anything in years. And yet, later that week, she took Rocky up on his offer and found her self at his mother's piano. She had rode her bike to the perimeter of his farm where she waited and watched for him to leave. After nearly a half an hour straddling her bike, she heard the back screen door slam. A moment later, she saw him head toward the back where he tended to the 'three stooges' in the yard.

She pulled up to the front porch and parked her bike. From the wicker basket dangling off the handlebars, she retrieved a canvas bag and slung it over her shoulder. She tiptoed up the steps and found the front door unlocked as he had promised. She gingerly sat down at the piano, determined to compose a song that would capture the essence of each of their lives. She assumed her playing would reveal her presence, despite the subterfuge she exerted in arriving. Yet, her intuition told her that he would not intrude on the moment.

Her hands hovered over the keys and impulsively played two chords. She played them again. And again. She flopped both hands into her lap and stared at the keys with a sigh. Nothing. She was getting nowhere fast. After a few more futile attempts to coax something from the two chords, Kookie had an epiphany. Her life – like the two chords and the melody struggling to emerge – seemed to be – well – stuck. So, in the same way that she had allowed her shop to evolve, she stopped trying to pry the two chords out of their repetitive hiccup and allowed them to shape the arc of the song. She decided to capture this very moment in the song.

Outside, Rocky smiled as he listened to her play. In between the bleating of the goats he could hear her voice, but he could not make out the words she was singing. He was pleased that she had accepted his invitation to *dabble* – as she had described it. While he enjoyed music – mostly country music – he was not particularly musical. Despite his lack of talent, he couldn't help but notice how the two opening chords seemed to hiccup back and forth, as if they were stuck on a broken record. This struck him as odd, but he convinced himself that his ignorance of the composition process was to blame for his confusion. Little did he know that she was intentionally staggering the chords to musically frame the lyrics that painted a portrait of their life journeys – consisting of taking two steps forward and one step backward. He considered heading to the front porch to better hear her voice but thought better of it – deciding it to be too voyeuristic. Instead, he meandered out to the apple orchard to take stock of the fruit.

Finally, she was able to scribble out some lyrics in a spiral bound notebook she pulled out of the canvas bag.

I don't know – what to say.
My tongue gets tied – the words get in the…
Way.
I've lost the meaning of what I am feeling
And it's getting me nowhere fast.

I've been here and over there

I've done it all once or twice.
This rocky road is filled with some holes
And it's taking me nowhere fast.

For heaven's sake – is it all give, no take?
I feel like I'll break in two.

I've been up and I've been down.
This spinning world goes round and round.
I get the feelin' this life I've been leadin'
Is taking me nowhere fast.

Guess I'll bide my time and take it slow.
The light is green, but I can't go.
This time of the season – I can't find a reason
For getting me nowhere fast.

I've played by the rules and I've paid up my dues,
But I still get the blues so bad.

Now some melodies with nice harmonies
Can bring you to tears or a smile.
Don't get me wrong – but I feel like this song…
And it's getting me nowhere fast.

She then removed a cassette recorder from the canvas bag sitting next to her on the piano bench and made a rough demo of the song. In her head, she could hear gentle brushes over a snare and a melancholy bass line that would fill out what otherwise sounded sparse in the song's embryonic state. She also knew that a real piano player could add some embroidery to it. Still, she was pleased with the way the repetitive chord structure framed the story. After all, it was all about the story – just as Joey had taught her.

Once she finished, she slipped out of the house as quietly as she had entered and peddled her way home with the song in her head and the basket on her handlebars. The next day she listened to the demo twice, before sending the cassette to Benny. Initially she worried that an original and contemporary song would compromise the nostalgic theme and feel of the album. After hearing the rough demo, Benny assured her that it did not – that a jazz trio would do it justice and give it the right feel to match the other tunes she had chosen. Indeed, it was her signature. A week later, Kookie made one last trip to L.A. where she recorded her song that would be the coda to the album of torch songs in memory of her mother.

The song, entitled *Getting Nowhere Fast,* was the only single released from the album. It was a quirky surprise crossover into Jazz as well as Pop/Rock that blazed the way for others like Ricki Lee Jones. Her stammering chords and cryptic lyrics resonated with both old and new fans and to her astonishment the song and album were also generally well received by fans and critics. Reviews oozed with speculation that she *and* her fan base had matured over time and that *Lonely Friday Nights* was an album that had been incubating for years. She had made the come back Joey envisioned.

In the meantime, Kookie maintained a rudimentary relationship with Rocky. He supplied her with goat cheese and plenty of tomatoes. But that was all she allowed him to offer or give her. He came to accept this. And the boundary she had erected didn't dissuade him. At the same time, neither did the margins she had established compel him to exert any attempt to encroach the emotional moat she had constructed. He simply made his presence known and patiently waited. This way, he knew she wouldn't have to wrestle with what she thought and felt about him…or them.

Chapter 52

While many patrons took advantage of the space, several stopped by only long enough to pick out and take some cookies with them. When working the counter, Kookie made an effort to strike up a conversation with the 'cookie monsters' – a nickname that patrons gradually adopted on their own – however small and fleeting to make a connection with everyone who came in. Over time, she had established a relationship with many of the 'cookie monsters' and the chitchat took on increasingly more depth as she checked in on how things were going. She had become a local icon.

One foggy morning, Kookie noticed a woman enter the shop who began to immediately survey the space, seemingly to soak in the ambience. The woman did not look familiar. The woman was wearing a long flowing skirt with a wide belt and a large buckle. A gauzy, beige peasant blouse completed her ensemble giving her a funky chic look. Her white hair was pulled back into a bun and her thick black horn rim glasses gave her a somewhat intelligent appearance. None-the-less, Kookie welcomed her as she did with all her guests.

"Good Morning. How can I help you?"

The woman had a Mona Lisa smile, exuding warmth and confidence. "Yes, it *is* a good morning, isn't it?" she replied with conviction. She continued to look about the place as Kookie patiently waited to take her order. "My, my…this is quite the little spot you have here. Reminds me of a little coffee house I used to go to years ago in Minnesota back before they became all the rage." The woman's reminiscing pleased Kookie.

"Minnesota? Where about?" Kookie perked up.

"South of the Cities – Winona."

Kookie said with a cheery look, "How about that – I'm from the Moorhead area. Small world."

"It is." The woman continued to take in the room, scanning the artwork and the coziness of the space. "And I must say you've done a nice job bringing back those days of old."

Her critique made Kookie smile. "What can I get for you? And, is it to stay or to go?" Kookie asked as her question seemed to bring the woman back to the moment.

"Ah yes…to go. I'm on my way to a workshop retreat over at the Institute. Someone from there is actually going to pick me up here in a bit. The info they sent out in advance encouraged all the participants to stop by and sample some of your goodies."

Kookie leaned against the countertop. "Oh, how nice. Yeah, the folks over there are good people and good friends of the shop. What kind of workshop are you going to, if you don't mind my asking?"

"Oh, it's a workshop for programmers of small NPR stations – mostly along the west coast."

"Really? How cool. I love NPR. You must be a programmer, then?" Kookie presumed.

"Yup…for a little station up in Wrangell, Alaska."

"Alaska!" Kookie exclaimed. "Ooh, I'd love to get up there for a visit sometime."

"I hope you do someday…it's lovely. Anyway, I decided to mix business with pleasure. After this I'm going to hop on the Coastal Starlight and head down to the Santa Barbara area where my daughter and her husband live. I love the train. They get to drive and I get to look out the window."

"Ooh, I'd like to take the train sometime. And I'm sure you'll have a nice visit with your daughter. And Santa Barbara is so lovely. Do you get to see her often?"

"Not as much as I'd like to. We actually reconnected recently after a difficult period apart…but things are good now," she sighed contently.

"I'm glad to hear that. So…what can I bag up for you?" Kookie inquired.

The woman peered into the display case, resting her hands on top of the glass. "Oh my…too many choices. They all look so good. Tell you what, why don't you pick out a half-dozen of your favorites or whatever your best sellers are – I'm sure I'll love them. Besides, that's one less decision in this life I'll have to make. Oh – and one large latte to go."

"Okie dokie! A half o' bag of faves and a large latte to go – coming right up," Kookie chirped as she began selecting and stashing her works of edible art into the bag.

As she puttered, the woman continued to gaze about the shop soaking it all in and then leaned her hip against the counter. "I'm so glad I stopped by here. I'm not sure if I would have if the institute folks hadn't suggested this as a convenient pick-up spot from the ferry. Speaking of which – during that short 20-minute voyage, I just happened to overhear two other women talking about your cute little place here. I thought I heard one of them mention something about you used to be a professional singer."

Kookie camouflaged her initial surprise by simply continuing to peruse her cookie shelf and plucking samples out of the display case with her tongs. Without looking up and without any apparent emotion she replied, "Yeah…that was a whole other life."

"How cool. Have I ever heard you? Did you record?"

"I dabbled. I'm one of those 'one-hit-wonders' who was lucky enough to have at least one more modest hit. But…" she sighed as she stood erect, handing the bag of cookies to the woman, "that was then…this is now. And I'm glad to be here now."

"My sentiment exactly," the woman beamed.

Kookie sighed, "Besides…I got tired of the business side of it. It's not all that glamorous, believe me. And, trust me, running this little place isn't the same…it's certainly not as cut-throat," Kookie informed her guest as she turned her attention to creating her latte.

"Oh, I know what you mean. My daughter, who I mentioned earlier…well that's what she thought she wanted to go into…the music *business* as opposed to performing music. In fact, she even did an internship with an agent or producer…and well anyway…somebody along those lines, during her senior year at UC Santa Barbara. She thankfully decided it wasn't for her. She and her husband now run a small winery up the in the mountains and they are doing very well."

The woman's story struck a chord with Kookie, as she momentarily flashed back to the young woman who was doing an internship with Joey. She couldn't help but wonder if this had been the woman's daughter. Joey had played a demo of the song from their little excursion to the library to both of them in his office and even offered it to her.

While Kookie pondered the possible connection, the woman from Alaska began to ponder a few things as well. There was something about Kookie she couldn't quite put her finger on. She ultimately dismissed it as the familiar down-home Minnesota sensibility that exuded from her. But there was no way she could know the woman now steaming the milk for her latte had sung the story of her life with the 'big ol' world' by singing the 'one-hit-wonder' Joey had written for and about the visiting lady so many years ago. Perhaps that's why she felt a strong connection – whether it was through her daughter who had tangled her way into Joey's life years ago or the song he had written about her.

Once again, both women stood silently, taking each other in. There was an uncomfortable space they now both occupied. Kookie began to realize that she was detecting a coy, knowing smile from the woman standing in front of her. Was it just happenstance that the institute recommended Kookie's place or was this simply a ploy? She toyed with the idea of exploring this further but ultimately chose not to. What difference would it make? The honking of a horn from a van outside interrupted Kookie's pondering.

"Oh, that must be my ride from the institute," the woman said as she turned to look over her shoulder toward the front door.

Kookie handed her the latte. "Well... here you go. That'll be $10, including the latte."

The woman handed her a ten-dollar bill and dropped a couple of ones into the tip jar.

"Oh, thanks!"

Again the two women held each other in their gaze for a moment. The woman from Alaska finally – and somewhat pensively – turned toward the door.

Kookie called out to her. "Enjoy your visit with your daughter!"

The woman turned and looked back over her shoulder. "I will. And thank you. Bye now."

Chapter 53

Welcome to People, Places, and Things – a program that is an introduction to some of the most interesting elements in our everyday world. I'm Stephanie Jenkins, your host. Today, we find ourselves in Langley, Washington, a charming little town on Whidbey Island in the middle of Puget Sound a few miles northwest of Seattle. Just off the lone main street of this hamlet on the waterfront is an inviting Craftsman style house with a yawning front porch that leads into a warm and welcoming space on the other side of the front door. Upon opening that door and crossing the threshold, one's senses are overwhelmed. The first is the sense of smell as the aroma of freshly baked cookies wafts through the air. Next, the rich warm colors of the wooden interior seems to wrap itself around you, like a comforting blanket. There is a gentle murmur of voices, much like the sound of a trickling stream. Rocking chairs and comfy lounge chairs invite you to sit and rest your weary bones and restless soul.

What is the name of the paradise, you might wonder? That's a good question as there is no sign out in front. Likewise, it's hard to pin down what type of place this is. Is it a bakery? A coffee shop? A café? A library or art gallery? In reality, it is all of those things. And yet, by mere word of mouth, everyone knows this little slice of heaven as Kookie's Place.

Kookie James is the host of this space. And that's precisely what she calls it – a space. She is a relaxed, middle-aged woman who has been welcoming guests --rather than customers – for the past decade. She says she wandered into town by accident and thankfully never left. We're here today to find out more about this person…this place…and the things that take place here. Thanks for sharing with us, Kookie.

It's my pleasure.

As mentioned in the introduction there is no sign out front or name for this place. So how did it become known as Kookie's place?

People actually started calling it the Cookie Place – with a C' – because I was simply baking and selling cookies here. I was busy doing that so I never got around to making a sign, let alone a name for the place to put on the sign. So, people just started calling it 'the Cookie place.'

And I believe even that name morphed a bit due to the colorful and playful cookies.

Yeah, in addition to the old standbys like oatmeal cookies, I started playing around with their appearance. Over time, some folks called them 'kookie cookies' and I guess that makes sense so the name sort of stuck.

I can see that. I need to share with our audience that your cookies are in a variety of shapes and images – some even meant for customers over the age of 21.

That was an accident as well. I started off making them look like the old 45 records we used to listen to and then I made peace signs and later some traffic lights. One day, with the input and inspiration of some friends, some more provocative shapes resembling various parts of the human anatomy came to life.

And along the way, people came to call you or know you as Kookie – with a "K" -- ...isn't that correct?

The name sort of fit.

So have you always aspired to be a cookie baker?

Goodness no. I fell into it quite by accident really. Cookies and milk are my ultimate comfort food. Something I always relied on, even as an adult. Funny...there's that old expression, 'that's how the cookie crumbles' but that's never been the case for me. Cookies convey stability to me. So, it just made sense that cookies became a backup plan to my original life plan.

And what was that original life plan?

Oh my, that was a long time ago.

Well, the 70s aren't all that long ago. I'm sure many of our listeners remember Bessie James, a popular singer with several hits and that, of course was...or should I say <u>is</u> you.

I suppose so.

And...you had a surprise reprise album not so long ago. What made you step away from the kitchen and back into the studio long enough to make that album?

It was a gift.

A gift?

Yes, for my mother who had just passed away.

I see. My, what a lovely gift. Very touching. Meanwhile, you do pull out the guitar and perform now and again don't you...here in your lovely venue?

When the spirit moves me. People politely listen. But I prefer to give the stage over to up and coming talent...especially local talent. I've been there...done that. I feel good about all that went on before but I don't dwell on it. I don't miss it. I don't regret it. Life's too short for that. So today I simply prefer to move on and tend to the space.

SPACE -- That is an interesting and consistent word you use to describe your place.

Yes it is. I started noticing space years ago. Like how art galleries provide ample space between exhibits so one could really take it all in without any distractions. I could hear how space in music evoked certain emotions. I saw how cathedrals literally generated heavenly space. Finally, I noticed how people...mostly frazzled people...lamented on how they just needed to carve out some space in their busy lives. I wondered what that might look like. And then I recalled some of my favorite spaces from my past. They were warm, welcoming spaces where people could have conversations and be with each other. I guess that's it...I wanted to provide a location to be and to be with. I hope that makes sense.

It makes perfect sense. And you seem to have successfully created that kind of space here.

Well, thank you. It really was an organic process. Things just evolved over time. I more or less stood back and watched which direction I would need to go in.

I want our listeners to know that on any given day they would enter into this...space, as you call it and...well what would they experience?

Comfort food. We have our signature cookies and milk as well as a very limited menu of comfort food.

Such as?

Homemade tomato soup and grilled cheese sandwiches...mac and cheese...homemade granola...

But there's so much more to this than food – isn't that right?

We have live music inside and outside on the patio when Mother Nature cooperates – usually Celtic music – but always local talent. We have an open mic night when aspiring singer/songwriters can try out their new songs with the caveat they engage in a salon conversation with their audience for a constructive critique. The space is also used for local artists to exhibit their work. Take a look at the walls and you'll see all kinds of artwork. We also have poetry readings and read-alouds.

Read alouds?

Yes. Someone...anyone really... comes in and picks up the book that is sitting on a small table next to a chair and reads it aloud for as long as they want.

And what is being read aloud right now?

To Kill A Mockingbird.

How lovely! I also believe your patio area is cigar friendly?

Yup. Cigars are a very Zen experience and an opportunity for conversation.

And customers...or guests as you call them…will also find a book exchange where one can drop off books and pick up another. Guests are also invited to pull out an array of jigsaw puzzles and backgammon boards.

Yup…it's all here.

Well…thank you so much for telling us your story. I'm sure our listeners are fascinated by this special space of yours.

I hope so. We're always glad to have guests venture in.

And that brings us to the end of this week's episode. Join us next time to explore exciting new People, Places, and Things. I'm you're host Stephanie Jenkins. I hope you join me next time!

Chapter 54

At first the NPR interview seemed to come out of nowhere but over time Kookie deduced that the woman who stopped by the shop on the way to the conference for programmers must have mentioned something about the place to the other participants. This, in turn, led to the broadcast that Kookie listened to in her bedroom by herself with trepidation. She feared she had said too much, revealing too much of her past. It was a mixed surprise that very few of her faithful 'cookie monsters' even mentioned the interview. Perhaps her clientele didn't listen to NPR. This, in an odd way, was a disappointment and a blessing in another way. In any case, Kookie was relieved that the broadcast seemed to create a slight bump in sales without generating prying questions about her past from her patrons. Before she knew it, life went on and the radio program faded away from her memory.

After one particularly busy Sunday, Kookie flopped down into her favorite oversized chair in the parlor area to catch her breath. It was a relative warm evening and she had the windows open. The phone rang. She debated whether to answer it. After several demanding rings, she wrangled enough effort to walk over to the wall phone.

"Hello?"

Given it was after hours, she didn't offer her standard "Kookie's" salutation.

"Hi. It's me."

She recognized his voice but uttered his name speculatively, just the same.

"Rocky?"

"Yup."

Despite being tired, she was pleased that he had called. "Hi. What's up?"

"My birthday."

"Your birthday?" she repeated with surprised glee.

"Uh huh."

"Well Happy Birthday! Did you do anything exciting or special to celebrate?"

"Not yet."

"What do you mean, 'not yet?'" she inquired.

"Well, I was hoping you might join me for some homemade ice cream…you know, to celebrate."

She paused. "You mean now?"

"Yeah."

"I guess so. Can you give me a few minutes?"

"Sure."

"Okay, I'll head over in…"

Rocky interrupted her, "I can come over there if that would be easier."

"Oh, I see. Well, yeah, that'd be nice. You don't mind?"

"No. It was my idea."

"Oh, right. Okay, then."

"Great. See you soon."

* * *

A half an hour later, she heard his pickup truck pull up in front of her house. Rocky came up the steps, tapped on the front door, carrying a wicker basket looped over his right arm missing its hand. In the basket, packed in dry ice, were a bowl of fresh homemade ice cream and a small jar containing light brown syrup.

She opened the door in her bare feet. "Happy Birthday!" she greeted him.

"Thanks."

"Want to come in?" she held the door open.

Rocky scanned the front porch. "It's so nice out tonight…why don't we just stay out here?"

"Sounds like a plan. Here…set your basket down on the table. I'll go in and get some…"

Rocky completed her sentence. "I brought some bowls and spoons."

"Gee, you thought of everything, didn't you?"

Rocky began unpacking the basket and served up the ice cream, topping it with the syrup from the small Mason jar.

"This looks amazing!" she exclaimed. "But I feel like *I* should be serving *you* some birthday cake."

"Don't worry about it. I made this big ol' batch of ice cream out of Curly's milk and wanted to share it. It's too much for me to eat – it'll just make me fat." He held up the small Mason jar and continued. "This is apple cider syrup made from my apples."

She closed her eyes as she let the spoonful of the delight melt in her mouth. "Oh my, God. I've never tasted anything like this before in my life!"

"Like it?"

"Like it?!?!" she asked incredulously – "I love it!"

"Yeah, the goat milk makes it pretty rich."

"No kidding! And this sauce…it's so sweet and spicy."

"I'm glad you like it."

She spooned another dollop into her mouth and closed her eyes. "Well, I wish I had known it was your birthday. I would have gotten you a present. I would have made you a cake."

Rocky pursed his lips and shook his head. "Oh, that's not necessary."

"Sure it is! What's a birthday without presents and cake?"

Rocky sighed deeply and tugged at his ear nervously. "Oh, I did buy myself a little something."

"Really? What?"

His deep grey eyes looked into hers, causing her to gasp slightly. She even raised one hand to her chest for a moment to keep her heart from leaping. He seemed to notice. She lowered her hand back down onto the table. He raised one eyebrow and then shifted his weight to rummage through the bottom of the basket with his one good hand as he continued to explain.

"Yeah, it was on an impulse…know what I mean?"

She did understand impulse purchases but said nothing. Expecting some kind of response but hearing none, he paused as if he had found what he was looking for and turned his attention back to her, keeping his hand in the basket. He was purposely concealing whatever it was.

"Funny thing, really. I was at the grocery store picking up a few things…coarse salt for the ice cream maker, for one. Anyway, I was standing in line at the cashier when I heard this music being played over the P.A. system and I suddenly recognized it. I knew I had heard this song before. I remembered hearing this odd little…oh, I don't know what to call it…a little stammer in between these two chords on a piano. It was making me crazy…know what I mean? Ever hear a song you can't quite put your finger on?"

His chatter surprised her in two ways. First was how much he was saying. Rocky had always excelled in verbal economy. Yet here he was, telling her a story. Second, she was surprised at how nervous his fleeting search in the basket and his ongoing comments had made her. It all gave her an odd sense of trepidation. After all, she just asked an innocent question out of curiosity and courtesy and it somehow was spinning into a mystery. She was barely able to muster a feeble, "Uh, huh" in response.

"Crazy thing was the cashier seemed to notice me just standing there…listening hard. She finally asked me if there was something wrong. I told her I was fine but that I was trying to figure out what that song was and where I had heard it before. She tilted her head up, craning to hear the music. Next thing I know she looks at me and says, 'Oh, that's *Getting Nowhere Fast* in a very matter-of-factual way."

She stopped breathing. Rocky looked at her as he raised the CD jewel case of *Lonely Friday Nights* out of the picnic basket and held it in the air.

"Well, that bit of information wasn't all that helpful. She said it like I was supposed to know what it was. I just paid and walked out the door. I got outside and stood there for a few seconds going crazy trying to figure out where and how I knew this song. So, anyway…I'm standing there when I noticed a record store at the other end of the street." He paused, continuing to gaze through her before gently tossing the CD case on to the table.

She swallowed hard and stared at her shadowed portrait on the cover. "I see," she offered meekly.

He reached over to pick it up and turned it over to inspect the backside. "Yeah…I found this and took it home to give it a listen."

"And? Did you…like it?" she probed cautiously.

He gingerly placed the plastic jewel case back on the table. He leaned back and crossed one leg over the other. He tilted his head and stared at her. He slowly began shaking his head in quiet disbelief. Without answering her question, he flatly announced, "I don't even know what to call you," seemingly changing the subject.

She was genuinely bewildered. "What do you mean?"

"I mean, are you Kookie or are you Bessie James?"

She licked her lips. "I guess I'm both."

"Uh huh," he replied unconvinced.

Rocky uncrossed his leg and stood up. He quietly paced back and forth on the front porch gathering his thoughts, so he could finally share them. "Well…needless to say I finally figured out where I had heard that song before," he informed her.

"I imagine so."

He didn't bother to reply. She couldn't discern his feelings from his gaze. It was either contempt or disappointment – perhaps both. She finally caved in to confirm her fear and asked, "Are you upset?"

He continued to glare at her. "Should I be?"

"I don't know. I thought you might be…" she let her speculation hang in the air.

"That I might be what?"

His firm voice un-nerved her. Kookie inhaled deeply, taking stock of the potential reactions. "I don't know…Pleased? Impressed? Surprised?"

"Surprised?" he repeated tersely. She had never heard or seen him like this before.

"Well, yes…but in a good way, I mean," she suggested.

Rocky rested his one good hand and the remnant of his other one on his hips. He looked at her and then spun around on one boot heel, wrenching his head away from her. He looked off and spoke to the darkness.

"Yeah, I guess you could say I was surprised." He stopped, collecting his thoughts before stumbling on. "I don't know what to make of this. I don't know why you did this, let alone why you didn't tell me about it." He shook his head in wonder combined with a modicum of disgust before adding, "I don't know what to think." He kicked a small rock with the toe of his boot off the porch, adding, "At best this is artistic plagiarism…at worst its betrayal."

"I don't blame you…but…

Without turning back toward her, he brusquely cut her off, "But what?"

His question truly stumped her. "I'm not sure."

Her flimsy response spun him around. "You're not sure???" he mimicked in disbelief.

She heard both the disbelief and irritation in his voice. For the life of her, she had never considered any particular rationale for keeping the tribute to him from him – until this moment.

"I guess I was afraid to."

His face softened and he slightly tilted his head. "Afraid?"

Again, his question prompted her to uncover a reason she had buried – not so much from him – but from herself. "I guess I was afraid of what it meant."

"And what might that be?"

She bit her lip and turned away. He waited patiently for her answer but she didn't offer one. He walked back to her and sat down next to her. She began to tremble as she fought back her tears. Her apparent contrition softened Rocky's irritation as he gently placed his one hand on her knee.

"Listen..." he quietly spoke.

She wiped a tear away from her cheek and turned to see his face had softened. "What?" she asked timidly.

He reached over to retrieve the CD from the table and pulled out the lyric sheet from the inside of the CD jewel case and opened it up to the song in question. He pointed to the printed words.

"A lot of these words are mine...things I shared with you."

She nodded. "Yes...you did," she acknowledged

"Well...I was...um...geez...I don't know...I mean you didn't even..." he stumbled over his feelings and words.

She didn't wait for him to reveal his disappointment that she had shared his story with the big old world. "I know...I know. That was wrong of me."

His gentle gaze confirmed her confession. She took a deep breath and attempted to undo what she had done. "Let me explain."

"I'm listening," his voice went flat.

"I didn't mean to...to betray you. That wasn't my intention. I was just so..." she paused to find the right words.

"You were so what?" His tone had sharpened with an edge once again and probed like a surgeon's scalpel.

"I was so taken by what you had shared. I was inspired to write about – no – to honor our shared journeys. It was sort of a tribute to you."

"Tribute? That's what you call what you did? A tribute?" he scoffed.

She clamped her eyes shut and pushed on. "And so…" she paused again, struggling to come to grips with the epiphany she had tried to conceal.

He waited patiently. "Go on…"

"I don't know. You had given me the words to express my own sense of getting nowhere fast. I can't explain it. It was almost like bonding…that's the only way I can put it. Up until then, I couldn't…*wouldn't* allow myself to feel…let alone articulate what I was feeling."

She paused, taking him in, assessing his response. His expression suggested he wasn't buying her explanation, forcing another succinct tact. "I want you to know that I didn't intend to steal your story. That wasn't my point."

His searching eyes were relentless. "What was your point, then?"

She rolled her head and flailed her arms into the air with exasperation. "I guess I was borrowing your words because I couldn't bring myself to…" she paused again.

"To do what?" He continued to press.

"To admit I was lost. To admit I was lonely. To admit that…"

Her sudden silence was not because she couldn't find the words. It was because she wouldn't allow herself to say them.

"I see." His flat acceptance of her clumsy and incomplete confession left her uneasy – even dizzy. Perhaps her state was due to the cosmic convergence of fate. She could not know how Joey had done the same thing when he wrote the song that would make her famous – when he appropriated the words and life story of the woman who had come into the cookie shop before.

Dazed, she tried to regroup and asked, "Do you believe me?"

"Should I?" he asked as he inspected the pained look on her face. Rocky finally chuckled half-heartedly. "I guess so."

His sudden levity lightened some of the guilt weighing on her. She sighed with relief and placed her hand on top of his that was resting on her knee. He glanced down at the gesture before looking up at her.

"I have to admit, though…" Rocky deliberately let her squirm for a moment with a pause.

"Admit what?"

"I'm not sure *what* to believe. Let's face it…you haven't been honest with me."

"I suppose not," she confessed as she slowly withdrew her hand.

Rocky ran his hand through his hair. "Look…I never knew who you were before…you know…before who you are now."

She slowly nodded her head. "I don't think I knew who I was either."

He rolled his tongue in the side of his cheek and asked, "Why didn't you tell me about your other life?"

"I was afraid to."

"Why on earth were you be afraid?"

"Because I thought you'd be infatuated with her…that other person…that recording star. Fame has a way of doing that to people. I haven't been able to trust anyone, really, for years out of fear they were just, you know…hangers on…even to a washed-up singer."

She hoped that part of the truth was able to slip through the cracks of her fragile alibi. Rocky looked at her, weighing the credibility of her explanation.

"You know…" Rocky paused, stood up and began to pensively pace on the front porch as he collected his thoughts. He finally stopped and looked at her as he raised his damaged arm "…when I lost my hand, I realized I had been holding on to something for a long, long time. The crazy thing is, once this happened…I was able to let go…literally and figuratively." An embarrassed chuckle escaped as he continued. "I know that must sound like a ridiculous cliché and glib metaphor but it's true. It was very liberating…you know what I mean?"

Rocky could tell by the way she looked at him that she didn't. He chuckled to himself again and slipped his nubbed wrist back into his front hip pocket. He heard her sigh deeply.

"No, I suppose you don't," he surmised.

He turned toward the night just beyond the yellow glow of the porch light that now kept the encroaching darkness at bay and added, "I guess I'm just wondering what it is *you're* holding on to…what you're afraid to let go of."

She felt her indignation rise. "I'm not holding on to anything!" she shouted.

He just looked at her. There was no judgment…no pity…no defensiveness…no anger in his face. This only infuriated her more. She leaped up to her feet and continued her tirade.

"My God, how can you say such a thing? Especially after learning how I let go of my whole career as a singer and ended up here in this dreary place!"

Her sudden outburst surprised her more than him. Rocky simply walked over to the small table on the porch to calmly gather up the empty bowls and spoons and quietly placed them back in his basket. He retrieved the CD and held it up in his hand as he turned to her.

"I'm not so sure. After all, why did you write this song? Why didn't you tell me about it?"

She just once again stared at him, letting her breathing slow and his words sink in. When she said nothing, Rocky put the CD back into the wicker basket, closed the lid and picked it up.

"I think there's something else you're holding on to," he said as he gave her a knowing look before walking back to his truck. She watched him drive away into the dark.

Chapter 55

It was the Fourth of July so it was a slow day with most folks out enjoying the holiday with family. Kookie even contemplated closing the shop but thought better of it. She figured she'd circle back with Doc and Ruthie and light some sparklers. Kookie was busy puttering with a new batch of cookies on the worktable with her back to the service counter, barely paying attention to the voice behind her.

"So…have you heard the new Pink Floyd album yet?"

Without turning around, she put the finishing touches on the cookies that had just come out of the oven as she responded to the question over her shoulder.

"No, I didn't even know they were still together," she replied as she spun around. "Oh! Hello. It's you!" she said calmly.

Tony just stood there with a grin. "Yup. It's me."

Bessie felt her checks flush as she pulled a stray strand of hair from under her hair net away from her face. "Yes. I see that."

"Surprised?" Tony smiled.

"Well yes, of course I am. How did you…"

"I heard the NPR story."

Kookie's head raised slightly in revelation. "Ah yes. But that aired nearly six months ago."

"I know, but I promised myself to track you down. And well, I just happened to be in the neighborhood so I thought I needed to see this place for myself." He glanced about the room. "Quite impressive."

"Thanks."

"Besides, I thought it'd be nice to see you."

Kookie rolled her tongue in the side of her cheek. "So, in the neighborhood eh?" she queried in an attempt to divert his motive.

"Yeah. In Seattle checking in on one of our markets."

"Markets?" Kookie puzzled.

"Right. Don't you remember, I oversee franchises of Tower Records – of course now it *should* be called Tower CDs I suppose. Anyway, we have a store here."

She leaned against the counter. "Oh right. Well, how's the store doing?"

"Great. This new grunge scene here has really taken off. That translates into sales."

"Well that's good."

"Like I said, I was in the area…heard the piece on the radio and thought I'd drop by and see what the buzz was all about." Tony turned and surveyed the cozy setting and continued. "I must say, it's everything they described. Very welcoming. Its very…you."

Kookie tilted her head with curiosity and smiled. "I'm not quite sure what that means. But, thanks…I guess."

"It would appear you've settled into the area…so you must like it."

She just nodded at the obvious.

"Rain doesn't get to you?" Tony asked.

Kookie shook her head and pursed her lips. "Not really. You get used to it."

The strained conversation slipped into even more strained silence until Kookie finally decided to bail him out. "So, can I get you a drink or a cookie?"

"Yeah, sure. I heard something in the story about your X Rated selections."

Kookie gave him a coy smile and stepped back to a special case of cookies that was elevated and out of sight from the service counter to retrieve a sampler tray.

"Well now…look at what we have here!" Tony exuded scanning the provocative cookies.

Kookie cocked her hip and placed one hand on it. "See anything you like?"

Tony chuckled as he stared at her for a moment. Kookie took note and just shook her head, annoyed. "I *mean* – do you see any *cookies* you like?"

He pointed to two round cookies with what appeared to be nipples. "What might these be?" he asked with a wink.

"Those are Ta-Tas – of the Caucasian variety -- you have to buy the pair – we don't condone mastectomies. They're your basic sugar cookie with some coconut and cinnamon flavoring. We have assorted colors to be fully inclusionary of all races."

"I guess I'll go with those."

"Why doesn't this surprise me?" she snarked coyly before adding, "A glass of milk to go with them?"

Tony laughed. "Sure, why not? I couldn't tell you the last time I had cookies and milk."

With a pair of tongs, Kookie gingerly placed the two cookies on a plate before pouring some milk into a mug. "That's what most first-timers say when they come in. Then they keep coming back…not just for the cookies."

Tony once again surveyed the warm room and content patrons. "I can certainly understand that."

"Have a seat…I'll bring your order over…we can chat a bit."

"That'd be great. What do I owe you?" he asked pulling his wallet from his back pocket. This sent a flashback to another time in the past when he pulled out his wallet. She couldn't help but smile.

"On the house."

"Really? You sure?"

Tony shrugged. Kookie watched Tony put his wallet back into his pocket as he made his way to a small table with two chairs in the parlor area of the cookie shack. Once he sat down, she delivered his order and joined him.

"You look good, Bess."

Kookie inwardly flinched hearing him call her by that name. "Thanks. So do you."

Tony just grinned. "It's been quite a ride for you. Fame and fortune…recluse…and now…cookie queen."

Kookie ran her fingers across the tabletop. "It's had its ups and downs."

"You look happy."

"I am."

"Really?"

"Really," she looked at him, daring him to doubt her sincerity.

"What makes you so happy? This is so far afield from singing in front of adoring fans. I thought that's what you wanted."

Kookie closed her eyes and sighed. "It was…in some ways. In other ways all of this," she gestured with both hand outstretched, "is what I guess I really wanted…longed for."

Tony scoffed. "Cookies? You longed for cookies?"

Kookie tilted her gaze upward. "No, not for cookies per se. But *this*…" she once again gestured to the room. "The intimacy this space has to offer. And I can tell you after all these years…it's not just me who yearns for this. I mean look at it…look at the people here."

Tony looked around the room. "It's so mellow."

"Exactly."

"I gotta tell you…I travel all the time and it's a busy, crazy world out there," he nodded out toward the front door with his chin.

"Tell me about it," Kookie confirmed.

"I don't know, Bess – or should I call you Kookie?" he finally corrected himself and waited for her response that never came and continued. "You're really on to something here. If only you could bottle it and sell it…you'd make a fortune."

Kookie chuckled. "I once said almost the same thing after I experienced a place much like this early in my career."

"You know…" Tony's thoughts trailed off.

"What?"

"You know…maybe you could…"

"Could what?"

"Could clone this place…this experience. You know…start a franchise."

Kookie shook her head. "I'm dubious of that. As I said in the interview, this was pretty organic. I didn't plan it. There's no formula for it."

"Maybe there is," Tony suggested with a raised eyebrow.

Kookie just stared at him, trying to read his mind. He changed the subject.

"So…what time do you close up here?"

"Around 4:00 or so. Why?

"It's Fourth of July. I didn't know if you had plans. If not, I'd like to take you out for dinner…catch up."

"Oh you don't need to do that, thanks."

"I know I don't *need* to…I'd *like* to…that is, if you don't mind."

"I suppose."

"Great, I'll pick you up around 6:00."

Chapter 56

Tony arrived on time in his rental car. He was getting out of the driver's side door when Kookie came bounding down the front steps. She was wearing a corduroy pair of cute overalls that showed off the figure she had maintained over the years. Under the buckled suspenders was a simple short-sleeved, white low-necked t-shirt lined with petite embroidered flowers. Sandals on her feet. Her hair was up in a bun. It was farmer-chic at its finest. Kookie's earthy beauty was dazzling.

"You look nice," he called out.

Kookie opened the passenger door and climbed in. "Thanks. Well then, do you need some recommendations on where to go? There are a lot of nice places here on the island."

"No, thanks. I've got it all planned."

He put the car into gear and drove south toward Clinton. As they approached the ferry, Kookie turned to her chauffer.

"Where are we going?" her voice tinged with suspicion more so than surprise.

"Not far. Just to the other side. Why don't you sit back and come along for the ride?"

The ferry ride was smooth, including the commute on the other side as they were facing oncoming commuter traffic. Once off the ferry in Mukilteo, Tony drove another mile or so, turning left into a small executive airport.

"What's this?" Kookie asked.

"Dinner."

"Dinner?"

Tony just smiled and looked at her out of the corner of his eye as he parked the car and pressed the button releasing the trunk hood. He opened the driver door and put his left foot out on to the pavement. Kookie remained strapped in her seatbelt with the passenger door still closed.

"You coming?" Tony asked wryly before exiting the car and slamming the driver's door shut. Kookie followed suit, watching him retrieve a small picnic basket from the trunk.

"What's all this?"

"I already told you…dinner. Come on, follow me," and he outstretched his hand that she warily took as he towed her toward the executive terminal. Once inside, Tony quickly scanned the waiting area when he waved and called out to another man standing off to the side of the room.

"Robbie!"

The man looked up and returned the wave as Tony continued hauling his reluctant dinner date by her hand. Robbie and Tony exchanged a soul handshake and a hug.

"Good to see you, man," Robbie said with a broad smile.

"You're looking good. I'm glad this worked out. Oh, here…Robbie, this is my friend, Kookie."

She took note of the name he used to introduce her.

"Nice meeting you Kookie. That's an interesting name," Robbie remarked.

"She's an interesting lady," Tony quipped.

She accepted his hand. "Nice meeting you. The two of you seem to be old friends."

Robbie smacked Tony on the back.

"Ol' Tone and me go way back."

"Yeah, we haven't seen each other in, oh, what, ten years or so?"

"At least that long," Robbie confirmed.

Tony turned back to Kookie.

"Robbie's going to take us out to dinner…isn't that right Rob?"

The buddy of old nodded with a grin. "Yup! Here…let me take that," Robbie replied as he reached for the picnic basket in Tony's hand. "Right this way," he announced with a slight bow and sweep of his arm toward an exit door.

"I don't understand," Kookie confessed.

"Robbie's a pilot. In fact, he works at Boeing right over there," Tony gestured to a large building just to the east. "He's taking us on a little sight seeing dinner tour."

"Dinner tour?" Kookie repeated.

Overhearing the conversation, Robbie raised the basket up in the air while continuing to walk ahead of them on to the tarmac without turning to look behind him.

Kookie just tilted her head in confused amazement as the trio approached a small red and white Piper Seminole airplane. Robbie set the basket down on the ground as he opened the door on the side of the tiny twin prop airplane.

"Hop right in!" he invited.

Kookie cautiously climbed into the tiny compartment and took a seat with Tony following right behind her. Robbie handed the picnic basket through the open door to Tony.

"Here you go. Get buckled in." Tony instructed them as he climbed in behind them and secured the door. He squeezed himself into the pilot seat located in the row in front of the two dinner passengers. Once strapped in himself, Robbie looked over his shoulder.

"Comfy?"

"It's pretty tight back here," Kookie replied.

Robbie smiled. "No, it's cozy...I must ask you to use the proper terminology." Then he turned his attention to pre-flight check and revved up both engines on the tiny airplane. On taxi to the runway, Tony explained the evening's itinerary over the roar of the two engines into Kookie's ear.

"Robbie's going to fly us up and down Puget Sound to look at the city lights and the firework displays. Dinner's right here," as he opened up the wicker basket crammed in between their two feet and began holding up and naming each course of the meal.

"Cheese...bread...salami...fruit...wine...two slices of Death by Chocolate cake...and...one red rose," he announced as he handed her a rose bud from the basket.

"Oh my, God! This is amazing!" Kookie cooed as the plane buzzed off the runway and into the darkening sky over the slate grey water below them. The noise of the engines did not allow for much conversation. That, however, was not necessarily a drawback as both of them peered out the window at the sparkling lights outlining the waterline of the sound on the rare clear night in the Pacific Northwest.

Tony removed a small wooden cutting board from the bottom of the picnic basket and deftly cut pieces of cheese and salami. He set the cutting board on Kookie's lap as he pulled a bottle of red wine and a corkscrew from the wicker box. Tony poured a glass of wine and handed it to her. She furrowed her brow and shook her head. Tony returned the furrowed brow and raised his shoulders in confusion. Kookie leaned over and spoke directly into his ear, "I don't drink." She immediately saw his spirit fall from his face, but reluctantly accepted the glass just to be polite – he had gone out of his way to make this special – she didn't want to hurt his feelings.

He leaned over and cupped his hand over her ear, "Just sip and nurse it…it goes so well with the cheese and salami." She nodded and took a sip. Her raised eyebrow displayed her surprised satisfaction. Tony gave her an 'I told you so' gesture with one hand and a nod of his head. Kookie shook off his condescending grin with a grin of her own and turned her attention back outside her window. Each of them nibbled away at the Spartan yet eloquent meal for the next 90 minutes as they first winged their way south toward Tacoma and then north back up the west side of the sound to the airfield in Mukilteo. The skyline of downtown Seattle shimmered and the exploding fireworks seemed like exclamations points to the lovely view. Tony turned away from his window to watch Kookie gaze out hers. At one point, he noted her wine glass was empty. He held up the bottle and gently tapped her shoulder inquiring if she wanted a refill, to which she nodded.

Once landed, Robbie carefully parked the plane and killed the engine. "So…how was that?" he asked, removing his headphones and craning his neck to the back seat of the plane.

"It was amazing!" Kookie exclaimed.

"Perfect, Rob…absolutely perfect! Thanks!"

"It was my pleasure. Besides, it gave us an excuse to touch base again. Let's not wait another decade, shall we bro?" Robbie exuded.

As the trio began to unwrap themselves from the cramped interior of the plane, Tony held up the wine bottle.

"Hold on. We can't get back into the car with an open container…here, let's kill this," as he poured the remainder of the wine into their glasses. As a novice drinker, Kookie was already feeling the effects of the first two glasses she had nursed in the past hour. Still, she had to confess it did taste good. After all these years of abstinence, she was surprised how much she actually liked both the taste and the slight buzz she was feeling. In their rush to get back to Tony's rental car, both of them essentially gulped, rather than sipped, the last of the wine.

The three of them exchanged hugs and farewells back inside the tiny, but elegant executive terminal.

"Wait a sec…let me make a quick stop to the ladies room," Kookie said.

She gazed in the mirror to touch up her hair and inspect her face, flushed after drinking the wine. She couldn't help but wonder what this whole evening was about and where it was going. Satisfied with her appearance, but still pondering Tony's motive, she rejoined him in the lobby.

Tony gently grabbed Kookie's arm to escort her to the rental car.

"That was so lovely, Tony. You went all out on this, tonight," Kookie said as they pulled out of the parking lot.

"It was fun, wasn't it?" Tony replied as he looked out the windshield.

"So how do the two of you know each other?"

"Oh, Robbie used to help fly in supplies for my franchise."

"He worked for Tower Records?"

"No," Tony replied flatly.

"Oh. Well what then?"

"He helped out with shipping for one of my side projects."

Kookie sensed Tony was being cryptic. She speculated what it was being shipped and what Tony's "franchise" might entail. She decided not to pursue the topic. Instead, she decided to change it.

"I noticed you're not wearing a ring," she observed coyly.

Tony kept staring ahead out the windshield. "Neither are you."

"So…is there anyone in your life?" she probed.

Tony sighed. "Not right now. There was. Things didn't work out."

"I'm sorry."

Tony shook his head. "Don't be. It turned out for the best in the long run. What about you…anybody in your life right now?"

His question shook her. No one had ever asked her this. She had never had to respond truthfully and painfully.

"No," was all she said. Once again, she found herself wanting to shift the topic of discussion.

"What a gorgeous evening. It was such an amazing way to enjoy the fireworks. I guess the only downside was we couldn't really talk, could we?" she added.

Tony nodded his head in agreement. "But we can talk now," he suggested.

"I'd like that," she confessed.

Tony turned to look at her and smiled. "I would, too."

She turned to look out her passenger window adding, "Where should we go to talk?"

Almost immediately, the car made a right turn into the parking lot of a hotel perched next to the ferry ramp. Kookie turned toward Tony and gave him a knowing look as he parked the car.

"I thought you wanted to talk?" she said accusatorily.

"I do. This is where I'm staying. We can go up to my room and talk."

"Uh huh," she muttered suspiciously.

Tony smiled at her as he turned off the ignition. "Besides…we missed the last ferry."

Kookie gave him faux scowl and wagged a chiding finger at him. "You timed this well…didn't you?" she accused him. He shrugged off her flimsy accusation and opened his car door. She sat in the passenger seat, shaking her head in disbelief as he walked around to her side and opened the passenger door. Tony offered a gallant hand, which she accepted, to help her out of the car.

They walked into the hotel and rode the elevator in silence. Walking down the hall, Kookie still felt the effects of the wine. She was such a lightweight given her lack of experience. She ran her hand along the wall to help maintain her balance. They soon arrived at Tony's room where he unlocked the door and held it open for Kookie. She froze as soon as she stepped across the threshold. The floor was sprinkled with red rose petals. She followed them past the bathroom door and into the room to find more on top of the bed. Kookie gasped slightly and held her hand to the base of her throat. She stood there, taking it all in – the romantic dinner in flight plus the rose petals – Tony had clearly gone over the top. She wondered what on earth was she doing, allowing herself to be swept off her feet in this way.

While pondering the reality of the moment, Tony walked up behind her and slipped his arms around her from behind, pressing up against her. Again, Kookie felt her breath catch as she raised her head and leaned back against Tony's chest. He loosened her bun, letting her hair fall. He nuzzled the back of her neck with his chin that was now slightly bristled with the day's growth of whiskers. She felt the hairs on her arms rise with goose bumps and her nipples unexpectedly harden. As Tony could feel her beginning to melt in his arms, he spun her around and kissed her gently on the lips. When he pulled away, Kookie ran her fingers through his hair and looked into his eyes. The firework display continued.

"Come here, you!" she grinned coyly.

Chapter 57

Kookie was in the shower when room service arrived with breakfast the next morning. She had hoped she'd be able to wash away some of the confusion and remorse she had incurred over the past few hours. How could she have let herself succumb to Tony's charms – *again* – after all these years? What did all of this mean? What was she thinking? What was she feeling?

She came out of the bathroom with a towel wrapped around her, toweling her wet hair with another as Tony was pouring the coffee next to the two plates filled with croissants and fresh fruit on top of the executive desk.

"Perfect timing!" he exclaimed as she sat on the end of the bed.

"WOW! Look at this!" Kookie gushed.

He handed her a cup of coffee before grabbing his own and sitting down in the lounge chair off to the side of the disheveled bed. Tony perched both elbows on the arms of the chair and gazed at her. She could feel him look at her as she sipped her coffee. To divert his attention, she leaned over to set the coffee cup down and grab a strawberry. They looked at each other while she munched on the fruit.

"Maybe we need to talk – since we didn't actually do much talking last night," she suggested.

Tony played coy. "What do you want to talk about?"

Kookie tilted her head in annoyance. "About this…about last night."

Tony nonchalantly set his coffee cup down on the side table next to his chair. He sighed before continuing. "Look…last night just happened."

"Don't give me that, Tony. Rose petals don't just happen to fall out of nowhere on the floor and on top of the bed."

He grinned. "Fair enough. But, to be honest, that's not the reason I came to your shop to track you down."

Kookie sucked the sweet red juice off her fingers before reaching over to pull a piece of the croissant off the plate. She popped the fluffy pastry into her mouth. "Uh, huh. So what was the reason if it wasn't to seduce me – which I'm chagrinned to admit this is not the first time you've done that."

Tony's grin broadened. "No, that was not the original plan. But I will admit that the idea of seducing you came to me after I saw you in the shop. You are as lovely as you were back in the day."

She continued to dry her hair with the towel in a futile attempt to distract his attention from her blushing face. "So, what was the original plan?"

"I already told you…yesterday in the shop." Her blank stare revealed her confusion so he continued. "You know…a franchise."

Kookie dropped both hands into her lap. "You weren't serious were you?"

"It's what I do."

Kookie shook her head in disbelief.

"Hear me out," Tony pleaded.

She sighed. "I'm listening."

"Two things. First, we brand and package your cookies."

Kookie rolled her eyes but Tony continued.

"Haven't you heard of Famous Amos? Mrs. Fields?"

"I have no idea who these people are."

It was Tony's turn to roll his eyes. "Both of them are making a shit-load of money selling cookies. But wait…"

Kookie interrupted, "But wait! There's more…if you act now, you can get the Ginzu knives at no extra cost! Her mocking didn't crack a smile or his armor.

"Secondly…" he paused dramatically to continue his pitch, "your…*space*…as you call it…*that*…" he emphasized, " is unique and special!"

This caught Kookie's attention. This much she agreed with. Was it possible to spread a little bit of that joy? "Go on," she said.

Pleased with her willingness to listen, Tony got up and began pacing the room in an attempt to quell some of his energy. "We create some other shops…like the one you have now…but we're very strategic and selective about the location. The building has to feel a certain way. The city or neighborhood has to have the right kind of vibe…perhaps a college town or some bohemian artist village."

Kookie's curiosity was piqued, but she remained skeptical. She recalled Margot's comment at the Amazing Grace Coffeehouse two decades earlier that you just can't clone some things.

"Any place you have in mind?" she asked mostly to be polite as opposed to being genuinely serious about his plan.

"I don't know. L.A. wouldn't be right. Berkeley maybe…it's a college town…that seems like a no-brainer. Maybe Carmel or Monterrey – but they may be too upper crust, if you know what I mean. Ojai is too far off the beaten path. It has to have some earthy granola funk as well. Perhaps Santa Cruz – it's a funky college town."

Kookie knew of Berkeley by reputation but knew next to nothing about any of the other possible sites. In all honesty, she truly wasn't all that interested in Tony's proposal. That is why she surprised herself when she heard what came out of her mouth.

"What about Santa Barbara?"

Tony pointed his chin up as he deliberated her question. "Hmm – that's a possibility. It has a college ghetto out by the university and the town itself has sort of a funky shimmer to it. I hadn't thought about it. We can go check it out if you'd like."

Her motivation for the field trip wasn't even remotely related to the folly of trying to replicate the space she had created on Whidbey Island. It was just an excuse – a cleverly veiled excuse – to see Joey again. For some reason, Tony's sudden reappearance rekindled the memory and warmth of the past. At the same time, she couldn't help but wonder what Joey would think of a space like the one she had created. The last two times she had been with him – their shared apartment in Hollywood and his office in Santa Barbara – ended on a bad note, which in hindsight she regretted. The last time she saw him he had, after all, offered one of his songs encouraging her to sing again. Instead of accepting his olive branch, she had reprimanded him. Both times a beautiful young woman had been part of the equation that seemed to add up to her resentment and regret.

Tony noted Kookie continued staring blankly out the window, hopefully pondering his plan. "So?" he asked not so much for her thoughts, but to bring her back to the room.

Kookie blinked. "Interesting."

"That's all?" Tony was somewhat taken aback by her bland response.

"No, that's not what I meant. I was just…you know…thinking. So, what are you proposing?"

"I'm proposing the two of us take a little trip. Scope out some of these places…just to feel them out."

"I suppose I'd never know for sure and I'd always wonder…" her thoughts trailed off but re-energized Tony.

"Does that mean you'd consider it?" Tony held his breath.

Kookie stood up and walked over to the mirror. She ran her fingers through her wet hair. "It means I'd check it out…maybe not all of those places. Perhaps start out with one."

Tony was relieved. He did not anticipate her willingness to consider his proposal. "Wow! Well then…when and where? Do you have any preference?"

"Oh, I don't know. How about Santa Barbara? Do you have any leads there?"

"I can get some."

"Well…I guess I'd be up for a little field trip."

Tony smiled. "It'll be a nice get away. Just the two of us. We can pick up where we left off and get reacquainted."

Chapter 58

Two days later, the two of them were on a plane headed to Santa Barbara. It was Kookie's first time away from her shop since her mother's death – not counting the off and on jaunts to record her last album in L.A. The trip back to Minnesota could hardly be considered a vacation, but in some respects, neither could this little impromptu junket. This was, supposedly, a business trip. In her way of thinking, this was…well…she wasn't sure what it was. In mid-flight she was able to discern it definitely was not a romantic getaway despite Tony's attempt to frame it as such. This truth revealed itself listening to Tony's manic preoccupation with the potential of a business venture. His random thumbing through the latest issue of *Rolling Stone* magazine seemed to simply generate a host of ideas and questions and unbridled speculation in a foreign language – infrastructure, profit margins, marketing, branding, scalability, tent-poling, moving-the-goal posts – all of which had next to no meaning to Kookie. He was obsessed with the business possibilities as opposed to the possibilities of them – together. She just looked out the window, tired of the one-sided conversation. Kookie couldn't help but think about that night in the attic at The House when she pondered if it was he who used her or the other way around. All in all, the main thing she recalled from that night was her resolve to remain in control and never again surrender to ill-conceived impulses. In many ways, the past two days was reminiscent of that night so many years ago.

They touched down shortly after noon and picked up their rental car. Kookie continued looking out the window – this time on terra firma – toward the mountains. The modest municipal airport was near the university. Tony pulled out the map the agent had provided at the counter and studied it.

"OK – here's the airport. It looks like we're only about 15 minutes from Isla Vista."

Kookie turned toward him. "Isla Vista?" she inquired.

"Yeah, it's the community adjacent to the university. I thought we'd start there. I have an appointment with a business realtor at 1:30." Tony looked at his watch. "Perfect timing! Any way, there's a former pizza joint up for sale. I thought we'd check it out."

Kookie shrugged. "Sounds like a plan," she offered flatly as she returned her gaze out the window.

Tony sensed the indifference in her voice. "What's wrong? Aren't you pumped about this?"

With a sudden sense of remorse, Kookie turned back toward him. "Sorry. Just a little tired, I guess. It's all a bit overwhelming." She feigned a smile.

Tony reached over and squeezed her hand. "I know. It can be. But trust me. This is my thing. It's what I do. It's like I have this sixth sense about properties."

He stopped his effusive assurance long enough to assess her response which was nothing more than a half-hearted smile and nod of the head. Tony removed his hand from hers and started the ignition. They exited the airport parking lot and ventured just a few miles along a freeway before pulling off into a hamlet of cheap, rundown apartment buildings and bungalows. The high-rise dormitories from the nearby campus dotted the horizon. What amounted to the downtown area – if one could call it that – was a hodge-podge of record stores, surf shops, head shops, and fast food joints.

They arrived to the shuttered pizza shop that was squeezed in between a bike shop and a laundromat. Its façade was a single door bordered by two large picture windows. The real estate agent met them at the front door and escorted them inside. Kookie made her way into the center of the room – stopped and stood there, carefully inspecting it. Despite being vacated for several months, the place still reeked of beer and cigarettes. The walls were covered with cheap paneling, lined with beat up, worn out naughahyde booths. The counter suggested customers came up and ordered from there. A few wooden tables and chairs filled the center of the room. While the real estate agent chattered on about location, location, location being so close to campus, Bessie made her way into the back kitchen area. Clearly the huge pizza ovens could work for baking cookies. That, however, was the only redeeming attribute of the entire dreadful venue.

Tony enthusiastically turned to Kookie. "So, what do you think?"

Keeping to her mid-western upbringing, Kookie politely deflected his question and the realtor's hopeful smile to camouflage her disappointment with, "Can we think about it and get back to you?"

The optimistic realtor expressed that they could take all the time in the world, as she handed each of them her business card. The three of them exited the way they came in and shook hands. Kookie and Tony climbed back into the rental car. Tony pulled a folded piece of paper out of his shirt pocket and retrieved the map from the dashboard.

"Well, that's one down. Let's see here..." he paused as he ran his finger over the map, attempting to locate their next venue.

"Tony?" Kookie meekly whispered.

Without taking his eyes off the map, he responded with a preoccupied, "Uh huh?"

Kookie cleared her throat. "Tony...we need to talk."

This captured his full attention. He expertly folded up the map and set it back on the dashboard before turning sideways to face Kookie.

"OK. What about?"

Kookie sighed and turned to look out the passenger window in search of courage. She finally turned back to him. "This. We need to talk about...this." She raised both hands gesturing to the interior of the car as well as what was churning inside her.

"What do you mean?"

She could hear the confusion and apprehension in his voice. She leaned her elbow against the car door and rubbed her forehead. Tony jumped in, hoping to salvage the moment.

"Look, I admit that wasn't exactly what we had in mind. But hey, there are lots of other possibilities. We just need to…"

Kookie cut him off. "No. Well, I mean, you're right…about this place," she nodded toward the pizza joint through the car window and stopped to collect her thoughts.

Tony spoke up. "I agree. Now…I know what you're thinking…you're…"

Kookie interrupted him again. "No, Tony. You don't. You *don't* know what I'm thinking."

Her abrupt rebuff silenced his presumed telepathy. "OK. Well then…what *are* you thinking?"

Kookie leaned her head back and sighed once again. "I've been thinking about it…everything over the past few days. Thinking about you showing back up in my life after all these years. Thinking about your idea…your dream of cloning the cookie shop. Thinking about us."

She stopped.

"And?" Tony probed.

Kookie flopped both of her hands into her lap. "This isn't going to work."

"What isn't going to work?"

"This. All of it. Us."

Tony placed both hands on the steering wheel as if to anchor him and his emotions. "I see."

"Don't be angry. Please, don't. I'm…I'm so flattered and overwhelmed by what's happened these past few days…by your energy and exuberance. Really, I am. But…"

"But what?"

"But I can't do this. You're chasing something and I'm thrilled you think you want me and what I do to be part of it…whatever that is…but…" Kookie could not complete her thoughts.

"I see." Tony stated flatly. "So…what now?"

"I'm not sure…other than there's no reason to take this…this charade any further."

He cleared his throat. "A charade?" he repeated with disbelief and contempt.

"No, no, no. Let me explain. Me…*I'm* the one playing a charade. I've just been pretending to go along with this…all of it…the franchise…us. I'm sorry, but I have to be honest. None of this is going to work."

"Well now…" Tony considered what to say next.

Kookie quickly surveyed the street. "Look…why don't you just let me out right here. I'll be OK, really I will. I'll make my way back home. Let's just…I don't know…call it quits before it has a chance to start."

Tony stared out the windshield, with both hands still gripping the steering wheel. Kookie gently placed her hand on his shoulder.

"Tony…please…"

He violently brushed her hand off and suddenly reached across the front seat to fling the passenger door open. "Get out," he said flatly.

He didn't shout, which in some ways might have been easier to take. It was not a request. It was simply an order. Kookie recoiled and sat there with one hand at her throat. Not raising his voice, he repeated, "Get out, I said."

Kookie climbed out and stood next to the car. The trunk lid suddenly released and popped up slightly. Taking the cue, she moved to the back of the car to remove her carry-on suitcase and set it down on the pavement after closing the trunk. The back tires suddenly squealed and spun, sending wisps of blue smoke into the air. The passenger door slammed shut with the inertia of the car lurching forward and down the street.

Kookie watched Tony drive off. She had let go. She leaned down to pick up her suitcase and stepped back up the curb and on to the sidewalk to discover the real estate agent still standing there, apparently a witness to the entire scene as she perused her notes in her black leather portfolio. Kookie nervously pulled her hair back with her hand and looked at the woman, raising her chin slightly.

"Are you OK?" the realtor asked shyly.

Kookie simply nodded.

"Can I give you a lift somewhere?" she offered.

Chapter 59

The kind real estate agent transported Kookie to a nearby Motel 6 where she was able to reserve a modest room for two nights. There was a nostalgic symmetry to this – given that the chain of economical motels were given birth here in Santa Barbara and that she and Joey had always stayed in one during their early years on the road.

Kookie called Joey, saying she was passing through town and wondered if he'd like to get together for lunch. He did. They agreed to meet at little bistro close to the beach. She took a cab, arriving first. Staring out at the waves, she was reminded of her previous life in Venice Beach. Her flashback was interrupted.

"Sorry I'm late. Waited long?"

Kookie turned to see Joey standing by the table. She rose and gave him a hug.

"No, not long. I'm glad you could make it."

"I'm glad you reached out."

The two of them gazed at each other for a moment without speaking. After ordering and eating with some small talk, Kookie was compelled to lean over the table during dessert to offer her observation from the meal.

"Joey, you don't look so good."

"I don't feel so good."

"Why? What's wrong?"

"Ummm…it's nothing." Joey fumbled with his fork.

Kookie sat back in her chair. "It's that girl, isn't it?" Joey's silence confirmed her hunch. "OK, Joey...what happened?"

"You were right."

She just looked at him knowingly. "I'm sorry."

"I'll get over it."

"I know *you* will...how is *she* doing?"

"OK, I guess."

"You guess?"

"I don't know. I haven't seen or heard from her. It's been almost a year."

Kookie sighed. "You haven't changed."

"Probably never will either."

"No, probably not." Kookie flopped back into the booth with an exasperated sigh.

"Joey..." she waited for permission to continue.

"Yeah?" Joey finally responded while continuing to play with the fork on the table.

"You amaze me. You want to know why?"

He chuckled, "I have a feeling you're going to tell me."

Kookie earnestly leaned across the table once again resting her weight on her elbows. "You have the uncanny ability to see into others' lives...their thoughts...their feelings. And then, you somehow take that jumbled mess and make sense out of it. You write a song and the listener starts to wonder, 'How did he know?' You can sense the meaning and feeling of someone else's song and add your own unique take on it and turn it into something totally new without compromising the integrity of it. There's a word for that." Kookie left him dangling and he took the bait.

"Which is?" his eyebrows raised in wonder.

"Insight. You somehow crawl into a person, a song, a story and reveal its meaning to the rest of the world. That's a gift."

Joey nervously twirled his thumbs as he listened. "Thanks."

Kookie once again leaned back against the booth. "But here's the thing…" she hesitated while she carefully considered dropping the other shoe. "As much as you're able to get inside other people's stories, you never quite allow yourself to get into their lives. You stand on the edge watching."

Joey felt himself tense up. "That's what storytellers do…we tell the story. We're not part of it."

"But you sometimes forget that you *are* in the story…your story."

"Look at us. Look how I entered your life and your story to guide you on to fame and fortune," he retorted defensively.

"We're talking about two different things here, Joey. Yes, you guided me. You've guided others."

Joey scoffed at her example and turned his head away in disgust as she continued.

"But that's just it. You're good at shepherding but you're not good at getting personally involved. You don't allow yourself to get close to anyone."

Joey turned to see her gentle but condemning inference. In their years together, their relationship was strictly professional. They had never been intimate with each other. Part of the demarcation of affection was Joey's ethos of refraining from the quid pro quo culture of sleeping your way to success that he knew many artists and managers engaged in. Joey also knew part of the boundary was due to something deeper.

"I did…once. A long time ago. Right before I heard you sing in that pathetic little coffee house. And you know what..." his sudden revelation stopped him from continuing.

Kookie looked at him sympathetically as she completed his thought. "Yes, I know…you let yourself get close again during these last few months to that girl."

"Her name is Laurel," Joey corrected.

"Laurel," Bessie repeated.

It gradually dawned on him what she had tried to tell him in his office that day he played the song for and Laurel. They sat in silence looking at each other before Joey made his confession. "Look…I never knew how you felt…about us. I never…"

Kookie interrupted him, "I know. It's OK…at least it is now. You never knew because you've always seen what you wanted to see. The flip side of that is you never see what you don't want to see."

"It's easier that way."

"Maybe. But it can get awfully lonely, too."

They sat quietly for several minutes, looking at each other the way old friends do. Time has a way of revealing things. Joey stared at her as she waited for him to ask the inevitable question.

"So...what about the song? Do you want it?"

"Her song?"

Joey nodded.

"What do you think?"

"I had to ask."

Kookie sat there, tilting and gently shaking her head as she looked at him. "Remember that night at *The Box* when you gave me that cassette of your songs?"

"Of course I do."

"Well, all these years I've known they were written for or about someone else."

Joey's brow furrowed slightly. Kookie waited patiently for his response that never came. "You know...you've never written a song just for me."

Joey looked down as he rotated his fork nervously, saying nothing. Kookie watched him for what seemed like an eternity. She waited. And waited. She had waited all these years for him to share his feelings for her. Kookie suddenly realized her faint hope that he would do so here and now was merely that – hope. This moment was the fulcrum of her own feelings. Up to now, she had cautiously triangulated what and how she was feeling about the three men who had taken a part of her away. And now, at the close of this odyssey, she had made her final discovery. Finally, she made a show of checking her wristwatch.

"I need to get going," she lied.

Her announcement brought Joey out of his trance.

"So soon?" He seemed genuinely disappointed as well as dazed.

Kookie nodded and bit her lip, trying to conceal her own pain. In truth, she wasn't leaving for nearly 24 hours when she would catch Amtrak's Costal Starlight around noon and cocoon herself in her own private sleeper car on the trip up the coast. She had made the reservation on a whim, partially recalling the nights she and Joey had spent in Union Station in L.A., imagining where those trains might take them. Funny – it was there in the waiting room of the art deco train station that Joey predicted he would find his way to Santa Barbara.

The two of them gazed at each other silently. Joey finally stood and offered a sad smile before turning and walking away. No hug. No kiss. No goodbyes.

Chapter 60

The Coastal Starlight snaked its way around Point Conception – California's 'elbow' – and clung to the continent as it made its way back up the coast to Seattle. Ensconced in her tiny sleeper compartment, Kookie gazed at the Pacific coastline outside the window. She watched the swells roll and break along the shore and was suddenly reminded of Doc. She recalled his succinct treatise on measuring the peaks and valleys of waves in the brain that day on the patio behind the diner – and how he studied what happened in the space between them. This prompted her to ponder the peaks and valleys of her own life – her father's death, the strained yet peaceful coexistence with her anesthetized mother, being in the spotlight with an appreciative audience, loneliness, allowing songs to emerge from deep within her – just to name a few. For a moment, she took pity on herself for having her career swept away from her. And then, watching the waves recede from the sand, she realized it was she who had done the sweeping. It was she who had turned her back on her voice – her audience. Her career had not, as she had pathetically come to convince herself over the years, crashed and burned. None of her listeners…Tony…Benny and Ron…and even Joey for that matter – had abandoned her. It was she who had abandoned them.

White specks bobbing on the brilliant blue water brought her attention back to the world fleeting outside her window. In a moment, she recognized them to be seagulls. She marveled at how they were content to float on the water, oblivious to the rise and fall of the waves' energy passing beneath and past them. In a strange way they reminded her of Rocky. She envied his spiritual buoyancy. His presence alone seemed to buoy her. Despite acknowledging this, she floundered in her own emotional flailing to stay afloat as to why she had kept him at bay.

As usual, the train was running late, falling victim to giving the right of way of the rails to freight trains. As a result, it was dark by the time it crawled into the San Francisco Bay Area. The sleeping car attendant converted the two facing seats in her tiny compartment into a bed as the train made its way out of Jack London Square in Oakland. Kookie propped herself upright and stared out the window as the train continued to creep along the waterfront. She looked out into the darkness to see a few lights shimmering along the shore on the other side of the black, still water in San Pablo Bay as the train approached Martinez, California – the home of Joe DiMaggio and according to urban legend, the Martini – neither of which had any significance to her. The compartment's tiny nightlight above her head cast her reflection on the window. She gazed right through her image and into the darkness. The gentle rocking and rolling of the train relaxed her, gradually lulling her to sleep.

Chapter 61

Knock, knock, Knock.

"Anybody home?" Kookie timidly called, straining her voice through the open screen door. She leaned up against the mesh and shielded her eyes in an attempt to see inside. Boot steps from another room replied. She stood back from the door, running her hands down to smooth out her summer dress. Rocky came around the corner from the kitchen wearing a black t-shirt and jeans.

"Look who's here," he announced with a smile. He opened the screen door as an invitation.

Kookie was suddenly embarrassed. She looked down, avoiding those intense eyes of his.

"It's been a while…so I decided to…well…I thought I'd stop by and say hello."

"Well, hello," he chirped playfully. Rocky stood there letting her squirm a bit just for the fun of it. The man of few words stayed true to character. Unable to bear his patient silence any longer, Kookie raised her eyes to meet his.

"Yeah, well…I just wanted to stop by. I hope I'm not interrupting anything."

Rocky gently shook his head. "Nope. But I was just getting ready to head out into the orchard. Wanna join me?"

His invitation was liberating. She was beginning to feel somewhat caged in and stepping outside would give her a little more breathing room. "Ooh, that'd be nice."

He motioned with a jerk of his head for her to follow him back through the kitchen and out the back door. The 'Three Stooges" bleated their greeting to her as they entered the fenced-in yard.

"Hi, girls," Kookie returned their salutation. All three goats trotted toward her, allowing her to scratch their heads. Rocky paused to watch the exchange. He then turned and simply continued his slow walk toward the trees. Kookie had to jog to catch up. Rocky opened the gate and waited for her. Once they both cleared the fence, he latched the gate and pointed to some trees a few feet away.

"These here are Pristines. They're comin' on and will be ready to harvest soon – mid to late July."

Kookie bent down to duck under some low limbs and then gently caressed the pale fruit with admiration. Rocky watched her as she ran her hand over the branches. He spotted one apple on a higher branch and pointed at it.

"This one's about ready."

"Is it OK if I pick it and try it?"

Rocky warned, "It might be a little tart."

Kookie scrunched up her shoulders and grinned mischievously as his smile allowed her to pick it. She held it up to her mouth and looked up at him with trepidation. She finally took a bite. Her closed eyes and puckered cheeks elicited a chuckle from him.

"I warned you," he playfully chastised.

She continued to chew and then swallowed. "It's good, though."

Rocky inspected her with a knowing half-smile as she continued to munch on the apple. This unnerved her slightly and to recover she turned and began to slowly walk down the path between the trees. When he didn't follow, Kookie turned and looked at him quizzically. He met her eyes with a wry smile.

"So…what's up?" he asked.

His abrupt inquiry didn't surprise her. This was simply Rocky being Rocky. In some ways, this is what she expected – even hoped for. At the same time, he allowed the distance to buffer them as she gathered the thoughts she had rehearsed. She raised her eyebrows. She walked back toward him and offered him a bite from the apple she was holding in her hand. Rocky smiled and reached over, touching her hand that gripped the apple and bit into it.

"What do you want to know?" she asked devilishly.

"What do you want to tell me?"

She took another bite from the apple and tilted her head. "This seems rather biblical, don't you think?" she suggested and folded her arms across her chest.

He cocked his head to one side. "What do you mean?"

She grinned impishly. "Well…here I am…offering you a bite of the apple and you want to know what's up. If I recall my Sunday School lessons, Adam got into a lot of trouble when he asked Eve that same question when he bit into the apple she offered him. Are you sure you want to go there?"

"Somehow I get the feeling I'm already in trouble," he grinned.

Kookie shook her head in mock disgust, then turned to continue her slow saunter through the orchard. "Well…I've been doing lots of thinking…since we last saw each other," she said over her shoulder.

"About?" Rocky asked as he slowly followed her.

"About what you said."

"And what was that?"

"Well, for starters you shared your past…some of it, anyway."

"Would it help if I told you I wasn't completely honest?"

His confession surprised her. "What do you mean?"

"I didn't tell you my real name."

Relieved, she chuckled. "So…are you going to tell me now?"

He smirked. "Lawrence."

She laughed aloud. "Lawrence?" she repeated incredulously, "Where did 'Rocky' come from?"

"Not sure. I think it might have something to do with the rocking of the boat I was working on. Someone called me that once and it just stuck."

She shook her head with a smile. "Well, that was very brave of you – not just revealing your real name but sharing bits of your past with me."

He let her compliment run off his broad shoulders. The levity had helped ease some of the weight but her smile dimmed as she continued. "Well, I'm afraid I was a coward."

"Coward?" he repeated somewhat perplexed.

"Yes. I didn't share my story. I was afraid to." She glanced down at the ground, embarrassed.

"I didn't ask you to. Besides – you're entitled to your privacy."

She nodded. "True. But that's not all. I was also thinking about some of the other things you said."

"Like?"

"Like I'm holding on to something."

"And?"

"I was."

"And you're not now?"

He had opened a door and was inviting her to cross the threshold. She nervously fingered the leaves on a branch, gathering the courage and words to continue.

"Well...I actually realized that I was grasping...reaching...trying to hold on to something...lots of things, I guess. And..." she paused.

He waited patiently, saying nothing, prompting her to continue.

She turned to him and said, "But...you can't let go of something you never really had...can you?"

"No. I suppose you can't," he confirmed in a gentle, manner-of-factual way.

Kookie sighed before launching into an abbreviated version of her quest. She spoke of the father she never knew and of a barely functioning mother. She confessed she had loved but had never been loved by anyone. Fame and fortune brought her loneliness.

Rocky listened, not saying a word. When she ran out of steam, she caught her breath before revealing the epiphany she had experienced on the train.

"I've been stumbling along for so long…and I told myself I had to get back up. I came to realize that everything I was looking for was right here…waiting for me. It almost seems like everything that came before was designed to bring me here…to this place…to you."

Hearing herself finally articulate what she had been refusing to recognize elicited a slight audible gasp. At first, she was embarrassed but that was soon erased by the sudden liberation of the true feelings she had kept to herself for so long. She watched and waited for a reaction.

Rocky leaned down to pluck a tall strand of grass and clinched it between his teeth. "Thanks for sharing."

She didn't expect anything more than his typical understated manner. "Thanks for listening."

He turned his head and gazed off into the distance. "There's one thing, though…"

She became flustered. What had she said or done? Had she said too much? Too little? Kookie finally mustered up a tentative response. "What's that?"

He turned his eyes back to her. "There's some truth when you said you can't let go of something you've never had. But...my guess is you have, indeed, 'let go'—maybe not of what you thought you were reaching for – but here and now – letting go of that baggage you've been luggin' around with you all these years."

Hearing this, a deep cleansing breath escaped from Kookie. She suddenly buried her face in her hands and sobbed. Rocky kept his distance. He did not approach her or offer a consoling hug. He simply accompanied her on her journey that had now come to an end. When she finally regained her composure, Kookie wiped the tears from her cheeks and looked up, before giving an embarrassed chuckle.

"My – I didn't see that coming."

"We never do," Rocky confirmed.

Kookie wiped her nose with the back of her hand. "My goodness – I'm a wreck."

Rocky offered a caring smile. "You know..." he paused carefully calculating his words before continuing, "I'm listening to everything you've told me...not just today, but things you've said in the past and it's got me to thinking."

Kookie took a deep breath and ran her hand through her hair. "Geez, I can only imagine what you think of me," she said with embarrassment.

Rocky shook his head with a smile. "No, no – I was thinking your story sort of reminds me of another story I read a long time ago."

Kookie sniffed one last time as she composed her self and asked, "Oh yeah? What story was that?"

"Ever read Homer's *Odyssey*?"

She blinked. His oblique question out of nowhere caught Kookie off guard. "In high school. Why?"

He sucked on the end of the grass and smiled. "I guess you remind me a little bit of Odysseus."

Kookie's head snapped slightly back as she chuckled aloud. "I do?"

Rocky merely nodded with a grin and offered no further explanation. "Well?" Kookie impatiently implored for some clarity.

He continued to casually stroll through the orchard with her tagging along. "Do you remember Odyssesus' oar?" he finally asked.

Exasperated, she retorted, "Geez, Rocky, I read that years ago. No...I don't remember."

"Well then, I guess that could be sort of a homework assignment," he said with a grin.

She furrowed her eyebrows. "What are you talking about?"

He just grimed at her.

She put her hands on her hips and shook her head in disbelief. "You want me to go back and re-read the Odyssey...that's what you're saying?"

His silent smile was his only response. Kookie suddenly felt very shy as she scuffed the toe of her sandal in the dirt. "So now what?"

Rocky sucked between his teeth. "What do you mean?"

"I mean us…where do we go from here?" she asked.

He leaned against the trunk of one his trees. "I'm not sure." His honesty stung. This was not the answer she wanted to hear. Rocky then added, "But I do know one thing, though."

She looked up with some trepidation. "What's that?"

"I'd like to go there…wherever that might be with you…when the time's right."

Kookie felt her heart skip a beat. "You're sure? After all I've said and done?"

He nodded. Then he calmly added, "But not today. We both need some time to ease into…whatever this is."

She bit her lip. "OK."

They looked deeply into each other. Rocky smiled and said, "Well then…you'd better get going…you have some homework to do."

Chapter 62

A few months later, Kookie rejoined her friends on the patio at Doc's Diner one afternoon after closing time. It had been a while since all of them had gathered for their afternoon ritual.

"So…tell us how this works." Ruthie commanded as she cut her cigar. Denise and Doc had already cut and lit theirs and were sitting back in their Adirondack chairs on the back patio of the diner waiting for a reply. Kookie was focused on slowly rotating her Rocky Patel cigar over the blue flame of the butane lighter, holding her audience in suspense. As soon as she finished torching her cigar, she passed the lighter to the matriarch of the group. Kookie sat back in her chair and drew from her maduro cigar, letting the blue smoke spiral up and away.

"There's not that much to explain," Kookie replied honestly.

Ruthie and Denise exchanged disgruntled glances. Doc just puffed away. Denise chimed in. "I mean, like…did you move in together?"

"Not really…well…sort of," Kookie replied unconvincingly.

Ruthie harrumphed impatiently. "What do you mean, 'not really?'"

"I mean, I have a toothbrush over there…he has one at my place," Kookie explained.

Denise scowled. "What are you? Some kind of nun or what?"

Kookie chuckled as she rolled an ash off her cigar into the ashtray. "No. We each have our own place."

Ruthie rose up in her chair with an air of approval. "Well now...that sounds downright old fashioned if you ask me."

"Nobody asked you," Doc chortled. Ruthie playfully whacked him on the shoulder.

Kookie scanned the circle of friends and continued. "I don't know...it just sort of happens. Our relationship seems to evolve on it's own. Sometimes I go over to his place...sometimes he comes over to mine. I'll help out with a few chores at his farm. He'll deliver his produce and cheese to my house. Sometimes we don't see each other for nearly a week."

Denise took a long draw from her cigar and raised her head to let the smoke escape along with her unbridled prurient curiosity. "So, how's the sex?"

"Denise!" Ruthie chided in shock.

"Well? All of us are wondering. I just happened to have the guts to ask." She turned to Kookie to add, "And?"

Kookie smiled. "Sometimes we just lay next to each other...and cuddle."

"Jesus!" Denise exclaimed. "I'd go for some of that as much as I would go for some hot n' heavy..."

Doc interrupted. "Good for you, Kookie. I'm glad things have worked out...for both of you."

Kookie looked deep into the old man's eyes. "Me, too."

Chapter 63

The days...the weeks...the months...the years settled into a comfortable, shared domestic routine, tucked in between the life of the cookie shack and the farm. More and more of her clothes took up space in his closet as did his in hers. Coming to terms on important topics of debate such as which way the toilet paper goes on the roller and how to 'correctly' wash the dishes ensued and were resolved. Soon, each of them could finish each other's sentences through shorthand conversation. Acceptance of each other's quirkiness such as putting up with Rocky wearing socks to bed because he had a severe case of terminal cold feet and Kookie's penchant for eating peanut butter out of the jar with a spoon while watching Monty Python solidified their shared existence in between the two households. They also surrendered to the inevitable changes in their appearance and bodies. Kookie's sandy hair had whitened and she kept it knotted up in a bun and a few wrinkles had gathered around the corner of her eyes. All in all, she had taken on a handsome look. Rocky had become barrel-chested and was beginning to bald on the crown of his head. Rituals and routines evolved organically – such as the unspoken expectation that the host made breakfast the next morning after the guest spent the night at one of their homes.

As they both seemed to tangle-up the sheets at night, Kookie especially relished the lazy mornings when they would both stir and wake up early at the same time and make love. Afterwards, they would spoon together in the glow of the moment. Because Rocky was inclined to go to bed early and be the first one up the next day she considered him a morning person. She, however, was a night owl as it was hard to decompress after the shop closed up around 9:00 pm. When at her place, as she did on the road, Kookie would soak in her clawfoot bathtub late at night. It helped her unwind. She had to settle for a shower at his house – accepting it as more of a utilitarian task rather than relaxation. Most often, she would wake up in his bedroom, finding his side of the bed empty and the aroma of coffee and bacon wafting through the house. When it was her turn to make breakfast, it was usually simple – homemade yogurt from milk provided by the two new goats Rocky bought after the 'Three Stooges' moved on to greener pasture. He let her name them – she chose Queenie and Sweet Pea. The creamy yogurt was topped with granola and blueberries in wooden bowls and eaten with wooden spoons that Rocky had hand-carved. Her culinary skills were limited in that respect. She rationalized she had to reserve her creativity and energy to oversee the 'kookies' and menu of her shop. Rocky merely chalked it up to the fact she was not a morning person.

One morning, while showering at Rocky's, Kookie lathered her body with Rocky's homemade soap – also made from his goats' milk. In the process, she felt something.

Rocky was just folding her mushroom omelet when she came into his kitchen. Having spent nearly a decade together, he immediately noticed the alarm on her face when she came into the kitchen.

"What's wrong?"

She blinked herself out of her glazed concern through a faux smile in a failed attempt to appear chipper. "Nothing," she lied.

He continued to look at her as he slid her omelet out of the pan and on to her plate. She took her seat at the table and began poking at the omelet with her fork.

"You look upset," he said as he sat down and held his coffee mug in his hand.

"It's nothing, I said."

He continued staring at her. "I'm not buying it. What is it?"

It had been a long time since she heard him speak so forcefully. She laid her fork down. "I found a lump."

He let the word sink in and said nothing.

She watched him ponder her report and then added, "In my breast."

He took a sip of coffee. "I see."

She raised her fork and took a bite of the omelet. "It's probably nothing…most likely a cyst," she remarked, chewing on the possible ramification of her discovery.

They sat in silence for a few minutes.

"Are you going to have it checked?" he finally uttered tenderly. He watched her continue to poke at her omelet for what seemed like an eternity. Still looking down at the breakfast he had made for her she simply said, "Yeah."

Chapter 64

A gentle Pacific Northwestern rain pattered on the roof as they lay in bed together the night she was released from the hospital. Kookie gingerly rolled onto her good side, sore from the surgery, turning away from Rocky. He cozied up next to her and wrapped his arm around her, over her nightgown and bandages.

"No. Don't," she said curtly.

He gently removed his arm and began to caress her back with his hand. He could feel her body shudder as she quietly cried. They listened to the rain long into the night. When the rain finally subsided, Kookie whimpered, "I guess now we're even."

Rocky silently juggled her words. "What do you mean?" he probed as he pulled her hair back and stoked her neck.

Her body rose and fell with her breathing.

"I mean..." she paused.

He waited.

"Now it's my turn to be incomplete," she whispered.

Rocky gently ran his stumped hand down her spine. Then he raised his head slightly and whispered into her ear, "You make me whole, Kookie."

Kookie rolled over onto her back and looked at him through the tears in her eyes. She stroked his face with the back of her hand. "So do you," she murmured.

He propped himself up on his elbow and looked at her. "I'm glad."

She smiled and took a deep breath. "Rocky?"

"Yeah?"

She ran her finger over his lips. "Did I ever tell you that I finally read the Odyssey like you told me to?"

Rocky chuckled – amused that she would share this – on a night such as this. "No – you didn't."

Kookie turned her head to look up at the ceiling. "Well…I think I figured it out."

"Figured what out?"

"The oar."

Rocky furrowed his brow. "You mean…Odysseus' oar?"

She nodded her head causing the pillowcase to rustle. Then she slightly grimaced in pain and wrapped her arm around her chest.

"You OK?" Rocky asked.

She closed her eyes and nodded. "Just sore…that's all."

He waited for her to continue.

"I guess…" she paused to gather her thoughts, "…I guess my guitar was like the oar."

"And?"

"And I know this will sound corny or stupid…" she hesitated.

"Go on," he coaxed.

"It's sort of like how no one knew what his oar was and they thought it was some kind of tool to separate the seed from the chaff. I guess I sort of did the same thing with my spatula in a weird sort of way. I ended up here where no one really knew what my guitar was to me and what it meant in my life. Instead, everyone saw me with a spatula in hand. Finally, Odysseus found a new home and life…just like I did." She turned to see a broad smile on Rocky's face. "Does that make sense?" she added.

"It makes perfect sense."

The two of them gazed into each other's eyes. She reached over to clasp his wrist where his hand used to be and added, "I've been thinking."

"About?"

"There's something I want to do…something I *need* to do."

Chapter 65

She listened to the ringing on the other end of the line. It rang and rang. She was just about to hang up when he answered.

"Hello?"

It was good to hear Benny's chirpy voice.

"Benny? It's Bess," she replied in a subdued voice. She hadn't used that name in years.

"Bessie, Bessie, Bessie! It's so good to hear from you! Do tell what convinced you to slip away from your domestic bliss and cookie castle in the hinterlands long enough to reach out to this old queen."

Her long silence un-nerved him.

"Bess? Are you there? What's wrong, dear?"

The silence continued.

"Bess – talk to me. You're beginning to frighten me. What is it?" Benny implored.

She cleared her throat. "I think I still owe you one more album – isn't that right?"

Benny sighed with relief. "For Christ's sake…is *that* what's troubling you? I told you long ago there's no need to fret over such a trivial…"

She cut him off. "Benny – listen to me."

Her abrupt command was uncharacteristic of her and it only generated more concern on the part of her long-time friend and collaborator. She could hear him swallow hard over the phone. "What is it, Bess?"

The usual bounce in his voice was gone.

"Benny…"

"I'm listening."

"I'm sick."

"Sick? What do you mean?"

The silence was deafening.

"I have cancer." She waited for him to respond. When he didn't, she asked, "Benny?"

She could hear him sniff a tear away. "Yes, my dear. I'm here…I'm here for you."

"I think it's time to make good on that contractual agreement I have with you."

Benny chuckled. "Of course. Anything you want. You know that…don't you?"

"Yes."

The two of them allowed their emotions to recede. Benny finally asked, "What did you have in mind?"

"I'm not sure just yet. But I don't have a lot of time."

"I understand."

"And…well…I was thinking about…um…something you said when we met at LAX…about working with Joey again."

"I'm listening."

"I thought we might…you know…bring him in on this little project in some way – you know…for some closure."

"Oh, my dear… Joey has fallen off the face of the earth."

"What do you mean?"

"I mean he's disappeared. Poof! Gone. Nobody knows where he is or what he's up to. To be honest – I don't even know if he's…" Benny didn't finish his speculation.

"I see." Her voice was weak and pensive.

"How about bringing Ron in?" Benny cautiously explored.

"Maybe. But I can't tour. I'm just too…"

It was Benny's turn to cut her off. "I think it would be good for you…for the *two* of you, I mean. And…if you don't mind me saying so…" her clairvoyance interrupted his gentle chastising.

"I know, I know…I owe him."

Another long pause prevailed – each waiting for the other to speak. After Benny could no longer endure the silence, he continued to gently probe. "Would you like to reach out to Ron or do you want me to?" Benny suddenly became aware of the ticking clock on the wall of his office as he waited for her response.

"I don't know. Let me think about it."

Both of them took her reply to heart, allowing the gap in their conversation to deepen. Finally, she spoke up. "We'd have to record up here. I'm afraid I can't…"

"Say no more. We…I can find a studio in Seattle."

His willingness to surrender to her need choked her with emotion. "But what about your beloved sound board? The walls of that studio would never forgive you," she tearfully lamented.

"Never mind about that. Now tell me…any ideas about…a theme? Songs?"

He heard her sniff away her tears.

"Not just yet. I thought the two of us could figure that out."

"I would be thrilled and honored."

Chapter 66

Kookie was busy sorting through paperwork and computer files at her desk in her upstairs office area on a heavy autumn afternoon. Off and on, she would pause from her work and gaze out the dormer window. The grey skies hung low. The trees stood bare. It reminded her of the impending weariness of winter she had experienced in Minnesota, but without the unforgiving cold. Warm tomato soup from Rocky's tomatoes and grilled cheese sandwiches with cheese provided by Queenie and Sweat Pea would be the lunch special on a day like this. Kookie could hear *Bach's Prelude and Fugue #24 in B Minor* – a favorite of hers that matched the mood of the day – playing below. Charon was downstairs running the shop. For the moment, there were few guests, allowing both of them to putter on their respective tasks which is why neither of them were aware of the white rental car pulling up outside.

The squeaking hinges from the front door announced the handsome gentleman. Charon looked up and momentarily paused as she was slipping today's batch of cookies off the tray and on to the cooling rack. His looks were striking. He had a strong jaw and warm brown eyes. His black hair was perfectly coiffed. He was overdressed for the laid-back venue, wearing a blue blazer over a light blue dress shirt, sans tie, and khaki pants. A small leather satchel was in one of his hands. He slowly took in the space as he made his way toward the counter – taking special note of the guitar perched in the corner of the parlor. Charon had to regain her balance as he came closer. Once he arrived, he set his bag on the floor and smiled. Charon froze with spatula in hand and mouth slightly agape.

"Good afternoon," he said in a confident and professional manner.

Charon, regrouping, set the spatula down and wiped her hands on her apron. Thoroughly smitten, a meek, "Good afternoon," was all she could summon in the way of a response.

He smiled and stood there patiently. When no further salutation or offer to serve him came from the shell-shocked Charon, he took it upon himself to bring their stalled interchange to life.

"Yes…well then…I'm wondering if Bessie James might be around."

Charon's shock and frozen adoration gradually shifted to awkward caution. Obviously she was now aware of her friend and employer's true identity, but she was wary about revealing that awareness – as well as her whereabouts – to anyone – especially this man. He could see her sizing him up and debating how to respond. Before she could answer, he offered a preemptive clarification.

"Or perhaps should I say…is Kookie here?" He reached into his inside coat pocket to retrieve a business card and handed it to Charon. "I'm David Tucker – a music journalist and podcast producer. I heard the NPR story about her some years ago. I thought I might follow up…so-to-speak…focusing on her music."

Charon stared at the card and then looked back up at the man on the other side of the counter. It was clear she did not have to protect her friend's identity, as he already knew of her previous life. It was equally clear that this man did not pose any kind of threat, other than infringing upon her privacy. She rolled her tongue inside her cheek, deliberating what to say and do. Mr. Tucker simply stood there – smiling – awaiting a response.

"I'll check," and she turned away with his business card in hand, before adding, "You can wait down here."

"Thank you. I will," he replied with a slight nod of regal-like appreciation.

Charon tiptoed up the stairs to Kookie's office. She stood at the open doorway.

Tap, tap, tap.

"Kookie?"

"Hmmm?" she hummed as she continued to stare at the computer screen.

"There's a man here who'd like to speak to you."

"Is he a salesman? I'm not interested."

"No. He's a..." she stammered and glanced down at the business card in her hand and added, "...he's a journalist."

Kookie spun around in her chair to face Charon. "A journalist?"

Charon nodded and outstretched her hand offering the business card to Kookie who carefully studied it. She rubbed her hand over her head to feel its stumble.

"What does he want?"

"He said he wanted to follow up on the NPR story."

Kookie rolled her eyes. "That's ancient history," and tossed the card on her desk and returned her attention back to the computer. After a few seconds, Kookie realized Charon was still standing in the doorway. She turned back around. "And?" she inquired.

"Um, well...he said he wanted to talk to you about your music. And...he seems very nice. He's quite handsome," she added.

Kookie chuckled. "Is he now?"

Charon nodded with a knowing smile.

"And he wanted to talk about my music, huh?" Kookie clarified.

Charon nodded again.

"And handsome?" Kookie asked with a wry smile.

"Very!" Charon confirmed.

"Well...we don't want to be rude now, do we?" Kookie mused as she got up from her desk, taking his business card with her. The two of them walked back downstairs. Charon stayed in the kitchen as Kookie walked around in front of the counter with his business card in hand.

He straightened slightly when he saw her approach and outstretched his hand. She watched him carefully to see how he would react to her appearance. She refused to wear a wig or a scarf. It was as if she purposefully brandished the impact of the chemo treatment in defiance of the cancer that had spread and was taking her life away day by day.

"I'm David Tucker." He maintained a calm and strong demeanor – seemingly oblivious to her appearance.

Impressed, she shook his hand. "Hi. I'm Kookie James."

Walking down the stairs, she had determined to use her new identity to help frame the context of their conversation. She thought that would detour things away from music.

He smiled, aware of her ineffective tactic. "Yes...well. I'm wondering if I might have a few minutes of your time."

"I suppose. Here...let's move over here," she gently ordered as she steered him away from the three guests who were scattered about in the parlor area to a cozy nook off to the side. Once seated, she took another glance at his business card and then up at him. "So...what would you like to talk about? Oh...can I get you a drink...coffee? Latte? Chai tea? A cookie?"

He was pleased – if not surprised at the progress he was making with the reclusive woman sitting across from him. He felt the need to accept her cautious but gracious invitation. "Sure. A latte would be great...thanks."

Kookie raised her head and her voice, "Charon!"

"Yo!" came from the kitchen.

"A tall latte!"

"Iced or hot?"

Kookie turned her attention to her table guest.

"Hot, please."

"Hot!" Kookie called back.

"Got it!"

Kookie readjusted herself in her chair. "Now…where were we?" she asked.

"Well…Kookie…or should I call you Bessie?"

She didn't reply – she merely looked at him with a coy smile.

He continued. "As I was saying…I have a column for *In The Spotlight* magazine and a companion podcast. I've been doing a feature now for several weeks…it's getting a lot of 'likes' online. People seem to be interested in the stories I'm producing."

She gave him a sly smile. "But I'm no longer in the spotlight."

He returned the smile and continued. "The series is called, '*Where Are They Now?*' Like I said, it seems to have garnered quite a following. The analytics suggest the audience is mainly aging boomers. There seems to be a nostalgic dynamic at work here."

Kookie nodded. "Uh huh. I think I see where this is going."

Charon arrived with his latte.

"Thanks," he responded.

"Anything else?" Charon inquired.

"No, we're good. Thanks," Kookie replied and turned her attention back to the handsome man as Charon left them alone. "Go on."

He took a sip from his latte. "Well, as I was saying…people are curious about recording artists from the past.

They want to know where they are now – hence the title of the series."

Her eyes burned a hole through him. "And you think people are curious about where I am now…is that what you're suggesting?"

He returned her hard gaze with an equally hard, "Yes."

She sat back, resting an elbow on the side of the chair to rest her chin in the palm of her hand. "Mr. Tucker, by now you…"

"Please…call me David," he interrupted.

She raised an eyebrow. "David…as I was about to say…I'm sure that you've deduced my current situation by now."

His suave smile faded. "I'm so sorry."

She waved off his sympathy. "How could you have known? Anyway, as you can imagine…I'm afraid I have other priorities at this juncture in my life…of what's left of it."

David gave a slight nod and pursed his lips. "Of course. I understand. However…if I might so bold…"

His tenacity appealed to her. "Yes?"

"The story I'm proposing…now that I'm aware of your situation…is all the more important. To share your legacy, I mean."

She smiled. Legacy. She had never considered the ramifications of the word before – the finality of it. There was a sudden flash of comfort to it in an odd way that gave her a sense of calm closure as well as an idea.

"I appreciate that." She paused, considering what and how much to share next. "I will tell you, however, that at the moment I have some other tentative ideas about..." she paused for a moment to carefully choose her words before continuing, "...my *legacy*, as you put it. I should add that you've given me an idea."

"And what might that be?"

"Well...there would be no story of mine to tell without Joey Michaels."

David cocked his head. "Joey Michaels?" he repeated. "How does he fit in?"

She chuckled. "He more or less discovered me – mentored me. He wrote my first hit."

"I don't believe I knew that."

She privately scoffed at his lack of historical knowledge, given his professed expertise and vocation. Despite this, she surmised a savvy journalist would have the where-with-all to track down Joey. And even if he did, she wasn't sure what would come of it. If nothing else, at least she'd know and would get some closure.

"My point exactly." She added. "He's spent his whole career in the wings while others took to the stage. He was never in the spotlight. Given the name of your magazine, it certainly seems like its time he was. Someone needs to tell his story. Besides, mine's just about over."

She could see the gears turning inside him. He appeared to be intrigued but not fully bought into the idea. She decided to sweeten the deal.

"Tell you what – I'm thinking about a new album – my swan song – so-to-speak. I consider it part of my therapy. I haven't actually started it – I'm just now getting it off the ground."

"Really?" David was pleasantly surprised, adding, "That's wonderful."

She sloughed off his compliment. "So…here's the deal – You can write about my project…. *if*…" she emphasized and paused.

"If what?" he inquired.

"If you do a story on Joey as well."

David looked at her and smiled. He outstretched his hand.

"Deal."

Chapter 67

"What time is it?"

Kookie nervously paced the parlor.

Rocky, calmly sitting at one of the tables, glanced at the hands of his wristwatch.

"Almost 9:00."

She chewed on a fingernail. "They should've have been here by now. Do you suppose they missed the ferry?"

"They would've called."

She walked to one of the front windows and cupped her hand against the glass as she peered out into the rainy darkness. Two headlights reflecting in the wet pavement made their way around the bend leading up to the house. The car slowed and tentatively approached.

"That must be them," she speculated.

She opened the massive wooden door and stood out on the covered porch bathed in the gold porch light. The car stopped. The headlights were doused and both car doors opened in unison. Rocky rose from his seat and joined her on the front porch. One of the figures opened an umbrella, invoking a chuckle from the die-hard Pacific Northwesterners who celebrated the rain rather than shielded themselves from it. The other simply dashed between the puddles and toward the steps with a briefcase raised over his head. Benny lowered and shook out his umbrella before setting it down on the porch. Ron followed close behind and set his briefcase down as he brushed his hands over his coat in a futile attempt to shake off the rain.

No one spoke. The four of them momentarily took stock of the reunion. Then, Kookie walked over to Benny and wrapped her arms around him. Rocky watched them tearfully tremble in their embrace. Kookie finally pulled herself away and wiped a tear away as she turned toward Ron who stood there with both hands in his pocket. She outstretched her arms and softly called out, "Ron." He removed his hands from his pocket and accepted her warm welcome.

"I'm so glad you're here," she whispered softly in his ear.

"Me, too."

Kookie released him and took both of her hands to wipe the tears from her cheeks. She then nervously ran them over her bald head. "Look at me…I'm a mess," she confessed.

"You're beautiful," Benny reassured her.

She suddenly realized Rocky was standing there, taking this all in and turned to introduce him.

"Oh…and this is Rocky," she gestured with one hand.

Ron was the first to extend his hand. "Ron Speilman. Nice meeting you."

Rocky extended his left hand and shook Ron's hand. "Nice meeting you."

Benny stepped up and offered his hand. "I'm Benny."

"So I presumed. I've heard a lot about you," Rocky responded with his outstretched left hand.

Benny flashed an embarrassed smile over to Kookie. "Have you now? Well…don't believe everything you hear," he said slyly.

Kookie took each of her guests by the arm. "Come on…let's get inside."

Ron bent down to pick up his briefcase as she escorted them into her space that was as warm and embracing as her greeting.

"Here…hand me your coats," she said.

Benny craned his neck surveying the cozy room as he slipped off his coat. "Oh my! This is exquisite! Mission-style craftsman, if I'm not mistaken."

"Thanks," Kookie replied as she hung the coat on a coat tree by the front door.

Ron took off his coat and handed it to her. "Bess…this is amazing," her former manager enthused.

She noticed Rocky slightly twitch his head to the side when Ron referred to her with the name that she no longer used. She then watched her guests as they continued to take in their surroundings.

"Here…let's sit over here," she gestured to one of the larger, well-worn butcher-block tables near the kitchen. "Can I get you something to drink to warm up with? Coffee?"

"No coffee for me," Ron chirped. "It'll just keep me up all night."

Kookie gave a wry smile. "Well then, how about a nice mug of warm milk with a cookie?"

Ron smiled. "Sounds perfect." He turned to Benny and Rocky at the table as Kookie headed toward the kitchen. "I can't tell you the last time I had warm milk and cookies," he added.

Hearing his remark, Kookie called out over her shoulder, "Almost everyone says that," as she puttered in the kitchen before adding, "Benny? How about you?"

He cleared his throat dramatically. "Um, no dear. I don't believe so. Perhaps something a bit more…spirited?"

Kookie turned toward him as she poured Ron's milk into a mug. "I'm afraid not, Benny."

He shook his head dismissively. "What was I thinking? Of course not. Well then, some coffee will just have to do, then, won't it?"

Rocky was settling into the moment, trying to make himself comfortable with the reunion. "So…how was your flight?"

"Oh, it was fine…the sun was just beginning to set," Benny chirped. "Seeing all those snow-covered volcano peaks out the window along the way was amazing."

"Yeah, the Cascades are pretty nice," Rocky agreed before resuming his usual quiet demeanor.

Kookie returned with a tray containing a plate of warm cookies, Ron's mug of milk, and two mugs of coffee with a pitcher of cream. She handed one cup of coffee to Rocky, "Here you go, sweetie."

Benny and Ron exchanged a glance and a smile as Kookie sat down. The men silently indulged in the refreshments for a moment as she gleamed radiantly. Benny took another sip of his coffee and with a sudden revelation, set it down on the table.

"Oh! And speaking of the flight...tell them what happened with that TSA agent at LAX," Benny quipped as he tapped Ron's arm. "Wait until you hear this...it's hysterical. Go on...tell them Ronnie."

Ron gave his head a swoonful sway as he recalled the moment. "Well, it *was* kind of funny," he began.

"Go on...tell them," Benny coaxed.

Ron leaned down to reach for his brief case. From it, he retrieved a cassette tape recorder.

"Oh my God!" Kookie exclaimed. "Where on earth did you get that antique?"

Ron set it down on top of the table. "These are actually hard to find now days. Luckily, I happened to still have this buried in a closet at the office."

Benny impatiently rapped his knuckle on the table. "So tell them what happened!"

Ron settled back in his chair. "Well...we're going through security at LAX...right? Well, I forgot I had this in my briefcase and this twenty-something TSA person pulls me off to the side and makes me open up my bag and pull it out. This pimply-faced kid glares at me and then looks down at the recorder and asks, 'What's this?' I couldn't believe it. I couldn't tell if he was kidding or not."

Kookie covered her mouth with her hand. "Are you serious?"

Ron nodded. "I'm totally serious."

"Go on!" Benny prompted.

"Well anyway, not only did I have to explain what it was to this kid…I had to show him."

"NO!" Kookie exclaimed.

Ron nodded. "Yup, I had to play a cassette so he could see and hear it before he'd let me through. Nuts, huh?"

Rocky grinned. "I guess we shouldn't be surprised. Cassettes are like Model T's to kids these days."

Benny added, "Millennials don't even play CDs – they stream everything now days. My God, they don't even know how to read an analogue clock! My, how times have changed!"

The four of them collectively chuckled and shook their heads.

"I guess we're just getting old," Rocky concluded.

"I suppose so," Benny agreed.

Kookie tilted her head slightly as she continued to make sense of the incident.

"So, I'm not quite I sure I get why you lugged this tape recorder all the way here."

Ron and Benny exchanged glances.

"Go on, tell her," Benny said to Ron.

Ron took a sip from his mug of milk and a bite from one of the cookies to stall long enough to consider what to say.

"Well…we were going to share this with you later as we discussed your project." He paused to look at Benny who just gave a slight nod of encouragement. "I guess now is as good as time as any."

Ron reached back into his briefcase. Kookie quizzically scanned everyone's face. Rocky simply raised his eyebrows in wonder when her eyes met his. Ron then tossed a manila envelop on top of the table. Kookie glanced down at it and then back to Ron.

"What's this?" she asked as she reached over to inspect the familiar handwriting on it.

"Open it," Ron replied flatly.

Kookie glanced around the table and then unclasped the flap on the end of the padded mailing envelope. A cassette tape tumbled out as she turned it upside down over the table. She held it up, inspecting it. Written in ink were the two words: 'For Bessie.' She held it in her hand waiting for further explanation.

Ron reached over and gently took it from her hand. He popped open the cassette tape recorder and slapped the tape inside and closed the lid. "I could have digitized this and played it to you on my phone but…" he paused. "…I wanted you to see this *as well as* hear it – the way he wanted you to hear it."

He hit the play button.

A piano played some opening chords. She immediately recognized Joey's voice as he began singing what was clearly a demo of a song he had written. His voice had lost the edge from his days as a rocker and since he had moved from the stage in a cover band to a desk as a producer and manager. None-the-less, to her ears, it was sweet. His voice went into a falsetto on the higher notes, which were in her range. He had double-tracked his voice on his little four-track recorder, apparently to give it a little more depth – perhaps even some sheen. She listened carefully to the lyrics that took her back to her past. The hook, *'just for me'* from the chorus specifically transported her to the last time she had seen Joey. It was clear that he was responding to her lament that she knew his songs she had recorded were written for and about someone else. She always wrestled with the fact that he had never written anything just for her. It was a rough and somewhat ragged recording…much like the way their relationship had become and ended. But it was a song 'just for her,' all the same.

Maybe I'm foolin' myself
but I thought our love was something special.
Now the coolness in your touch makes it all seem so superficial.
When did you feel it slippin' away?
Is it me? Is it you? Is there somebody new?
Is there anything left we can save?
Nothing you say can make it easy for me.
Try as you might, I'll be crying tonight.
I still want you back can't you see…Just for me.

How could you leave me once you have me believing
Our love was all that mattered?
Your change of heart completely caught me off guard
And my dreams were all but shattered.
I wish you'd tell me just what you need.
Is it give? Is it take? Is it luck? Is it fate?
How can I make you need me?
A broken heart can take a lifetime to mend.
But I'll be alright alone here tonight.
It's best you don't stay and pretend...Just for me.

I made a place for you in my heart.
How could we grow so far apart?

If love has its seasons...its rhymes and its reasons,
I swear I've never seen them.
I'm never sure and so insecure but something keeps me reachin'
For love, real love -- No empty fantasy.
I thought you were the one and my life had just begun
Cause' you showed me what loving could be.
I'd like to think I was important to you.
And that you needed me at least partially
For more than a memory or two...
Just for you.

The short demo clicked to an end. She had to remind herself to breathe. Kookie looked up at Ron waiting for the backstory to the song.

"Joey sent this to me years ago. I've held on to it all this time – hoping I could eventually share it with you," he explained.

Kookie turned to Benny. "Did you know about this?" she implored.

He shook his head. "No, my dear – not until I reached out to Ron about this project."

She turned to look at Rocky who gave her a warm look. "I have a feeling this is what you were reaching for," he said lovingly.

She stared at the ghost hiding inside the tape recorder. "My God, it's even in my key…you can hear him stretch when he goes out of his range."

Benny nodded with a smile. "Indeed. That song is totally you, my dear. It's as if it finally consummates what you had with Joey – or should I say – always wanted from him."

Stunned, she wiped a tear away. She scanned the faces of the three men she had come to know, trust, and love. She took a deep breath and exhaled. "Well then…" she paused and smiled, "…let's start recording with this, shall we?"

Chapter 68

The cookie shop continued to thrive. Charon changed little in the way of operations or vibe that first year she ran the place. There was no reason to change anything. Cookie monsters remained loyal. This would have pleased the founding "kookie monster." The only tweak of the space was creating a modest, unassuming shrine in the corner of the parlor. A thumbnail-sized framed portrait was perched on a small candlestick table. The guitar named Prudence rested in the corner next to the heavy leather chair and fireplace hearth.

One late, warm Sunday afternoon, Charon noticed a man who looked to be in his sixties enter the space. He was carrying a small canvas tote bag. His grey hair was pulled back in a ponytail while wisps of his equally grey chest hair poked through the open collar of his tropical shirt. The color of his hair was made more striking against his bronzed skin. Peeking out from the bottom of his light, gauzy drawstring pants were well-worn flip-flops on his leathered feet. Charon watched him lift his sunglasses up on to the top of his head as he scanned the room. The chalkboard with the menu printed in multi-colored chalk above the counter seemed to catch his attention. He sauntered toward the counter and set his canvas bag down by his feet.

"Hello. Welcome to Kookie's. What can I get for you?" Charon asked as she wiped her hands on her apron.

The gentleman calmly perused the chalkboard and then surveyed the 'kookies' on display. A smile came to his face that had not been shaved for a few days and a faint chuckle escaped.

"I believe I'll have a glass of milk."

His simple order surprised her. He struck her as a hard-core caffeine addict.

Charon nodded before asking, "Anything else? Want to try one of our kookies? Right now we're showcasing our specialty Ta-Ta cookies – all proceeds go to fight breast cancer." She pointed to the comically risqué 'kookies' with the pink nipples in the display case with her finger.

The gentleman smiled. "No…I don't believe so. Just the glass of milk. I will, however donate something to the cause," he said as he wrestled his wallet out of his back pocket. He fished a $100 bill out of his wallet and stuffed it into the jar on the counter labeled, SAVE THE TA-TAs! Charon was already on her way to retrieve the milk and failed to notice Benjamin Franklin's sudden appearance in the jar.

"Just a glass of milk coming up! Would you like it warmed?" Charon asked from the cooler.

"No…cold is fine." The man suddenly added, "Oh – and could I have a small empty plate – if you don't mind."

Charon finished pouring the milk into a glass and reached over to hand him a plate. "Here you go. That'll be a dollar."

Without another word, the guest reached back into his wallet and handed her a single dollar bill.

"Thank you. Well…you must be visiting," Charon surmised.

"How can you tell?" he grinned.

"You're way too tanned to be from the Pacific Northwest."

The man smiled at her observation as he returned his wallet to his back pocket and his attention back to Charon. "It's my first time in these parts. I live down in Mexico."

"Mexico!" Charon exclaimed with surprise.

The man just gazed at her without offering anything more in the way of conversation. Taking her cue, Charon provided a simple reply.

"Well…welcome. Please…make yourself at home," Charon said with a nod toward the parlor.

"Thanks. I believe I will." He leaned down to grab the canvas bag and then he carefully set the glass of milk on the small empty plate. The man gingerly carried the balanced glass on the plate toward the parlor area just as the phone on the wall rang. Answering the phone and taking the "to-go" order diverted Charon's attention from the curious man from south of the border and back to business. Soon she was thoroughly caught up in the hum of guests coming in and out of the shop. As closing time approached, Rocky made his way in from the back door as he did every night.

"Oh good…I'm glad you're here. We had a late rush. Can you give me a hand clearing up?"

Ignoring the irony of her euphemistic request, Rocky smiled.

"No problem," he called out and grabbed a bussing tub to gather up cups, glasses, and plates left scattered about the parlor.

Charon began closing down the cash register when Rocky returned. The perplexed look on his face alarmed her.

"What is it?" she asked cautiously.

A smile slowly replaced his initial look of confusion. "Come here – I want to show you something."

Charon finished shoving the remaining cash and loose change into the bankers' bag and cinched it up with the drawstring. Then she made her way around the counter carrying the bag to follow Rocky, grabbing the donation jar along the way. He stopped near the fireplace and nodded toward the tiny table next to the leather chair.

She looked in the direction of his gaze and then quizzically at Rocky.

"What?"

"I thought chocolate chip cookies were off limits here," he quipped.

"They are," Charon replied flatly. "…always have been. I don't believe a chocolate chip cookie has ever come out that oven – she wouldn't allow it," she added.

Rocky once again nodded toward the table. Charon turned to look.

Next to the table, a single red rose was slipped in between the strings of the guitar resting in the corner. On the table was a glass of milk next to a plate with two chocolate chip cookies.

* * *

Acknowledgments

I'm so appreciative of the many folks who helped me throughout this project. My own beloved teacher, Phyliss Zimmerman, had a profound impact on me as a person and on my musical appreciation. She lives on in many of these passages. Thanks to Tiffany Martin and Jennifer Helgerson from the Gresham Writers' Group for their input early on. Many thanks to Nannette Taylor who put a great deal of time and energy in reading drafts and providing feedback. The continued support and cheerleading from Sherrey Meyer encouraged me to press on with this story. She and friends from Moreland Presbyterian Church who read the prequel, encouraged me to write Bessie's story in this sequel. Neil Tesser's article about the Amazing Grace coffeehouse in the Fall 2011 issue of *Northwestern* magazine was extremely helpful in capturing the vibe of that venue. My affection goes out to Gordon who introduced me to the Zen of Cigars – I miss sharing a stick and conversation with you – and I appreciate how you shared your vision of an amazing 4th of July adventure that found its way into this story. Once again, I am deeply grateful to Aimee Altamirano for bringing the voice of Bessie to life on these pages. I'm also pleased that Jordan played the guitar on the recording of *Bring You To Your Knees* – my son plays it much better than his old man. Finally, and as always, my eternal gratitude to Julie who, like a true trooper, slogged through drafts of the manuscript and endured my incessant ruminations.

About The Author

Marshall Welch spent nearly 30 years as a professor and administrator at the University of Utah and Saint Mary's College of California where he focused on scholarly writing and teaching. Prior to his academic career, he was a professional musician as a singer/songwriter playing in bands and recording radio/TV commercials, a breakfast chef, and a gravedigger. Since retiring, he has focused on writing fiction. He now lives in the Portland, Oregon area with his wife where he enjoys his grandchildren, hiking, and making ginger beer and sourdough bread when he's not tending to his wooded acreage overlooking Mt. Hood. For more information go to his website at: www.marshalljwelch.com

About The Singer

Aimee Altamirano majored in Music at Portland State University in Portland, Oregon and is now pursuing her Masters Degree in Music Education.

Back Story

An old coffee table picture book of Santa Barbara plays an unexpected role in bringing together three souls for a disastrous Thanksgiving dinner. Joey Michaels is a washed-up singer/songwriter and manager who is hanging on to his career and past as it spirals away. Laurel Burgess is a wry and insightful college intern who endears herself to Joey through a string of carefully planned outings designed to help him re-enter the world he struggles to understand. Gale Rivers, a bohemian waitress who has reinvented herself in Alaska, finally realizes her life-long dream to visit the beauty of Santa Barbara only to have it become a nightmare. Their lives intersect during an impromptu Thanksgiving meal together that reveals secrets from the past and present that ultimately sends each of them running away in different directions to rebuild their lives. In the process, Joey captures the experience in songs that are eventually recorded and released by an up and coming singer, Bessie James -- we learn her story in the sequel BACK UP. Years later, two seemingly random radio broadcasts bouncing off the ionosphere provide the balm to heal their wounds and the courage to carry on. Told through a series of flashbacks and flash-forwards, Back Story is truly the backstory of three people exploring who they are and who they hope to be. A unique feature of the book is embedded QR codes the reader can scan with their smart phones to hear original songs that are part of the story.

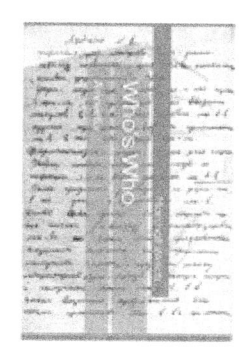

Who's Who: A Novella

Onnie Thomas is 16-years old. She likes to listen to heavy metal music, smoke cigarettes, steal from the convenience store, get high in the cemetery, and walk along the railroad tracks in her hometown of Stafford, Kansas. Her luck finally runs out after getting caught siphoning gas into a friend's car. She is ordered to complete community service hours at the local library. While archiving books, Onnie stumbles upon a bundle of letters hidden in a 1940 volume of Who's Who written long ago by a girl her own age. The yellowing pages from the Big Chief writing tablet reveal a tragic secret buried in the past. Moved by the passages, she is compelled to search for the mystery author with the hope of returning the time capsule to her. Her quest ends in an unexpected friendship bridging two generations with a bittersweet balm that heals the terrible wounds inflicted long ago and the teenage angst of living in today's digital world.

GRAVE MATTERS

What better way to learn about life than working in a cemetery? This is exactly what happens to the main character, Martin Stevenson, in Grave Matters. Martin alludes to the lost year he has left behind when he stumbles into employment as a groundskeeper in a cemetery in the middle of Kansas. There, he secretly takes up permanent residence camping in an obscure corner of the cemetery. The reader sees life through Martin's eyes as he digs out from his past and interacts with the quirky characters he works with. Martin serves as a muse as the reader learns lessons of life from the stories and experiences told by his co-workers. Through these lessons, Martin comes to find some of the answers about life he has been searching for through the experiences framed by death. Each chapter is an episode that takes place in the cemetery, spotlighting each employee and their unique experiences. In the end, both Martin and the reader come to realize that a person's identity and life are not shaped by what we appear to be nor by the compartments that constrain us, but by how we live our lives.

Made in the USA
Coppell, TX
30 August 2021